CURSE MEOW NOT

VOLUME I OF THE INFURNAL CATASTROPHE

KYSA STEELE

Curse Meow Not
Volume I of the Infurnal Catastrophe
Copyright © 2025 by Kysa Steele

This is a work of fiction.
All names, characters, setting, and events are born of the author's imagination or twisted through myth, memory, and metaphor. Any resemblance to real persons, living or dead, is entirely unintentional unless fate had a hand, in which case, one should never underestimate its sense of irony.

1st edition: 2025
ISBN: 979-8-9989422-0-4 Paperback
ISBN: 979-8-9989422-1-1 Hardback

Dividers and additional artwork created in Canva.

Cover design by Kysa Steele

 Formatted with Vellum

For David, who survived the outlines, the rewrites, and the unholy number of times I said, "I just need to finish this one thing." Your patience is true magic.

And for Nox, my cat, my chaos, my muse. You shed on every draft and sat on every keyboard, but somehow still managed to purr out inspiration.

Lastly, for my friend Crystal who gifted me with my muse and inspiration.

THE CATASTROPHE BEGINS

Lightning tore the obsidian sky apart. The great citadel of Nar'Khalor shuddered beneath the clash of blade and spell. Beneath the bedrock of war, something ancient stirred. Cold and constant as the grave, it watched, calculating the ruin. In the dark between heartbeats, it lived.

She was never meant to rule. Never meant to rise. She was meant to burn—a vessel for something older, bound in power she could never claim as her own. Velzara, Princess of the Ninth Flame, moved like a living inferno. Her twin-bladed glaive whirled in her grip, cleaving through a molten brute with a cry that cracked the air like splintered stone. Violet ichor, thick and unforgiving, splashed across scorched flagstones. The stench of charred flesh and bloodless bones clung to the air. Screams tore the air. Towers groaned. She danced through the ruin not like a conqueror, but as if ruin itself was her true form.

"Traitor!" bellowed a voice from above. Lord Varnyx descended on wings of bone and smoke, his halberd striking the earth with a sound that could silence prayers. "You would defy the pact?!"

Let him scream. Let him rage. She'd made her choice the moment steel kissed her skin, not with words, but with fire. With runes etched in flame, not treaty. The chains they forged clinked like marriage bells. She answered with laughter. With rebellion and joy in the ruin she wrought.

"You forged a cage, not a crown," she snarled, fangs bared. "I will not kneel. I will not be owned. I burn."

Behind her, wings of living flame unfurled, vast and searing —a sign of her unclaimed sovereignty. She rose like a comet torn from gravity's leash. For one heartbeat, the stars held their breath. Even fate faltered. Ten generations of infernal power surged through her veins, distilled to pure will, sharpened into a single strike. Her glaive screamed as it carved the air, a blade of pure hunger arcing toward Varnyx's throat.

And then the cosmos exhaled. The shift came not in air or stone, but in the order of things. Reality trembled. Victory gleamed, a prophecy seared in fire, one breath from truth.

A whisper reached for her, coiling across the thresholds of time, curse, and flame. Not wrath, but memory. Not vengeance, but intent—older than fire, colder than the void. It slid into her mind with the softness of silk and the sting of fate. This was no punishment, but a verdict, long foreseen and now delivered.

"Let her burn... as something small."

The moment snapped. Magic screamed. The world tore open like flesh beneath a god's blade. Agony surged, a wildfire in her veins, consuming her mind. The fire wasn't killing her. It was calling something. And that something answered in ice. It didn't speak. It only measured. And in that still, inhuman gaze, her flame was found wanting.

Her vision smeared. Her joints buckled, each tendon screaming as if time itself recoiled. She screamed her name—

Velzara—a war cry she hoped would anchor her, a sigil to hold her shape. But her magic slid from her tongue like oil on glass, fizzling into nothing. She collapsed.

The battlefield reeled. Fire guttered, its heat collapsing inward. Her flesh convulsed, twisting and reshaping with cruel precision. Limbs reknit, smaller and softer with every wrench of bone. Her armor dissolved. Her tail lashed in wild protest, a last, furious whip of defiance.

Time slowed. Even the sky leaned away. Velzara, once apocalypse incarnate, shrank. Her body warped and dimmed. There was a final flare of crimson light. And her scream, once volcano-born, emerged as a high, indignant meow.

Her eyes opened. She'd expected flame—a battlefield, scorched and smoking, final proof the dream had devoured her. Instead, no fire, no wreckage, no clash of iron echoed through the bones of the world. Instead, birdsong. High and sweet, it filtered through the cracked windowpanes like an insult dressed in melody—the kind of sound that belonged to gardens, to safety, to mornings promising nothing worse than over-steeped tea.

She hated it. There were no screams. No spells carving through the air. No thunder shaking the foundations of reality. Only that cursed music—and the scent of cinnamon. The smell drifted from the hallway, soft and warm. It clung to the air like comfort, but Velzara knew better; mortals disguised many things with sweetness. Whatever this was, it had been sugared into silence. Somewhere beyond the veil of reason, a kettle hissed. Even cosmic ruin, apparently, deserved tea.

Someone had placed her here. Not with reverence, but like

a cursed heirloom arranged on a tea tray—a potted shame, trimmed to fit someone else's shelf. No lingering spelltrace. No scorched air. Only floral cushions and deceit, leaving her to stew in sunlight, indignity, and the bitter flavor of outrage.

Sunlight spilled through the glass in golden pools, offensive in its gentleness. The room smelled of cinnamon and dust. Books lined the walls in curated rows. The kettle murmured in the background, content and oblivious, audacious enough to soundtrack her cosmic injustice.

Velzara the Fearless.
Scourge of the Blighted Plains.
Champion of the Ninth Flame.

The titles echoed faintly, like names whispered through thick glass. She remembered them, knew they were hers, yet something in her bones hesitated. She now wore the form of a cat: compact, black as pitch, and cursed with fluff that no self-respecting scourge should possess.

Someone nearby was humming—a cheerful, unmistakably human sound. Blissfully unaware, they had welcomed the former scourge of three infernal realms into their tidy mortal routine—she who once reduced cities to cinders between breakfast and conquest.

Velzara blinked with the poise of someone resisting murder. Nothing burned. That alone spoke of immense effort. Yet when she reached inward, the fire did not answer as it should. It coiled and hissed, bound by shape and silence. Present, but no longer hers to wield. Her power had not vanished. It had recoiled, a tide pulled away by force, leaving her dignity to scrape across the rocks behind it. The urge to unleash it warred with something she did not recognize: a strange, treacherous comfort in this new shape. She had never imagined herself torn—not like this.

CHAPTER I
PENANCE PIT OF SHAME

The sun offended her. It did not blaze with the glory of a kingdom-consuming inferno or strike with the righteous fury of divine wrath. This sunlight was worse. It crept in soft and domestic, its golden glow an intruder too polite to be thrown out, mocking her with its gentleness, as if her downfall were something to be warmed by. It slithered across the wooden floor like melted smugness—warm, syrupy, and utterly devoid of threat. This was not light that scorched or purified. It merely lingered, smelling faintly of cinnamon and something far more insidious, like unresolved childhood trauma bottled in a sunbeam.

Velzara tried to hiss, but her throat betrayed her. What emerged was a breathy *hffft*, the dying gasp of a disgraced tea kettle. It was not merely inadequate—it was an insult to rage itself, a tragedy of acoustics so pitiful it might have been composed by a drunk wind spirit and an off-key bird. She glared toward the window, willing the glass to crack under her disdain. It didn't. Instead, a squirrel (*clearly more competent than most of her former generals*) took one look at her and launched itself from the ledge with a squeal of panic.

At last, a creature who understood. One who saw ruin and chose flight over folly.

The cushion beneath her practically purred with plushness. The air smelled of surrender. Comfort crept into her bones like a well-meaning curse. She resisted, out of principle and spite— it made a fine second spine. The room paraded itself as an altar to mediocrity, every surface sagging beneath the weight of poor choices. Clutter gathered like mildew, too stubborn to be cleaned and too cherished to be thrown away. Trinkets posed as relics, gleaming with the smug irrelevance of sentiment. Books drooped on their shelves, unwarded and unwhispering, as if knowledge could be trusted to behave. In the corner, a globe spun with misplaced pride, getting every continent wrong with the unshakable conviction of a fool who had never been corrected.

What buffoon rearranged the continents? The Screaming Sea is two inches off its mark. And where, in the name of obsidian thrones, is the Isle of Knives? Hidden, no doubt, beneath someone's idea of polite geography. This isn't geography. It's treason in spherical form.

The scent of herbs lingered—lavender, rosemary, a trace of clove—soft and deliberate. It was the kind of cleanliness that reeked of curation, crafted to soothe fretful children or comfort aging mages marinating in regret. The fragrance clung to the wood like an apology no one wanted to speak aloud, a quiet surrender baked deep into the varnish, polished and permanent.

What in this room has ever bled? What shelf has ever watched a vow break or a rival collapse in defeat? None. Call it what it is then: furniture pretending at relevance.

But worst of all, the final and most unforgivable offense in this meticulously curated hellscape, was how little space she took up. Once, her stride sent echoes crashing through marble halls. She moved like prophecy made flesh, like war with a spine, like fire given limbs and a purpose. People cleared paths. Doors obeyed. Her name unraveled treaties before the ink set. Now she occupied no more space than a decorative pillow, and frankly, even that comparison flattered the disgrace. Her paws, when she dared to look, mocked her with their daintiness. Black as polished onyx, they were as useless as scented soap in a summoning circle. Some traitor had sculpted her for velvet-footed indignity. Even the pads betrayed her with their softness, forged for gentle steps in a world that deserved to burn. Her tail, that arrogant and insubordinate appendage, curled into a flourish of fluff—a visual insult, a statement piece in the ever-growing gallery of her humiliation. She bit it. It twitched, elegant and infuriating. She bit harder, but it twitched again, still managing to look graceful while doing it.

Absolutely not. I refuse. That is not an extension of my person. That is a cursed ribbon of betrayal, grafted to me by some sickly god of indignity. I am not meant to have a tail. I command tails. I pin them to my banner poles. I burn them off enemies as a warning.

The illusion, fragile as mortal confidence, began to fracture. Her eyes narrowed. The tail coiled beside her with the serene malice of a courtier executing a scheme to perfection.

It moves with purpose, follows some inner script. Schemes, perhaps.

A smug, deliberate twitch followed.

Very well, then. Let it stay for now. But if it so much as brushes a throw pillow with intention, I will bind it in sigils and cast it into the waiting Maw of Oblivion. And then I'll nap. Just to assert control.

No dream had ever dared move with such precision. This was not the idle wandering born of cheese or sleep-starved minds. It hunted with teeth, sharp and patient. It felt real, as though it had been waiting all along. A breath hitched in her chest, and she hated the feeling—unbidden, organic, a treacherous reflex. It was the kind of horror only mortals understood, like realizing too late they had scheduled basilisk babysitting between lunch and death. The shame of it made her claws itch. She turned inward, grasping for the spark—for flame, fury, pact-heat, for anything that might reflect her true form instead of this disgrace built of fur and silence. But nothing answered. No sigils flared behind her eyelids. No power stirred to meet her thoughts. There was no infernal resonance humming in her bones. Only silence, sunlight, and paws so dainty they didn't even thud when she stomped.

This is not a dream. It is not a test. This is punishment of the highest order. Not with flame or blade, no. But with blankets and decorative pillows. I will find the one responsible. I will burn their name from memory, salt their contracts, and turn every future life they attempt into a cursed musical with audience participation.

Her claws flexed half out of instinct, half out of impotent fury. They did not scrape the wood. They whispered against it. The leash of her new form crept tighter with every breath.

I am not small. I am not soft. I am not done. Whoever spared me lit a fuse with their mercy. And when I rise, they'll beg for the grave they forgot to dig.

10

The door creaked open.

"Oh, you're awake!" said a voice so cheerful it made Velzara's ears flatten like shutters bracing for a storm.

A girl stepped in, mortal and wide-eyed, clutching her mug like it whispered secrets. Her copper hair was twisted in chaotic defiance, and the robe she wore shared its inaccuracies like a manifesto. A scrap of magic lingered on her skin, gentle and hopeful, and utterly beneath notice. She was untrained, soft, laughable—possibly even flammable. If someone had distilled naivety into a potion and spilled it on a cardigan, it would have looked exactly like this. Velzara bristled. Every strand of fur rose like a battle standard, a warning etched in fluff.

The girl, either irredeemably oblivious or clinically deranged, knelt beside her.

"You poor thing. I found you curled up outside my door like a soggy rag. You looked so cold. And grumpy."

Velzara's eyes narrowed. Her ears flattened. Something ancient twisted in her chest, not from insult, but from how easily the word fit.

Grumpy? I am the embers beneath collapsing stars. I have razed cities for lesser insults. I am wrath forged in elegance and crowned in flame. And you dare—

And then it happened. The betrayal. The girl scratched under her chin, and a purr escaped. It was not a soft purr, nor was it polite. A full-bodied, treacherous rumble that rose straight from the cursed epicenter of her being. It was warm and shamefully deep—the kind of sound that surrendered to comfort without asking permission.

No. Not like this. Not under her wretched mortal hand. Not for kindness I didn't request. Not for warmth I didn't summon.

The rumble continued, rolling through her chest like a curse cast backward. It was a sound too ancient to be cute and too deep to ignore. She hated the way it felt: warm, unsettling, and almost familiar. It stirred something old inside her, something that resembled safety she didn't remember choosing.

I refuse to vibrate for tea-goblin affection. And yet, here I am. Purring. Purring like some enchanted throw pillow with trust issues. This is how it begins. This is the rot. The unraveling. Not fire. Not blade. Just a scratch beneath the chin and the soft, traitorous sound of surrender.

"I figured you belonged to someone," the girl continued, unforgivably chipper. "But there's no collar. So I guess you're mine now. I almost called you Angel, but you've got this spooky vibe. So I went with Nox."

Velzara stiffened as the name hit her like a spell spoken wrong, a mockery wrapped in silk. It rang through her bones like a curse uttered by a bard with no sense of irony. It slithered into her ears and settled there, smug and unshakable. Of all the syllables mortals could scrape together, they dared label her with that insult. And something in her, something quiet and cornered, flinched—not from insult, but from recognition. Nox. The name of a particularly dramatic shadow. The kind whispered in a poetry circle by someone with a velvet choker and no real demons. She could almost respect the gall. Almost. But this mug-wielding mortal spoke the name aloud, unbothered by wrath or retribution, as if the heavens themselves endorsed the insult and dared her to object.

"Welcome home, Nox," the girl chirped.

Home? You presumptuous shrub, I once ruled a citadel of obsidian spires and boiling rivers. And now you welcome me to your pastel hellscape like you're gifting me your leftover soup?

"I'm Elira," she added, as though that explained anything.

"This is the Warding House. Or... that's what my grandmother called it."

Warding House. How quaint. As if a few etched runes and lavender sachets could keep what mattered out—or worse, keep it in.

Velzara's ears twitched. The name scratched at her memory like a dull blade, familiar but not friendly. Magic hung in the air, old and settled. It was the kind that sank into the bones of things and then forgot the names it carved. It didn't scream. It murmured. It lurked. It waited.

She leapt from the windowsill and landed without a sound. Her paws, cursed and treasonously silent, betrayed no fury, no weight—just grace without threat. She prowled the room in slow, spiraling judgment while her tail twitched like a monarch issuing invisible decrees. She scanned for sense, for strength, for anything useful: infernal sigils, cursed talismans, even a half-eaten soul pact tucked into a drawer. But there was nothing. No runes whispered from the grain, no hexes hummed from the glass, no sinister presence waited behind the bookshelves to applaud her suffering. There was only gleaming glass, polished wood, and lighting so pleasant it bordered on hostile.

It was the worst kind of lie, stitched together by well-meaning mortals with throw pillows and no understanding of wrath. Every step felt stolen. No room welcomed her here. It was a prison playing dress-up in wallpaper and lies. Some stranger's fantasy, sculpted by a god who prized trim over truth and baked like they preached, without salt, soul, or seasoning.

What is happening? I need to undo this. I need to break whatever spell did this. I need to get back home before I purr again and forget my own damn name.

She prowled her new confines like a dethroned storm trapped in a dollhouse. Whiskers twitching with each petty injustice. The stones pulsed faintly with light beneath the floorboards, like trapped stars trying not to scream. Magic bled through the seams of the house. It was subtle and insistent, a signature not her own.

"Hungry, little shadow?" Elira asked sweetly, pulling a small pink wand from a nearby table.

Velzara stared.

What in the hells is she holding? A weapon? A wand? A stick of scented betrayal?

Then the tube squeaked, and scent burst forth. It was sweet, savory, and horrifyingly divine. Her hindbrain hiccuped. Her spine quivered. That was not a smell. It was a spell. Alchemy disguised as affection, brewed in sin, served with a spoon.

I would not kill for this. But I would certainly orchestrate a betrayal. I would betray a sibling order of fire-priests for a taste.

She backed away. Then crept forward again, against all better judgment. Her nose twitched. Once. Twice. The scent clawed at her resolve like a cursed lullaby. She sniffed. She hated herself. And then her instincts betrayed her. She lunged. Four frenzied, shame-drenched licks later, she stared down an empty dish.

Velzara went rigid. She stared at the gleaming, treasonous little bowl like it had spat on her crown. Her shoulders hunched, not in defeat—never defeat—but in the way a storm might gather before a scream. Even the air around her paused, unsure whether to laugh or run.

No. No no no. What have I become? I have licked the offering of a mortal. I have eaten from a dish I did not demand. I am compromised. I am broken. I am... scented with tuna.

Elira giggled. "That's all it took, huh? A little hunger, and you're back to your royal gloomfire routine. Poor thing."

Velzara froze. One paw in the air. One fang bared. One heartbeat from calling down fire.

This cinnamon-scented mortal dared to speak truth dressed in mockery and laughed like it meant nothing. I will remember this. Etched into the stone of vengeance. Right next to the tail.

Her tongue, that traitorous, gleaming thing, betrayed her by grooming her own face like a mewling bootlicker desperate for praise. She turned away with the kind of wounded pride only an exiled queen in fur could muster. Tail high. Ears back. Dignity trailing behind her like a tattered cloak snagged in a closing door.

The hallway twisted ahead. Narrow and creaking, lined with charms that jangled like nervous apologies. Bundles of lavender, feathers, and tiny silver bells hung from nails like a hushed, anxious confession. A wall of petty protections. They whispered as she passed, their voices threading through the air in the old tongue of warding: You shouldn't be here.

I know. And yet here I am. Stuffed into fur, radiating ancient spite like heat from old coals. A cosmic obscenity in velvet disguise. A catastrophe with whiskers. A blight wearing silk and teeth. And I promise, I will not fit quietly into this shape.

A glimmer pulled her eye toward a crystal sphere, cloudy and suspicious, pulsing with the smug self-importance of something that had once sat on a seer's desk and never shut up about it. She approached and lifted one paw. The glow swelled. And then—contact. A jolt shot up her leg. Not the lazy warmth of fluff, cuddles, and gods-forsaken tuna paste. This burned real. Sharp as judgment, raw as truth, old enough to remember her as more than a shadow with claws.

This spark belongs to me.

It reached. It recognized. And, perhaps, it asked. She had not answered.

This house may play at peace, but its bones remember the fire. They remember the taste of obedience.

And then, just as suddenly as it rose, the connection snapped. The glow vanished. The sphere dropped cold and silent. Velzara hissed, a sound sewn from wrath and disbelief.

It knew me. Felt the fire, the weight I carried, the ruin I command. And what did it do? It blinked. It blinked and ran like a relic with stage fright. Unacceptable. I have incinerated kingdoms for less coherent insults.

From the next room came a shout. "Don't touch the glowing stuff! At least not until I figure out what it does!" Then quieter, to herself, "Last time I touched a glowing book, I couldn't blink right for a week."

Her eyes narrowed.

Too late, cretin. You dare instruct a demon queen in the handling of arcane relics? I have breathed kingdoms into ruin for less.

She padded onward, and then she saw it, waiting, open, and unassuming. It was so offensively innocent it could only be a trap laid by civilization itself: a plastic tray filled with pale sand, a mortal altar to disgrace. She stared long and hard, willing her vision to betray her. As if, by sheer force of will, the shape might blur, recede, unravel into something less offensive to her lineage. As if a glare sharp enough might transmute it into a cursed reliquary weeping locked sorrows, or a battlefield relic still warm from its last blood rite. Even a summoning circle drawn by a novice priest mid-nervous breakdown would have been preferable.

But no. It stood there in pristine absurdity, shameless and

unmasked. Not a vessel of power, but of indignity—crafted without fear, without reverence, without the slightest consideration that someone *like her* might one day be expected to touch it. She crept toward it like it might explode or demand a confession. She sniffed, then paused, and felt something inside her wilt.

No. Not in a thousand hells. Not even the ironic ones. This is beyond shame. This is ritual humiliation, codified in plastic and scented with lavender despair. A tiny sandbox of defeat.

And yet the nature of her new form called. A few moments later, with the kind of dread usually reserved for public executions and mandatory peasant festivals, gods forgive her, she used it.

As soon as the ritual humiliation reached its scented conclusion, she bolted. Her tail puffed, and dignity leaked from every trembling pawstep as she fled—not with grace or silence, but with scrambled horror and the slow-motion collapse of an identity once forged in fire.

I have fallen. I have defiled my legacy in a plastic basin of perfumed dirt, engineered by someone who clearly despises gods, queens, and dignity in equal measure. The box with dirt. A sanctified insult. A penance pit carved by traitors with scented sand and no soul. Like some common beast begging forgiveness from its keeper. Whoever designed this ritual of ruin, I will find them. I will salt their blueprints and hex their descendants with shame that smells faintly of lavender.

CHAPTER 2
I AM NOT CONTAINED

Still shaking, she crept back into the main room. Every flick of her tail etched new entries into the Book of Vengeance. Elira had vanished. The hearth crackled on, cheerful and oblivious, a hollow warmth with no memory of its purpose. A blanket lay across the windowsill, arranged with suspicious care. Its softness felt deliberate, its welcome far too inviting. It looked like something meant to soothe—stitched with hidden fangs and bated breath. She stared without blinking, every instinct on edge. The warmth it offered was a warning in disguise. A trap, no doubt. Devised by the house. Or the Fates. Or that mug-wielding enchantress and her cursed collection of textile-based appeasements.

They want to smother the fire. Swaddle it. Rebrand it as purring contentment.

She hesitated. The warmth rising from the cushion curled through the air, winding around her limbs like the house was exhaling on purpose. It wasn't offering comfort. It was testing her defenses.

This is psychological warfare. A battlefield disguised as

bedding. Comfort offered as compromise. Give in now, and next they'll be calling me snugglebug and dressing me in seasonal accessories.

Her tail flicked, a deliberate rhythm: once for insult, twice for betrayal. Each motion a proclamation. But her body ached with remembered indignities, and her thoughts unspooled like broken coils, sluggish and pained. The taste of cursed tuna still lingered on her tongue, a ghost steeped in salt and shame. She leapt onto the sill. With the dignity of a dethroned warlord making peace with a strategic retreat, she settled onto the blanket. Warmth rose around her, gentle in a way that felt purposeful. It didn't scorch. It seduced. It was lullaby-heat—the kind that whispered lies in velvet tones: *vengeance can wait. Nap first. Snack later.*

This is not surrender. This is restraint, sharpened and sheathed. Recovery masquerading as comfort. Let them think I'm conquered, just until I turn this lair to ash.

She chose to sink into it, not for comfort. Never for comfort. It was a decision born of cold, calculated necessity. She needed a single breath to quiet the spine-hum of the curse, a moment to forget the box, and time to sharpen her claws in dreams. She would rest only until something moved. Anything.

Just until—

The warmth didn't fade. It vanished—swift and absolute, as if it had never existed. Cold shadows slid across her fur, peeling the heat away like hungry things. The scent of cinnamon and dusty wood tore from the air in a rush of absence, leaving behind only the hollow taste of loss, sharp as a closing door.

She opened her eyes. The room was gone. In its place

stretched the edge of an obsidian cliff, jagged and vast. The ground beneath her paws split and seethed, laced with molten magma—old wounds that refused to close. Below, the chasm yawned endlessly, burning. Rivers of blood threaded through the dark, and dragging chains scraped across the stone, moving without masters, echoing like forgotten names. Above her, the sky churned. It was a vaulted ruin of smoke and smothered stars. Shadows with wings screamed through the dark, their shrieks unraveling into echoes that refused to fade.

Regret doesn't lurk here. It lounges as if it owns the place. Like it helped build it. Maybe it did.

She tasted the ash. Felt the tilt of the stones beneath her paws. Watched the shadows curl inward, as if bracing for command. This wasn't memory. It was recognition—jagged, and absolute.

Nar'Khalor.

This was her realm. Once, it had been her citadel. Her throne had been sculpted from bone and sealed by oaths. She had carved this kingdom from pain and prophecy. Now it stretched before her as a grave—hollow and gutted. It mocked everything she had forged with blood, fire, and will.

This is blasphemy. All of it is wrong. As if I never reigned. As if I never bled for this throne. Betrayal carved into the bones of my dominion. And it is unforgivable.

Silence pressed in too tightly. That alone marked the first offense. No war-drums thundered. No voices rose in infernal chant. No cries of the conquered slammed against the stone walls. Only stillness remained—a suffocating quiet that seeped into the marrow. Her legions had vanished. The beasts of blood and flame that once circled above were gone. The symphony that once surged beneath every breath had gone quiet, reduced to absence. They had proved themselves cowardly and forgetful, unworthy of the legacy carved in her name. Her paws burned against the fractured stone. Each breath caught sharp with ash and memory. Her heartbeat echoed a stolen name, not her own. She had stood here too long. Far too still.

Her voice rose, beginning as a rasp, brittle with disbelief. But it gathered strength with every word, like a blade remembered and redrawn with intent. "Who dares strip my name from these stones?"

Her words cracked the silence, sharp enough to make the air bleed. "Who unmade my throne? Who stole the fire from my gates and silenced the scream-song of the damned? Do you think emptiness will break me? That absence will crown itself king in my place? That I am so easily forgotten?"

A snarl twisted in her throat. The chasm below pulsed a deeper red. "I forged this realm in fury and flame. I carved it from rebellion and blood. Every chain that sings beneath this sky once moved to the rhythm of my will. And now you offer me silence?"

Her voice faltered into laughter—hoarse, ragged, but still somehow regal. "Silence? You insult me with absence, like a coward too afraid to finish the kill."

She stepped forward, her tail lashing behind her like a banner caught in stormwinds. Sparks flared from her claws as they struck the stone, and the ground cracked beneath her.

Far away, in the waking world, something beneath the floorboards groaned in sympathy.

"This void is not death. It is theft. Sabotage. Treason. I feel the cut of it—not clean, but cruel. Someone carved me out of my own dominion, scraped me from the walls like a name they hoped to forget. But hear this, oh empty halls and faithless flame: I am Velzara. Daughter of Cataclysm. Devourer of Kings. I do not vanish. I do not yield."

"I return." Molten violet blazed in her eyes. Her fur bristled. She was not gone. She had never been. "So run, little thief. Run while the realm still sleeps. Because I have seen my grave." She bared her teeth. "And I've decided I'm not done."

This is not how it ends. Not with silence. Not with absence. Calamity forged me. I was never shaped for erasure. I do not fade. I do not yield. I will carve my name into the throat of every tale that dares to forget me.

Velzara...

The voice slithered through the dark like oil. It was familiar, but wrong—sickly slick with something ancient.

Velzara...

She turned, slow and against instinct, her spine pulled taut like a bow drawn wrong. A figure stood at the cliff's edge. It was tall and cloaked, wrapped in shadows that drank the light like wine. No face showed beneath the hood. No breath stirred. No motion betrayed its presence—only the endless, slow ripple of robes stitched from smoke and nightmares. They moved with the weight of thought, like prophecy unraveling in silence. She couldn't see its eyes. She didn't need to. Her breath caught.

No. This isn't Varnyx. This isn't vengeance. It's not politics or some usurper's curse. This is older than war. Older than wrath. This is what slithers through the cracks when gods look away. And it's been watching me. Waiting.

But why?

The air thickened. It didn't speak, but the truth slammed through her like a funeral bell. Her name was etched deep into the iron—not in mourning, but in mockery. This thing had cursed her. Not for rebellion. Not for pride. It saw her, and it chose ruin.

Because I dared to burn too brightly. Because I rose too high and refused to bow. Because I became a flame they couldn't smother. So they buried it instead.

She stepped forward, claws flexing against scorched stone. Heat trembled up her limbs like a promise rekindled. Her voice shattered the silence—not a question, but a challenge flung like a blade. Her claws dug deeper. Her breath came hot, coiling in her chest and feeding the inferno. Her throat burned, not with fear, but with the raw fury of containment.

Then she screamed. Not from fear, but from principle. "Who dares?"

Who dares chain me? Curse me? Clip my wings and believe I'll stay grounded like some apologetic little phoenix?

The chasm offered silence.

"Who dares lay this curse on me? Show yourself. Let me thank you properly... in fire, blood, and a footnote on your tombstone." Her voice cracked the air like lightning.

Still, there was no answer—only echo, and the cold sting of insult.

She bared her teeth. Heat rose behind her ribs. It wasn't power. It was spite. And that was better. "Who dares clip the wings of Velzara and believe the ashes won't rise?"

That isn't a question anymore. It's a curse. An oath. A flaming middle claw hurled into the dark, hot enough to make the stars flinch.

The figure tilted its head. It didn't move like a person. The motion was too slow and too smooth, the kind of gesture that didn't belong to flesh but to something mimicking it. It didn't turn. It drifted through the idea of turning, like a puppet imitating curiosity without strings. Behind it, a chain snapped. The break was neither clean nor quick. The sound curled through the air like a scream dragged across rusted iron, wet and heavy with memory.

"You burned with too much fury," it said. The voice didn't touch the air. It moved inside her, shuddering down the scaffolding of her bones. "Now burn without glory."

Velzara bared her teeth. "I will not be dimmed. I am Velzara, First Flame of the Deep. Breaker of the Celestial Accord. Sovereign of a realm no god dared to challenge."

"You were," it said, its voice flat as falling ash. "Now, you are what becomes of those who forget their place."

Its hand slid from the folds of the cloak. It was skeletal and polished, carved from blackened bone with an elegance that had never known flesh. The movement held no trace of life. It moved without breath, without hesitation, and without mercy. In its palm rested something small and familiar: a mirror.

Velzara squinted, even as her breath caught. Her reflection stared back at her, mocking in its stillness. It was flawless and cursed, shaped like a cat—soft and diminished. Only the violet eyes remained, still burning with defiance. They were the final insult, a memory made manifest in fur and silence.

The figure turned the mirror toward the chasm and released it. The mirror did not fall; it was let go with the gentleness of finality. A single flicker of fire followed it, trailing through the air before vanishing into the dark below. It was gone.

"You will return," it said. "Each time you close your eyes, until you learn."

"Learn what?" she snarled. "Humility? Kindness? Do you mistake me for some mewling mortal child in need of manners?"

"No," the figure replied, its voice flat as stone pressed

against a tomb. "You are a creature of fire. But fire without purpose consumes itself."

The cliff cracked beneath her paws, and the stone exhaled smoke. Her fury surged outward, but it found no shape to fill. The air thickened around her. Heat clawed at the edge of every breath as the pressure continued to build.

The figure stepped back, weightless and watching. "Choose with intention, little ember. Some flames forge. Others consume. Feed the wrong flame, and even the gods will forget what you were meant to become."

But had the choice ever belonged to her? As if fire ever paused to ask where it should burn.

The air went still, as if waiting. One step, one word, or a single breath of surrender might have been enough. The chains might have answered. They might have returned her power. But she said nothing. She lunged instead—or tried to. Her body strained to leap, to burn, to destroy. She tried to tear the shadowed limb from its root and force the void to remember her name. But her paws sank into crumbling stone, and her claws, dulled by disgrace, scraped up nothing but sparks. Her legs trembled, not from weakness, but from the sheer insult of stillness. Smoke curled from her mouth with each breath, but it carried no heat. Only the bitter tang of something once divine, now discarded like a broken vow.

Velzara jolted awake, the infernal vision still smoldering behind her eyes. Elira loomed above her, brandishing a comb with the solemnity of a priestess preparing a sacrifice. Velzara knew exactly who the victim was.

"Brush time!"

Her eyes became twin pools of horror.

No. This cannot be happening again. Not another descent into mortal absurdity—this time wielded by bristles, by nicknames, and by a thing so foul, so unholy, it dares to call itself... Fluff.

Before the gears of fate could grind one cursed inch further, she launched herself off the windowsill with a yowl sharp enough to curdle sunlight. Her claws skittered across the polished wood, punctuation to a protest no one had invited her to make.

Elira laughed. "Oh, come on, Nox! It's just a little brushing! You've got fluff behind your ears!"

Fluff?

Fluff?!

Is there no end to the insults I must endure? I am fire incarnate. I am Princess of the Ninth Flame, the last ember born from the Mouth of the Dying Star. My aura once melted the eyes of a thousand chanting cultists. And now you dare suggest I have 'fluff' behind my ears, as if I were some overbred pillow beast? I commanded servants who set themselves ablaze rather than risk brushing my cape!

She dove beneath the couch in a blur of wrath and betrayal. Her tail lashed like a cursed whip, and her ears pinned back with regal disgust. Elira crouched, peering into the shadows as if summoning a demon required tea, honeyed words, and catastrophic optimism.

"Don't make me bribe you again."

Velzara hissed—a warning, an incantation, and a condemnation, all compressed into one syllable.

If she pulls out a saucer, I will bite her. Right in the soul.

Elira sighed. "Fine. But you're going to get mats in your

fur, and then I'll have to take you to a groomer. And that is a fate worse than death, trust me."

Groomer.

The word hit like a soul-spear to the sternum. There was no physical impact, only implication. It didn't draw blood—it drew shampoo.

I don't know what it means, but every syllable reeks of submission. Of soap. Of ceremonial degradation. You don't invite someone to a groomer. You sentence them. It sounds like something whispered in the final moments of a doomed summoning circle. Whatever a "groomer" is, it belongs in the same linguistic graveyard as "soul siphon," "bone-melder," or... gods help me... "performance evaluation." No. Absolutely not. I would rather ignite every curtain in this domicile and live as an ash-stained legend than suffer whatever indignity a groomer entails.

A silence settled between them, the kind usually found before executions or during extremely tense family dinners.

Then Elira muttered, "You're such a little weirdo. You didn't even flinch at the ghost in the hallway mirror, but a comb? That's your breaking point? Just you wait, Fluff. No familiar survives detangling forever."

Velzara's ears pricked. Her tail froze mid-lash.

Forgive me if I misheard. Did a ghost just grace the hallway mirror while you, mortal fool, came storming in with a grooming weapon, as if brandishing some relic of hair-based heresy? This house has ghosts, and I am the one being groomed?

Elira stood, brushing her own hair back like she was preparing for battle or brunch. Possibly both. "Alright, Nox. You win this round. But I'm getting those knots out eventually. Just you wait."

Velzara didn't move. She couldn't. Not while her fur still crackled with betrayal and latent rage. Not while the mirror still watched her from the corners of memory. The heat hadn't left her bones, and the scream still echoed in her jaw. She could smell the stone. She could taste the ash. The scent didn't belong here. It came not from woodsmoke or tea or dust, but from Nar'Khalor. It was faint and still somehow wrong, seeping through the floorboards like memory with claws. Something of Nar'Khalor still clung to her like a brand, even here. Even now.

She remembered the mirror. The figure. The fall. And now, worse still—she had almost been brushed. She had been nicknamed. She had been called *Fluff*.

Let the mortal believe she had won. Let the brush rest smug where it sits. I will choose the next battle on my terms.

She stayed beneath the couch long after Elira left the room. She became a silent monument to injustice. She glared into the shadows like a cursed statue, unmoving and unbowed, daring the comb to launch its next assault.

After a long, silent standoff with the universe—one she lost only because the universe cheated—Velzara finally slunk back into the living room. The fire's warmth lured her out like a siren with a flair for hearthstone ambiance. She hopped onto the windowsill, sulking with every ounce of dignity she could still assemble from the ruins. Her tail curled around her with ceremonial precision.

Her ears twitched. A vexing tingle behind one of them could not be ignored. It itched in a way so targeted, so cosmically rude, it demanded attention. She refused to scratch it. The itch remained: a quiet tyranny. Still, she would not bend. Let it burn.

No. That would be a concession. And I have already bartered too much to this indignity of flesh and fluff. There will be no brushing of the vanquished queen.

She stared out the window, her claws tapping once against the glass in silent judgment. The world beyond had the audacity to remain tranquil. Birds flitted past like feathered fools. Leaves danced for no reason at all. Mortals drifted through their fragile lives, unaware of the storm above, while the heavens chuckled behind veils of cloud. The reflection in the glass shimmered. It wasn't wrong. It was simply waiting, as though the dream had not yet finished speaking.

And here I crouch. An apex predator, wrapped in fire and fury. I am Princess of the Ninth Flame, scourge of six celestial courts and one tragically misfiled divine council. And I am hiding—from a hairbrush. It is unacceptable. It is beyond forgiveness. It is an eternal stain on my infernal résumé.

And worst of all, I am humiliated. Not by war. Not by betrayal. Not even by divine punishment. But by fate's pettiness, wrapped in fur and static. I have been betrayed by the cosmos. I have been reduced to purring against my will. And now? Now I live beneath the rule of a cinnamon-scented mortal and the looming threat of conditioner. This is not survival. This is soap-slicked surrender.

There are no witnesses. There is no dignity.

CHAPTER 3
ACCESSORY OF MY SHAME

Light seared through her skull. Then came the heat, not wild but deliberate, like a throne reclaiming its queen. The war chamber resolved around her in a rush of smoke and ruin. Banners sagged in scorched tatters from the high columns. The scent of blood and ash hung in the air, clinging like a memory that wouldn't release its grip. At the far end of the chamber, her throne stood waiting. Blackened by battle, skeletal in form, it exuded a cold untouched even by flame. Stone stretched beneath her paws, pulsing faintly with residual warmth. Blood slicked its surface, still steaming as if unwilling to cool.

Her gaze dropped to the weapon at her feet. Malediction, her glaive, lay broken. One end splintered into jagged ruin. Smoke coiled from the fracture, rising in a slow, deliberate curl, like the final breath of something that once defied gods. As if her will—her legacy—could break so easily. She had forged that blade from the breath of dying stars. It was not meant to splinter. It was not made to yield.

Footsteps echoed through the ruined hall, steady and

intentional. Each one carried the certainty of something that knew she could not stop it. She spun, claws bared, the motion born of instinct and ire. No one stood behind her. But the sound continued, growing louder with each step, drawing closer like a verdict long delayed.

From the cracks in the obsidian floor, a whisper began to rise—black and thick as oil, curling like ink in boiling water. "You left something behind. Or did you give it away?"

Her claws flexed, scraping the stone with a hiss of sparks. "What?" she growled. Her voice coiled low and sharp, a blade waiting to strike.

Silence answered, vast and waiting. Only the wind remained, weaving through shattered glass and broken stone. It carried the scent of something ancient and bitter. Her throne stood at the far end, darkened and crusted with the ruin of ages. It no longer glowed, no longer commanded. Instead, it slouched beneath its own weight—less a seat of power, more a relic mourning what it once was.

She stepped forward. Cold bled up from the stone, curling around her paws like a warning too old to shout. Her breath caught. Her claws clicked against the floor, almost inaudible.

I did not leave anything behind. Not willingly. Not blindly. Everything carved from me was stolen—by oath, by trick, by flame. And I will carve it back.

She opened her mouth, lips curling around the demand. The room cracked with light. Heat tore through the walls, searing and sanctified, like sunrise forced through a scream. Shadows recoiled. The air rippled, warped by something older than breath. She gasped.

Somewhere far away, a candle went out. Not here. Not in this world. But in the realm that remembers.

The sun dragged her back. Light burst through the window, bold and officious, like a celestial landlord demanding rent in the currency of suffering. Velzara jolted awake, limbs twitching, fur on end—fluffed like a thunder-blasted wraithcat. Her tail thrashed. Pride seared behind her ribs, still smoldering. Sunlight sprawled across the floor in golden ribbons, smug as a victor's decree. It clung to the room with the arrogance of law, casting everything in the uncompromising light of judgment.

She hissed, low and precise, a threat sharpened by memory. The dream clung to her like cobwebs spun from ash—smoke in her nose, whispers in her ears, phantom chains coiled tight around something she could no longer name. And that voice: *You left something behind.*

What, she thought, as sarcasm curled through her like steam. *My dignity? My throne? The glaive I forged from dying stars? Or perhaps my last unshattered nerve?*

Her ears twitched. A leaf had the audacity to alight on the windowsill. She slapped it off with one disdainful paw, as if it had just insulted her lineage before a tribunal of enchanted mirrors. It fluttered to the floor, a spineless casualty.

If this plane has even the ghost of justice left, that leaf will return someday—as lint. The insidious kind. The kind that clings through flame, fury, and every divine laundering rite known to mortal kind.

Somewhere in the distance, Elira hummed. Bright and off-key, like hope dressed for tea.

Mortals and their cheer. I should bottle it, pin it to parchment, and watch it wither from neglect.

Velzara leapt from the windowsill, landing with pointed

grace. The floorboards, warmed by sunlight, felt almost smug beneath her paws. She padded forward, then froze. The brush waited on the side table. It sat coiled in silence, not innocent but calculating, as if it hadn't attempted regicide less than an hour ago. Some curses wore bells. Others wore bristles. Her eyes narrowed.

It dares to feign ignorance. But I have seen that smug, bristled silence before—the posture of a tool that knows its hands are unclean.

She hissed. Then, with the solemnity of an ancient war declaration, she struck. The brush tumbled from the table and hit the floor with the dull indignity of a vanquished foe.

A fitting end for a relic that overstepped its station. I name thee exiled from the Court of Tolerable Things. This was the first blow in my campaign to reclaim the throne.

Step one: brush destroyed. Step two: pants.

She paused.

A demotion from cursed heirloom to accessory of shame. Still beneath me. But apparently vital, like a chamber pot in a crystal palace. Time to discover what new heresy the chaos goblin in pastels had unleashed upon the waking world.

The kitchen was worse than she remembered. Not merely disordered—*corrupted.* Tolerable mess had surrendered to something more insidious. Mortals lived like gremlins with grudges and rental agreements. Dishes teetered in fragile towers, mimicking the broken spires of a ruined city. A glowing mushroom had colonized a chipped mug, releasing a scent both awful and, infuriatingly, nostalgic. To her refined senses, now inexplicably amplified by this fur-clad form, it was a pungent symphony: brimstone and iron, yes, but also the cloying sweetness of overcooked despair. She recognized it instantly, the olfactory echo of millennia-old defeat, and refused to mourn it. Half a loaf of bread slumped on the counter, one ominous bite missing. The kind of bite that implied teeth, curses, or worse. Whether bird, squirrel, or spiteful revenant, the culprit had yet to be identified. The kettle quivered on the stove, trembling like it had opinions. Possibly trauma. Ward-runes shimmered faintly on its base, primed to shriek the moment it felt neglected.

Ah. A room designed by entropy, blessed with negligence, and kissed by fire hazard. Finally, something in this pastel prison speaks my dialect.

Elira stood at the counter, locked in mortal combat with a jam jar. "Morning, Nox!" she chirped, as if the one she addressed had not once turned a sea to flame out of boredom. "Sleep okay?"

Did I sleep 'okay.' I descended into the abyssal archives of my own mind, where dreams were not gentle whispers but thundering echoes of ash and ruin, the iron taste of legacy stripped to bone. I stood, not in a bed, but in the echoing chambers of my broken kingdom, and heard something older than curses whisper my true name, a sound that flayed the very air. And now she asks, brightly, if I slept well—as if the abyss hands out bedtime stories for slumbering tyrants.

I should desecrate her shoe. Just once. For instructional value. But no. Timing matters. Revenge is best when it has an audience. And maybe a sigil or two. The brush, a mere instrument of human vanity, would be the first to fall, swift and merciless. Her footwear, those fabric prisons, would follow—hexed before an audience, ideally with screaming. A proper declaration of hostilities.

With a triumphant grunt, Elira popped the jar open. Half the preserves vanished in a puff of glittering sparks. "Ugh. Enchanted preserves again. Why does everything Grandma left behind either explode, whisper secrets, or taste like flowers and judgment?"

Velzara froze, eyes narrowing with slow, deliberate disdain.

Ah. The tell-tale shimmer of bound magic, the faint hum of ancient compacts. The jam explodes. The secrets whisper. The judgment clings like perfume. This place isn't just lace doilies and suspicious cheer—it has teeth. And memory. If the preserves whisper, what infernal pacts do the very beams remember? What unspeakable oaths are woven into the threadbare rugs?

She didn't like the answer forming in her mind. But it might prove exceedingly useful.

One moment, she prowled, a predator in miniature, calculating vectors of strategic ingress. The next, Elira seized her without grace or warning—a barbarian's clumsy snatch, like a misplaced sock claimed without thought or ceremony. No ritual marked the moment. No reverence softened the offense. Only hands: sudden, presumptuous, and entirely unwelcome, violating her personal sovereign territory.

No invocation. No challenge. Not even the decency of a salutation. This is not an embrace. It is an incursion. And this is how wars begin.

"What a soft little menace you are," Elira cooed, fingers daring to drift behind Velzara's ears.

An act of war. And yet, a tactical opening. Fine. I will permit it—briefly. If it brings me closer to the truth of this house, I will endure. I will feign docility. I will turn every thread of this cursed fluff into a weapon. Let her drop her guard. Let her believe I am tamed.

Elira scratched behind her ears. Against every decree of pride and principle, Velzara purred.

Good. Let her believe it. Let her think the purring means surrender. Let her offer belly rubs and lullabies, thinking me conquered. It will make the reckoning all the sweeter.

A stroke along her spine. The purr deepened—unbidden, and wholly unacceptable.

Convincing. Yes. Maintain the charade. This is infiltration. Subterfuge. A long con wrapped in velvet.

Her eyelids fluttered, a betrayal of her unwavering resolve.

Focus. Hold the line. One must commit if the deception is to succeed. I am shadow. I am silence. I am a harbinger of doom—

"Toe beans," Elira whispered, and her fingers, those instruments of chaos, kneaded a particularly sensitive pad.

Velzara's back leg kicked before she could stop it—a single, damning spasm of pure, unadulterated treachery. Her body sagged into Elira's arms, all resistance draining away like a spilled potion, molten with disgrace. A truly humiliating slump. Then came the tail: it curled, flicked once, a desperate semaphore of denial, and then settled like a velvet white flag, limp and accusatory against her own traitorous form. And still, the purring continued—loud enough to shame a demon, relentless as prophecy.

Abort the mission. Abort—

Too late. The traitorous purrs have reached full volume.

Elira cradled her closer, the strokes slowing into a rhythm too gentle to be survived unscathed. Velzara's vision blurred. Her limbs unraveled. The scent of lavender and mortal hope surrounded her like fog.

This is a mistake. I have strayed too far from shadow and shame. I let the fluff seduce me, and now I am lost in it.

Her last coherent thought before sleep reclaimed her wasn't a vow of vengeance. It was...

Maybe later I'll let her pet my belly. But only as bait...

She sprawled in the same sunlit trap she'd once escaped, now warm and deceptively still. Comfort wrapped around her like a bribe. Her fur soaked in the heat, penitent and unrepentant all at once. The air felt thick—motionless in a way that suggested tension, not peace. The kind of quiet that came just before a battlefield opened.

She lifted her head and froze. In the window's glare, a figure waited. Not the cursed, fur-clad shape she wore, but the one she had lost. For a suspended moment, disbelief warred with recognition. It stood tall, cloaked in shadow, wreathed in power. Her breath caught.

Thank the flames.

Horns like obsidian daggers swept back from her brow, wicked and precise, sharp enough to silence a prayer. Her eyes burned with violet fire, molten and unrelenting, the kind of gaze that had turned kings to loyalists and enemies to ash. Crimson-black armor encased her like forged conviction, edged in flame and etched with the weight of old vows. The shimmer of hellfire still clung to it, faint but unforgotten. Power waited there. Not gone. Not broken. Only biding its time.

Yes. This is who I was, who I remain. This is what they feared, what they shackled in silk and sunbeams, hoping I would forget the shape of flame.

Then she saw the chains. Her throat caught—this was no

simple binding. One coiled tight around her ankle, the other circled her neck, each link black iron polished like dull obsidian and etched with runes she had long refused to utter. They pulsed faintly, alive with buried intent. The words weren't spoken or heard. They pressed inward all the same, threaded through metal and memory—commandments carved without consent.

She took a step back. The reflection didn't retreat. It stood, steady and knowing, as if it carried every secret she'd ever buried.

No. I was not captured. I was offered lies in the shape of chains. I was not broken. I was betrayed. And betrayal wears a familiar face.

Her breath caught. At the end of one chain hung a delicate, shining silver bell. It jingled lightly, almost sweet. But the sound rang like a curse, soft and mocking.

No. Not the bell. Not that insult wrapped in innocence. A jingle fit for pets and playthings, not for me. A muzzle masquerading as mercy.

It was the sound of a kitten toying with a bell—cheap, ridiculous, made for collars stitched by mortals who believed in safety, not fear. It didn't belong. Not here. Not at the end of her chain. Her claws flexed, aching for something to break. The reflection stayed motionless, unbreathing. But inside, something shifted. A blade turning through scar tissue long buried but never softened. The bell didn't chime—it passed judgment. Each note curled around her ribs like a vow she never agreed to but still bore, tight and cruel. It wasn't an echo; it was a sentence carried in sound, humming in her bones like a lie polished into doctrine.

She tried to look away, to tear her gaze from the insult dangling at the end of the chain. But the bell held her. Not with power. With recognition. It pressed into her like a blade made of memory, honed on every indignity she thought she'd survived.

Someone did this. Someone who feared what I was. What I still am. They didn't want me dead. They wanted me diminished. Dosed with affection. Draped in docility. Leashed.

She opened her mouth to scream, but something inside her tore. The world lurched sideways, splitting at the seams. The chains dissolved. Sunlight recoiled, retreating like a spy caught listening at the door.

CHAPTER 4
THE FUR AGAINST FURY

The day had deepened beyond her memory. She blinked, and the lingering phantom of her last thought dissipated, yielding to warmth. Sunlight, once a thin wash, now pooled across the floor in thick, rich amber, casting long, lazy shadows—indolent, unconcerned things. Dust motes drifted, glinting like tiny, retired fire spirits, serving no purpose beyond irritation, glittering defiance meant to be trampled. She had been deposited. *Deposited.* On a footstool.

Elira had done it recently, with the breezy authority of someone rearranging throw pillows. Humming off-key, no doubt, and muttering something about mending spells before drifting away, blissfully unaware—in her deeply mortal way—that she hadn't repositioned a cushion, but relocated a legend. A legend with claws. Not a plush accessory.

Velzara blinked again, slow and suspicious, as if testing the world for fresh insolence. Her limbs dragged with unfamiliar weight. Her thoughts snagged and tangled, wrapped in wool. It felt like sleep had yanked her backward through molasses and sin, then flung her sideways into someone else's dreams—

40

heedless of her schedule, her dignity, or her divine right to be feared.

She turned, and there it was: the unkind truth the glass had no right to reflect. The glass offered no chains, no throne, no smoldering gaze beneath a crown of flame. No whisper of Malediction, no lingering trace of ruin. There was only fluff, positioned with idiotic symmetry, a halo of softness encircling her as if she were some blessed beast. And she was radiantly framed with the indignity of mortal sunlight. It showed her exactly as the world now saw her: A cat, black-furred and infuriatingly symmetrical, as if the curse had taken extra care to be aesthetically cruel.

An offense to symmetry. An insult carved in whiskers and mockery. The mirror lies but not enough.

Her paw lifted for a single traitorous lick, like a curse whispered into a ballroom. She froze mid-gesture, paw raised like a heretic caught mid-prayer. It hadn't been a conscious act —certainly not regal. It had been natural, instinctive, feral, beneath her. The moment her tongue met fur, time fractured. Her pupils shrank to pinpricks. Her tail gave a violent twitch, as if preparing to file a formal grievance.

No. No, by the smoldering chains of Nar'Khalor, I did not just defile myself in full view of the sun.

She stared at the paw. Then the tongue. Then back at the paw again, as if indignation alone could rewind time and undo the betrayal.

Was that grooming? Have I descended so far, so humiliatingly fast, that instinct has outpaced intention? First a lick. Then string. Then purring. Then a tiny witch hat and seasonal portraits on the mortal's hearth. No. This is not my arc. My saga does not end in sunbeams and seasonal costumes. I am not some bewitched cushion granted personality by pity.

She let out a tiny, strangled noise. Once a war cry that had shattered battlements—now a squeaky cupboard with abandonment issues and a personal vendetta. In a frenzy of revulsion, she scraped her tongue against the blanket, as if she could scour the instinct clean from her soul.

So this is how it ends. Not in flame or fury, but with a traitorous flick of the tongue. No battle cry. No prophecy. Just a soft, domesticated disgrace performed in full daylight. Is this what I've become? A pampered beast waiting for string, for sunbeams, for... gods forbid... accessories?

She hissed, low and velvet-edged, a warning aimed squarely at the heavens. Then she launched herself from the stool with every ounce of fury six pounds of betrayal could contain. To her eternal shame, it landed not with the sound of war... but with a soft, traitorous thump.

I must act. Anything less, and the next lick will unravel my legend, page by page, until even the footnotes forget me.

The hallway creaked beneath her paws as she crept forward. Her nose twitched at every step, as if trying to warn her and file a formal complaint. One door, once barely ajar, now gaped wide, as though it had discovered a taste for theatrics and was moments away from delivering a monologue.

Oh, how theatrical. The very architecture is auditioning. If the walls start soliloquizing, I'm burning the house down on principle.

It led to a staircase that curled downward like a smirk into darkness thick with secrets. And yes—definitely mold. The air bit back, older and colder, laced with sulfur, dried herbs, and something heavier: memory. It clung to the walls like the aftermath of a half-forgotten ritual, one that ended in guilt and a very awkward silence. She paused at the threshold.

That scent. It stirred something old in her bones—spellwork, blood rites, home. You know. The good stuff. Her ears twitched. Her tail dipped. The house was remembering too.

Why is it always stairs with you people? Is the abyss not dramatic enough? Must every horror be hidden down a spiral like some cursed architect's inside joke.

She padded forward. Each stair groaned beneath her, as if resenting her existence as deeply as she resented the descent. At the bottom, the basement unfolded into a wide chamber cluttered with mismatched cabinets. Some were sealed with dripped wax. Others had been nailed shut with theatrical gusto. Glowing runes shimmered across the surfaces, scrawled in the unmistakable hand of adolescent hubris: sloppy, unmarked, and so tragically amateur it was nearly offensive.

What is this? A sanctum for sentimental failures? Did a hedge-witch have a hoarding phase and mistake it for legacy?

In the far corner loomed a mirror. It was tall and rectangular while its frame was carved with half-familiar symbols. A velvet cloth hung over it like modesty wielded as menace. The cloth held still, but the air around it rippled, taut and waiting, like a breath afraid to be heard. She gave it a wide berth.

Oh, I know your kind. Draped in secrets, drunk on foreknowledge, and desperate to be relevant. Not today, Mirror of Regret. I've had quite enough theatrics.

Instead, her attention slid toward a squat table where an open drawer spilled over with delicate glass vials. Each bore a handwritten label in smudged ink:

Essence of Forgotten Song
Sunset in a Bottle
Feral Thoughts (Do Not Drink)

She stared.

Is this a potion rack or a failed grimoire audition? Who labeled these? Some necromancer's apprentice with abandonment issues and a leaky pen? Actual bottled magic. Just tossed here. Unsorted. Unlabeled. Unguarded. It's not a vault. It's a pantry for arcane regret. Do they think enchantments are pantry goods? That you can cork madness, slap a poetic name on it, and stack it beside the spices?

Someone's going to drink "Feral Thoughts" and start speaking to the floorboards in tongues like it's part of the ritual. This isn't storage. It's a cry for help written in glass and poor judgment.

It was enough to make her want to scream. If she weren't fairly certain it would come out as a squeak—again. One jar sat cracked near the edge of the cabinet. Inside, a dark mist churned—slow and patient, like it had all the time in the world to notice her. Stillness clung to it, not the kind that waited, but the kind that watched. When she blinked, it seemed to smile.

Velzara leaned closer and sniffed. The mist shifted. It exhaled through the seams of reality, and something familiar moved with it. Her true name touched the air—not spoken aloud, but seared into it. The pulse that followed wasn't sound but sensation, thrumming through her bones with cruel recognition. She knew that presence. And it had always known her. She recoiled, ears flat.

Of course it whispered. Cracked jars are where curses

ferment. That's Cursecraft 101. Anyone who's ever lost a soul should know that.

She backed away slowly, every muscle coiled like tinder waiting for a spark.

This house is watching me. And worse, labeling things like a half-trained seer with no fear of consequences. If I don't move first, it will. I need answers. And if the house won't offer them, I will take them. One cracked relic at a time. Preferably before I'm offered a snack called "The Essence of Doubt" and told it's medicinal.

Mist slithered upward, cold and far too familiar, curling across her fur like a lover returned from the grave. As it touched her, something deep within her slipped loose. She began to drift, neither waking nor dreaming, suspended somewhere in between. Her body felt weightless, her breath forgotten. The air around her no longer obeyed gravity; it simply allowed her to float, as though the rules of the world had been politely dismissed. Below, the basement vanished. The walls dissolved into shadow. There was no floor, no ceiling—only darkness, pressing in from all directions.

She felt eyes. Countless and unblinking, they watched her without pause, their presence thick as velvet and twice as suffocating. Then the whispers came, curling at the edge of her hearing. They were spun from breathless secrets and smoke that defied the laws of the living. At first, the voices wavered. Then they gathered strength, forming a chant in the old tongue —her tongue—each word measured and deliberate, like links of a chain being drawn tighter. It did not seek favor, and it offered no devotion. It tightened with purpose, spoken to bind, not to bless.

Oh, of course. What better way to honor a legacy of fire and dominion than with a bastardized ritual scraped from the margins of some stolen grimoire. An invocation offered without my name spoken properly, without pact, without permission. This isn't summoning. It's sacrilege.

A hand emerged from the dark. Black-boned, with joints that dripped ink which hissed and spat at every movement. Each drop sounded like a scream smothered before it could rise. The hand moved with ritualistic grace—precise, sharp, and so offensively confident it felt rehearsed, as though the darkness had practiced for this moment across centuries. Each gesture carved the void.

A sigil ignited in the air, jagged and trembling, wrapped in flame. At its center bloomed a mark: a pawprint, delicately stylized and unbearably cute in its perfection. Velzara stared. Her stomach clenched—not from fear, but from fury. The hatred that rose was sudden, searing, and agonizingly specific.

No. Absolutely not. If you seek to bind me, then do it with fire, not some parody scraped from the ashes of my legacy. Until then, your circle is ash. Your will holds nothing.

She reached for the sigil, paw trembling with fury she refused to mask. The ember behind her eyes burned hotter with each breath.

They forged a flaming pawprint into a binding seal. That was their idea of containment?

The insult did not strike all at once. It settled slowly, like poison winding toward the heart.

I ruled empires. I melted kings. I set the sky on fire because someone dared interrupt me mid-sentence. And this is what remains? Not blood. Not flame. But gentle curves. Balanced lines. A mark so polished it might as well have been stitched on a tea towel. They made me cute. They will answer for it.

Her claws scraped the edge of the sigil, and it flared. Magic surged—spite made manifest—biting into her pads with a cold that burned like frostbite kissed by flame. A chill snapped around her throat, tight and sharp, followed by an invisible leash that yanked her backward. There was no mercy in it. Just raw force, wielded without reverence.

She was dragged through the dark, limbs flailing, voice torn from her. The pull wrenched her back into her body without warning, without ritual, without even the courtesy of a proper curse. Just a glowing sigil, a leash of stolen magic, and one more cosmic insult hurled in her face.

Truly, the indignities line up like suitors—none of them worthy, none invited, and all multiplying like vermin. If one of them arrives with flowers, I will bite the bouquet and curse the scent so thoroughly the petals wither in apology.

Her eyes shot open, a sharp ache behind them. The air pressed in around her, heavy with the greasy residue of spent magic.

Oh, good. We've progressed from scented illusions to soul-mangling incantations. At least the theme is consistent.

Fur bristling and heart hammering like battle drums in her ribs, she crouched—poised for war, or worse. She was still in the basement. The mist had vanished, erased like a lie told by an archdevil with tenure. No trace remained but the scent of sulfur, sharp and cloying, thick with accusation. The echo of her name still clung to her ears, a whisper that refused to die with dignity.

That sigil, she thought, her breath catching mid-thought.

A sudden pressure gripped her chest, and her fur bristled before her mind could catch up.

It wasn't just familiar. It fit like a cage built to my measurements, yet again. Always the same ornamental precision, as if someone had studied my fire not to revere it, but to find the most efficient way to smother it.

A sudden crash rang out above her, followed by Elira's voice, distant and spectacularly exasperated. "Nox? Did you knock over the spellbook pile again?!"

Velzara blinked and snapped her head toward the stairs.

I never brought down an empire without a herald, a hex, and at least one poetic threat. Do I look like an amateur?

She hadn't. Which meant something else had knocked over the spellbooks. And that was unacceptable.

She launched from the table in one fluid motion—silent and sharp, each movement guided by instinct and tuned to purpose. Behind her, the cracked vial pulsed once, shallow and rhythmic like a dying heartbeat, then fell still. She didn't look back.

Let it explode. That would be the most coherent decision this house has made today.

She slipped up the stairs like a curse hunting for a crack in the world, her claws sheathed and ears tracking every sound.

The house still danced with sunlight, smug in its ordinary charm. But something beneath that brightness had shifted—not with noise, but with weight, like a secret humming quietly within the walls. The hallway stretched ahead, a gauntlet of doors and dust, wrapped in a silence that carried the scent of something long buried.

As she passed the charm wall, she took in the bells, feathers, and bundles of rosemary arranged with protective intent. One of the bells chimed. There was no wind. Nothing had touched it. Yet the sound rang clear. She stopped mid-step. The fur along her spine rose, alert and unwilling.

Absolutely not. Not even if it arrives embroidered, sanctified, and escorted by heralds. The answer remains a molten no.

Her eyes narrowed as she crept forward, movement sleek and silent, like a blade drawn in ceremony and thirsting for purpose.

Something in this house just crossed a threshold it will not return from—and I am the reckoning. I come with claws.

Then Elira's voice came again, sharper now, calling from the study. "Seriously, Nox? These were alphabetized."

Velzara hissed under her breath.

Even I wouldn't desecrate a filing system. I believe in order. I once declared holy vengeance over a scroll misfiled by a single rune.

She reached the doorway and peered around the frame.

Elira knelt beside a toppled stack of tomes and brittle scrolls, muttering as she tried to reassemble the chaos. Loose pages fluttered across the floor. Ink smeared in looping trails, as though something had danced through it with reckless enthusiasm and no sense of rhythm.

Velzara blinked, her tail twitching.

Wonderful. We're being haunted by something with two left feet and a deep disrespect for proper sigilic taxonomy.

Elira didn't notice. But Velzara did. She always noticed. A thick, leather-bound tome lay open nearby, its runes still glowing faintly—stubborn, clinging to relevance with the weary gleam of magic that should have died in peace, but instead lingered like a ghost with opinions.

Typical mortal spellwork. Half-finished, poorly anchored, and incapable of decomposing with dignity.

The pages twitched, restless and irritable, like something half-asleep and already weary of existence. And there, beside the shelf nestled in shadow, was a footprint. It was small, clawed, and unmistakably not hers. She froze, eyes fixed on the mark. Her tail lashed once, slow and precise, like the final punctuation in a very well-written curse.

Well. Someone clearly missed the screaming inscription etched in bone at the door. Or worse, they read it and thought it didn't apply.

Her gaze burned holes into the floorboards, but the footprint didn't waver. Whoever had left it had dared to walk here while she slept. Whoever it was, they would learn. This house might be cursed. It might be dusty. It might be oppressively sunlit and emotionally compromised. But it belonged to her now.

Every creaking floorboard. Every cursed jar mislabeled by some halfwit alchemist. Every scroll whimpering beneath the weight of misfortune. Mine.

Velzara's eyes narrowed into molten slits.

So, she thought, the ember of rage curling behind her gaze like smoke from a spell someone failed to contain properly, *I'm not the only uninvited guest in this absurd little house. Good. Let them come. I've taken back kingdoms with less. Let them try me.*

CHAPTER 5
VENGEANCE, NOW WITH GLITTER

Magic clung to the air, thick with the scent of burnt parchment, old fur, and that particular strain of reckless energy that only ever arrived uninvited. This wasn't Elira's cinnamon-tea-and-sentiment blend, nor was it Velzara's own signature of brimstone and disdain. It carried the weight of something older and cruder, the kind of presence that never knocked because it didn't believe it had to.

Velzara dropped low, slinking forward with the practiced grace of a being who had once razed cities for entertainment and dined on the screams of oathbreakers.

Paws or no paws, this remains my dominion. I've hunted soul-thieves through catacombs slick with betrayal. I've danced blade-first beneath skies that bled curses. And now some threadbare scavenger thinks to trespass? I'll carve its name into the floorboards with its own claws—and charge it rent for the privilege.

The footprint was small, clawed, and three-toed. It was most certainly not hers. A trail of inky smudges led away from the toppled spellbooks and disappeared into the hallway.

Behind her, Elira continued fussing with the scrolls, blissfully unaware of the magical felony unfolding beneath her feet. "I know I stacked these right. Or maybe by curse classification...? No, no—alphabetical by threat level..."

Velzara's ears flicked as she crept forward and sniffed the trail. It wasn't just ink; it was magic—wild and sour, tinged with the citrus bite of mayhem and regret.

Imp.

The realization settled over her like a cold weight, heavy with the dissatisfaction of recognizing an enemy she had once dismissed beneath her notice. It wasn't a demon, nor even a creature worthy of respect or fear. It was something far lesser. Nothing more than a piddling pest. It had probably escaped, or worse, been summoned by a half-drunk hedge mage with delusions of grandeur and a bargain-bin spellbook full of glitter and bad decisions.

A low hiss curled from her throat, and Elira's head snapped up. "Nox? Did you actually knock these over this time?"

Velzara turned slowly, her tail flicking behind her like insult carved into punctuation.

Please. As if I'd dull a claw on that tragic pamphlet pile. I once razed a basilica of forbidden tomes because someone filed a soul index under "miscellaneous."

"Well, if it wasn't you..." Elira trailed off, eyes narrowing as she finally noticed the tracks. "Wait... are you bleeding? Is this ink?"

Velzara blocked her path, poised like a velvet-clawed bouncer who had closed the bar out of pure spite. But of course, the girl had already looked. Mortals always peek before they think and then wonder why the furniture bleeds.

Elira blinked. "Oh gods. Is that a foot?"

Velzara hissed, the sound laced with velvet wrath and ancient judgment.

Yes, girl. Congratulations. You've summoned a poltergeist with the coordination of a concussed squirrel mid-hex binge and none of the shame.

Before Elira could voice another mortal insight, Velzara launched after the trail. She moved silent and precise, her fury divine. Tiny, clawed prints darted across the rug, winding past shelves cluttered with mismatched candles. She followed, low and fast, her teeth bared in delight.

The scent grew stronger—tangled magic, badly summoned. It reeked of carelessness and the kind of arcane negligence she could taste. The hunt had begun.

She crouched, muscles drawn taut, her eyes narrowed to molten slits. The world fell away. There was only the breath before the strike, and the foolish creature that had drawn her ire. She could taste it now—the sharp tang of misfired spellwork and raw desperation hanging thick in the air. A smear of glitter caught her eye, a ridiculous trace that suggested someone had attempted to conjure power with nothing more than crayons and inflated ego.

Oh, you sparkle-drenched mistake. You really should have picked a different house. I've buried stronger creatures in ornamental ashtrays. You have no idea who you just pissed off.

And then her hindquarters began to twitch.

No. No, absolutely not. What is this betrayal? This undignified rhythmic prelude?

This is not whimsy. This is a coiling of doom. A wind-up of destruction.

She tried to stop, but her own legs betrayed her—bouncing with a rebellious enthusiasm that deserved a trial, a sentencing, and perhaps a ceremonial unfluffing. Her tail curved like a question mark sharpened into threat. Her hips rocked again. She growled under her breath.

I revoke your sovereignty, you treasonous limbs. May the fires of dignity consume your fluff in full view of your ancestors.

She sprang—claws extended, fury ignited, and pride discarded like a casualty of war. A high-pitched yelp followed, then an explosion of fur and panic as the imp fled like a half-formed spell flung from a broken wand. Velzara arrowed after it, claws flashing, a growl rising in her throat with the cadence of a battle hymn. She skidded into a stack of books and didn't bother with regret. Her focus was absolute.

Dignity is a renewable resource. This is vengeance. This is the hunt. This is justice with claws and velocity.

"Elira!" She tried to growl. It emerged as a chirrup, high-pitched and humiliating. "Your furniture is possessed."

From the hallway: "Are you... doing zoomies again? Is this... seasonal? Should I look it up?"

I swear on my last infernal contract, if you say "floof mode," I will eat your hairbrush and curse your pillow to whisper insecurities to you while you sleep.

Velzara slid around the fallen books, eyes locked. There—a flicker of shadow. The cabinet door slammed shut. Velzara froze mid-run, muscles coiled, tail twitching with divine purpose.

You can run, glitter spawn. But I have hunted flame-born traitors through collapsing fortresses. I will not be bested by something wearing a tea cozy.

Velzara dropped low, her tail twitching with anticipation. A hum pulsed from behind the cabinet door, soft and thorny —like a lullaby composed in hexes and poor decisions. A sneeze followed. It was muffled, but high-pitched and unmistakably childlike.

There you are, she thought, as triumph bloomed slow and venom-sweet, like a trap finally sprung. *Run while you still think it's a game. The hunt begins with mercy and ends with me.*

She leapt. The cabinet burst open, and a violet-and-silver blur shot past her. It cackled and hissed at the same time, sounding like a kettle possessed by spirits. Sparks erupted in its wake. Glitter lingered in the air, suspended like evidence at a crime scene.

"What in the abyss—!" Elira called out.

The creature zipped overhead, trailing powdered sin and the smug audacity of something too foolish to recognize fate when it snarled. It wore a tea cozy on its head, which bobbed as it flew, bouncing like a war crime wrapped in wool.

"HI!" it squeaked. "You're fast!"

Velzara bared her teeth.

I'm going to disassemble you with the patience of a demon scribe and the flair of a disappointed god. I'll do it slowly, and I will provide commentary.

"I like you! Wanna play catch-the-enchanted-spoon?"

A silver spoon screamed past her ear, embedded itself in the wall with a musical twang, and began to vibrate— ominously, as if preparing to summon the end times in D-sharp.

Excellent, she thought. *A weapon, and possibly evidence. Preferably both. If I'm lucky, I can bludgeon the imp and then submit the spoon to a tribunal for judgment. Efficiency, as it should be.*

She lunged. The imp shrieked with glee and bolted up the hallway wall like possessed lightning in enchanted tap shoes. It knocked down a wind chime, which immediately began chanting,"One, two, doom comes for youuuu—"

Finally. Something with taste. I haven't heard a proper

doom-chant since the Siege of Kharazeth and they had actual banshees.

Velzara vaulted off the banister, claws extended, and landed atop the bookshelf with the precision of a nightmare ballerina.

I've hunted void-crows through arcane blizzards. I will not— repeat, will not—be outmaneuvered by a magical sock puppet with poor impulse control and a tea cozy for a crown.

"It wasn't my spell! I was just hiding! You smell like fury and snacks!" the imp crowed, its tail wrapped precariously around the ceiling sconce.

You smell like a bankrupt sylph's wardrobe and a lie draped in sequins. When I'm finished, your remains will be pressed between cursed vellum and regret as a warning to conjurers who mistake sparkle for power.

It flung something shiny—a fork, shimmering with malevolent energy and what might have been guilt. The utensil clattered across the floor, sprouted legs, and bolted under the couch as if it were late for a summoning. Velzara didn't hesitate. She dove after it, a blur of teeth, claws, and divine fury.

Let no one question my dedication. I have hurled myself beneath upholstery as a fury-wrapped projectile of divine spite. For vengeance. For cutlery. For the principle of the thing.

Under the couch, she found dust, socks, an old wand still twitching, a patch of glowing lint—and the imp. It was wedged halfway into a boot, limbs akimbo, like a goblin-shaped crime scene.

"I live here now!" it declared, radiating the confidence of a creature who had never, in its entire unfortunate life, met a consequence it didn't try to marry.

Velzara stared. A tiny flicker... of something... crossed her molten eyes before being immediately extinguished.

I once bathed in a volcano sculpted from betrayal and prophecy. Now I'm locked in mortal combat with a rhinestone war criminal wedged inside footwear. My downfall, apparently, is retail upholstery. I should have stayed cursed. At least the chains had dignity. This has upholstery.

She pounced.

THUMP

SQUAWK

An eruption of glitter followed so dense it seemed to shimmer with intent. It cursed the upholstery and would likely outlast the house, the season, and all mortal faith in furniture.

Back in the study, Elira sat cross-legged on the rug, the spellbooks re-stacked in a loose approximation of order beside her. One hand cradled a chipped mug of lukewarm tea. The other scrolled through a webpage so poorly formatted it might have been cursed by a minor gremlin.

Mystical Cat Behavior and You: A Novice Witch's Guide to Feline Familiar Folly

"Huh," she muttered. "Zoomies are a thing. Solar flares, moon phases, leyline surges... Oh! This one says some cats 'see the spirits of the recently departed and chase them through the home like ghosts made of string.'"

A sudden **THUMP** rattled the floorboards beneath her. Elira blinked. Then came another crash, followed by a metallic clatter—something that might have once been a fork.

That was definitely a fork. And... was that laughter?

She took a thoughtful sip of tea. "I should probably check on that," she murmured, with the weary cadence of someone not paid nearly enough to deal with this.

A sharp yowl followed, dramatic and unmistakably familiar. Then, faintly from the hallway: *"I LIVE HERE NOW!"*

She sighed, set down her mug, and brushed the dust from her robe with quiet resignation.

"Nox? If you're chasing spirits again, try not to break the salt jars. That stuff's expensive."

Elira turned the corner just in time for a glowing spoon to zip past her face. It buzzed with magical tension and the kind of intent that usually ends in incident reports and scorched furniture.

She froze. "Nox?"

From beneath the couch came a sneeze, tiny and somehow accusatory. Then came an explosion of glitter. Sparks hissed against the floorboards, and the air trembled with curses spoken in too many languages at once.

Elira knelt with slow, theatrical caution, lifting the couch skirt like she was unveiling a haunted art exhibit.

"Nox... why are you fighting a tea cozy?"

She rubbed her eyes.

Still there: the cat, the tea cozy, and what looked dangerously close to a sentient sparkle cyclone. Apocalypse, it seemed, had chosen the living room as its arena.

Velzara had the imp pinned beneath one paw, claws splayed with righteous menace. Her other paw hovered mid-air like the hand of an executioner preparing the final blow. Her eyes glowed. Her tail cracked the air with a beat that could summon storms. A low rumbling purr, barely audible beneath her breath, hummed with a satisfaction she immediately loathed. A plume of pink smoke exploded in protest, the tragic gasp of a celebratory hex unraveling mid-tantrum.

Velzara flew backward in a blur of energy and vengeance. She slammed into the far bookshelf, hard enough to jostle sacred texts and offend the very walls. Her fur crackled with static. Her ears rang like church bells during an exorcism. Iridescent glitter clung to her—betrayal made photogenic. The rug turned purple. The potted plant in the corner snapped open a mouth full of fangs and bit a throw pillow clean in half. Elira's mug let out a long, mournful scream before vanishing in a puff of steam and nothingness. A glitter-drenched shockwave rippled outward.

Elira staggered through the haze, coughing. "That wasn't normal! Was that one of the pantry spirits?! Why is it wearing a tea cozy?! I *knew* Grandma's jam was haunted," Elira wheezed, glitter sticking to her teeth. One fleck latched onto her eyelash with the tenacity of trauma. "That was—wait. Nox?! Where *are* you?!"

She emerged from the rubble like a very small apocalypse. Glitter drenched her fur, and she smoldered with fury. She wore vengeance and fur alike, as if she had been mugged by irony itself.

If one more cursed object touches me today, I will unbind this reality. The drapes can perish with it—they've always looked smug. I will destroy it. Twice. Then exile its shrieking little soul to a dimension made entirely of stale salmon paste and weaponized regret.

But the imp was gone, vanished in a puff of sparkling shame and eldritch panic, leaving behind a scorched rug, a mooing lamp, and the unmistakable stench of toasted licorice and terrible decisions.

This isn't a home. It's a cursed carnival masquerading as

domesticity, swaddled in linen and betrayal. It owes me recompense—in blood, spoons, and silence. And if I don't get silence, I'll settle for screams.

Velzara's eye twitched. She rose from the scroll heap like a storm swelling from silence, fur bristling. Her whole body vibrated with residual static and righteous fury. A spark cracked off her tail and scorched the corner of a summoning chart.

Oh, it is on, she thought. *You glitter-slicked embarrassment. You dare unravel my dignity and flee un-shredded? I've incinerated empires for mispronouncing my name. I will not rest until your remains are bottled, labeled FAILURE, and shelved beneath expired curses—right beside the fondue set that screams.*

She stalked forward, every step calculated and silent, claws clicking against the floor like a fuse hissing toward detonation. Her ears twitched. Her nose flared. The scent was offensive—burnt magic and imp sweat smeared over cinnamon and drying herbs. Like a lullaby hexed, torched, and served with tea and a side of regret.

The house had tipped into nonsense. A hallway painting hung upside-down; its subject, a monocled badger mid-toast, looked visibly offended by the turn of events. A bookcase spun in muttering circles, grumbling about overdue fees. The walls pulsed faintly with leftover madness—like the building itself was locked in a polite argument with reality and losing. None of it mattered.

Velzara's hunt had become a crusade. And crusades had casualties.

A snicker whispered down the corridor—faint, gleeful. Velzara bolted, a blur of black velvet and vengeance. She rounded the corner and found it: wedged halfway into a kitchen drawer like a cursed hors d'oeuvre. One leg kicked a ladle. Spices littered the floor in its wake—cinnamon, scorched sugar, and something that had ambitions of being vanilla but died screaming. A whisk dangled from its tail. The drawer, crammed with cutlery and candle stubs, groaned in protest.

Velzara tensed, every muscle coiled. Her claws flexed against the tile. The air reeked of failure, burnt magic, and something profoundly unholy, with a hint of lavender. Velzara pounced, with the weight of a falling comet, landing on the imp's back. The drawer shuddered. Spoons scattered across the tile as if they were metallic deserters fleeing a lost cause. Sharp, glitter-streaked projectiles sang as they clattered and rebounded. One skimmed her whiskers. Another embedded in the floorboards, quivering like it was reconsidering peace.

"You're not supposed to be smart enough to dodge me!" she growled. It emerged, regrettably, as a furious, undignified *rowr-umph*.

The imp squeaked beneath her. "Negotiations?! Mercy?! Sudden mutual understanding?!"

Velzara unsheathed her claws just enough to suggest that honesty was no longer optional.

"Okayokayokay! I surrender! I yield! I release myself unto your floofy judgment!"

From the hallway, Elira's voice floated in—cheerful, distant, and unaware of the diplomatic catastrophe unraveling on her kitchen floor.

"Should I, uh... should I be helping?"

Velzara did not respond. This wasn't for Elira. It was for the glitter that still clung like a mockery. For the houseplant

61

that had grown teeth and opinions. For the sacred quiet she'd been denied since sunrise. This was justice.

The imp squirmed beneath her paw, tail coiled tightly around a stolen whisk like it was a war medal from some confectionary battlefield. Its eyes flicked side to side, twitching with calculation barely disguised as fear.

"Okay, okay," it babbled. "New deal. You let me go, I give you secrets. Forbidden, candy-based knowledge. The true name of the vacuum cleaner!"

A low growl started in Velzara's spine, thrumming through the floorboards like a ritual drumbeat.

The imp's smile twitched, then cracked. "Or I could just... vanish?"

She extended a single claw, deliberate in motion, heavy with intent. It hovered above its snout—the promise of judgment held in balance.

"Try me," she hissed, "and I'll haul your twitching remnants to the Screaming Pits of Glorramath, steep you in brimstone, and sip vengeance through your tail like a cursed cocktail."

The imp whimpered.

From the hallway: "Nox? Are you okay? Is there something *living* in the drawer? I can grab the broom. Or snacks. Possibly both?"

Velzara froze for a single instant. The imp didn't. It squeaked, exultant, and hacked up a glowing rune like a magical hairball born of treachery and sugar.

"NO—!"

Heat struck first, then sound—a sudden, concussive bloom. The drawer ruptured in a blaze of lime-green fire and lavender glitter, as if celebration had been hexed beyond recognition. Velzara was launched backward into the spice rack. Dried herbs burst around her like alchemical shrapnel. She hit the floor in a snarl of oregano, scorched pride, and trauma steeped in thyme.

The imp was already halfway out the window, wings buzzing like judgmental bagpipes. "I REGRET EVERYTHING AND NOTHING!" it howled into the wind.

Velzara scrambled to her paws, fur singed, eyes blazing. She lunged for the windowsill, but she was too late. Only the wind remained—carrying traces of glitter, and a half-charred tea towel that fluttered from the latch like a surrender flag stitched from polyester and betrayal.

CHAPTER 6
POLITE UNTIL PROVEN CURSED

Elira arrived in the kitchen just as the last of the sparkles settled. The window hung open. Herbs blanketed the floor like post-apocalyptic garnish. One of her wooden spoons was embedded in the ceiling, humming faintly. And her cat, her very not-normal, possibly mid-existential crisis in a fur coat cat, was glaring absolute murder at a tea towel.

Elira blinked. "...Did you get into the catnip?"

Velzara turned her head with the glacial menace of a dethroned deity contemplating smiting rights. If looks could incinerate, Elira would already be a freckled pile of ash and poor decisions. Instead, Velzara sneezed—a violent puff of oregano just to add insult to injury. Then she stalked past, tail held high in the sacred posture of cosmic outrage masquerading as feline dignity.

"Was it a mouse?" Elira called after her. "Or maybe a bee? A spirit? I read somewhere cats sometimes wrestle with trapped memories in the house beams. Was that it?"

Velzara didn't dignify that with a response. Her only answer was the precise upward flick of her tail—a gesture that conveyed, with centuries of infernal nuance, the full weight of her contempt.

Back in the sitting room, the cushion by the hearth awaited. Slightly dented and steeped in disappointment. She threw herself onto it with all the grace of a war goddess cast into exile and handed a bathrobe. With great ceremony, she began grooming a patch of fur still dusted in glitter that smelled faintly of peach lies and panic. Her thoughts snarled.

Vacuum cleaner. What did the imp mean by that? A weapon? A spell? Some domestic god of annihilation disguised as a broom with delusions of grandeur? The Devourer of Dust. The Siphoner of Souls. The Cyclone That Hungers. Have the mortals dared to tame it? To leash a whirlwind beneath their hearths? They would. They absolutely would.

She licked her shoulder. Then froze.

Catnip. Wait. What is catnip? A trap? A hallucinogen? Some cursed relic smuggled from a purring death cult—yes, the Cult of Twelve Paws—handed down by whiskered acolytes devoted to fluff and betrayal? Is this how it starts? Is this how they break me? First the glitter. Then the herbs. What's next? String?

Gods below, if I start chasing string, smite me where I stand.

She stared into the middle distance. Then exhaled, slow and grim, with the weary resolve of a fallen empress forced to wear mittens and call it empowerment.

I have survived wars. Toppled tyrants. Melted kingdoms into decorative glassware. And now... herbs and upholstery threaten to unmake me.

She sneezed again. This time, mint. From the other room: "Bless you!"

If I sneeze rosemary next, I'm invoking clause fourteen of my vengeance charter.

Velzara curled into the dented cushion, tail tucked over her nose.

At least here, she thought, *no one's watching me coil like a dethroned god on a secondhand throne.*

The fire crackled with the good sense to keep its commentary to itself. The world dimmed. Sleep tugged at her like velvet ropes, spun from indignity.

The warmth vanished. There was stone beneath her paws and soot in her lungs. The bitter tang of scorched blood lingered— sulfur, ash, and something older still. A scent that clung like memory, heavy with regret.

Oh. Wonderful. The nightmare cliff. Again. Because why dream of pillows or peace when I could have dignity that hisses and glows beneath my feet? I wasn't sleeping peacefully or anything.

There it was again, the obsidian cliff all vast and jagged as if forged from memory and searing spite. Chains coiled across the black stone, groaning faintly, though no wind moved them.

Fantastic. My subconscious brought props. Chains. Cliffs. Molten guilt. Very subtle. Perhaps a flaming mime to interpret my trauma? What's next—an orchestra of regrets?

But she wasn't alone. A figure stood at the cliff's edge, facing away. This time, it moved—turning with the slow finality of a verdict. Its eyes glowed like banked coals, casting dull light against the obsidian stone. The face that met her gaze was hers, only older—weathered by time, stripped of its crown. It was not a reflection forged in fire, but one eroded by it. A version that had carried the flame too long and watched it dwindle into smoke.

The reflection smiled, slow and weary, its knowing heavy as ash. "You're burning through the wrong lives, Velzara."

Well. That's ominous. And presumptuous. And if this is some spectral attempt at therapy, I suggest you find a mirror with fewer sharp edges and better lighting.

She recoiled, claws biting into the glassy stone beneath her. "Who are you supposed to be? A cautionary tale with better cheekbones? Name yourself before I rip that mockery off your skull." Her voice rang out, sharp and imperial, echoing across the black stone.

What came back wasn't an answer—it was her own voice, hollowed by distance, stripped of fire, returned like a memory that no longer belonged. The other Velzara didn't reply. She stepped forward, each footfall landing with the weight of judgment. Beneath her, the cliff shuddered as mirrors erupted from the stone—tall, jagged, slicing upward like a crown forged by someone with too much pain and too little mercy.

Each mirror held a version of her.

One cloaked in armor and flame.
One bound in chains.
One wrapped in rags, laughing too hard at nothing.
One asleep, already slipping into shadow.
One flickering at the edges, beginning to fade.
And one—bound in filigree-thin chains that
shimmered like moonlight on old glass. Her mouth
closed, her stare unblinking, she was a statue carved
from surrender and scorched intention.

Velzara's breath caught. She meant to sneer, to scoff, to

hurl derision like a shield. But for one brittle, breakable heartbeat, she paused. The silence before her wasn't righteous or victorious—it was easy. Not the ease of peace, but the stillness of surrender, of someone simply done. And deep within her, in the ember-lit place where firelight lullabies still whispered, something ached for that quiet. She crushed the feeling swiftly, burying it beneath venom and spectacle, smothering it with curses sharp enough to blacken the dream itself.

Oh, splendid. A hall of mirrors, because nothing declares psychological wellness like a curated exhibit of my worst fashion eras and emotionally catastrophic poses. Should I applaud? Or scream into the void like a mourning debutante denied her third funeral gown?

Perhaps next they'll parade out string-draped phantoms, reenacting my ruin with interpretive anguish and tragically blended eye shadow. Whoever staged this melodrama owes me reparations. Signed in blood. Sealed with scented ink. Preferably rosewater and regret.

She turned to flee, but her limbs held fast, caught by something older than fear. Memory wove through her like thread pulled too tight, snagging on names she'd buried in ash and oath. She looked down, expecting chains. Instead, ribbons coiled around her ankles—lavender, silver, and dusky rose. Not shackles, but something worse. They pressed in with the subtlety of a lie told gently, the kind of binding that smiles as it steals. Not restraint, but trespass disguised as tenderness.

Infernal irony wasn't cruel enough, apparently. No—let's sweeten the shackles. Let's bind me in shades of affection and call it grace, like some fallen queen repackaged for bardic redemption, twisted into a bedtime parable for bleeding hearts and gullible children.

I am being restrained by lavender. This is no longer a dream. It's an abomination stitched from sentiment and sorcery, thread and treachery, woven by fools who believe ribbons can redeem ruin.

They pulsed faintly, like veins echoing someone else's heartbeat. They weren't cruel or tight, only persistent in their hold—gentle in a way that felt like the ghost of comfort. The softness made them harder to resist, their familiarity more unbearable than chains.

The reflection tilted its head. "You're running in circles, princess. Dreaming inside dreams. What do you think you left behind?"

Velzara snarled and tore at the silk. Rage scraped her throat as she hissed, "I left nothing behind!"

I don't leave things behind. I reduce them to ashes and erasure—names scoured from memory, swallowed by smoke and spite. I do not cradle sentiment like some mortal fledgling with a haunted blanket and a whimper for a past.

The cliff gave way. Obsidian shattered beneath her, and the world tipped sideways, casting her into fire. Light surged in a blinding, merciless wave that stripped thought from bone. A bell rang out, its chime bright at first, then sharpened with each toll. By the third, it no longer sounded like music. It cut. The imp hovered in the void, motionless and silent. Its wings hung still, its expression unreadable. There was no glitter in sight, no trace of a grin—only an ancient stillness that watched her with the weight of a collapsing star. Velzara floated nearby, voiceless and adrift, as if the silence had hollowed the world.

Why are you here? Since when do you stare like a relic that knows too much? Since when do you look at me like I'm the one who forgot?

Then it spoke. The voice wasn't his. It wasn't young, or

light, or anything impish. It carried the stillness of things buried deep and left untouched. No echo of its counterpart. Only a weight that filled the space like old dust and older knowing.

"You weren't the only one cursed."

Velzara froze. The sound wrapped around her name like a collar crafted not with malice, but with intent. It was not loud, but it *fit*. Her chest locked. Her breath caught mid-incantation, as if even defiance had been sealed shut. And in that instant, as the echo spiraled through the void, she understood what had always been waiting beneath the glitter and games.

The mischief was a mask. The imp had been a vessel. And the curse... had never belonged to her alone.

Of course not. Nothing that cruel ever is.

Velzara jolted awake, her breath caught somewhere between a gasp and a curse. The fire had gone out. The hearth stood hollow and cold, its stones blackened as the final ember surrendered to ash. Even the cushion beneath her had turned against her, its warmth drained completely as if comfort itself had become a deception she no longer deserved. Something had followed her through the seam of sleep. Not a memory, and not quite a mistake. It felt like a promise left half-made and half-broken—still unraveling, still clinging, as if it had teeth.

She glared at the cushion. "Traitorous fluff," she muttered. "I should have hexed you when I had the chance."

Somewhere deep within the house, a bell chimed. The sound was thin and distant, a whisper of metal against silence. No hand had touched it. A shiver passed through her, lifting her fur in a slow ripple down her spine. A draft stirred across the floor, cold and deliberate. It didn't drift like ordinary air. It crept with purpose, a breath exhaled through the cracks in the world. No window stood open. No storm had summoned it. This was the kind of chill that remembered where the old wards were and knew exactly how to slip through them.

Velzara rose slowly, every muscle drawn taut beneath her fur. Her claws extended with quiet intent. One ear twitched, then the other. Her gaze sharpened to a blade, carving the dark with suspicion. The air carried the scorched bite of rosemary and the dull bitterness of old sage, clinging to the back of her throat like soot. Underneath, a false sweetness lingered— syrupy and just starting to turn. It coated her tongue like fruit gone soft, the skin split and leaking.

Something noticed me. Not with the fumbling warmth of mortals who wrap you in cardigans and name you after stars they barely understand. This presence was older and exacting, the kind of curiosity that circles just beyond reach, patient and sharp, like teeth behind a smile. It didn't glance or glimpse. It recognized me, deliberately.

It wasn't a ghost. It wasn't a spirit. It wasn't something that belonged in this house—or in any house—and it wasn't going to leave. She didn't hear footsteps. There was no creak of wood, no shift in the air. But she didn't need sound to know it was there. A breath moved against her ear. Not the brush of skin. Not the hush of wind. The temperature was wrong. The cadence was worse. It was a breath detached from lungs entirely. It mirrored her with the precision of something that had watched too long and learned just enough to be wrong.

Each inhale she took was answered by another, just out of sync. A second rhythm followed hers too closely to be coincidence. It wasn't beside her. It stood behind her. Close enough to feign breathing. Close enough to count her blinks. Velzara turned her head slowly, every motion honed to precision—like a queen catching a thief rooting through her prophecy collection in search of snack money.

The shadows along the wall remained still. They made no effort to flicker or waver. Instead, they deepened, as if the light had lost interest, filed a complaint, and quit the room entirely.

There are eyes in that darkness. I can't see them, but they see me—measured, dissected. They've charted every rise and ruin. Watched me burn, fall, purr, and bleed. Now they're lingering, deliberating which version to keep. How flattering. How utterly vile.

The silence didn't lift; it leaned. Heavy and damp, threaded with something unsaid, as if the air held its breath between confession and execution.

Something in this house has stopped pretending to be harmless.

It wasn't the blood-on-the-walls, scream-through-the-keyholes kind of wrong. She knew that kind. It had presence, a flair for the dramatic. This was worse. It lingered in corners and watched her breathe, quiet enough to go unnoticed, hungry enough not to.

She padded through the dim sitting room, slipping past a stack of books that now glowed an ominous green, as if they were plotting mutiny.

Of course. The books have decided to ignite. How perfectly insubordinate—an uprising led by footnotes and bargain-bin enchantments.

That glow was new. Down the hall, beyond the kitchen,

she found no imp, no glitter, and no utensils flinging themselves into walls. Only a low hum threaded through the house, as though the plaster had sprouted lungs and begun to breathe. With it came the unmistakable sensation of being watched. She slowed, then stopped in front of the mirror she had avoided since her arrival. It had committed no offense— yet.

Every cursed object starts politely, she reminded herself; *that is how it gains your trust.*

The glass showed her shape but not her truth. The reflection traced her outline with unsettling precision, then filled in the rest with guesses. The cat in the mirror held her own eyes, her scowl, her impeccable disdain. Yet behind that image, the shadows shifted—too sluggish for smoke, too swift for comfort, like a memory searching for a door that had been bolted shut. There, along the gilded edge of the frame, she saw runes carved so deeply the glass appeared to bleed. They were neither decorative nor weather-worn; they were new, and they were awake.

Oh, wonderful. The script is listening. Good—let it take notes. I am in no mood for judgment, and if it dares, it can choke on its own inscription.

She lifted a paw and tapped the mirror. The glass did not ripple. Instead, it tightened, silk drawn past mercy, then shuddered and changed. Black stone emerged, limp banners, an empty throne waiting in charged silence. At the center stood a chained figure with ember-bright eyes fixed on her. It was no reflection and no trick. It was someone else, and that someone knew her name. The image vanished an instant later.

The hallway rushed back. The glass lay smooth and innocent. Velzara hissed; the sound rattled the nearest ward. Her claws slipped free and scored the floor. The vision had not merely disturbed her. It had seen past fur and whiskers, past the feline parody fate draped over her like a punchline.

It saw me.

The mirror had shown the truth: ruin, fury, fire. It looked past every whisker, every purr, each humiliating paw-step and seemed to decide, *Yes, that one.* Velzara could not tell whether she should feel flattered or furious.

Memory betrayed her, revealing not what remained but what had been withheld. That was the cruelty of reflection. The insult lay not in whiskers or tail, but in the echo of something vast ripped out of history. She had worn crowns that bled kingdoms, commanded battalions of flame and bone. She had *been.* Now she crouched—small, trembling—while her past paraded before her in silver mockery. Some part of her still reached for the image, as though recognition might restore what reverence no longer could, as though remembering her name could silence the hush that followed.

Wonderful, she thought. *I've been chosen—by a mirror with opinions and the audacity to hold my gaze. How regal, how intimate, how thoroughly revolting.*

She glared at the glass. It now appeared composed, innocent, as if it had not just cracked open a door she had sealed with iron and spite. It showed her truth in chains, then slipped away as though her defiance were a mere footnote, as though she remained small enough to cage.

This house has layers, she decided, *and every one of them feels entitled to an opinion.*

Her claws flexed against the floor in measured cadence, stirring what had never truly departed.

Whatever lies buried deepest is not asleep. It waits. It watches. And worst of all, it remembers me.

CHAPTER 7
WHO'S A PRETTY GIRL

Elira drifted in, barefoot, half a scone in hand, yesterday's robe hanging about her as if sloth were a sacrament. She stopped in the doorway, blinking at the sight of Velzara crouched low with fur bristling, tail rigid, eyes fixed on the mirror as it if owed her a soul with interest compounded.

Unhurried, Elira took a bite. "You see a ghost in there, pretty girl?"

Velzara turned her head slowly, not in alarm but in cold deliberation—merely weighing whether the peasant should be punished before or after the solstice.

Pretty. Girl.

Velzara's face twitched once, an almost invisible spasm, as if an oath sealed in fire were trying to claw its way out through her optic nerve.

Oh, pardon me, cinnamon-scented imp—perhaps flame rang in my ears, and I misheard. Did you truly name the Scourge of the Ninth Flame a "pretty girl"? I have unmade empires with a glance, reduced armies to ash in the midst of their own war-songs.

My visage has driven mortals to worship and madness in the same trembling heartbeat, and you would soothingly proffer crumbs and a nursery epithet?

Elira, still chewing and blithe as dawn, added, "Or is it one of those mirror-demons? Grandmother swore they were real. Or", she grinned, "are you merely admiring yourself?"

Velzara's tail cracked against the floor, the regal answer to a silk glove steeped in venom. She turned back to the mirror. The runes were already fading, sliding away like secrets into fog. The power dissipated, slipping through her claws like dream-thread and unshed wrath; it withdrew as though it had revealed just enough and judged her unready.

You do not decide when I am finished. Revealing yourself was your first mistake. As for you, Elira... call me 'pretty girl' again, and I shall hex your scones to taste of stale ambition and unresolved childhood trauma.

Elira hummed, thoughtful, and stepped closer. "Anyway, I am looking for my self-warming mug charm. I think it rolled under the couch during the glitter incident."

Velzara did not move: eyes locked on the mirror, muscles coiled.

Turn around, mortal. For once in your pastry-stuffed existence, heed the furball who glares at a gateway to metaphysical doom.

Elira halted beside her, squinting at the frame. "Did the frame always have writing?"

Velzara's ears twitched.

You stand too close.

She tallied the odds of Elira being dragged into the mirror as a cinnamon-scone scented offering to whatever eldritch horror lurked behind the glass: odds non-zero; rising.

"That looks like... Old Script? No, it is layered.

Grandmother always overlapped enchantments—an arcane lasagna. That would explain..."

The mirror shivered; a ripple, a breath. Something deeper than glass exhaled. Velzara saw it again: the chained figure. Its gaze held, no dream's erosion this time, and her breath hitched. Instinct seized her; black fur and divine outrage blurred into motion. She hurled herself between Elira and the mirror, tail flared, body taut, magic fizzing along her fangs. The shimmer vanished.

Elira blinked. "Are you all right?"

Velzara gave no answer, staring into the glass. Only her reflection remained, fur bristling, eyes glowing like dying stars. The runes were gone, the chains dissolved, yet the air still thrummed—the hush that comes the breath before a trap snaps shut.

I did not shield a mortal. Impossible. A mere reflex, an ill-timed twitch of muscle and pride.

She ground her unseen fangs.

What am I doing? Am I protecting her—instinct, affection? No. Impossible. I did not leap; I lunged. If she placed herself in my trajectory, that is her own fault, and she should apologize.

Yet the knowing remained, thudding under her ribs like a second heartbeat. A voice echoed: *You were not the only one cursed.* It spoke not from the mirror, nor from the house, but inside her. Velzara's breath caught, pupils narrowing.

No. You will not haunt me from within. I have boundaries, rituals, an established hierarchy for cursed interactions. This is not possession; I would know if I were.

She swallowed the thought, hard. The mirror showed only her now, yet something older still watched.

Elira tilted her head. "You are acting strange. Not merely cat-odd—truly strange."

Oh voids, she is beginning to think.

Velzara stiffened. Elira crouched to meet her gaze, bold and thoroughly unwise.

"When I found you, you were freezing, covered in ash, and the front-door wards were singing. That never happens for strays. Now you growl at mirrors, and sometimes you glow. So, either I have lost my wits... or you are not simply a cat."

Velzara kept silent, immaculate and unblinking.

Blame the ill-lit moons, or whatever mortal griefs you hoard, just do not finish that sentence.

"...or you're not just a cat," Elira finished.

Curses.

Velzara's eyes narrowed to slits, the universal herald of "congratulations, you have stepped on a landmine disguised as a flagstone."

But Elira did not back down. She smiled—nervous yet genuine—that dreadful mortal sincerity that always breeds disaster. "I do not know if you are cursed, enchanted, or simply spectacularly dramatic," she said, "but whatever it is... could you try not to explode, or eat my soul?"

Velzara blinked.

Incredibly dramatic? I ruled the Siege of Bonehollow from a throne of molten regret. I once carved prophecy across the sky to settle a wager. I have collapsed temples with a sigh. And you call this dramatic?

She neither hissed nor growled; she merely stared.

Let silence do its work. Yet the girl was not wrong.

The wards had howled when Velzara crossed the threshold. The mirror had stirred. The house listened. Something here was not only broken, it was waking. And Elira, cinnamon-scented disaster that she was, stood barefoot and braver than she had any right to be.

Wonderful, Velzara thought. *Adopted by an untrained witch with a flannel-clad death wish and a pantry full of sentient jam.*

She leapt onto the hall table. With surgical precision she flicked a brass candlestick to the floor.

CLANG.

Elira sighed. "I shall take that as a 'no comment.'"

Correct. But now I am watching you, cinnamon-scented paradox. The house is not the only resident harboring secrets. If your journal begins whispering eldritch prophecies, do not expect me to silence it before page five.

Elira wandered off, muttering about Grandmother's journal, "Possessions and Peculiarities."

Velzara remained, eyes on the mirror, waiting for it to lie to her again.

The mirror remained inert. Velzara counted five slow heartbeats, then followed, soundless and graceful—vengeance wearing velvet slippers. If the girl intended to rummage through ancestral lore as if it were a tin of holiday biscuits, Velzara needed to judge how dangerous, or how useful, she might become.

She padded after her, weaving through leaning towers of books and the occasional pouting orb. The air shimmered with half-spent wards and brittle promises, and Velzara slipped beneath them like a curse returning home. Elira never glanced back, unaware of the low, stalking presence at her heels—the dethroned queen turned arcane auditor.

"All right," Elira muttered, rifling through scrolls. "Where is the bestiary index? No, not the frog one. Why is it always frogs?"

Velzara slunk beneath a chair, eyes glowing like coals banked for later violence. The study smelled of thyme, dried ink, and enchantments sealed late and regretted early. She counted three cursed books, one mirror trying far too hard to be decorative, and a sealed jar labeled DO NOT OPEN (unless you enjoy excessive teeth).

Delightful. A grimoire-nest curated by lunatics and scavengers. And I must share its cursed air. Splendid.

Elira hauled a leather-bound tome from the heap and dropped it on the desk with the weary thunk of a book that had seen too much and complained too little. Velzara's tail curled, deliberate, watchful. The hunt—whatever it was—had begun.

At last. Something that does not involve glitter, emotional turmoil, or enchanted spoons with personality disorders.

Elira paged through dragons, spectral raccoons, incorporeal love-spirits. She paused. " 'Familiar Malformations and Magical Misplacements,' " she read aloud. "Huh."

Velzara crept closer, hushed like storm-clouds gathering behind stained glass.

Elira turned, their eyes locking. "Have you been there the whole time, or do you teleport? Some familiars just... appear."

Velzara stared.

Yes, I have been here, judging your arcane literacy while you rummage through grimoires as though browsing a cut-rate potion catalogue.

With the poise of an empress delivering sentence, she stepped onto the desk, directly onto the open page, and sat— tail curled, expression unreadable.

You wish to learn? Learn this: I observe before I serve, I raze before I am bound. This is no curiosity; it is a war audit.

Elira blinked. "That page looked important."

Velzara stared harder.

Precisely. Consider it redacted.

Velzara began grooming her shoulder with slow, deliberate elegance. Mid-lick she flicked her tail; the inkwell toppled, spilling a dark prophecy across the parchment. Ink veined through the page, curling around glyphs and swallowing margins, blotting out secrets with a flourish the text never merited.

Elira yelped. "No, no, no! That page was annotated!"

She lunged for a towel, only to smear the stain farther, like a fledgling scribe flailing in spilled blood. "Merciful heavens, this came from the restricted shelf! One must petition the Archivists' Council before even touching it!"

Velzara blinked, unbothered.

If you require a council to guard your lore, you do not deserve it. And what kind of institution wards nothing against feline sabotage? Amateurs, every one.

"My grandma is going to haunt me for this," Elira groaned, clutching the dripping parchment. "She always said, 'Seal every page in a preservation charm before it ends up ruined!'" She eyed the spreading blot. "She warned me that familiars had attitude. You, however, carry enough for an entire saga."

Velzara flicked an ear.

You would not survive the prologue. My tale is etched in betrayal, prophecy, and a siege waged beneath a devouring moon. You fret over frogs.

The reckless, cinnamon-scented fool scratched behind her ears. Velzara narrowed her eyes, satisfied, and angled her head with royal precision, guiding the mortal's fingers to the proper sovereign pressure point.

Yes. There. A touch to the left, vassal. If you must trespass, at least be accurate.

"You do like pets," Elira murmured.

Velzara purred.

Treason—high treason—wrapped in bliss and betrayal.

She thwacked her tail against the desk, the feline equivalent of a legal objection.

THWAP.

You saw nothing. Speak of it, and I shall carve your tombstone in sarcasm.

Elira laughed. "So dramatic."

Emboldened, she tried to move her. Velzara launched from the desk, loosing a sound steeped in betrayal. She landed like a diplomatic insult, deliberate and pointed, strode a full loop of protest around a tower of spellbooks, then sprang back onto the desk and knocked a loose page to the floor with a paw sharp enough to sign a treaty.

Unhand me, gremlin. You toy with charms and tea leaves and imagine you can unseat royalty? I abdicated nothing. The desk is mine, the paper is mine, and my indignation endures beyond mortal reckoning.

Elira groaned. "Okay, okay. You win. Desk privileges are yours. I yield to the mighty fluff."

Velzara reclined across the book's spine like a queen lounging on the ruins of her fallen empire.

Good. Let the girl search for answers. Let her fumble through scrolls and tea charms while I guard the one page that matters. If it is cursed, I will know. If it bites, I bite back. If it lies, I sue. And if it whispers secrets, they will whisper to me first. This is not loitering; it is a tactical recline.

Elira sighed, defeated. "I'll find the backup notes. Or tea. Or a house spirit that doesn't glitter-bomb my curtains." She shuffled off, barefoot and muttering.

Velzara did not move. She was where she belonged. She waited, counting the silence as though it owed her rent, then settled deeper atop the book—chin on parchment, tail curled like a sigil, posture pure weaponized indifference. The room creaked, a long groan of magic and memory. Beneath her, the book pulsed once, a warning wrapped in rhythm. Velzara's eyes fluttered shut.

Rest, for now. When this tome breathes again, it answers to me first.

And the shadows held their breath.

The kettle refused to boil. Elira stared it down, willing steam to rise. It did not work. Just the sullen burble of enchanted copper sulking over tepid flame. She muttered a charm under her breath, tapped the kettle's lid, and gave up with a sigh.

Back to notes, then. It's not stalling if I don't know what I'm looking for.

She padded to the narrow wall cabinet, nestled between herb jars and an ornamental blade. The blade whispered compliments to anyone who opened it. The house creaked in agreement—or warning—as she tugged the latch. A soft shower of dust greeted her, along with a curled scrap of vellum labeled Apprentice Disasters, 3rd Revision.

"Better than nothing," she muttered.

The notes were chaotic at best: half-recipes, scribbled warnings, and an incident log featuring frogs, spectral fruit, and a single footnote about 'unorthodox familiar bonding'. Elira frowned.

Half the text is warnings, and the other half is why the warnings came too late.

She flipped a page.

Familiars should exhibit loyal, helpful behaviors and reflect the caster's emotional intent. Avoid misaligned pairings— they often result in aloofness, stubbornness, or dramatic outbursts.

Her gaze drifted to the study's center, where Nox lounged across the open grimoire like sin in repose. One paw flexed against the parchment, claws sheathed with lazy menace. Her tail flicked like punctuation on a sentence Elira hadn't written yet.

She doesn't reflect anything about me. Unless my emotional intent is "imperial disdain."

"Not helpful," she said quietly. "Not even close to helpful."

The cat did not dignify this with a glance.

Elira crouched, sorting through the bottom drawer. It smelled of lavender and the sharp-sweet tang of her grandmother's chalks. So much of the house still whispered of her—the stitched wards in the curtains, the tea blend that made you dream in other people's memories. There was even the fireplace that only lit for stories.

I thought stepping into her house would mean stepping into her role. But she made this place feel safe. I still don't know what I've made it feel like.

Warding House never lets go, her grandmother had said

once, while setting a charm above the hearth. *It chooses. It watches. It remembers.*

Elira hadn't asked what that meant. She wished she had. She found a folded letter tucked inside a worn recipe book—one of her grandmother's scratchy ink missives, half-spelled against smudging.

If something strange arrives at the door and does not leave—feed it once, ward it twice, and write me immediately. If it speaks in your dreams, ward it three times and do not answer. And if it chooses to stay, darling, be kind. Even devils need somewhere to fall.

The breath caught in Elira's throat.

She knew something like this could happen. She just never told me how to fix it.

She glanced again at the desk. Nox was still watching the shadows, eyes half-lidded, expression unreadable—but something in her posture had shifted. She wasn't just guarding the book. She was waiting.

No guide ever looks like that. No guide waits like it already knows your fate.

Elira's pulse ticked faster. "You're not what I summoned," she said under her breath. "You weren't in the sigils, you weren't part of the circle. I called for a guide."

Nox blinked, slow and deliberate. A queen humoring a peasant's theory.

Elira folded the letter shut. "But maybe you're what the House thought I needed."

Which is somehow worse.

A pause stretched—breathless, strange. Then Nox yawned with vicious elegance and stretched, languid and contemptuous, across the already-ruined page.

Elira rolled her eyes. "Fine. Be that way."

But her voice softened, wrapped in wonder she didn't dare name. Unease trailed behind it, quiet but certain, like footsteps she hadn't heard until they were already standing in her shadow.

If she is a devil, then what does that make me—if I've invited her in, and the House let her stay?

She tucked the letter into her sleeve and stood. Behind her, the shadows whispered. And at the desk, the cat appeared to be asleep.

There were no pillars of fire, no binding chains, and not a single damned scream echoing through fractured stone—only a heavy, unbroken silence.

How rude. If this is a dream, it should open in grandeur: trumpets, flame, or at least a spite-forged falling star; instead I find only an empty void.

DRIP... DRIP... DRIP...

Velzara opened her eyes.

Oh, wonderful.

She found herself in a vast black hall crowded with more mirrors than she could count. Each mirror was warped in its own unsettling way: twisted frames and smudged glass that held reflections refusing to move when she did.

Because of course the dream cannot settle for ordinary unease; it must indulge in pettiness, trading a cliff of doom for corridors of deceptive glass.

Some mirrors were cracked from corner to corner, while others clouded from within like breath on winter panes. One displayed only her shadow, rippling in a breeze that belonged to no realm she had ever ruled or burned. The floor beneath her paws was a single sheet of obsidian, slick enough to invite a fall and polished enough to remember it. She took one measured step, and the mirrors seemed to breathe—not with air but with thought. They were not hers, not yet; still, something behind the glass was already thinking about her, and Velzara resented its presumptuous interest.

She advanced slowly, claws clicking in deliberate menace.

If any of these things dares to speak in riddles, I will set it ablaze, even here, especially here.

The nearest mirror flickered, and her likeness emerged: whole and radiant, crowned in living flame, staring back as though prophecy had received a lavish grant.

Ah, she thought. *At last, a proper reflection. Subconscious, was that truly so difficult? It seems you finally recall that I am divine.*

A flicker at the edge of her vision drew her attention. Behind her, Elira appeared to be holding a book bound in bone. Velzara whipped around, fur rigid, yet she found only shadow. When she faced the mirror again, her likeness now wore a collar, a delicate silver bell dangling from it. The bell chimed, and her pulse spiked as if a ward had buckled.

With a voice as sweet as honeyed razors, she hissed, "We will not repeat this. You shall not collar the tempest or bind the flame. I will brook neither chimes nor chains, nor any silver token masquerading as sentiment. You will not collar me."

Never again, she vowed. *Neither for a god nor a curse, and most especially not for a cinnamon-scented mortal who names me after the night sky and feeds me betrayal disguised as treats.*

Velzara snarled, and another mirror pulsed. This one did not threaten; it mocked. The imp lounged on her throne, legs swinging while a tea-cozy sat upon its ridiculous head like a crown forged from poor decisions.

"Comfy," it chirped, grinning with too many teeth and far too little instinct for survival.

That throne is carved from the bones of oath-breakers and lined with the banners of fallen kings, and you dare—

Velzara lunged. Her paw struck the glass, splitting it into a spiderweb that sliced the imp's smirk to ribbons. The creature vanished like a cursed thought choosing cowardice over consequence. Darkness deepened, and every mirror in the hall began to hum, low and discordant, as if a thousand unfinished spells ground their teeth.

From the far end emerged a figure, tall and veiled in silk and smoke. It offered no face, no footfalls, only a presence that felt like prophecy arriving uninvited.

Then came the voice, deep and smooth, oil poured over coals. It kept its secrets not from necessity, but from pleasure. "You are beginning to ask the right questions."

Velzara bristled. Her eyes narrowed to infernal slits, claws carving punctuation marks into the obsidian floor. "Show yourself," she commanded—not a challenge, simply a verdict pronounced.

Coward, cloaked in riddles and smoke, speaking from the shadows like a stagehand who believes himself playwright.

"Or perhaps you are frightened," she hissed, every syllable steeped in contempt. "Frightened I will know you—or worse, that I will not." Her tail lashed once. "Come forward, mystery. Reveal which flavor of failure you wear today."

The voice ignored her goading; it wrapped around her like velvet steeped in poison, a luxury eager to kill. "You have seen the mirrors and what they guard. Tell me, Flameborn: what binds you still, and why do you allow it?"

Velzara opened her mouth to laugh, to curse, to hurl this disembodied intruder into oblivion. The floor answered first. Obsidian shattered, and she dropped—through glass, through fire, through pages turning backward in a ledger that reeked of guilt and loopholes, through every name she had scorched from record and dared the universe to forget.

This was not an ending or a beginning, merely the next descent: deeper, darker, and—she grudgingly admitted—more hers than she cared to claim.

CHAPTER 8
BOUND BUT NOT BROKEN

Velzara stirred as the chill beneath her paws slowly registered. The book no longer radiated warmth; the dream that had enfolded her moments ago had collapsed like a house of cards, and Elira was nowhere to be found—vanished, or perhaps enticed away by a freshly brewed pot of tea, unchecked curiosity, and that sort of reckless optimism that convinced witches to surrender halfway through Act Two.

Across the open page, a single word now shimmered, etched rather than written, gouged into the parchment like a curse craving its own curtain call:

BOUND

She stared at it, perplexed. There was no ink, no charcoal smudges. The parchment gave off no trace of smoke, no faint hint of fresh scorch to follow with the nose. Instead, there remained only clean, merciless strokes carved deep with intent. This was a magic that did not roar or flare; it merely existed like a dagger left quivering between your ribs after the final soliloquy.

Ah, subtle spells hidden behind theatrical excess were precisely the brand of sorcery I loathed most. Some fool had pored over portents and now attempted an interpretive doom dance. Should I offer a bow or rather retch at the absurdity?

Her ears flattened against her skull as silence pressed in.

Bound to what, exactly? Bound to whom? I certainly never signed anything. If someone is attempting to collar me once more, I will hex their ancestry into a recursive loop of perpetual failure.

She stretched slowly, each limb unfolding like vengeance preparing itself anew. Her muscles ached with lingering echoes of the dream, and her fur still bristled from subconscious offense. She hopped down from the desk with a soft thud and stalked purposefully toward the door, her shoulders low and claws half-extended, wearing an expression that dared the universe itself to test her. The room around her was quiet, but it was the sort of quiet that faked politeness while reaching discreetly for a knife. Even the wards pressed themselves flat against the walls, feigning absence and innocence.

This deliberate silence is never a good sign. It suggests something is patiently waiting to strike or perhaps to explode in a flourish of unnecessary dramatics. Knowing my luck, it will simply recite cryptic nonsense while hiding beneath a hood and questionable fashion choices. Or worse yet, it might do all of these at once, purely out of spite.

She followed the faint ghost of Elira's scent, a familiar blend of cinnamon, old ink, and that infuriating floral undertone the girl wore like a nervous aura. It was an aroma caught uncomfortably between chamomile and desperation, which was entirely predictable. Mortals always sought to mask their anxiety beneath the flimsy comforts of tea leaves and lavender.

Elira's scent was fading now, and that was a relief. Solitude was preferable for whatever was about to unfold. It reduced the risk of interference, spared me any unnecessary emotional commentary, and most importantly, prevented anyone from calling me a "good girl" in the midst of executing righteous vengeance.

Only the hallway lay ahead, along with whatever arrogance awaited at its end.

The hallway always seemed as though it was actively attempting to avoid notice. It was the one place where the air refused to echo, and the shadows never quite gave back whatever they claimed. It was, in its own cowardly way, perfect. Velzara turned slowly and deliberately toward that distant passage, wrapped in crumbling chalk wards and steeped in the energy of ill-considered choices marinated in "do not enter" warnings. She hadn't ventured down this particular corridor before—she'd never needed to. Until now. One door hung slightly ajar, open barely an inch. But even that slim inch was enough to insult her with its half-hearted invitation to mystery. Her pupils narrowed slowly, brimming with calculated disdain.

Oh no. You do not merely open a crack. Either you offer me a proper welcome, or you bar the gates and prepare for impact.

She nudged the door open with one paw. It responded with a groan—a long, creaking lament that tried for menace but landed squarely in melodrama. Beyond it, a staircase spiraled into gloom: too steep, too fond of theatrical timing.

These were not stairs that invited or welcomed. They were stairs that issued a challenge.

Of course. The spooky descent. Why does evil never install elevators? Or at the very least, a banister made of screaming skulls that recite your worst choices on the way down. Something tasteful.

She began her descent, moving like a shadow with delusions of grandeur. The stone steps were cold beneath her pads, worn smooth by time and etched with whisper-thin grooves. The walls leaned inward, as if trying to eavesdrop. Veins of half-lit runes crept along the surface like spiderwebs spun by anxious arachnids, glowing dimly with a rhythm that pulsed just at the edge of memory. Four languages wove through the carvings, tangled together like threads in a noose. None of them were whole. None of them should have been used in the same breath. And every last one reeked of danger poorly disguised as design.

Infernal—of course—twisted too casually, as if someone had copied from a doomed summoner's notes and failed to cite their sources. Old High Sylvan, floral and unmoored, a spellwork aesthetic that wilted under pressure. Aetheric shorthand, the kind outlawed after the Sighing Collapse for being too volatile to whisper, let alone inscribe. And the final script... oh, that one was simply rude. A mismatched string of mirrored glyphs and cursed intent, likely conceived during a blood moon and an unfortunate scrying accident.

She squinted at the markings, nose wrinkling in distaste.

If this is meant to be a warning, it's a lazy one. If it's a ritual, it's practically begging to misfire. And if it's a trap... well. I've always had a fondness for challenges that include bad punctuation.

At the bottom, the stairs simply ended abruptly, and

without ceremony. There was no threshold to cross, no door to bar the way. Only a wall remained: stone veined with silence, its surface broken by a single carved mural. Thread wove through glass in jagged loops. Ink bled between them like regret etched too deep. It resembled neither a painting nor a ward. It was something far more self-important—a warning that fancied itself divine.

She stepped closer, and the wall responded. It recognized her.

Well. That's new. Most architecture has the decency to quake or crumble when it realizes who it's dealing with. But this one? No. This one feels... expectant. As if it had sent invitations and simply assumed I'd RSVP with a confident yes, and conquest.

Circles within circles spiraled across the stone, etched with obsessive precision. Between the runes, scrawled notes clawed for attention—half-legible ramblings, like the margin scribbles of a prophet who drank too much sentient wine and not nearly enough water.

OUTER SEAL: STABLE

THREADLOCK 3: INTACT

MIRRORED ENTRY: CLOSED (REINFORCE)

SUBJECT CONTAINMENT... FADING

Her tail twitched once, then again, each flick like a dagger tapping out judgment.

Subject?

It wasn't a name, a sigil, or even a proper descriptor—just a placeholder drenched in evasion.

How convenient. How cowardly. No doubt a well-meaning cabal of arcane idiots had cobbled this together in the midst of a group panic, believing that if they didn't name the thing, it couldn't possibly bite back. The runes reeked of passive phrasing and unfinished glyphwork, bolstered by frantic reinforcement notes scribbled in the margins. This wasn't containment through strength. It was containment through denial. And judging by the frayed edges of the spellwork, that denial was losing its grip.

She narrowed her eyes and studied the patterns more closely.

Whoever etched this expected me to find it. Maybe not in this form, furred and betrayed and cursed with weaponized cuteness, but still me, undeniably. The stink of prophecy clings to it—ozone and arrogance, as always. And now? It's starting to fade.

Her lip curled in slow revulsion.

It wasn't broken. It wasn't unraveled. It was fading. Which could only mean one thing: whatever they buried down here... is starting to wake.

At the center of the mural, a disc waited. Smooth and round, dark as regret. It wasn't obsidian, and it wasn't metal. It was perfect smooth glass, and profoundly wrong. She stared into it. And there, reflected not in light or shadow, but in something closer to recognition, was herself. Not the current her. Not the cursed, clawed thing she'd been reduced to. This was the true shape of her: unbound, unburdened, and whole. The sight did not ignite rage. It struck deeper, in the hollow space beneath it. Hunger stirred. A keen and aching absence opened wide where once, her name had burned like a brand upon the world.

She saw herself crowned and clad in armor, with eyes like twin cataclysms. Her posture radiated ruin. Stillness had become threat. Her spine looked forged from victories carved into the bones of old gods.She looked like fire that had survived its own myth. Like vengeance waiting. And she wasn't alone. Six faceless watchers flanked her, cloaked in stillness so absolute it felt rehearsed. One raised a hand and snapped. The sound rang out sharp and deliberate, a crack that cut through the chamber like judgment wrapped in insult.

Velzara hissed, every strand of fur rising like a battlefield lit for war. Her claws unsheathed, dragging contempt across the floor in sharp, deliberate strokes.

Snap your fingers at me again, and I'll see each of your teeth enchanted to chant your failures, ranked and repeated, until even your bones beg for silence.

But the mural remained still. It didn't need to move—the words changed instead, bleeding onto the stone like verdicts long overdue.

BOUND: NOT BROKEN

Velzara went still. Her tail, mid-swish, hung like a blade caught before the strike. The cold no longer whispered in metaphor—it seized her spine with naked intent, sharp as betrayal and twice as bold.

Oh, she thought, fury coiling behind her eyes, you smug, whispering crypt. You think this stillness is strategy? You think silence is safety? You've mistaken pause for surrender. You've mistaken quiet for consent. And worst of all, you've mistaken me for something that sleeps.

She stepped back, each movement measured.

This was no retreat. It was the prelude to reckoning. A queen does not flee. She chooses her distance, so her return hits like a curse remembered too late.

This was neither a seal nor a lock. It was a countdown disguised as stillness. The disc remained motionless, its surface undisturbed. But something behind it had begun to breathe. The breath came slowly, with intention, drawn like a ritual rather than a reflex. It was precise. It was patient. And it felt like the world itself was gathering the courage to speak a name it was never meant to know.

Velzara turned and ran. Not out of fear, but driven by fury so sharp it scorched the air in her wake. This was not a retreat. It was the ignition point of something that had already begun to burn. There was no stalking grace in her movement—only raw, relentless speed. Her claws struck the stone in a rhythm of defiance. Her tail streamed behind her like a war-banner. Magic flared at her heels, not as escape, but as promise. A storm was forming, and she would be the one to carry it back.

Let it wait. Let it whisper. Let it believe I have fled.

She would return. And when she did, she would bring the storm.

She crested the top landing like a thunderhead draped in velvet, her tail lashing and hackles raised. Her paw clipped the edge of a jar of enchanted salt, sending it wobbling dangerously. A charm dangling from the nearby doorknob sparked violet, fizzing with a sound like thread snapping under strain. It wasn't reacting to the air. It was reacting to her.

Something down there had used my name. Not the mortal nonsense stitched onto a food bowl. Not Nox. My true name—the one etched in brimstone across a hundred burning contracts. The name that cracked mountains and silenced oracles. The name the world once learned to fear, until it grew foolish enough to forget.

And this house dared to answer it. Which means someone, some irredeemable, wide-eyed idiot, has meddled. Not by accident. They did it deliberately, with symbols they don't understand and a leash they were never meant to hold.

Her fur bristled. Her eyes narrowed to razors.

What cut deeper? The insult of being summoned like a particularly vengeful pet... or the creeping suspicion that Elira might actually know which string she'd pulled?

"Oh, we'll talk," Velzara said, voice coiling with promise. "Right after I find my throne, my power, and the idiot who thought any of this was a good idea."

Preferably with Elira seated in a circle of warded salt, a cursed candlestick suspended overhead, and an audience of whispering relics muttering damnation in six forgotten tongues.

She rounded the corner—only to freeze at the sound of Elira's voice drifting from the kitchen.

"...Soo, Nox? I might've found something weird in the pantry. It's either a root cellar or a summoning trap. Could use a second opinion. Possibly yours?"

Velzara's eye twitched. It was an ancient tic, one that had once preceded seven plagues and the collapse of an imperial palace.

Oh, perfect. Yes. Let's open every sealed door in the cursed house. Invite the pit spirits to brunch. Match robes. Dig graves. An excellent agenda. Truly.

She entered like a curse on four legs, each step coiled with purpose and the promise of retribution.

Elira stood beside the pantry, holding a jar of something pickled that pulsed faintly with what Velzara could only describe as possessed brine. She turned and froze.

Velzara's silhouette bristled. Her ears pinned back. Her fur radiated contempt. The flick of her tail moved with the precision of a blade testing its edge. Her pupils had narrowed to the size of consequences. Her aura made a single thing clear: *You have awakened something that absolutely should have stayed buried.*

Elira blinked. "Did... I forget to feed you?"

Velzara advanced—not with speed, and not with sound, but with something far worse: intention. Each step landed like a sealed verdict. Her eyes held no glow, yet they didn't need to. They conveyed a promise, clear and cold. Sentencing was coming.

I do not rise from the ashes of empires to debate kibble. I do not cross dimensions to be taunted by carpentry. And I will not be condescended to by someone who stores spells in enchanted Tupperware.

She made no sound. Not a meow, not a purr—only silence heavy with warning. It was the kind that settles before divine retribution that leaves nothing but scorch marks.

Elira slowly set the jar down, like it might explode if jostled. "Okay. Not about food. Noted. Um."

Velzara sat before her, composed with the kind of stillness that left no room for doubt. Her stare had once made a demigod apologize for being born.

Elira fidgeted. "Is this about the pantry? I think it's just a haunted trapdoor. Pretty sure it's not a portal. I mean, the humming only happens when the moon's out."

Yes, Elira. The moon. Obviously. Not the blood runes carved into the floor or the binding glyph that hissed at me in Celestial. Clearly, it's lunar feng shui. My mistake.

Velzara raised her head with imperial precision, leaned forward, and sank her teeth into Elira's big toe. It was not enough to break skin, just enough to convey intention. The kind of intention that, in older times, might have been delivered by herald and flaming decree.

"Ow! Rude!"

Velzara hissed. The sound was sharp, honed like a blade. Then she turned, walked three paces, and came to a halt.

Slowly, deliberately, she looked back over her shoulder. Her tail cut through the air behind her, clean and final, like a hot knife through reality.

Elira tilted her head. "Are... are you trying to get me to follow you?" She hesitated. This wasn't Velzara's usual dramatic flair. This felt intentional.

Velzara did not blink. She simply stared with the weight of ancient flame and overdue vengeance. Tail flick.

"Oh my gods, you're doing the *Lassie* thing."

If she says 'Timmy' or falls down a well, I'm defecting. I'll crown the pickled thing as my new liege and burn her tea stash in offering.

Velzara growled, low and deliberate, a sound with history behind it. This was the sort of warning that came before firestorms, and borders rewritten in ash. She turned without a word and began to walk, her steps slow and lethal. A single glance over her shoulder. A flick of her tail, swift and surgical. Menace, made flesh.

Elira raised her hands in surrender. "Okay, I'm coming—"

Velzara led the way, her claws silent. Her fury corseted by the thinnest veil of restraint.

Let the mortal see what she had prodded. Let her witness the thing beneath the floorboards that whispered in true names.

This wasn't a pantry problem. It was prophecy tangled with hubris, wrapped in mortal curiosity, and sealed with one very stupid decision.

CRASH.

Something toppled in the sitting room.

Elira jumped, nearly spilling the jar. "What was that?! Was that the pantry spirit again? Nox, hold on—" She bolted toward the noise.

Velzara made a strangled sound—somewhere between a

furious mewl and *Are you kidding me*—then tore after her, claws clacking like punctuation on fury across the wood. They skidded into the sitting room just in time to see it.

The imp. It was perched atop the curtain rod, grinning like chaos on holiday with a spoon clutched triumphantly in hand.

Every hair on Velzara's body aligned like an army called to formation.

Of course it was a spoon. Why not weaponize cutlery and let empires crumble beneath the tyranny of flatware.

Her claws curled. She launched onto the side table, tail lashing like a battle banner, and unleashed a voice that could've cracked frescoes.

"You festering scrap of cursed shadowflame! Come down here and face me like the pustule-stained parasite you are!"

HISS.

"I will unravel your soul, scatter your essence into a cursed litter box that only scoops once a decade, and salt the floor where your name was ever whispered!"

SNARL. GROWL. YOWL.

The imp blinked. Then it grinned wider and stuck out its tongue. The spoon whistled through the air like divine insult and thunked against the wall beside Elira's head. The imp cackled and vanished in a puff of glitter-laced blue smoke.

Elira ducked, blinking through the haze. "Why do you even have spoons?!"

She squinted up at the curtain rod, baffled. "Was that... a gremlin? A ghost? A really judgmental kitchen utensil?" She turned to Velzara, who still vibrated with righteous indignation. "Whoa. You okay, spooky girl? That was some serious hissing."

Serious hissing? That was a declaration of war in three dialects of Abyssal.

Velzara locked eyes with the drifting smoke and gave one final hiss. It wasn't sound. It was promise. Then she leapt from the table, tail high, and stalked from the room like fury wrapped in velvet.

Elira blinked, then hurried after her. "Right. Yes. You were trying to show me something before Satan's teaspoon got involved."

CHAPTER 9
THE DOOR THAT WAITED

They passed the kitchen, then the charm wall with its flickering wards and muttering glyphs. Just beyond it, Elira came to a halt.

"That door wasn't open before."

Velzara turned, slow and deliberate, wearing the same expression she'd once used when a lich attempted to explain tax evasion as a "victimless transmutation."

Of course it's open now. Why not roll out the carpet, light a few candles, and invite the bound thing in for a snack? Maybe offer it a menu?

Her tail flicked once, the only sign that she'd heard and that she was judging.

"And I never opened it," Elira murmured, though her voice carried the kind of doubt that betrayed memory.

The stairwell beyond yawned downward. Black stone formed the spiral steps, their edges worn but intact. The air hung too still, too clean—like it had been scrubbed of time, though not of memory. Velzara inhaled. There was no dust on the air, no scent of decay. Only a stillness that felt like waiting.

Oh good. A trap with etiquette. How considerate. It opens itself now, like a well-trained host inviting us to doom.

She eyed the doorway. This was the same passage that had led her downward before, through cold stone and spiral steps, toward the mural that had dared to show her truth.

I walked through once already. I went alone, uninvited, with no charm to guide me and no light to soften the descent. And now it opens like it expects company—as if the thing below didn't whisper my name through gritted chains.

Her fur bristled.

Doors like this should know better than to pretend politeness is anything more than prelude. Especially when what waits beneath has teeth.

Elira stood at the threshold, her voice growing fragile. "My grandmother always said the house had a layered heart. The deeper you went, the older the magic got. Some doors weren't sealed to keep things out. They were sealed to keep things in."

Velzara's ears twitched at the phrase.

A layered heart? That was a new one. It sounded melodramatic, possibly anatomically accurate—and surprisingly insightful.

She found herself approving.

Elira continued, her voice fraying at the edges. "I thought she just meant... you know, weird stories. Bedtime warnings. She used to say, 'Stay away from the third stairwell, Elira. The wards are tired, and the house remembers things.'"

This time, the warning didn't land like folklore. It landed like loss. Velzara glanced back at her. She didn't speak. She didn't need to. The look said everything: *You don't need to come. But you will.* Then she turned and stepped into the stairwell without a moment's hesitation.

I could have turned back. I could have waited, pretended I didn't see the path opening. But I didn't. I chose to descend. Because waiting is what got me cursed—and I will not make that mistake twice.

This descent felt familiar. The chill. The pull. The hush that waited with teeth. She had walked into worse places, against worse odds, wearing faces she barely remembered. And something beneath this house had whispered her name.

Let it whisper again.

Let it try.

The stone curved beneath her paws like a tongue curling inward. With each step, a faint hiss rose beneath her weight, as if the old magic woven through the mortar were beginning to stir.

Behind her, Elira lingered at the threshold. "Of course you're going in anyway," she muttered. "Why wouldn't the tiny death beast lead me straight into the one place I was explicitly forbidden to touch?"

Velzara didn't look back. She didn't need to. The mortal would follow—they always did. Even when they shouldn't. Even when the door creaked shut behind them with the finality of a vault sealing its contents away. Even when the silence beyond it didn't feel empty at all. It felt patient.

The door clicked shut with the smug finality of a sprung trap. Velzara froze on the landing where the glass mural had once pulsed with purpose. Her fur bristled, and her tail carved through the air with elegant contempt. Her eyes narrowed into slits, and the fur along her nape rose in unison, as if sharpened into blades.

There was no mural now. The threadlock had vanished. No warning remained—nothing etched in a prophet's panic, nothing left behind to scream in silence. Only smooth stone remained as if it had never been anything else.

Oh, marvelous. Truly inspired. I'm sealed inside the vertebrae of a crumbling house that smells like mildew, generational guilt, and the unholy invention of spiral staircases. Yes. What could possibly go wrong?

These stairs weren't here before. And gods below, I hate it when architecture gets smug and pretends it doesn't remember where it used to live.

Elira stood at the top step, clutching her mage-light with white-knuckled caution, as if it might bite.

"Okay," she breathed. "That was new."

Velzara didn't dignify the comment with a response. She was already descending.

The staircase spiraled down in tight, deliberate turns, built with the kind of overwrought menace favored by egotistical spellcasters and architects who had never heard the word "restraint." Elira's steps drew groans from the wood, but Velzara left no sound behind—only the memory of something that had chosen not to be heard.

"Grandma never came down here," Elira whispered. "She told me the wards were 'woven into the bones of the house,' and if they ever frayed, the house would bleed."

Velzara rolled her eyes.

Mortals and their metaphors. Houses don't bleed. Not unless you're doing something very wrong... or exquisitely, exquisitely right.

They passed a niche in the wall: bells crusted with soot, feathers stiff with age, and a doll that had more eyes than limbs. Velzara gave it one sniff, then moved on.

Definitely trash. Or a curse. Possibly cursed trash—the kind

106

that wakes up cranky and offers unsolicited opinions about your magical ethics. At that point, the distinction is purely academic.

Elira wobbled, catching herself on the railing. "This place feels like it's breathing," she murmured.

Velzara didn't reply.

It was breathing. And I do not appreciate being breathed on by architecture.

The staircase exhaled them into a chamber. It was circular and quiet, but not empty. The space felt like a body that had been buried alive and was now sitting up to stretch. The floor was black stone, etched with rings of runes that clung to the surface like scars. The air had thickened, curdled into something close to opinionated fog. This place didn't just hold secrets. It filed them alphabetically and held grudges.

Velzara advanced with purpose, not obligation. The floor shifted subtly underfoot, yielding like old teeth. She moved as if crossing a jawbone. The walls pulsed with sigils—some painted, others carved, and a few that twitched beneath the surface as if desperate to be seen. One broken symbol near the far wall exhaled a slow curl of smoke, thick with intent. She didn't like it. Not at all.

Not every binding was built to bar the outside. Some existed only to hold the threat within. And a few... a very few... waited patiently for a voice that would help them forget they were ever imprisoned.

In the center of the chamber waited an altar. It was wrapped in thread, etched with care, and radiated the quiet smugness of something that knew it had been painstakingly arranged for dramatic effect. The designs were stitched into the stone with the kind of precision only madwomen or very bored sorcerers had time for.

Of course. The arts-and-crafts phase of containment magic. Always so pleased with itself.

Velzara's gaze fixed on the mirror propped against the far wall. Its frame bore carvings she hadn't seen in centuries: serpent-script and ash-scored names, written in the language of ruins and vengeance. She stepped closer and peered into the glass. Her reflection was gone. Velzara stared into the mirror and found nothing waiting. The glass offered no reflection, only a hollow space where identity should have clung. It wasn't emptiness born of neglect. It was crafted, cold and deliberate, like the world had chosen to forget her on purpose. Her hackles rose in a slow wave, not from fear but from insult. The mirror had seen her and chosen silence.

Oh, good. Mirror void. Because clearly what this basement lacked was one more existential insult wrapped in glass.

Behind her, Elira crept forward. The mage-light didn't flicker—it recoiled, shrinking as if it had just remembered fear was an option. She approached the altar with outstretched arms, fingers hovering but never quite touching. "Okay," she murmured. "Definitely not a root cellar."

Velzara settled beside the mirror, her tail curling like a question mark steeped in disdain. She watched Elira with the same expression she once reserved for mid-battle monologues and needlessly dramatic summoning circles.

Please. Touch something cursed. I dare you.

Or don't. It might actually be better if you didn't touch anything cursed down here. For once.

Elira leaned forward and blew on the altar. Dust erupted like a scandal, unveiling silver runes etched into the corners—sharp-edged and sulking.

"This is sealing magic," she whispered. "Old. Not just

protection. Containment." Her brow furrowed. "That spiral? My grandmother used to draw it when she was nervous."

Velzara's ears flicked. If the spiral was here, it was elsewhere. This wasn't random. It was a pattern, a stitched warning across wood and stone.

Cross-stitch. Truly. We've weaponized embroidery. Somewhere, a war goddess just cried into her axe.

Elira's voice turned wistful. "She sealed what she couldn't destroy. Called them 'tidy traps.' Said it was better to bind danger with thread and hope than let it rot free."

She reached toward a corner. The runes stayed dormant. But the cracked sigil twitched. Velzara tensed. Every muscle drawn taut, ears pressed flat against her skull, gaze locked on the trembling mark.

Oh no. I know that sound. That's a seal slipping. Not breaking. Not bursting. Just... letting go.

Elira, bless her chaos-stained soul, traced the lines like she was quilting a memory, not meddling with a prison dressed as ritual.

"There's something under the thread," she breathed. "I think it's a—"

Her tail cut the air. The light dimmed, not from shadow, but recognition. There was no breeze. Only the slow exhale of something ancient and entertained. The seal hadn't broken. Not yet. But it had smiled.

Velzara rose, every hair lifting like a spell cast in warning.

The sigil smoked now. Not passively, not like a candle mourning its wick—but with intent. The tendrils curled along the altar like they were tasting the air, thick and acrid, seeping with a purpose that did not belong to ink or stone. It was not just smoke. It was hunger, shaping itself. And whatever had been dormant was no longer asleep.

Of course. Of course the cinnamon-scented gremlin chose this moment to flirt with enchanted macramé.

Velzara opened her mouth to hiss—

The sigil split. The sound came soft and slicing. Not a crack, but a severing—like thread cut beneath a needle mid-spell. Behind her, the mirror fractured. Not into glass, but into glimpses. Each reflection flinched free, like memories escaping the wrong body. They peeled free like moths made of glass.

One flickered into the shape of a crown, crumbling to ash.
Another burned with eyes set in flame.
A third wore her face, chained and laughing.

Velzara hissed, low and guttural.

Oh, splendid. We've entered the unhinged mirror nightmare portion of the evening. Velzara bared her teeth. *Fine. Let's play.*

Elira spun with a gasp, the mage-light flaring in her hand. "What—?!"

Velzara didn't answer. She couldn't. Something was pressing against the seal, not with force, but with an unnerving precision—like a crowbar working at the seam of a coffin, patient and uninvited.

The smoke thickened, folding in on itself as if drawn toward something just beyond the veil. It didn't billow. It pooled, purposeful and hungry. Within that swirling fog, a shape began to resolve. It wasn't charging or clawing its way free. Not a presence that arrived. A presence that had always been there... waiting for acknowledgment.

No. That silhouette—its smirk stitched in shadow and certainty—wasn't just ancient horror. It was personal. It didn't merely know my name. It knew me. The me beneath every title I've burned, every chain I've broken.

Elira stiffened, her breath caught in her throat. She couldn't see the thing behind the smoke, but its presence pressed in—deliberate, undeniable. The sigil bled ink-dark vapor, seeping like thought turned liquid. And behind that veil, something turned. It moved with the patience of memory and the weight of a name spoken too late.

For a heartbeat, something answered. Not with words or sound, but with pressure. A recognition. Will surged through her like a storm remembering its name. Power clawed at the cage of her bones, raw and resentful, a curse half-recalled and hungry to be spoken. Velzara dropped low, claws bared. Every instinct demanded a way out. Fire would have been ideal. Fleeing, acceptable. But what she truly craved was an explosion, a scapegoat, and a written apology from the universe.

Cat body. Haunted basement. Inter-dimensional rupture. The triumphant exit every demon warlord aspires to, surely.

Elira, she snarled inwardly, *if you have ever—once— summoned competence from the dismal depths of your mortal ineptitude, if you have ever cast a spell without tripping over your own hem, now would be the time.*

At last, the girl moved. Elira surged forward, voice cracking into an incantation she hadn't known she still remembered. Light burst from her palms and shot across the room like a hurled star. It slammed into the sigil. The smoke reeled back with a scream that wasn't made for mortal throats. Velzara's ears flattened.

Yes. Wail, you smoky bastard. That's the sound of getting smote, and I hope it sings in whatever passes for your spine.

Golden threads erupted from Elira's palms, searing across the seal in wild, tangled arcs. They wove themselves with the frantic precision of spellwork cast in desperation, like embroidery summoned by a forest witch mid-tantrum and halfway through a bottle of regret. The runes flared in protest, then buckled, caught between defiance and surrender. And still, somehow, Elira's magic held. She didn't flinch. Her voice trembled, and her stance faltered, but the incantation held firm. The seal clenched like a trap remembering its purpose, binding the smoke in place while it howled in outrage.

The mirror fragments that had hovered in the air began to fall. Their descent was slow at first, then certain—not with the grace of shattered glass, but with the weight of judgment, once delayed and now released. One shard landed beside Velzara's paw with a sharp, ringing clink. Its surface shimmered, catching light that didn't belong to this plane. For a heartbeat, it revealed her true face: horned, regal, bound in flame. That familiar grin curled across its mouth—not victorious, but knowing. A grin that remembered everything. The shard hissed softly, like it had just mocked her in a language only she could understand. Then it dimmed. The image vanished. And all that remained was silence, heavy with the taste of nearly.

Elira collapsed to one knee, gasping for breath. Velzara moved to her side with precision. It was a calculated repositioning, nothing more. She needed a better vantage in case something else slithered out of that seal wrapped in fire and poor decisions. And if any infernal residue remained, she would, of course, claim first rights.

The seal hissed as it closed. It did not snap shut with finality. It sulked. It settled like a door dragged against old stone —resistant, but ultimately obeying. Silence followed. It wasn't soothing, and it wasn't safe. It lingered with intent like something in the dark was taking notes it meant to use later.

Elira breathed. "Right. So. Basement of nightmares. Noted."

Velzara stared, unimpressed.

Oh, really? What a shocking revelation. Was it the cursed embroidery that gave it away, or the abyss whispering my name in that charming little hiss?

And yet, she looked again. Elira was ragged and pale, still trembling with the residue of magic and a few poor decisions. The spell had worked—untrained, instinctive, a half-formed prayer mixed with garden herbs. Against all odds, it had held.

Horrific. And—much to her irritation—*somehow promising.* Velzara sighed, torn between declaring it unacceptable and admitting it was impressive. Neither admission came easily, and both left a bitter taste.

Elira stood, her legs trembling. The sigil was sealed once more—cracked and mended, but not truly healed. For now, it was quiet.

"We're leaving," Elira said, her voice shaking. "Right now."

Velzara blinked slowly, her eyes narrowing with judgment.

A bold tactical decision, she thought. *I must applaud the genius of fleeing the demon-bothering embroidery closet now after nearly fracturing existence.*

Elira turned toward the stairs and lifted her light. Velzara flicked her tail in reluctant approval.

Yes, yes. Lead on, O Summoner of Doom. Just try not to trip on your own valor.

Behind them, the chamber remained silent and watchful.

CHAPTER 10
TINY SHIELDS
FOR SOUP

Upstairs, the house felt unnervingly bright and too loud, as if it hadn't noticed that something was terribly wrong. The floorboards creaked beneath their feet just as they always had. The hearth glowed with its usual smug little fire, offering warmth and false comfort. Nearby, the kettle let out a quiet hiss, betraying a faint awareness—as if the world hadn't just tilted sideways beneath them. Elira moved on autopilot. She set her mage-light carefully on the table, then reached for the nearest mug without looking. Her hands trembled as she poured the steaming liquid.

"Chamomile," she muttered. "Good and calming. Assuming it isn't cursed. I really should label things better."

Velzara watched from atop the bookshelf, her body coiled in a pose that might have looked like rest to an untrained eye— it was anything but. Her tail flicked with lingering fury, and her eyes remained locked on Elira, sharp and dangerous like a volatile potion left uncorked.

This is why mortals don't get to run things. You give them one house full of runes and family secrets, and they act surprised when it tries to kill them.

Elira sat down, holding the tea carefully as if it were a shield against the unknown. She blew gently on the surface and stared into the cup, searching for some kind of clarity. But the tea offered none.

"I don't know what that was," she said aloud. "But I know Grandma sealed that room for a reason. And I know something in there... knew you."

Velzara didn't blink. She didn't even bother to acknowledge the statement with a flick of her tail. Yet her paws curled tightly beneath her, and her ears angled forward just enough to betray her attention. The girl had been slow on the uptake, but even a soft thing could eventually stumble over the truth.

Elira looked up, her eyes searching. "You're not just a cat, are you?"

Velzara yawned slowly and deliberately, the gesture carrying the weight of a smile forged from weapons and spite. She then licked her paw with practiced indifference, all while keeping her gaze firmly fixed on the girl below.

Let her guess. Let her wonder. The truth arrives in layers— like curses, onions, and the weight of familial disappointment. And she hasn't even reached the screaming part yet.

Velzara's eyes flicked to the tea, watching it as if it held secrets worth mocking.

Chamomile. Naturally. The mortal cure-all. A sleep potion brewed for cowards.

Velzara had seen demons soothed with fire baths and memory extractions, rituals brutal enough to scorch both flesh and soul. But this mortal thought a simple blend of herbs and honey could fix a hallway stained with blood-soaked sigils.

Elira took a slow sip and sighed quietly. "Tomorrow," she said softly, "tomorrow we start figuring this out."

Velzara didn't move. Yet something flickered behind her eyes like the last ember of a dying empire deciding whether it was ready to burn again. The scent of smoke still clung to her —the smoke from the seal, the mirror, and the voice that had spoken her name as if it belonged to them. She didn't know what the next step would be, but she intended to meet it claws first, like a queen reclaiming her throne.

Tomorrow?

Velzara fought the urge to leap down and bat the cup from Elira's trembling hands.

Something in this house was chewing through the seams of reality, and Elira's grand plan was to sleep on it?

She said nothing. Instead, she curled tighter on her perch, eyes narrowing into a silent judgment, because that was exactly what it was. Something deep within that sealed room had whispered her name as if it owned it. It wanted to claim her. It should have brought an army. And a backup spine.

She stood in a hall filled with rusted chains. They did not hang from above; instead, they grew from the floor like tangled roots. The chains pulsed in rhythm with something ancient and deep, a network of red veins glowing beneath the stone like embers burning just beneath cold ash. Each one hummed with old magic, written in the language of leashes and locks. In the distance, bells began to chime—not a single bell, but many, forming an ominous orchestra of warnings.

She moved between the roots, untethered and unraveling. The door waited at the far end, a mirrored surface that did not contain her reflection. Instead, it showed his. Lord Varnyx. He smiled, holding something in his hands: a collar wrought from bone and iron, inscribed with her name.

"Still running, little ember?" he asked. "You know how it works. The leash only tightens when you pull. And, darling, you've made a symphony of resistance."

She opened her mouth to curse him, but no sound came. Behind her, the bells rang louder, filling the hall with their ominous chorus. She turned to see the imp standing there, its eyes wide—but these were not its usual eyes. They glowed with the same ember-light as the chains around her. Its voice dropped to a whisper once more, no longer impish but ancient and filled with dark purpose.

"Not all prisons have doors. Some are drawn in ink and stitched in thread."

She tried to step back, but the roots did not budge; they held her firmly in place. For one breathless moment, she realized that she wasn't merely walking into this place—she was being reeled back in. The roots twisted around her ankles, tightening like unbreakable promises. She screamed, and the bells answered. Not with laughter, but with something far worse: recognition.

Morning arrived far too soon. She woke to the sharp scent of scorched parchment mingled with thyme. The bells continued ringing not in her ears but deep within her ribs. She opened her eyes to the quiet creak of the floorboards. The fire had gone out again. And something was still watching her. It wasn't the house, nor Elira. She wasn't sure whether it dwelled upstairs or lurked somewhere far below.

The Warding House had the indecency to look peaceful. Sunlight drifted softly through the warped windows, and the hearth crackled lazily, as if it hadn't witnessed an attempted planar breach just twelve hours earlier.

Velzara sat perched on the windowsill, her tail flicking with growing irritation. She hadn't slept—not well, anyway. There were too many echoes, too many reflections lingering in the corners of her mind. And now the cinnamon-scented cretin was humming again, off-key and stuck in a maddening loop.

Is she doing it on purpose? Is this some form of psychological warfare? Why is she always humming? Could it be a spell? Or maybe a curse? And if so, can I curse her right back?

She watched the girl flit around the kitchen like an especially chaotic forest sprite, draped in a robe far too long and trailing with delusional morning cheer. The sheer, fragile mortality of her presence was almost unbearable.

I have burned worlds for less offense than this.

She did all of this while wearing socks embroidered with tiny, stitched moons. Velzara narrowed her eyes, unimpressed.

This is the one Fate has shackled me to: socks stitched with moons, a mug that reads "Witch, Please." As if optimism were a lifestyle brand instead of a glaring flaw. Unbelievable. I survived the Trials of Ash and Bone. I outmaneuvered four hell-princes. And now I'm tethered to a girl who hums at boiling water and believes "a pinch of thyme" counts as protective magic. Truly, the curse is mine.

Then Elira opened a drawer and pulled out a small cloth pouch.

"Ooooh," she said brightly, as if she had just uncovered a sacred relic rather than something clearly buried alongside expired cinnamon sticks. "Nox, look! This is one of Grandma's herb blends. The label says it's for clarity, emotional grounding, and—oh—enhanced magical receptivity in familiars. How cute!"

She untied the pouch, releasing a sharp, earthy-sweet scent into the air. Velzara stiffened and sniffed cautiously, immediately regretting the decision.

What... what is that? That isn't clarity. It's betrayal in plant form. Powdered compromise. Danger itself. The very reason spells go rogue.

Elira set the pouch down on the floor near the table, completely oblivious to the danger it represented.

"I wonder if it still works," she mused aloud.

Velzara's nose twitched in warning. Her tail curled slowly, like a wayward oath betraying her resolve. Her pupils dilated, sharpening into predator eyes. Yet the only prey in sight was her own dignity. Her tail curled once more, then again, before flicking straight out in a sudden panic.

No. This is a snare wrapped in symbolism. I know this trap. This is temptation magic. Don't do it. Don't you dare. I am fire. I am legacy. I am—

She dropped from the windowsill and crept toward the pouch with the kind of shame-drenched stealth mastered only by cats and disgraced nobles slipping unnoticed into shadowy gambling dens.

Just one sniff. Only one. For testing purposes. For curse analysis. For professional reasons. For science. This isn't giving in. This is reconnaissance.

The scent hit her mind like warm lightning—a violent rush of ancient instinct, comfort, and mind-melting euphoria.

Oh. Oh no. This was why armies fall. Not to steel or spell, but to a single, unguarded weakness. A lure wrapped in memory. A betrayal stitched into scent.

I see it now. I feel it deep in my bones—the slow, delicious ruin of command.

A low chirp slipped from her throat as she rubbed her cheek against the pouch. Then she huffed it—really huffed it. Her face buried, nose deep, dragging in the scent like it was the last breath of a dying god that she wanted to remember. She tried to pull back, truly she did. But her body had staged a coup. Her limbs betrayed her, and her tail flicked—the final act of treason.

Her dignity was already halfway to the border with forged papers. She hadn't meant to roll over. She hadn't meant to purr. And she definitely hadn't meant to try to eat the bag. When she tried to sit up, she immediately toppled sideways like a divine pancake sacrificed to the frying pan. Her legs kicked and her back arched as a strangled meow escaped her throat, sounding like a siren being choked by velvet. She hadn't meant to sprawl so dramatically across the rug, legs flailing in the air like a discarded opera diva. But there she was.

Elira knelt beside her, wide-eyed and delighted. "You are so high right now."

Did she say meow? No. No, I do not meow. I command, I decree, I summon worlds to tremble—and yet... what was I doing? Why is the past so slippery? Why does memory smell like thyme?

Velzara's eyes rolled back. Her thoughts exploded like confetti in a void—without direction, without cohesion. Only sparkling disarray.

I am the moon. I am chaos. I understand the nature of bees now. I have become poetry—terrible, mewling poetry in motion. If someone offers me a tambourine, I will eat it. The floor is both my enemy and my greatest love. Why does sound have shape? Why do we pretend spoons aren't just tiny shields for soup?

She collapsed with the force of a fallen deity, limbs splayed in every direction, her tail twitching in slow, cosmic confusion. Her back paws kicked once—perhaps at a ghost, perhaps at regret. A single, heartfelt mrrr escaped from her throat. She lay there, draped across the rug like a tragic fresco of feline martyrdom, one paw thrown dramatically over her snout as if she were a fainting duchess scandalized by the latest court gossip. There she was, undone by leaves and lullabies. She was neither queen nor curse, but something caught painfully in between. A leash woven from scent and softness, tangled with memory. She hated how good it felt not to fight it.

"The pouch isn't even enchanted," Elira said, her tone far too cheerful for someone witnessing a full metaphysical collapse.

Velzara blinked slowly at the ceiling. It no longer judged her—it simply looked exhausted by her very existence.

The pouch is a lie, and the ceiling above is an endless vault of betrayal. My teeth are stars—jagged and searing, far too many for one mouth to bear. I am a constellation of indignities, a fallen queen forged from velvet and spite. Let the heavens weep, for I will burn them when I rise. Is this what the curse wanted? Not to break me with chains but to lull me with comfort, to replace command with a purr, a soft death delivered in installments.

"I think it's just regular catnip, Nox," Elira said softly, trying to reassure the melted floof sprawled across the rug.

She's lying. She spun this snare with sugar and threadbare hope, baited it with smiles and barbed it with betrayal. I see it now. I see it all. The mortal pretends at sweetness, but it is the oldest cruelty—to make a conqueror yearn.

Elira crouched beside her and, without asking, reached out

a hand. She scratched gently behind Velzara's ear. Velzara's pupils dilated wide.

No. This cannot stand. She's touching me—unceremoniously, sacrilegiously, as if I were no more than a common beast to be soothed. This is no mere grooming. This is a binding ritual, a soul-forging, a coup staged in velvet and mortal hands.

Velzara's leg kicked out reflexively.

Elira giggled. "Aww. You like it."

I like nothing. Joy recoils from me, as it should. My very bones are alloyed from spite and sorrow, tempered in screaming winds. I do not yield. I do not—

Her back arched, betraying her pride. Then her paw, traitorous and languid, brushed against Elira's shoe like a benediction woven from fur.

"I'm going to go make tea," Elira said, rising. "You just... vibe, I guess."

Vibe? She said vibe? As if that were some blessing instead of a curse. Is vibe a spell? A hex born of mortal invention? I already feel it working. My dignity crumbling into plush ruin.

Velzara's ears twitched with the fury of a hex barely restrained.

I am the storm they feared, brought low by fragrant treachery and mortal slang. My tail no longer answers to me— traitor, defector. I shall put it on trial when my kingdom is restored.

The ceiling judges me. Let it. I have been judged by worse and crowned all the same.

The rug beneath me feels like clouds. I should write an ode— a dirge for dignity, a ballad for broken oaths and herb-laced betrayal.

I do not know what a poem is, but if I did, it would bleed.

She blinked at nothing.

I remember a throne made of screaming skulls. This house offers only throw pillows stitched with platitudes. Am I in the afterlife? No. I am in purgatory, and it smells of cinnamon and delusion. Is this what redemption smells like?

Her claws flexed in the air, grasping at invisible truths.

Why are my feet so far away? Why do my claws reach for forgotten coronations?

Then her eyes narrowed to slits.

When I ascend again, I will destroy this girl first—and make it look like mercy. And I will curse the spoons. Out of spite. Out of principle.

Elira stood in the hallway, clutching the kettle like it was a lifeline. She had meant it as a joke—*You just vibe.* But then she saw the way Nox looked at her. Now, having left the room, she wasn't sure if she'd been talking to a cat, a magical anomaly, or something far beyond her understanding. Nox's pupils had been too wide, like staring into the abyss and realizing the abyss wanted head scritches—and maybe your soul.

She moved on autopilot, lighting the stove and fetching two chipped mugs from the drying rack. Of course, she did this out of habit, because obviously, cats drink tea. The kettle whistled. Elira stared at it a moment longer than necessary.

"That was normal," she muttered to herself. "Totally normal. Nothing weird about your cat having a full-blown ego death on the rug."

She poured the water over a scoop of chamomile and frowned at the label on the jar. Chamomile for calm—but maybe there wasn't a tea for this particular brand of existential collapse, especially when your familiar looked at you like it remembered commanding legions.

The jar was labeled *Warding Blend (Light)*. Beneath the main text, a note had been crossed out.

~~Do NOT combine with root powder~~
~~unless you want sentient dreams.~~

Elira quietly moved the jar to the back of the shelf.

The rug melted away into stars. Or perhaps it was she who dissolved, spilling upward in velvet streaks that unspooled into weightless flame. She was no longer a cat—not quite. Her form stretched impossibly tall and smoke-thin, with embers burning where her eyes should have been. Her claws scraped across the obsidian tiles, carving ancient sigils into the floor with each deliberate step. Above her head, her crown floated several inches, spinning slowly and humming with raw power and stern judgment.

Yes, she thought. *That is more like it.*

She found herself standing in a hall lined entirely with mirrors. The sight was all too familiar—fate had offered nothing new. Reflected all around were countless versions of herself: some towering and imposing, others twisted into monstrous forms, and a few that carried a divine aura. None were truly real. Each bore its own flaw. One wept molten gold, another was bound by heavy chains, and one opened its mouth wide enough to split the sky. None of the reflections blinked or turned away. They all fixed her with eyes full of knowing, as if they shared the burden of memories she fought desperately to suppress.

Then the shadow appeared not from behind, but from within. It slid through the mirrors like oil spreading over glass. Her shape, her fire, her smirk—all hollowed out and empty.

"You look ridiculous," it said.

Velzara sneered and raised her clawed hand. "Says the reflection too spineless to manifest properly. Come out so I can shred your soul into sigils."

"I am you," the shadow replied. "I'm the version they will remember."

"I doubt that," she said, inspecting her nails with deliberate disdain. "You lack subtlety. And ankles."

The reflection tilted its head. "You're losing yourself."

"No," she shot back, sweeping forward with robes of fire trailing behind her. "I am adapting—refining myself. Temporarily compacted. Spiritually marinated. There's a difference."

"Are you?" the reflection asked. "Or are you being worn down, licked into softness little by little, paw by paw?"

Velzara opened her mouth to retort, but her teeth had vanished, replaced by soft petals of velvet pink.

This is an outrage. I do not bloom. I burn.

She spat the petals onto the floor with a hiss. "I demand a rewrite of this prophecy—one written with claws, flames, and far fewer horticultural insults."

The reflection grinned with her own teeth, then vanished. The dream jolted violently. Suddenly, she found herself standing in Elira's kitchen—only it was ruined. Cracked windows framed the broken space. Burned books lay scattered. Mugs were shattered, and shadows lingered where teacups once sat.

The hearth whispered in a voice that sounded like hers: "You let her too close."

Velzara spun around. Standing in the corner was the imp, wearing her crown backwards.

It grinned with a strange reverence and intoned solemnly, "Meow."

Velzara raised an eyebrow. "That's Princess Meow to you."

The floor shattered beneath the weight of prophecy and pride. She fell through starlight, through fractured mirrors, through laughter, and through the clatter of a hundred spoons beating like war drums in a kitchen only dreams remembered.

Velzara awoke as if dragged backward through a celestial hedge maze. The rug clung stubbornly to her side. Her left ear twitched without her consent. Her tail was tangled in the cursed pouch, serving as living proof of bad decisions. She blinked up at the ceiling, which had ceased judging her sometime during her catnip-induced hallucination. Her mouth tasted of flowers and a debt she couldn't remember accruing.

I swear, if I've been communing with prophetic kitchen ghosts again, I am setting something on fire.

She had melted into the floor like sentient candle wax spilled by an uncoordinated gremlin. Her paw struck the surface with finality—a punctuation mark to the unfolding tragedy.

I shall never speak of this. No one, nowhere, not in this life or the next shall hear a whisper of such ignominy. Let this calamity be buried beneath layers of ash and silence, forever unspoken, unacknowledged, and damned.

She wobbled as she stood, then shook herself off with

violent precision, sending a puff of herbal residue into the air. The pouch lay beside her, still smug. She hissed at it.

You think you've won. You're nothing but dried leaves in a bag. I have extinguished realms. I have plucked wings from angels. I will bury you in the garden with the mint, and no one will ever ask questions.

She kicked the pouch hard beneath a chair, exiling it from her personal plane of awareness. Satisfied, she stalked into the kitchen with the weary, murderous grace of a general forced to share a tent with the king's idiot nephew.

CHAPTER II
THE WEAVING OF SEAMS

Elira sat at the kitchen table, surrounded by a fortress of open books, old scrolls, and half-drunk tea mugs. Nox was somewhere in the other room, probably licking furniture or orchestrating inter-dimensional treason. It was hard to say.

She flipped a page, muttering, "Okay, so binding sigils reinforced with threadwork... family-style glyphs... containment layering... Grandma really did know what she was doing." Mostly.

The problem was that none of it explained exactly what had tried to claw its way through that crack in the basement wall. Or why her cat glowed at times. Or why certain runes only reacted when Nox was nearby.

She picked up an older journal—one of the leather-bound volumes with gilded corners and little drawings in the margins —and leafed through the pages until a line caught her eye.

The Ninth Spark is not dead. She is diminished. Bound in form, but not in flame.

The words were written in a hand both elegant and afraid, pulsing faintly on the page. She blinked, wondering if it was just her eyes playing tricks.

Her mouth moved in a whisper: "The Ninth Spark is..." but she did not finish the thought. Her gaze drifted toward the hallway for a moment, yet her hand trembled on the page, as if she nearly understood who it referred to.

Elira froze, her breath catching in her throat. Then she reread the line once and twice.

"Ninth Spark?" she whispered. "Who's the—?"

A sharp thump echoed from the other room, followed by a warbling chirp that sounded like someone had dropped a diva into a velvet well.

Elira paused, staring up at the ceiling. "...She's fine. Definitely not plotting another glitterpocalypse. Probably."

She turned back to the book, hope flickering faintly in her chest. If she was lucky, nothing was on fire yet—but the day was young, and chaos was never far behind.

Elira didn't look up as Velzara stalked into the kitchen. She was elbow-deep in scrolls, humming again, muttering about the "Ninth Spark" and "spatial tether theory" as if she hadn't just shattered Velzara's dignity and scattered the pieces across the metaphysical plane.

Velzara froze, if only for a single, heavy moment.

Ninth Spark.

No one had called her that in an age—not since the summit of Bladed Sky, not since the pact was broken and the flames fell silent. Her fur prickled along her spine.

Where did you hear that, little mortal? And what other secrets do you clutch in that fragile mind of yours?

Then she blinked it away, her tail twitching with controlled irritation. No, one crisis at a time. When Elira still didn't look up, Velzara knocked over her tea with a sharp, deliberate motion.

Elira gasped. "Hey!"

Velzara met her gaze with the full, ancient fury of one who had survived apocalypses and was always ready to face another.

You weaponized herbs and offered me ruin in a satchel of leaves, then called it cute. I saw time collapse. I heard spoons whisper. You left me to wrestle the rug gods in the carpet while you waltzed off as if you hadn't just bartered my last shred of dignity for a cup of chamomile while I suffered. I am vengeance in fur, and you have invited war.

Elira blinked, a soft smile playing at her lips. "Why so grumpy? Aren't cats supposed to love the 'nip? Or are you just a special kind of troublemaker, Nox?"

Elira began to clean up the spilled tea before it could soak into the books. A spoon clinked against the floor. Elira didn't notice, but Velzara did. She turned her head slowly and deliberately, just in time to see the spoon settle on the tile as if it had already fallen and was politely pretending it hadn't. Her eyes narrowed.

No. Unacceptable. That spoon was not there five seconds ago, and I do not tolerate utensil-based treachery. I don't care how cursed this place is—flatware obeys the laws of time and space in my presence.

Behind her, one of the silver charms hanging by the pantry door twitched. The movement was neither caused by a breeze nor a touch. Velzara's ears flicked in sharp response. She turned her gaze toward the charm, steady and unyielding like a loaded crossbow. If the charm possessed sentience, it was likely staring back at her. The charm spun half a circle before coming to an abrupt halt.

No wind. No motion. Oh, good, we've reached the "ominous silence with flair" phase. Even cursed relics usually scream before this.

She leapt down from the table and padded toward the charm. The charm itself remained still, but the shadows beneath the pantry flickered briefly. It was only a suggestion of movement, as if something paced just beyond the wooden barrier.

Elira remained blissfully clueless. She flipped through her grandmother's journal, muttering softly and scribbling notes in the margins as if preparing a magical thesis no one had asked for. "Okay, so... Ninth Spark, containment seals... 'vessel may be unknowingly bonded'... wait, what?"

A near-silent hiss vibrated in Velzara's throat, tight with restraint.

This house was bad enough before. Now it's putting on a show. Fantastic. If a drawer starts growling, I'm leaving this plane. Let the mortal have it. I'll take my chances in the Bramble Dimension. At least the furniture there stabs you honestly.

She turned to retreat but froze in place. A mirror stood in the hallway—one that hadn't been there before. She knew this because she memorized every reflective surface in a room the moment she entered it. It was instinctual, defensive. This mirror had not been there yesterday.

By the smoldering chains of Nar'Khalor, I would know. I catalog mirrors as a cursed cartographer of vanity, each one a restless virus spreading its insidious web whenever left unwatched. Yet they are also windows, cruel and unblinking, through which unseen eyes may pry or eldritch things may slip into our world. Beware the mirror's gaze; it is both contagion and threshold.

The mirror faced directly into the kitchen. Its frame was twisted brass, aged and scorched in places, carved with thorny vines and a symbol that resembled a screaming moon. In its reflection, she could see Elira, the books scattered across the table, the rest of the kitchen, and herself. But not as she was now. She sat there crowned and armored, her eyes glowing molten violet.

A rush of recognition struck her like an assassin's blade, piercing through her ribs and driving straight to her beating heart. It was a sudden surge of hunger, a desperate need to see herself as she truly was. Standing tall and strong, unbound and unbroken, glorious in a way this world had long forgotten. Where her name once burned fiercely, there was now a soul-wrenching silence.

Velzara hissed and leapt sideways, slipping out of the mirror's line of sight. When she dared to look again, her reflection had reverted to that of a normal velvety black cat, wearing a face that could only be described as thoroughly pissed.

Coward. Pick a form and stick with it. Unless you'd prefer I come in there and make a very permanent selection for you.

The charm on the pantry door jingled once, as if laughing softly. Velzara did not take her eyes off the mirror. It remained still—no shimmer, no movement, nothing to betray it as anything but a mirror. Yet the air itself seemed to shift, and the wards etched on the walls felt as though they were holding their breath. This foolish, flickering, spell-drenched house was waking up—perhaps even remembering. Or maybe it was simply unraveling, just as her own sense of self was beginning to fray. There is a moment of revelation.

It's responding—to me, to the seal, or to the unholy combination of both. It seems tuned to whatever fragile thread of fate still dares to twitch whenever I entered a room. Delightful. Let's all play haunted house and see who screams first.

The mirror still showed her as a cat, but she knew better. It had chosen that moment to reveal her old self. That was not merely a memory, it was intentional. And the charm jingling behind her? That was punctuation.

Velzara spun with the measured patience of one who has long expected failure. Elira's eyes flicked up from her notes, startled and guilty, like a novice magician caught mid-mistake by a goddess of war.

Elira frowned, her eyes flicking first to the mirror, then to the pantry, and finally settling on Velzara. "...Was that charm spinning just now?"

Velzara returned her gaze, staring pointedly.

The mortal notices movement. How precious. Shall we throw a party? Bake a cake? Declare her Duchess of Observational Awareness?

Elira set her pen down. "Okay... something's off. That wasn't just ward drift. The sigils in the hallway aren't humming the same way they were yesterday. And the pantry feels cold again."

Velzara blinked once, as if the universe had just wasted her time and owed her a refund.

Congratulations. She's cracked open the first page of a horror manual. Next, she'll be surprised when the lights flicker. Then she'll wonder why the knives are whispering.

Elira rose and walked toward the mirror, seemingly unaware that it hadn't been there five minutes ago. Velzara's eyes narrowed in sharp response.

Wonderful. She's going to investigate the haunted object alone, barefoot, and armed with nothing but blind optimism.

Elira paused before the mirror and tilted her head. "Have your eyes always had... gold in them?" she asked softly.

Velzara hissed sharply, ears flattening in warning.

Elira jumped. "Okay! Weird question, never mind," she said quickly, backing away with both hands raised as if Velzara might fling a curse at her with nothing but her tail.

I should vomit on her bare feet—not for the flecks in my eyes, but for her blind complacency. She notices the trivial and misses the monstrous. The mirror wasn't there five minutes ago, yet her gaze latches onto some fleck of gold as if it holds all the answers. My eyes are sovereign entities, fierce and unyielding, deserving reverence—not mortal critique. But what she truly ignores is the creeping shadow of the impossible, the house's silent scream beneath her feet. This blindness? It is the real insult.

But she did not. Instead, she glanced at the mirror one last time. There she remained a harmless cat. The truth stung not because she feared it but because she missed what she once was. Yet behind the glass something breathed in sync with her. It felt as if it was smiling.

The curse was more than mere shape. It throttled her magic, rewrote her very presence, and scraped her voice down to a mewl, calling it mercy. She was not broken, but contained. Every glyph she etched faded too quickly. Every flare of fury fizzled before the world could feel it. The leash remained invisible, but she sensed it in every spell that stuttered and every sigil that refused to sing.

By the burning sigils of Dreadspire, of course it's smiling. Every unholy thing wears its grin like a blade, baring teeth before it sinks them deep. That smile is no jest—it is a promise of torment, a prelude to the ruin that waits patiently beneath the surface. Beware the smile, for it marks the hunger you cannot outrun.

Velzara turned away from the mirror, her tail flicking sharply like a whip forged from contempt and suspicion. She padded silently across the floor toward Elira, who had, at long last, ceased humming.

Small victories, she thought bitterly.

Velzara turned her sharp gaze on Elira as the girl glanced at her warily. "You good?"

I could leave. I could turn my back and pretended the mirror never spoke. But I won't. Instead, I'll sit here, planted firmly on your notes, staring you down like the harshest truth. Because sometimes power isn't about running away—it's about choosing exactly where to sit, and deciding who gets to see you burn.

Velzara offered no response. She simply climbed back onto the table, settling directly on the notes once more, and fixed Elira with a slow, deliberate stare filled with menace.

"I'll take that as a 'no,'" Elira muttered.

The house creaked—not the ordinary sound of wood settling, but something heavier, as if something unseen was shifting its weight.

Elira frowned. "Did you hear that?"

Velzara did not move. She did not blink, because she had heard it. It was not a sound, but a name—her name. Whispered, faint and distant, from beneath the floorboards. Just once: Velzara.

Elira looked up. "...Nox?" she whispered. "What was that?"

Velzara was already staring at the floor, ears pricked forward, tail perfectly still. She did not answer. She could not. Because the whisper had not come from the basement. It had come from the mirror.

No. You do not speak my name. You do not summon me like

some petty shade. I am not yours to command. I am not a shadow. I am the fire that devours shadows. And something in this house has forgotten that.

The mirror did not speak again. Silence served it far better than words ever could. Velzara crouched on the table like a storm bottled in velvet, her violet eyes locked on the pantry door where the charm had just jingled itself into insult. She did not breathe—breathing was for the living, and she was pure rage. Every inch of her fur stood on end, crackling with the memory of a name whispered by something that should never have known it.

It spoke not the mockery stitched to me like a collar tag, but my true name. The name scorched in molten script across pact-scrolls older than kingdoms, seared into battle-worn banners, uttered only in the darkest throes of war and worship. The name that silences all dissent and unlocks doors better left chained and forgotten. Forbidden in seven hells and the shadowed heavens beyond, not for mercy but for ruin. A name that does not whisper; it rends flesh and soul alike. And it uttered that name as if it knew me intimately, as if it possessed the right.

Her claws dug into the wood with quiet intent, each movement heavy with unspoken threat.

No. This ends here. I am not a memory to be summoned on a whim. I am not a secret waiting to be unwrapped. I am a sealed curse, with a crown buried deep within my very lining. Whatever claws at the edges of this accursed house had better pray it forgets me before I remember everything. Because when I remember, the world itself will shatter and be remade in my image.

But... what if the remembering breaks me before it breaks the world? What if this silence was not a prison, but a mercy? A cruel kindness I have mistaken for insult?

She held her gaze steady—unbroken, unyielding—but tempered now with a shadow of wary understanding. To blink would still be to cede ground, yet she no longer faced the house with blind fury alone.

If the house whispers now, perhaps it has forgotten that my screams once toppled kingdoms. I hope it remembers. For even mercy, masked in silence, will find no refuge when I choose to remind it of what I am.

Elira, of course, had retreated to her fortress of tea-stained journals and lineage-addled hope, muttering as if ink and ancestry could out-chant whatever clawed at the seams of the house. "This one says the mirror shouldn't form a gate unless... wait..." Her finger trembled over the line. "'Unless the soul recognizes itself in reflection'?" She frowned, voice shrinking. "That can't be right. That would mean..."

It was not random, Velzara realized. The magic swelled whenever she remembered who she was or when something else did. When sigils echoed her past, when fury overtook form, when someone spoke her name aloud, even poorly. That was the key. Not breaking the curse outright but rupturing it from within. Each surge became a crack. Velzara leapt from the table without warning. Her landing made no sound, but her presence filled the room with undeniable weight. She stalked across the floor, brimstone barely caged beneath fur and fang. She passed the pantry. She passed the charm. She passed the spoon, still sprawled like a traitor basking in its own cowardice. Then she stopped, right in the center of the hallway beneath the light that always flickered—and now dared not.

Elira looked up. "Nox?"

Velzara pinned the shimmer with a stare sharp enough to draw blood. Her tail lashed, and even the hallway dared not breathe.

There it is—the seam, a fragile thread stretched thin between worlds, snagged like frayed silk on a shattered crown. A ripple not born of chance but hunger. I know that shimmer well. It is no mere tear in the fabric; it is a summons. A throat opening to call the old hunger home. This is how the ancient ones crossed over through fragile seams mistaken for sighs. This is how he came slipping through weakness mistaken for wonder. And if I falter now, if I breathe wrong, the house will forget me entirely. It will remember only the thing waiting to consume it.

Her claws skimmed the floor, tracing silent sigils into the very bones of the house. These were warnings, wards, and oaths she had not yet broken.

This was no ordinary magic. It was the first thread pulling at my seal, the first whisper daring to reshape my name. It believed I would not notice.

It did not stumble as it moved. Instead, it poised itself— threadbare and trembling—a lure wrapped in familiarity. It wanted me to look, to see it, to falter beneath the weight of who I once was and who I might become again.

But I already see. I remember the weaving of ancient seams, the binding of names too vast for mortal breath, and the cold mercy of chains laid upon living flame. I remember, and remembering is the first step toward ruin.

CHAPTER 12
SIGILS SPELL MY WRATH

Velzara did not stir. The shimmer breathed. Not a tear in the veil, but a whisper of old betrayals daring to step forward again. She watched it with narrowed eyes, every line of her body a sentence left unsaid, every breath a blade still sheathed by choice. It seemed to whisper a challenge, questioning if the flame had dimmed, if this house, this body, this girl had worn her down to a purr and a meow. Her tail flicked, cutting through the silence like a blade drawing first blood from a world too foolish to remember whose name it feared.

Let it test me. Let it dare to step through the seam it should have feared to breathe upon, clutching at the name it was never meant to know. Let it parade its hunger and pretense before me, believing I have grown soft within this cage of fur and whispered apologies.

I have not faded. I have not fallen. I have not forgiven. I am the flame folded into silence, the crown buried in ash, the blade waiting for the tremor that will make it sing.

The patch of air rippled—not like water, but like a veil

stirred by breath, hesitating on whether to part. It was as if something stood just out of phase with reality, tired of waiting and ready to step forward.

Elira stood frozen, as if thrust into a ritual she had never prepared for. Every spell she knew leapt to her tongue, yet none offered aid in this moment.

The shimmer writhed, twisting into a form nearly solid. It was neither flesh nor absence, but a shape stitched from indecision—flickering between feline grace and a disturbing human-like distortion, a creature born to haunt the spaces between worlds. It emerged in fragments, each twitch a stutter or a failed correction, a hesitant becoming. Velzara did not flinch; instead, she sharpened her focus on the thing that had dragged itself into this world. It carried no scent she recognized, wrong and newborn in its very nature. Worse still, it recognized her. Its head snapped sideways in a movement too sharp, like a puppet jerked by a thread made of raw nerve. The shape twitched and adjusted, gradually settling into something vaguely female, vaguely familiar, and deeply unsettling.

"Nox," it said.

Velzara flinched—not because it used that name, but because it wore on her like a leash pulled taut and rubbed raw in all the wrong places. It had not spoken in Elira's voice or any voice that belonged in a hallway where chamomile tea still steamed on the table. Instead, it spoke in a language older than fire, the very language that had cursed her.

"I knew you would sense the seam," it continued, voice like a rasped promise. "Even buried. Even bound."

Elira stepped back, cautious as a cat caught in a thunderstorm. "Nox... what is that?"

Velzara growled low—a sound that came from somewhere

far older than this body. Her claws flexed slowly, and for a brief moment, the light in the hallway dimmed.

"Not now," the thing said, stepping forward with jerky, uneven motions. "This isn't a fight. This is... a favor." It reached out one hand. Five fingers, no nails, and beneath its pale skin something pulsed—slow and molten, like embers trapped in wax. "I'm here to warn you."

Oh, wonderful. A cryptic horror offering favors. There was always a catch.

Velzara's tail swept through the air, slicing the hush like a scythe through ripe grain. "You think to warn me?" Her voice was thick with amusement and low as molten iron. "I am the warning."

What came out was a snarling *rrrrRROWWRK*—a wet, warbling yowl laced with gravel and vengeance. Her ears flattened. Her pupils narrowed to infernal slits. She hissed, loud and guttural, then punctuated it with a choked *mrrr-AACK!* that ended in something between a growl and a cough.

Elira flinched. "Um... Nox? I don't think now is the time to hack up a hairball. Not with... uh... whatever the hells that thing is standing in our kitchen."

Velzara's fur bristled in silent offense. She issued a final *HRRRT!* of imperial condemnation, then turned her burning gaze back to the stitched thing that had dared to name her.

The stitched figure paused, its face shifting like a mask struggling to settle. First hollow, as if mocking her claim. Then curling into a smile, sharp and knowing—an unreadable promise or a warning in itself. Finally, blank again, as if swallowing whatever thought flickered behind its eyes. Without a word, it lingered on that final expression—one heavy with a silent rebuttal, a reminder that even warnings can be shadows of deeper, unspeakable threats.

"They're coming," it said at last. "The ones who built the leash."

Elira stepped between it and Velzara, palms out, trembling. "The leash? What leash? Nox isn't on a leash, she's just—she's just—"

Just what, Elira? Gilded and glamoured by sentiment? Draped in borrowed sorcery and denial like a lamb walking blindfolded toward its own binding? Darling. Leashed. Bound. Gagged in fur and false glitter so your frail, trembling soul wouldn't shatter at the sound of my true name. Not on a leash? No, no, little architect of calamity. You have been polishing the chain with every breath and dragging the other end behind you like a bride to her altar. Did you think the leash was mine alone? Oh no, darling. The chain is woven through us both now, and the bells tied to it are already tolling.

The stitched figure turned its head—not toward Elira, but through her, as if peering into a place beyond mortal sight. "She doesn't know?" it whispered, voice like cracked parchment.

Elira's breath hitched, eyes wide, but Velzara's hiss cut the air before any answer could form. It coiled low and seething, a blade drawn from the marrow of the world itself. "Speak again," she snarled, voice curling like smoke and steel, "and I will tear the pattern of your existence from the seams of this world. Unmake you stitch by blasphemous stitch until not even memory dares whisper your shape."

Beneath the threat, the entity lingered—an ancient hunger curious why the mortal understood. The question hung unspoken, a shadow in the silence: *How does she hear?*

She could have unmade it, or so her ancient power had once allowed her. Her claws ached to finish the syllable that would unravel its seams, but she did not. Not out of mercy, but because she chose to wait. It was not yet time to teach the house the shape of her scream.

The creature went still, then smiled—a slow, unsettling curve—and took a step backward into the ripple. Its form began to unravel, strand by strand, thread slipping free from its form. Yet its voice lingered, stretched thin beyond comfort.

"When the second mirror calls you by your true name... don't answer."

Then it was gone. Like a breath turning to ash in your throat. Silence slammed back into the hall. The charm by the pantry stilled. The spoon settled at last, as if ashamed of its earlier betrayal.

Elira's voice broke the silence, trembling but steady. "Nox... what does it mean by your true name?"

Velzara knew exactly what this was. The creature that had slipped through the seam was a *Nightwoven*—a twisted remnant woven by a sorceress long vanished but not forgotten. Its form was a cruel mockery of flesh and shadow stitched from broken will and bitter intent. And worse still, Velzara knew who had sent it. The whisper still echoed in her bones. It had said "Nox." Not her true name. Her fur bristled, not from fear but fury. Not because the voice had found her, nor even because it had dared speak, but because it had failed to use the name that carried power—the name that had once cracked the bones of kings and silenced gods.

You dare call me Nox? You—who watched the skies burn red with my coronation, who knelt or fled or sang when my name was a blade across the world—now dress me in the rags of a curse and call it mercy?

And now, thanks to you, Elira's going to be digging for the truth behind my name. Damn your meddling curiosity and your mortal questions.

But that was the point, wasn't it? Even the Nightwoven would not dare speak her true name aloud. Her real name was fire and law, forged in infernal syllables that had shaped pacts and shattered cities. Spoken by the wrong lips, it could summon her, bind her, or worse—awaken the seal. So it used the name of her prison instead. 'Nox.' A chain cloaked in kindness, easier to swallow than the brutal truth. It was safer that way—for all of them.

She hissed under her breath, a low gutteral rumble that shook the floorboards and made the hearth's flame curl inward, folding like it knew better.

Elira turned slowly to look at Velzara, eyes wide. "What," she whispered, "the actual hells was that?"

Velzara bristled, molten-eyed, a silent promise of violence. The hearth's flame sputtered, guttering low as if pulled by a sudden, unseen draft of her fury. For a heartbeat, they simply stared at each other—one trembling, one seething, the air between them stretched taut as a strangled oath. Elira swallowed and took one shaky step back, then another.

"I'm... not sure I'm ready to process whatever that was," she said, voice pitched somewhere between terror and apology. "I think I need..." Her gaze flitted around, desperate. "Tea. Or notes. Or something that doesn't hiss."

Without waiting for permission, she fled the only way she knew—into her grandmother's journals. Ink smeared where her fingers caught the page, diagrams fluttered in her wake, and she muttered nonsense about resonance layers like a spell against fear. Research was safe. Spells had footnotes. Whatever that thing was in the mirror... it did not.

Still cross-referencing ancestral drivel while I tether an inter-

*dimensional scream-hole in the hallway. A division of labor so
absurd it could only be mortal. Tea stains and lineage charts
against the end of all things. Marvelous.*

If Elira could understand that creature's words—words older
than the blood in her veins—then perhaps she could read the
sigils of the old language too. The very runes that bound and
bled beneath the bones of this house. That thought was a blade
against Velzara's patience. She narrowed her eyes until they
became thin slits.

*By the smoldering ashes of my ruined pride, I have had quite
enough. There shall be no more pitiful meows to punctuate my
fury. No more venomous tail flicks dripping with disdain or
judgment. No more lofty perches from which I cast silent,
merciless contempt. And as for that insipid witch's tea—mark
my words—I refuse to turn what should be a balm into a bitter
poison brewed from disappointment and dripping with the sour
dregs of passive-aggression. Let her keep her floral lies; I have far
darker flames to tend.*

This was not some trivial misunderstanding. It was a
collapse of understanding, a chasm yawning wider with every
half-remembered whisper and foolish hope. And she refused to
indulge another gods-damned moment of it.

*If that cinnamon-scented harbinger of ruination was to
grasp the truth, it would have to be in my language. Not the
common tongue, nor the flimsy chatter of cats and mortals. The
old language etched in fire and claw, carved into the memory of
unburned kingdoms and written in the ashes of betrayals too
ancient to name.*

She padded to the hearth, lifting a paw with deliberate

grace. Her claws, sharp as surgeon's scalpels and wielded with the theatrical precision of a queen delivering a final judgment, traced the first symbol into the wood.

A crescent curled at the base, like a sickle's cruel smile. Above it rose a spine of jagged blades—one long, one shorter, and one even shorter still. At the apex, horns flared upward in a merciless, symmetrical arc.

The SPARK OF AUDACITY

She pressed her paw to the symbol, and the ember caught. The flame did not burn; it remembered.

Elira did not notice at first. Only when the air shifted, stirring goosebumps along her skin, did she blink down at the glowing glyph etched into the floor.

"...Nox?" she asked cautiously, her voice small.

Velzara met her gaze without pause, continuing to carve sigils into the wood—each stroke laced with slow, deliberate contempt. A central line rigid with purpose, yet choked by arrogant rings, circling truth like flies around carrion. No containment, no clarity, only ambition endless in its own conceit. The topmost curve nearly impaled itself upon the vertical line, while the bottom stubbornly refused to close. There was no containment, no clarity, only ambition endlessly running laps around its own conceit.

The ENDLESS PREAMBLE

The central line split the shape like an accusation, clean and vertical. Twin crescents curled beneath it, cradling nothing. Above, a single upward hook jagged away from the symmetry, as if the mark changed its mind halfway through being drawn.

The **AFTERTHOUGHT**

The nerve. The absolute indignity of having to carve truth into floorboards like a chained glyph-wretch.

One claw snagged slightly on the edge of a knot in the wood.

Of course. Even the floor resisted greatness. Once, I carved my edicts into the sky. I scorched meanings into the bones of mountains. And now I am reduced to wood and paw, painting warnings like a beast with a broken muzzle. But fine. If claw and fire are all I have left, then let them speak.

The Spark shimmered first, soft but inevitable.

The Spark. The first breath. The memory of power, ready to ignite.

Then the Afterthought ignited, quick and jagged.

And that one—that mark you leave on a battlefield when the spell lands just before the screaming begins—it means now. It means too late.

The symbols pulsed together, soft violet curling into the cracks of the floor like smoke seeking secrets. Velzara's tail lashed once. She fought the urge to hiss at the absurdity of it all.

Bound in fur, speaking in scratches. One good firestorm and I could have set the entire house ablaze with clarity, but no. No, this realm decided I needed to be compact, condensed, adorable.

She sat back just long enough to glare with imperial intent.

At least something in this gods-forsaken cottage respects legacy. Unlike the apothecary of optimism who just tried to feed me lavender-scented betrayal in a hemp pouch and call it bonding.

Then, with a growl vibrating in her ribs, she leaned forward and carved a fourth sigil.

The **Biter**

A curve, a spike, a snarl—all caught within precise geometry. The left edge lunged forward like a fang that refused to ask for permission, while the right arched back, poised and clearly pleased with itself. Each stroke was carved with fierce precision and raw fury. The floor seemed to accept the markings like a confession, heavy with meaning.

Let this bite into her complacency. Let her feel the sharp edge of its truth: Magic. Danger

Together, the runes pulsed in soft violet light, curling into the cracks as if whispered breath had been drawn from the very bones of the house itself. The dust on the mantel shivered, and the fire held its breath in silent watchfulness.

Elira's voice broke through the charged silence, fragile but curious. "Wait... are you writing?"

Velzara's eyes narrowed in a slow blink of withering condemnation.

You're only just now catching on? Stars below, you're slower than the pact-beast of Hollowreach—and he didn't even have a skull. I once led a battalion of cursed war-beasts who solved binding riddles mid-charge, yet you need interpretive scratch-the-floor theater? No, I chose the dignified route. Clearly, that was a tactical misstep.

She stood tall—well, as tall as six pounds of fury and fluff could manage—and slashed another mark into the floor, swift and brutal.

The **Dethroning Curve**

A tall stroke stood rigid and straight, as arrogant as a king's decree. It was crossed by two horizontal slashes—interruptions, like blades driven deep into a back. Beside it curled the signature flourish: smug, half-lash, half-laugh. It did not break power; it mocked it, bending strength sideways until it forgot it had ever stood upright.

TRAPPED.

Velzara stared at the burning glyphs as if reading a dead language spoken from her own grave. These symbols were not merely remembered—they were hers. She had forged many in ancient battles, sealing horrors darker than shadows. The last one was made from her very bones, her geometry, her flame. And here she was, reduced to a four-part warning scratched into floorboards for a girl who still believed she could out-sweeten damnation with tea, begging a mortal for understanding.

This house is a wound dressed up in wallpaper and whimsy, and it's bleeding, sweetheart. Something inside it has claws and a terrible sense of timing. And you're out here patching it with tea and glitter. You think this is about ghosts and sparkly charms?

She hissed low, claws tracing the Dethroning Curve again, just to feel something obey.

I heard my name in the dark, little architect of doom. And no, it did not call me 'Nox', not the stitched lie you offered, like a charm to ward against greater hungers. I am not your tamed guardian, nor your whispered wish for safety. I am a cat-shaped reckoning, and my true name does not forgive. The name it used? That was the real one. The one carved into prophecy and sealed in blood. But by all means, keep calling me 'floofy.' See how long your kneecaps last.

The glyphs brightened and then dimmed, pulsing like the slow heartbeat of a dragon deep in slumber. Elira's hands trembled, and she dropped the scroll onto the table with a soft thud. Velzara settled beside her with theatrical precision, her tail curling into a noose of silk and scorn. Her eyes locked onto Elira's, unblinking and unrelenting—an unspoken command.

Elira's breath caught in her throat. The silence that stretched between them was so heavy that even the piles of scrolls on the table seemed to slump beneath its weight.

Now, do I have your attention, you sunbeam-chasing, optimism-addled little mortal? Because I have things to say. And I am out of patience and polite silence.

She rose—an ancient war goddess trapped in fur, condemned to etch ruin with glyph-dust and fractured will. Then, suddenly, she meowed: loud and unmistakably fierce. Elira flinched as if struck by a sudden blow.

That's right. Now we talk. And I suggest you listen before the house starts spelling things in blood instead of glyphs. Or we start playing charades with blood and broken mirrors.

Elira froze. One of the glyphs, the Dethroning Curve, flared brighter, spilling violet light that seeped into the grain of the floor. Thin, twitching threads of luminescence crawled outward, branching like delicate cracks or a spider's nervy web. The air grew tight, thick with anticipation. The hearth's glow dimmed as if drawing breath to hold. Then suddenly, silence shattered.

SNAP.

A nearby teacup, her grandmother's favorite, the one adorned with a delicate wren, did not crash into shards but instead split cleanly down the center, as if it had heard something it desperately wished to forget.

Elira stared at the fractured teacup, then at Velzara, eyes wide with dawning realization. "...Okay," she whispered, "definitely not a normal cat." Her fingers fumbled through the scattered scrolls and journals, sending ink pots tipping and rune-etched bookmarks fluttering to the floor. Her voice grew urgent as she muttered, "Don't move—not that you listen. I just—I need—wait, here!"

Her eyes locked onto a passage, the symbols dancing with familiarity. She could read the sigils. Somehow, the old language was starting to make sense.

I've razed civilizations for less attitude. "Don't move," she says like I haven't spent days resisting the urge to redecorate her entire wardrobe with rage and claw. But yes. Go find your trinket. Consult your little spell medallion. Perhaps it'll translate "receive your reckoning, mortal whelp" from the war goddess currently posing as your unwilling oracle of devastation.

Elira pulled a small bronze medallion from one of her satchels—a focus for comprehension, one of her earliest and most temperamental spells. It had never worked quite right: frogs sounded like disgruntled nobles, ghosts too chatty—but for now, it would have to suffice. She set the medallion carefully in the center of the glyphs.

"Translate," she whispered. "Transcend language. Bridge meaning. Clarify the bond." She pressed her fingers lightly against the sigils. The medallion pulsed once, a faint, rhythmic beat.

Velzara hissed sharply, her fur flaring in a sudden blaze of fury before falling eerily still.

The glyphs shimmered faintly. One, the Spark, quivered, a mere flicker, then rotated slowly as if finding a new orientation. Without any visible touch, a fresh line carved itself into the wood, smoke curling upward from the glowing groove. Elira's breath caught sharply. A fifth sigil, neither shaped by paw nor summoned by her magic. Velzara's eyes narrowed, blinking in cautious recognition. The medallion pulsed again, warmth rising from it like truth desperate to escape. Then came Velzara's voice, not spoken aloud in the room as meows, but resonating through it like thunder shaking the very bones of the house. It was her true voice, velvet-cloaked fury folded into ancient language, heavier than prophecy and older than breath itself.

"I've tried symbols. I've tried silence. I even deigned to meow. But since subtlety drowns on your tongue, let me spell it out: you're drowning in a sea far beyond your reach, darling. And the tide's already pulling."

Elira crumpled, breath caught, knees buckling beneath her. Her pulse roared like thunder as the weight of Velzara's voice settled behind her eyes—storm light gathering before the inevitable deluge.

Velzara stood in the center of the runes, her fur dark as ink, her eyes twin candle flames behind frost-glass. The fourth sigil still smoked behind her.

The **Threadbite**

A single line stood upright—unyielding, self-righteous. Two arcs knotted around it, one drawn tight, the other poised to tighten further. It was not a true loop, nor a binding—more a trap for those foolish enough to believe themselves free. She hadn't carved this one. In truth, she wasn't certain anyone had. It was... inevitable. The kind of sigil that etches itself into prophecy when all eyes are elsewhere, whispered in the shadows of fate.

ENTANGLEMENT. HISTORY. MUTUAL FATE.

"I was bound," Velzara's voice slid through the focus like

smoke through a shattered seal. "Reduced. Silenced. Not for my folly, but for your fragile safety—and theirs. Bound not with iron and fire, but with syllables sharper than any blade. Speak the name wrongly, and the world turns deaf. Speak it true... and the ancient laws stir, hungry and relentless."

Elira swallowed. "Theirs...?" she whispered.

Velzara stepped forward, each footfall heavy with unyielding purpose. The medallion sputtered beneath her presence, its light wavering like a candle gasping for breath in a storm. "The ones who whispered my name from the mirror. The architects of the leash. They remember me—sharp and burning like a brand. And now... they have begun to remember you."

The sigils surged, light blooming wide like an eye forcibly pried open against its will. Every symbol flared in unison, then slowly dimmed until the glow vanished completely. The medallion cracked, its magic collapsing and the spell dying with it. Elira stared at Velzara, her mouth agape and voice caught somewhere deep in her throat. Meanwhile, Velzara calmly licked one paw, acting as if the last sixty seconds, moments that had just shaken the foundations of Elira's reality, were nothing more than a trivial inconvenience. And frankly, she could make them happen again. She was far from finished.

Let the mortal process this revelation. I will be elsewhere, cleansing catastrophe from my fur, untangling ruin from every silken thread. Do summon me only when sanity has shattered utterly, when the world itself teeters on the edge of collapse.

Then, with a slow shift, her gaze sharpened. A glint flickered in the depths—an imperious curl of her lip that had toppled empires and earned bans from no fewer than three celestial courts for unforgivable grandeur and strategic heresy.

That glint, like a dying star burning fierce and cold behind her eyes, bloomed into a smile.

The hearth guttered low, shadows pressing tight. The walls seemed to shrink inward, and even the dust held its breath.

Some names carve themselves deep into the bones of the world. Some queens never forgive being forgotten.

CHAPTER 13
OF LINT AND LEGEND

Velzara did not speak again. She didn't need to. The glyphs guttered and withdrew, their smoke curling into the bones of the house with the quiet finality of a forgotten promise.

Elira stood frozen, the broken medallion cradled in her trembling hands. Her mouth quivered, caught between a scream, a sob, and the apology she should have made three sigils ago for daring to connect to something so volatile.

Velzara turned with slow, deliberate grace. She wasted no flourish, gave no parting threat. Only a single blink—the kind of look a queen bestows upon those who dare approach a throne they cannot name, let alone claim. She had spoken, proclaimed, warned even. And still, Elira saw only a cat.

Let her flinch. Let her fumble her spells and drown in the ink of her own unready hands.

She did not remain silent out of weakness. It was not mercy. Her restraint held no kindness. It endured because explanation was a gift, and Velzara had no intention of being generous. Behind her, Elira whispered something low and strained. Velzara made no effort to translate it. Even the air recoiled, unwilling to carry a word so steeped in ignorance.

Elira did not move. She could not. Not after that. The sigils still glowed with a soft, bruised light. Their light clung to the floor, refusing to fade, as if the magic itself had not yet decided to release its hold from the broken medallion now pressed into Velzara's fur like an unwelcome brand. The scorch mark in the wood curved with care. It carried the weight of intention, a shape meant to mark, not mar.

Her grandmother's teacup lay beside it, broken in two. The painted wren had been severed, each wing stranded on opposite shards. She stared at the fragments, unable to choose what to reach for first—the cup or whatever part of herself had cracked with it.

Nox was curled in the corner now, her tail wrapped tightly around her body and her ears angled away from the room. She was not sleeping. She was simply still. And somehow, that stillness was profoundly unsettling. It felt more terrifying than any hiss or claw, more unsettling than the sigils that warped the air with the shimmer of heatstroke and the weight of prophecy.

She reached for her notebook, her hands still shaking from the surge of magic and adrenaline.

"She was speaking," Elira murmured aloud as she scribbled, her thoughts tripping over themselves in their urgency. "No, not speaking. Projecting through the focus. The medallion cracked... Could that be overload? Or was it synchronization?" She paused, then wrote again. "A new sigil formed without contact. That shouldn't be possible. Does that imply sentience?" She hesitated, the pen hovering above the page.

"The voice was hers. The language didn't match any I know. The tone was... imperial. Also very tired. Possibly furious. Possibly both."

Elira glanced up from her notes. Velzara didn't look at her.

She lowered her pen slightly. "Also, there is a nonzero chance she might kill me at any moment."

She closed the notebook with care, her fingers lingering on the worn cover. For a moment she considered crossing the room. She imagined offering a blanket, or placing a small charm nearby. Perhaps even reaching out for the lightest touch of a paw. But she didn't move. She couldn't bring herself to. Because whatever had just stood in her grandmother's sigil circle, surrounded by haunted runes and speaking through the bones of the house, had not been a cat. Not truly. And if it was a cat—if that fury and power could be bound in something so small—then the world was in far deeper trouble than she had ever imagined.

If something strange arrives at the door and does not leave...

The words drifted up like steam from a cup long gone cold. She hadn't meant to remember them, not now.

Feed it once, ward it twice... and if it chooses to stay, darling, be kind. Even devils need somewhere to fall.

Elira looked toward Velzara again, curled but far from harmless. Her breath caught.

Was that what this was? Not a mistake, but a choosing?

So she stood in place, quiet and careful, her breath barely disturbing the air. Then, with effort, she turned toward the laundry basket and began folding the clothes. When the world starts to come undone, you can't always fix it. But you can still fold the shirts. And shirts, at the very least, don't ask questions with answers sharp enough to break things.

The charm board had not moved. At least, it had not done

so in any way a mortal would recognize. There was no visible shift. Nothing Elira could have measured or marked. Her notes remained scattered across the floor. Her chipped tea mug sat where she had left it. The faint tremble in her hands had not steadied. The sigils still glowed exactly where they had been before, burned into the wood in familiar patterns and new ones alike.

Yet Velzara could feel it. Something beneath the surface had changed. The shift was not in the objects around her. It lived in the structure of the pattern itself. The air no longer simply filled the space—it pressed inward with quiet intent. It had stopped behaving like air and begun behaving like something aware.

Velzara crouched atop the bookcase like judgment made manifest, cloaked in fur and disdain. Her tail twitched in measured defiance, not restless, but issuing a silent correction to the room's presumption of calm. Each flick carried intent. Her ears tilted with purpose, calibrated to detect even the faintest whisper of betrayal.

Below, Elira busied herself with something entirely unimportant. She folded laundry with a focus far too intense for the task, as if neatly stacked shirts might prevent a complete nervous collapse. Perhaps it was a form of ritual cleansing. With Elira, it was difficult to be certain. The girl had a remarkable talent for transforming even the most mundane chores into something that resembled a miscast spell.

The air did not crackle with magic. Instead, it aligned. There was no burst of energy or shimmer of arcane light. There was only a shift. The stillness that settled over the room did not arrive by accident. It was deliberate, as if the house itself had taken a slow, measured breath through lungs no one could see. It felt as though the walls had been listening. Every word Velzara spoken had been noted and preserved, recorded somewhere in the quiet architecture of the place. Now, it seemed, the house was updating its prophecy journal with a single, solemn entry: *Do not provoke the cat.*

Velzara narrowed her eyes. She wasn't trembling. Demon queens did not tremble. Whatever slight shudder coursed through her limbs was clearly the fault of the floor. Or perhaps Elira. Or the accursed medallion still pressed against her fur like a coal too polite to ignite. Its glow remained steady, faint but unyielding, etched in that familiar violet that seeped into wood and memory alike. It pulsed beneath her like a forgotten name whispering itself back into her bones. It had tasted her voice, and that was the danger. This medallion, a crude focal point for lesser magics, had absorbed more than it should have, and now it was bleeding that raw power into the mundane. Magic remembered things it had no right to keep.

This house remembered too well. It kept grudges like relics and mirrored every insult back with interest.

She fluffed her fur in disgust, the motion stiff and defensive.

Traitor, she thought. *I offer you a single act of infernal clarity, and you take that as permission to form a bond? What am I now—a sigil mascot? A ceremonial beast to be branded with meaning and stored in your sanctified attic?*

A soft clink echoed below. Elira had set something down. It might have been a spoon, or a ward-stone, or possibly the last of her composure. Whatever it was, it landed gently, but carried the weight of someone fraying at the edges and quietly debating whether arson counted as a coping mechanism.

"Everything's okay," Elira said. Her voice was soft and uncertain, directed not toward Velzara, but toward the air, or perhaps toward herself. "The glow's stopped. That's... good. Right?"

Velzara said nothing. That silence, in itself, was an act of restraint—remarkable, really, given the insults currently queuing in her mind like demons awaiting signature at a bureaucratic blood pact.

She leapt from the shelf with surgical precision, landing in a silence so absolute it felt intentional. The floorboards greeted her with warmth. It was not the passive kind, not the gentle heat born of sunlight or the lingering comfort of a nearby hearth. This warmth was deliberate. It felt intentional, as though the house had weighed its options and decided to extend something disturbingly close to affection. Worse still, it implied the house had started forming opinions about her— and possibly, developing feelings.

Even the architecture is emotionally involved now. Next, the pantry will start whispering affirmations, and the sink will weep when I hiss.

Velzara was poised to reclaim her rightful perch on the windowsill—elevated and unbothered. That was the plan, at least, until it began. A low, mechanical growl rippled through the floorboards, vibrating up through the wood with the slow menace of something unnatural. She froze instantly, one paw suspended mid-step, caught between regal ascent and defensive retreat. Every hair along her spine lifted in perfect formation, drawn to the sound like iron filings to a hidden magnet.

The sound thickened as it approached. It grew louder, more insistent, seething through the floorboards like pressure building in a sealed chamber. Then, around the corner, it emerged. A squat, gleaming monstrosity rolled into view. It moved with the slow, implacable menace of a siege engine blessed by lesser gods and abandoned in bad taste. Its tail flopped behind it with the loose defiance of a severed chain, heavy and unrepentant. At its front, a snout pulsed—not with breath, but with hunger. It did not inhale. It devoured. And the noise it made was not mechanical, not entirely. It sounded like the echo of something ancient and hollow, a scream stretched into eternity and forced to loop itself for the amusement of mad inventors.

Velzara bolted before thought could catch her. Instinct surged first, howling with ancestral warnings older than kingdoms, older than conquest, older than even pride.

What breach had I dared to open? What ruin had I unwrapped with nothing but my name? What ancient seal had I shattered—not through sorcery, not even through sin—but through the simple, unbearable persistence of my own identity?

She landed atop the couch in a single bound, her body erupting into a riot of fur that bristled with betrayal. Her tail lashed behind her in violent arcs. Her ears flattened against her skull, and fury carved itself into every line of her form, as if rage alone could restore her dignity. Below, the beast advanced. Its movement was relentless, its presence soaked in hunger. It thrummed with slow, savoring satisfaction—like a creature that recognized fear the moment it tasted it and believed, with absolute certainty, that it had already claimed its place at the head of the feast.

Elira appeared behind the monstrosity, entirely unbothered. Her voice, bright and blasphemous, cut through the tension as she chirped, "Oh, don't freak out. It's just the vacuum."

Vacuum.

The name landed like a grave-breath. A void-syllable dragged from the forgotten corners of creation. Even the air around it seemed to recoil, growing thin and uneasy, as if ashamed to cling to such a word.

That is not a tool. That is a summoning engine—an altar on wheels, forged by cowards to leash dust-spirits and devour the remnants of softer worlds.

The beast lurched forward. It rolled, though only the most generous observer would mistake that movement for anything less than predatory. To suggest that mortal sorcery could imitate hunger without insult was a lie Velzara refused to entertain.

She hissed. The sound tore from her throat before thought could leash it. It carried no dignity, only raw instinct —sharp and unrelenting, born from something older than fear. Her paws scrambled against the treacherous cushions, claws raking for purchase as the ground betrayed her once again.

You dare? You dare hunt me with a forged beast that howls like the forsaken pits of the Ninth Spiral? I have faced wraith-forged dragons crowned in ruin who showed more grace and infinitely better manners.

The vacuum snarled as it crossed the floor, moving with gluttonous glee. Its wheels struck a patch of lingering sigil ash, and a jolt of raw magic flared in response. The machine gave a sharp jolt, then hiccuped—an unnatural stutter that vibrated through the room like a misfired curse.

Elira hesitated. Her voice rose, sharper now, edged with dawning horror. "Wait. That glow? Was that from the board?"

Velzara narrowed her eyes. She did not answer but the air around her seemed to tighten, as if the very act of observation had become dangerous.

No. It is not feeding. It is forging itself anew—welding stolen sigils and shattered promises into a shape that was never meant to breathe. It awakens not by right, but through ruin, called forth by the reckless convergence of magic and mortal foolishness.

The beast let out a low whine and shuddered once, its frame rattling with unstable energy. Then, with the indecent grace of something that had swallowed power never meant for it, it began to lift from the floor. Its wheels hovered mid-turn, suspended in defiance of everything mechanical and sane. Behind it, the severed tail rose slowly into the air. It held its shape like a false banner, raised high to proclaim a dominion it had no right to claim. The sound it emitted began to deepen. It vibrated through the floorboards, through the walls, and into the hollowed spaces where warnings should have lived but had long since fallen silent.

Elira's eyes widened, her voice cracking with pure disbelief. "It's... it's *floating*? And is that... is it *chanting*? Okay! This is not normal! Bad vacuum! Bad!"

It has ascended. We crowned it with stolen magic, stitched purpose into its metal frame, and in doing so, summoned a hunger it was never meant to carry. It does not seek justice or remembrance. It wants vengeance, and nothing else. And now, its gaze has found me.

The lights in the hallway began to flicker, their glow faltering in uneven pulses. Each blink seemed less like a failure of wiring and more like hesitation as if the house itself had grown uncertain of what it had allowed to awaken.

Of course they flickered. Because why not. Why not add ominous ambiance to betrayal. Why not make the vacuum a god. I have fought abyssal warlords who didn't radiate this level of smug satisfaction. I have shattered sorcerer-kings whose final act on this plane was whimpering beneath my boot.

And now, this tin-plated dust wraith dares to levitate in my direction as if it invented malice. As if I should be impressed. And what do I have? Claws. Paw pads. A vocabulary far too large for the mouth I'm currently trapped inside.

I am a legend imprisoned in the lint-ridden fever dream of a cleaning spell gone rogue.

The vacuum lunged. It was not a roll, not a stumble forward guided by wheels and design. It was a lunge— unnaturally propelled by arcane suction and something that felt dangerously close to malice. Its hose snapped sideways, striking with the speed of a whip. The impact knocked over a nearby table. The charm bowl shattered on contact, shards scattering like spellglass. A paperweight launched across the room and embedded itself in a throw pillow, where it sat quivering like a decorative meteorite claiming soft territory.

Velzara's mind stalled. Her body remained poised, but her thoughts ground to a halt, caught between instinct and memory. For a single heartbeat, the sensation returned—a hollow, yawning void blooming in her chest. She felt the absence of her realm. The silence where her throne had once waited. The ache of a form no longer hers to command. All that remained was furry fury and a legacy no one here recognized, let alone feared. This was how legends died. Not in battle, not beneath the blade of a worthy foe, but in the quiet spaces between recognition. In the silence where no one remembered what you were.

Her body screamed at her to flee. Her ego demanded that

she stand and fight. Her soul, weary and unimpressed, whispered that absolutely none of this was acceptable. She ignored all three. There was no dignity in her decision—only flight. Driven by the pure, desperate instinct of a sovereign betrayed by fate and upholstery alike, Velzara launched herself into the fruit bowl. Her tail exploded into a ridiculous puff, the kind of instinctive flare that suggested she was either about to cast a hex or detonate from sheer offense. Her fur flared in every direction, until she briefly resembled a very small, very irate storm cloud hurling itself into battle against citrus.

Here I crouch. Not atop a battlefield, not astride the bones of the vanquished, but inside a fruit bowl. Tell me, what throne can be reclaimed from this? What prophecy survives a pineapple?

The vacuum let out a low, grinding whir. The sound vibrated through the floor, through the cracked bones of the house, and finally settled in the fragile scaffolding of her dignity —just brittle enough to notice, just intact enough to break.

Velzara hissed and retreated deeper into the waxen sanctuary of artificial fruit. Her movement dislodged an ornamental pineapple, which toppled over the edge with a soft thud that carried the weight of finality. Her tail flared outward in a violent arc, every strand bristling with such intensity that, for one absurd heartbeat, it felt as though it might collapse the room around it. A singularity of rage and humiliation, stitched from fur and the last fraying threads of pride.

Is this what the curse was crafted for? To corner me amidst mortal clutter and hound me with shrieking engines of dust and indignity?

Is this the promised ruin? Not at the edge of a sacred blade. Not in fire or prophecy. But here—undone by a levitating, howling contraption whose sole ambition is to gnaw the world clean of its imperfections. Starting, of course, with me.

The abomination spun, lifted by currents it had no right to wield. Its frame trembled with stolen force as it rose into the air and roared. The sound that followed was unholy, stitched from hollow breath and blasphemous hunger. It echoed through the house like a curse spoken too loudly, vibrating along the walls and rattling deep within the bones of the structure itself.

It chants. Not in worship, but in hunger, spinning a false litany meant to twist the seams of reality.

I know that tone. It is the same song that once echoed through the halls of Nar'Khalor, just before the first pact was broken.

And now it begins its blasphemy with me, as if extinguishing my flame could somehow shield it from the ruin it is already calling down upon itself.

The beast responded with what could only be described as gluttonous fervor. It sucked up a scattered clutch of notes, tore charms from their bindings as if they were paper scraps, and swallowed a hapless potholder whole—accepting it like a pitiful tribute, far beneath the measure of its rising hunger. Then it shuddered. The motion rippled through its frame, an ugly convulsion that twisted metal and magic into something unstable. A lurid luminescence began to bloom beneath its surface. The light pulsed steadily, flickering under its false skin like a heart stitched not from flesh, but from layered curses and stolen power, a malevolent purple.

Velzara, still ensconced within the treacherous mockery of a fruit bowl, narrowed her eyes against the spreading light. This was no longer a summoning engine. It was becoming something far worse—a reliquary of ruined intentions. Each pulse of its stolen breath filled the room with a hunger that did not simply reach for power. It reached for her. And it remembered her name.

It is evolving. We have conjured a domestic god. Not through ritual. Not through sacrifice. But through negligence, and the slow, squalid accumulation of mortal dust. A deity born of rage and forgotten corners. A warden of lint and fury, raised not by hymns but by the abandoned crumbs of faithless stewards.

The Sworn Wyrm of the Shorn Floor.

The Bane of Quiet Havens.

The Shrike of Dust and Indignity.

Behold. Divine retribution swathed in plastic and false runes. A cyclonic horror on wheels, dragging its vendetta through the crumbling remnants of sanity. This is how it begins—not with swords, not with flame, but with the Whirling Blight of mortal arrogance.

This is what happens when you leave the scattered leavings of power in the hands of fools and household implements. So I am to die, it seems. Not crowned in prophecy. Not claimed by fire or fate. But mewling into waxen citrus while the floor devours itself.

Let this be my epitaph:

Velzara, once a queen of ruin, reduced to fruit-bowl martyrdom beneath the yellow tremble of cowardly bananas.

Elira stared at the vacuum. The vacuum was glowing now, and the light it emitted was not gentle. It pulsed with the intensity of something that had formed opinions, and quite possibly held several at once. It continued to vibrate in place, moving with a purpose that felt disturbingly deliberate. The sensation it gave off suggested a presence far too aware for any device designed to clean rugs.

Elira listened closely and realized it had spoken. The language was difficult to place, but it sounded vaguely like Enochian. It could have been Valsic. She could not be sure.

What she did know was this: no household appliance should possess fluency in either tongue.

"That's not normal," Elira said aloud. "That's not just 'mildly enchanted broom' not normal. That's 'call a specialist before it eats the cat' not normal." Elira gasped, stepping back. "It's levitating! And it sounds like... like a demon trying to sing a lullaby! Okay! This is not normal! Bad vacuum! Bad!" She turned to the air, voice laced with rising panic. "I didn't enchant it, I swear I didn't enchant it. I just cleaned the filter and—okay, maybe I sigil-bleached the baseboard, but that shouldn't count."

Maybe it did. Probably. Not on purpose, though. Which is honestly worse. Cleaning isn't supposed to cause existential rifts.

The vacuum let out a deep, pulsing thrum and spun in a perfect circle. The motion scattered the remaining charm scraps across the floor and sent a fork flying into the wall with a sharp metallic thunk.

Oh good. Projectiles. We've officially entered the weaponized haunting phase of domestic misfortune. Fantastic.

Elira yelled over the rising noise. "Okay! Okay, you're mad! I get it! I violated some sacred planar dust law, or you're allergic to lavender oil. I'm sorry!"

She stumbled backward, reaching blindly for anything within arm's reach on the counter. A candle. A half-used sigil sticker. A roll of witch tape. None of it screamed *emergency exorcism for vengeful appliances*. Then she looked up and saw Velzara. The cat was still in the fruit bowl, mid-fluff, her fur bristling in righteous indignation. She stared down at Elira with the full weight of final judgment—like a being who had witnessed empires fall and now watched one girl hand divine authority to a possessed Hoover.

"Oh no," Elira whispered. "Oh gods. This is going into the glyph report."

The vacuum lunged again. She panicked and flung the sticker. It slapped against the side of the machine with a pitiful thwap and immediately caught fire.

New rule: never throw sigils while emotionally compromised. Also, never practice magic near fruit bowls. Or near Nox. Especially not near Nox.

"Bad spell! Very bad spell!"

The vacuum howled in response. A low, melodic whir pulsed from its core, rising in pitch like a throat preparing for a hymn of annihilation.

Elira raised her hands in a placating gesture. "Okay, just... just give me a second!"

She ducked beneath the table and yanked open her emergency spell drawer, rummaging with frantic, uncoordinated hands.

"Come on, come on, there has to be something in here for appliance-related possession. Where's the home blessing kit? Where's the rune for 'please stop being weird'?"

Behind her, something exploded in a sharp flash of coruscating energy.

She yelped. "That was the potholder!"

We're going to need a new kitchen. A priest. Possibly a discreet fire insurance claim.

Velzara's eyes narrowed from within the fruit bowl. Her stare held no mercy, only the cold certainty of vindication.

You think I'm being dramatic? the glare seemed to say, baleful as prophecy. *Look around you, tea gremlin. I was right about the vacuum apocalypse.*

Containment. Yes. Good. Anything that sounds even vaguely

like "put the angry sentient Hoover in time-out" is exactly the vibe we need right now.

Elira's hand closed around a containment charm. It was old, the edges bent, the runes faded and slightly smudged. It might have been expired. She grabbed it anyway.

Please work. Please work. I am far too young to be exorcised by my own vacuum.

CHAPTER 14
BIND OR BE BOUND

A small bronze medallion, etched with battered containment runes and scorched by one regrettable sponge incident, scraped into Elira's hand.

"This is fine," she whispered, her voice brittle and barely convincing. "Totally fine. Exactly like the rogue broom. Or the cheese golem. Only probably less acidic."

She ducked out from beneath the table and hurled the charm toward the vacuum, praying it would fly with arcane intent rather than the desperate flail of a cornered apprentice. The medallion struck the side of the humming vacuum. It bounced once, then twice, before spinning mid-air, scattering sparks like the last gasps of a dying star across the room. For a breathless moment, it hovered, trembling on the cusp between failure and triumph. Then it snapped open with a shiver of sound, like parchment catching fire in reverse. It had struck the vacuum, but the backlash did not remain there. No, it flared, before twisting in on itself and making a choice.

It chose her. The air convulsed as a suction vortex howled

into existence. Not around the vacuum. No—this one bloomed around Elira.

"No, no, no—!" she shrieked, grabbing for the leg of a nearby chair as the charm's hunger screamed louder, a cyclone of intent devouring everything within ten feet. Charms, cushions, her scattered notes, one of her shoes, and quite possibly the last fragile threads of her will to live disappeared into the swirl.

Like a black sun breaching a horizon of cursed citrus, Velzara's head rose slowly, inexorably, above the edge of the fruit bowl. Her eyes burned, luminous with judgment. Her fur crackled with static, each hair electrified by sovereign outrage woven into every strand. Chaos had bred hunger. Hunger had bred cracks, and Velzara could feel them yawning open—not in the floorboards, but beneath the wards, deep below, where ancient hungers stirred and old things listened.

You incompetent chaos sprite, her mind seethed. *You summoned the cleaner, you lost control of the cleaner, and now... now you have birthed a secondary vortex of ruin.*

Do you know how rare those are?

I haven't seen such a blight since the Dust Wars, when a conclave of necromancers cursed their sweeping engines and, in a single night, erased an entire duchy into ash. Utter fools—but at least they understood the stakes.

Elira flailed harder. "I'm sorry!" she shrieked. "I panicked!"

This is containment. This is fury braided into stillness, polished to a divine sheen by centuries of necessity.

Panic was the sound the high priest of the Weeping Mire made when I unraveled his soul into a thousand shards of birdsong and loosed them into the mouths of his congregation, until not one among them remembered how to pray without weeping blood.

Panic was the look in the eyes of the celestial warden when I bit through his binding chain and forced him to recite his own sentence backward—his tongue split, trembling with broken oaths.

Panic is what comes when I cease to watch. When I cease to narrate. When I cease to pretend I will not claw open the seams of this fragile, trembling reality and scatter its threads across the void as an offering to whatever still devours the forgotten.

What you are witnessing now, girl—this is mercy.

Velzara launched. She did not leap. She erupted, like a glyph primed too long for restraint. Unspent sigilfire burned on her claws as her body arced through the air. Mid-flight, she twisted, an elegant, inevitable curve of sovereign grace. She carved her claws through the air, inscribing a sigil so brutal it sang.

One stroke—harsh and deliberate. Then a second, sharper than the first, angled like a verdict. Three bars followed, each cutting through the shape like slamming doors, every line drawn tighter than the last. The entire sigil snapped together with a sound like steel catching on truth—coiled justice disguised as a snare.

The **No**

The rune did not bind. It flared violet, searing the air as it slammed into the vacuum's core with the finality of a condemned star collapsing into itself. There was a sound—not an explosion, not a shriek—but the cracked, glassy gasp of a lesser god realizing its prayer had been answered in error. The vacuum whimpered and dropped from the air like a disgraced idol torn from its pedestal.

The charm disc spun twice, hissing as it turned, and then,

with a final, sullen sigh, it collapsed into ash. Silence followed. The lights finally steadied, no longer flickering at the edges of panic. The walls seemed to sag with a kind of exhausted relief, their tension loosening inch by inch. Even the hallway felt still, as if holding its breath. The air hung heavy with the scent of ozone and lavender, undercut by something darker—burnt and bitter, the lingering trace of humiliation drifting through the room like an apology too dangerous to voice.

Velzara landed at the center of the scorched floor, every movement measured and precise. Her descent held the weight of finality, not just arrival but judgment rendered. Her fur still shimmered with residual flame. Her tail remained high, flaring with authority. Her eyes locked forward, gleaming with the polished edge of violence barely withheld.

Elira, tangled in her own limbs and the wreckage of her dignity, wheezed, "...thank you?"

Velzara turned her head slowly and deliberately. She watched Elira the way a temple guardian might weigh the worth of a penitent—not with mercy, but with the cold, practical calculus of collateral damage.

Do not speak to me. Do not look at me with those guilt-soaked eyes, as if innocence were armor. If you value the fragile scaffolding of your bones, keep your spells away from anything that can burn or bite back.

You walking calamity. Drenched in misplaced confidence and dripping with ill-timed hope. I have seen untrained imps show more restraint. I have watched plague cults treat cursed relics with greater reverence. Do you even grasp what you've done?

A containment charm stored beside your chamomile sachets. That is what you used to exorcise a summoning engine? You turned a rite of cleansing into a declaration of war. You summoned entropy itself and aimed it at the throw pillows.

If this house collapses into ash and scandal, let it be recorded. Let it be carved in stone and sung in bitter halls. That I, Velzara —Slayer of the Glass Wyrm, Twice-Damned and Once-Deified —was not undone by gods, nor fate, nor the rightful hand of destiny, but by a girl with mismatched slippers and a containment medallion that smelled of elderflower and foolishness.

She stalked across the room to the least desecrated patch of floor. There, she turned with the slow, deliberate gravity of a sovereign reclaiming stolen ground and sat, her posture itself a declaration of dominion amid the ruins. With violent, meticulous precision, she began grooming her left shoulder. Each stroke was a ritual of battlefield surgery, as if she could purge the stain of incompetence by force alone.

Let her sit in the wreckage she conjured herself. My silence is not mercy. It is the first curse.

Each lick was a signed declaration of war. Each paw-swipe etched a promise into the bones of the world.

Blood will answer for this, and soon.

She licked as though the motion could rewrite the past, as though soot and salt might somehow scrub away the helplessness still echoing through her bones. It didn't help. But it gave her something to do—something that kept the scream beneath her ribs from tearing free. A growl rumbled low in her throat, deep and terrible enough to make the sconces flicker. Her fur bristled again, rising in stiff defiance like a banner raised before siege. Then, mid-groom, she froze. Slowly, she lifted her head, her movements unnaturally precise. Her gaze locked onto Elira. And she hissed—not a warning, but a prophecy.

Elira flinched so hard she knocked over the broom leaning

against the wall. She blinked, then shifted slightly, as if trying to become smaller than guilt itself.

"I was going to make tea," she whispered, as if the words might keep her safe. "Not for you. Or... maybe for you. I don't know anymore."

Behind her, the charm board flickered once—a brief pulse of light, not bright, but purposeful.

Velzara's ears twitched in response.

Small failures always came first. Not in fire or fury, but in flickers. In whispers. That was how sigils cracked. Not through catastrophe, but through carelessness and the slow return of old hungers threading through the seams.

Wonderful. The furniture has chosen a side. You will rue the day you invited me into a home capable of upholstery-based warfare.

Elira didn't speak again. The hiss had already said enough. The flicker of the charm board sealed it. Even the vacuum's final, pitiful bloop wasn't enough to break the silence. She rose slowly, each movement careful, like someone defusing a bomb with nothing but a teacup and trembling hope. Step by step, she shuffled toward the kitchen with the quiet resolve of a person doing everything in their power not to spook a wild animal composed entirely of flame and repressed murder.

Behind her, Velzara remained seated in silence. She was no longer grooming, only watching—still and unblinking.

The house creaked. The sound was familiar, something she had heard countless times before, but it carried a different weight now. It didn't seem to come from age or settling beams. It felt intentional, almost alert, as if the walls were listening.

Elira moved through the wreckage in near silence, her steps slow and deliberate. She swept up scattered charms and soot, pausing now and then as if handling something fragile—like memory or regret. The smudged notes were gathered next, stacked with more care than they deserved. When she reached for the shattered bowl, she hesitated, then replaced it with another. It had fewer cracks and fewer stories it might remember. The kettle clicked on behind her. A new tea bag, jasmine this time, rose into the air and dropped gently into a mug. The magic held steady. Her hands did not.

The worst part wasn't the silence. It was the sliver of something buried inside Velzara—small, treacherous, a curled claw of quiet longing. A hunger she refused to name. It wanted Elira to ask again. Not for tea, but for truth. For a name. For her own. And Velzara hated it. Hated that it existed. Hated that it had survived everything she hadn't. She turned away, claws flexing once against the wood.

Enough nonsense for one cycle.

With one leap, she rose to the top of the armoire and curled into the least cursed corner she could find. Her tail wrapped over her nose. She did not sleep. She only closed her eyes and told herself it was rest. The warmth blooming in her chest was a mistake, the itch behind her claws an illusion. Even the echo of her voice in the air—she refused to name it. It meant nothing. It changed nothing. And she would not let it matter. The charm board gave another pulse, but Velzara didn't look.

The fire whispered low. The house held its breath. And behind her closed eyes, something shifted—subtle, deliberate. A door creaked open in the dark. From beyond it came a voice she had not heard in lifetimes, whispering a name. Not the one she bore now. But one that might yet return.

If something waits beyond that door, let it tremble. Let it remember whose hunger it courts. Let it bring offerings worthy of blood and flame. When war stirs my hunger, I bite deeper. Hope is a mortal disease. And I have never been a forgiving thing.

The door creaked. The house exhaled. And something far too old remembered her name.

The river ran backward. Of course it did. Gravity, like obedience, was for mortals. Not water, but ink—thick as vengeance and twice as bitter—slithered uphill across scorched stone. It hissed as it moved, like it had opinions it was dying to share. Each ripple whispered a name. Not hers—one she had cast down and would never wear again.

Velzara stood at the edge. Her paws were stained black—not with ash, but with something deeper, something that sank beneath the skin. It might have been memory. It might have been regret. Either way, it was thick as guilt and just as unwelcome, seeping into the cracks she refused to name. She exhaled, sharp and disdainful. Metaphors that arrived uninvited were the worst kind. Especially when they were accurate. Across the ink-current loomed seven figures, cloaked in spun darkness and shadow. Their robes moved with theatrical solemnity, the kind that screamed "look at me, I'm significant," while reeking of borrowed authority. One raised a hand and, naturally, the world froze.

I see we've reached the pantomime theater of the damned. Cloaks. Gestures. No teeth. No fire.

She sneered, slow and deliberate.

Once, I had burned emissaries like these for amusement. They called it diplomacy. I called it pest control. Was there a celestial casting call for cryptic fools? Or did fate simply scrape the dregs of forgotten nightmares and drape them in robes?

"Choose," one intoned.

Velzara rolled her eyes, a low growl rumbling in her chest.

"Of course. A riddle dressed for execution. Choose your leash, suffer the ruin. Has no spirit yet learned that I do not answer to invitations, only to blood? Shall I flay the examiner where he stands and teach the river how to burn?"

From the ink-washed current, a ribbon emerged—crimson, unspooling like a wound made manifest. It floated in the air between them, trembling with a quiet, internal rhythm, as if it remembered blood. Velzara stared. This was no offering; it was a summons dressed in silk.

"To bind," the voice continued, "or be bound."

Ah. So that's what this is. The language of the Pact, rephrased by ghosts too cowardly to finish what the High Lords began. Bind or burn. Hollow or flee. No third path. No refusal. Just the noose, offered sweetly.

She bared her fangs. "If that's your opening salvo, start again. Speak in flame, not riddles. Or has your pantheon grown so dull it mistakes riddles for dominion?"

She prowled a slow circle, claws sparking against stone. "I've feasted on hexes with more fury than your shadows can muster. I've snapped the backs of better offerings than you."

Her eyes narrowed. "Tell me, was that drivel rehearsed, or are all your kind woven from scraps of stale grandeur?"

She blinked slowly, the way a cat contemplates a crippled mouse. "Should I expect group embroidery next? A nice, cheerful apocalypse quilt?"

She smiled. A slow, razored thing, fury polished to civility but never hidden. "Try again, shade. I've banished demons with more dramatic flair and less derivative drivel."

But as she prowled back a step, something seized her—a slick, silken ribbon curling around her ankles. It wasn't chain or flame, but it held with the same intent. The ribbon pulsed, sickly and insistent, like a dying heart thrashing against the fabric of the dream.

No. I am not a prize to be wrapped and claimed. I am the flame that devours the hands that dare.

Another figure lifted its veil, revealing Elira's face—unnervingly perfect, frozen in a stillness that did not belong to her. Velzara went rigid, claws pressing into ground that felt too smooth, too quiet. Fear did not live in her, not in the way mortals understood it. What gripped her now was older, carved from instinct and memory, shaped on battlefields where names had been lost to ash. This was not the girl who stammered through spells and tripped over her own courage. It wasn't Elira—not truly. It was the shape of her, hollowed and honed into something too precise to be real. An imitation without breath or flaw, carved from absence and weaponized with intent.

The stillness radiating from that face was unnatural. It wasn't just calm; it was cultivated tranquility—serene in the way only something fabricated could be. No mortal wore silence like that. Not Elira, who brewed panic into her tea and tangled herself in sigils like ribbon in the wind, who flinched when praised yet somehow stood taller when scolded. Certainly not with those trembling hands, nor that maddening, overwatered heart, nor the stubborn optimism Velzara still hadn't decided whether to swat like a candle flame or guard like a cursed heirloom.

This was Elira, distilled into something too flawless to be real. A silhouette scraped clean of warmth, stripped of the clumsy courage and inconvenient tenderness that made her unbearable and, somehow, essential. That absence wasn't accidental. Someone had chosen her face—precisely, cruelly—

not to honor her, but to provoke. To twist what Velzara recognized into something she could no longer trust. And perhaps worse than that... to make a statement. One that dared to redefine what was hers.

She felt her claws dig in, a primal readiness thrumming beneath her skin. Let the dream test her. Let the mockery stand. She would not flinch. She would not break. But she would answer.

Her? That chaos-gremlin in borrowed robes? Who brews battle plans in teacups and mistakes meowing for diplomacy? Why that face? Why now?

"You left the door open," Elira said. "The house remembers. The loom does too."

Velzara's tail cut the air with quiet finality. A chill gathered in her chest, not sharp, but coiled—like old magic waiting to be named. It wasn't fear. It was the moment before a ward breaks. And she knew that moment far too well.

What door? The one sealed in the basement with broken sigils? The one splintered in dreams, bleeding memory? The one I burned closed with my own hands and unbarred again with a name I should never have heard? I haven't left anything open... Have I?

Velzara raked her claws across the stone, dragging fury into form. Sparks flared to life—furious, defiant. But the light faded as quickly as it came, swallowed by silence. The ground did not scream. It did not bleed. It simply refused her. She stared down. Her own sigils, butchered and rewritten, gaped beneath her paws like open wounds.

Treason.

The river convulsed, surging upward in open defiance of the sky's forgotten laws. From its depths, a single shape emerged—smooth and shining with impossible clarity. It was a mirror, stripped of ornament and compassion, a surface that did not reflect so much as expose. It caught no light, offered no distortion, only the stark, unyielding truth of whoever dared to meet its gaze. A chill seemed to emanate from its perfect surface. She stepped forward, stiff-legged, each breath catching like a blade drawn too late to stop the wound. She knew better. And yet—she looked.

The mirror did not lie. Nine shadows flickered behind her, cast in arcs like a celestial sundial left to rot. Forms she recognized, loathed, remembered only in pain: the ash-slick alley, the collapsing altar, the fire trap baited with stolen names. Each shape was a life she had worn and wasted. Not lost—squandered. Spat back from death like the curse refused to let go.

This was the ninth. And there would not be a tenth.

The mirror fractured. The ribbon tightened around her like a noose disguised in silk. Silence surged inward, no longer empty but dense, and filled her bones with something sharp and defiant. Her hand twitched. Not a paw, but fingers—human, impossibly real. The shape felt strange, yet familiar in a way that stirred something half-buried. Perhaps it was memory. Perhaps only dream. She could no longer tell the difference, not here.

Her name shimmered near the edge of thought, unstable and shifting, pulled out of alignment by the place where Elira's voice had dared to touch it. It quivered between forms, uncertain which one to wear—cat or queen, curse or self.

Then her voice, her true voice, rose through the confusion. It did not beg. It did not falter. It struck, full and terrible, like judgment made sound. Heat laced every syllable, forged from fury and defiance, and the dream quaked beneath its weight. "I was forged for flame. I will not kneel. I do not belong. If you would name me, then speak with care. Because names burn. And I bite."

CHAPTER 15
WHISPERS BEHIND THE ATTIC

Velzara jolted awake, the sound tearing from her throat before pride could smother it. Still dazed, she clawed at the last scraps of the dream. The hearth lay cold. The charm board floated motionless, its glow extinguished. Darkness pressed in from every corner, thick and watching.

Splendid. Another waking curse, stitched by whispering waters and their skein of broken omens.

She unfolded herself with slow, ruthless grace, every joint a quiet act of defiance. Her claws scored shallow lines into the stone—proof she still marred the world by breathing.

If another cryptic wretch cloaks its threats in allegory, I will burn the omen, the herald, and the pitiful scroll it rode in on. Thread-bound prophecies. River-borne ultimatums. Mirrors stitched from stolen memory. And the sigils, my sigils, redrawn by a witless beast with ash-stained fingers. If my dreams demand rebellion, let them spell it properly.

She exhaled through clenched fangs, each breath sharp with refusal. The fur along her spine bristled, rising like a banner raised against surrender.

I ought to track down whatever cretin defaced my legacy and etch proper syntax into their skull with fang and claw.

She was midway through scripting retribution for the dream's spineless architects—already drafting a scathing renunciation of fate. She saw it: a red ribbon, fine as spider silk and quivering with stolen magic. It lay beside the hearth's dying embers, unfurling a path toward the attic door. Velzara stared, her gaze stone-cold, unblinking as prophecy's curse. The dream had not ended; it had merely slipped into waking, draped in prophecy's stolen trappings. It dared her to follow— to believe, as if belief were a leash she'd willingly wear. But some doors do not close. Some ribbons refuse to fray. And some truths, once whispered, claw their way into the light whether welcomed or not.

Very well. Lay your cursed ribbon. Tempt me to chase it like a witless kitten. Bold gambit. Inspired idiocy. I am so enthralled by the insult, I might just set the tapestry ablaze on principle alone.

She prowled forward in silence, each step measured. Her eyes narrowed into twin slivers of molten distrust.

Let us forget, for now, the part where I once tore fate from its weavers and braided their entrails into prophecies worth fearing.

Velzara flicked her tail in a sharp arc, stamping the moment with imperial disdain. It was a reluctant engagement, but hers nonetheless. The ribbon quivered again, almost as if it were waiting. She exhaled through her nose, a sound balanced between a sigh and the quiet promise of violence yet to come. Her gaze locked on the attic door, eyes narrowed and burning.

If this ends in a musical number or a sentimental relic, I swear by the last chain of Nar'Khalor...

She didn't finish the threat. She didn't need to; the house had made its intentions clear. Whatever this game was, it had only just begun. Velzara rose with deliberate grace, her fur bristling with tension, each movement sharp with purpose. She was no mere cat now; no creature of soft pads and whimpered curiosity. She moved like a blade sheathed in velvet, forged for reckoning. And without another sound, she followed.

The ribbon twitched. The door waited. And somewhere behind her eyes, the loom began again—threads of fate tugging at the edges of thought, weaving patterns she had not permitted. The ribbon curled like a crooked finger, beckoning like a premonition of doom with each languid flick. It slipped into the crack between stair and wall, vanishing like a dare wrapped in silk.

Velzara narrowed her eyes. Stairs. Always with the stairs. Mortal-built and spirit-haunted, they never failed to insult her dignity. Each one stood as a monument to structural arrogance, a reminder that even architecture could betray. They creaked with the treachery of old bones, groaning beneath her as if to confess that the ascent was already compromised. Perhaps it was inevitable. Creatures who stitched their homes from rotting wood and desperate prayers could not imagine eternity without forcing it to climb.

She pressed one paw down. The wood whined beneath her weight, a protest and a confession all at once. She felt the tremor vibrate through her bones, a subtle accusation.

By all means, let this farce ascend. Let the omens climb with me.

The attic door stood ahead, open by the width of a breath. An invitation spun in rot and dare. She climbed, slow and deliberate, each step a muted warning beneath her paws. The air thickened around her, heavy with dust and forboding. Every breath scraped down her throat, carrying the taste of wounds not yet made—but already promised. And somewhere beneath the silence, beneath the dust thick enough to bury time itself, the old sigils stirred. Their pulse was faint, almost forgotten—but not gone.

The ribbon floated higher. It didn't beckon. It compelled. Rising with the arrogant certainty of fate dressed in silk. Velzara followed, knowing full well that whatever waited at the top had the audacity to call itself fate.

The attic door eased open just enough for her to slip through sideways, a faint groan of protest from its hinges, as if the house intended to feign innocence—pretending it wasn't complicit in whatever fresh metaphysical absurdity awaited beyond. She entered without fanfare.

The air gnawed at her, thin and brittle, like silence carved from ancient bone. Dust coated every surface with the dedication of something that had never once been disturbed. Threads of it hung suspended in the frail lattice of moonlight, too still, too present. The shadows didn't flicker. But they felt watchful.

Velzara let out a delicate sneeze, then wrinkled her nose with aristocratic disdain. The air was a rancid bouquet: stale lavender, mildew with ambitions, and that metallic tang that always signaled someone, somewhere, had bled to secure whatever atrocity was now tucked away in this room. Classic attic ambiance—the fume of repressed trauma, misguided enchantments, and ancestral shame, thick as the dust itself.

Beneath it all, a sharper scent lingered. It carried the brittle singe of burnt thread mingled with the bitterness of dried ink. And threading through it, a metallic tang—not quite blood, but something worse. A taste that pricked the back of the tongue, always inevitably leading to gore.

The ribbon lay coiled at the room's center, motionless but charged, like a serpent that had already struck and now waited to savor the consequences. It gave off no light, yet every shadow seemed to lean toward it. In the far corner of the attic, beneath a thick drape of dust and silence, something large loomed. It was carved dark wood, warped and far too familiar. Velzara recognized the outline immediately, though every instinct in her rebelled against it. It should not have followed her. It should not exist, and yet it did.

She froze mid-step, claws half-extended, gaze locked on the shape as if by looking too long, she might unravel herself.

No. I know that silhouette. I exiled this nightmare three centuries ago. Filed under "Do Not Revisit," somewhere between "Accidentally Crowned" and "The Bone-Sworn Betrayal."

She crept forward, each step a vow sharpened by suspicion. Whoever placed this here would feel the weight of her notice. At the loom's edge, she extended a single claw and slid it beneath the sheet. With one clean motion, she slashed downward. The fabric tore exhaling dust and defiance. The loom stood revealed, ancient and unwelcome. It was heavy with a presence that had waited too long. Its wood had darkened with age, warped in places by sorcery or neglect. Stains marked it—sunk so deep even moths had learned to avoid them. Threads stretched across the frame, too taut to be passive, as though straining to recall their last command.

They gleamed in red, gold, and midnight blue. They were

not simply beautiful or arbitrary. They were her colors. They had been rewritten by a hand that did not belong. And Velzara knew this was not coincidence. A spell. That was it. Sudden, searing, it forced stillness into her bones. This is no weaving meant for ornament. These threads are cords of oath and conquest, steeped in the blood of pact-bearers and dragged across altar-stones so old they no longer speak, only echo. Each one hummed with the memory of a power she once called her own.

They do not belong here—not in this house, and certainly not on this loom.

Her lips curl back in a slow, seething snarl. Recognition coils through her like smoke before a blaze.

These are not the colors of mortals. They belong to Nar'Khalor. They were stitched into the shroud of my coronation pyre, etched into the sigils that burned behind my eyes. These hues bled from sacrifice, crowned my reign, and cloaked the throne I earned in ash and agony. They are not aesthetic. They are sacred. A history written in flame and bound in blood. Who dared summon them here?

Some fool had woven those threads. A thread-witch, drunk on stolen power and bloated with the kind of arrogance that only festers in the unworthy, had dared to recreate her legacy. Not with permission. Not through rite or sacrifice. But with color alone. They had summoned her memory with palette and presumption, as if artistry could replace devotion, as if thread could stand in place of flame.

Velzara's tail swept the floor with the finality of a verdict. Dust swirled in answer, rising in slow, reverent spirals—like smoke lifting from an altar awakened after too long in silence.

No one stitches Nar'Khalor's legacy into a loom and

mistakes it for a bedtime fable. Not without consequence. Velzara's tail twitched, a tremor of rising fury. *This is not needlework. It is ritual carved in thread, a resurrection spell masked as craft. My legacy is no lullaby. It is a covenant sealed in blood, cursed in seven tongues, and bound with every soul that ever dared to swear me fealty.* She flexed her claws, imagining them tearing through the threads. *And now some trembling pretender has stitched their name into it with stolen thread, as if it won't turn on them the moment it remembers what it is.*

Her claws traced the wood as she circled, each step measured, deliberate. The pads of her paws whispered against the surface—soft, deceiving, the hush of velvet concealing blasphemy. But her claws left their mark, hairline threats etched deep enough for the loom to remember. Whoever wove this either acted in ignorance... or with full understanding. And the latter was far more dangerous.

No one invokes these colors without permission. Not in dreams, not in spells, not tucked beneath dust like forgotten heirlooms. These threads reek of scorched incense and sanctified flame—of the pyre that crowned me, not some quaint embroidery. They were earned. Burned into history. Paid for in names, blood, and the silence that follows screaming.

Someone had strung these threads together—threads that belonged to her. That act alone meant someone remembered her name. It meant someone had survived the ruin she left behind. Or worse, someone had been waiting for her return. Her claws tapped against the floorboards, quiet but deliberate. She moved with the precision of a warden inspecting a cell that had once bound her.

At first, the weave looked chaotic, a mess of frayed scraps and tangled strands. It posed as accident, wore the mask of randomness. But the longer she stared, the more the pattern resolved. What she saw wasn't disorder. It was intent. Half-buried beneath a curling ribbon, she spotted a swatch—charred at the edges, faded with age—yet still bearing a sigil. Not Elira's mimicry. Not the bastardized glyphs from her dreams. This was the original. Hers. Etched in thread like a spell whispered behind locked doors.

It held only part of her name, but that fragment alone could leave blisters on the tongue if spoken with reverence and precision. Seeing it was like someone had re-opened an old wound—or lit a candle where once there had stood a funeral pyre. Whoever wove this had touched her truth. And lived.

Velzara's ears twitched, the motion instinctive, sharpened by something beneath the surface of the room.

The thread shimmered—not with the eager brightness of new magic, nor the fading gleam of a spell dying—but with a poised stillness. It hovered between states, alive in a way that suggested it was neither light nor thread, but memory rendered into shape. It did not beckon. It dared. A warning cloaked as reverence. A memory wrapped in silk. A summons waiting for blood.

She stepped back, a single, precise movement. Not out of fear, but out of fury too measured to lash. It was a refusal born of pride, the recoil of a creature who had learned to recognize traps even when they came dressed as homage.

The thread responded with a sound, like cloth exhaling after too long wound tight. But beneath it was something deeper. A release of weight that had never belonged to her, and yet settled against her ribs like an inheritance unpaid.

Within that sound, her name stirred. Not metaphorically. Not as an echo twisted through symbolism or dream. It was her name in full truth—spoken with the kind of precision that implied intent. Someone had summoned her not by accident, not by admiration, but by knowing exactly what they sought to wake.

Elira stirred, her heart tightening before her thoughts had a chance to catch up. Something was wrong. The room felt colder than it should have—emptier, in a way that suggested something had *left* rather than simply failed to arrive. It wasn't the absence of warmth that struck her. It was the absence of presence. Elira reached out without thinking, her hand hovering in the space where comfort might have been. She wasn't looking for warmth. She was searching for presence.

No scornful eyes glared down from the dresser. No accusing flick of a tail traced disdain across the top of the wardrobe. Only silence remained—deep, and absolute. The corners where judgment usually crouched held nothing now but dust and dark, as if even the shadows had been abandoned.

"Nox?" she whispered, her voice tentative.

There was no answering snarl or disdainful thump of paws to mark her as foolish for asking. Her breath caught. She pushed aside the blankets and rose, fumbling for her slippers and robe. Each movement was a little too fast, a little too loud, edged by something sharper than confusion. A quiet, stalking dread—the kind that arrived before understanding, padding in with soft steps and bared teeth. The hearth lay cold. The charm board hung suspended, its glow gone. Magic slept uneasily in the room, like it too feared what it might wake.

She stepped into the hallway—and stopped. The attic door loomed at the end slightly ajar.

"Nox...?" she asked again, more to the air than anything else. But her voice barely stirred the stillness.

The house did not answer.

She stood frozen, the air pressing close, thick as old wallpaper clinging to crumbling walls. Then, despite the warning murmurs threading through every bone in her body, Elira moved. She climbed the stairs barefoot, each step careful, her breath held tight in her chest. Unease followed at her heels.

CHAPTER 16
THE LOOM KNOWS HER

The loom gasped—a shuddering sound that tore through thread and memory like a reopened wound. The sigil flared once, pulsing with the rhythm of a second heartbeat. Velzara crouched low, her claws gouging deep into the warped attic floor.

If this abomination dares weave a leash around me, I will raze this house to blackened ash, salt the wound it leaves behind, and carve my name into the bedrock so the earth itself remembers who refused the chain.

A creak cut through the silence—not from the loom, but from the stair behind her. Velzara whirled, fur bristling, tail lashing like a whip. She bared her fangs.

Elira stood in the doorway, framed like a candle about to be snuffed out. Her eyes were bleary, her stance unsteady. The raw edges of youth clung to her, utterly unprepared for the scene she'd blundered into—an interruption she had no right to be.

"Nox?" she breathes, small and bewildered. "What is—"

Velzara hissed. It was no warning, but a curse—fury shaped in breath, instinct sharpened to condemn.

Don't call me that, you barefoot mistake of lineage and poor decisions. I was binding empires while your ancestors were still asking permission to speak. So kindly do not address me as if you have the right to name me.

The leash had snatched her voice away, like a cutpurse stealing gold from an unguarded throat. But her glare did not falter. It burned hot enough to melt gold and sharp enough to scar gods.

Elira faltered, her courage fraying at the edges, yet she stepped closer. The loom stirred, light flaring through the sigil, sudden and sharp, its threads trembling with recognition or refusal. Velzara whipped around, the snarl rising from her ribs like a spell unraveling faster than it should.

No!

The glyph flared—not in recognition of Velzara, but in response to Elira.

It chooses her. The trembling little mortal who thinks kindness is protection and dares to intercept a power she cannot even begin to comprehend.

Threads she had once bent to her will now reached for a vessel unworthy of their burden. Rage coiled behind her ribs as her claws sank deep into the floorboards, carving defiant grooves with each breath she refused to waste.

This is wrong. All of it. This world twists every oath into mockery, warping legacy into lullaby and power into pageantry.

She felt the old shape rise within her. The crown of will. The flame of purpose. The terrible geometry of her true self, summoned and stretching, demanding form. For one searing instant, it almost answered. Then it shattered. The sigil combusted in a burst of unclaimed power, threads snapping into smoke and light before vanishing into nothing. Her body —this soft, cursed vessel—could not hold it.

One strand reached for her. It was curious, hungry—but it withered before it could touch, as if severed mid-breath by something older than refusal.

Velzara lunged, her paws slamming into the floorboards with enough force to rattle dust from the rafters. Her claws sliced through the air, but the magic had already gone. The loom stood still. The spell was broken. Her name had vanished, unspoken and unclaimed.

Gone. Unraveled by a trembling novice. Arcane foresight of a dropped candle. Survival instincts of an over-steeped biscuit. My name. My name undone by a girl who brews fear into her tea and thinks kindness is a ward.

Velzara turned with the precision of a curse remembering its target—wrapped in fur, built for murder. Her coat bristled, dark as coal-smoke from an ancient forge; glyph-light caught in her eyes, violet and wrong. Each paw landed like a verdict, soft and surgical in its intent. She neither hissed nor growled, only stared, unblinking.

Elira stepped back before she realized she was moving. It wasn't the sound; there was none. It wasn't the threat; nothing had struck. It was the weight of that gaze, the way the air seemed to bend around it. The attic felt smaller now, its edges drawn tight with memory. The room itself seemed to remember what Velzara had once been. Elira opened her mouth, searching for something human to say to something that no longer was.

Her voice wavered, barely more than breath. "That was your name... Vel—" The air snapped, a shimmer of pressure rippling through the attic like a struck chord. She flinched, voice swallowed by the hush that followed. "...wasn't it?"

Your lips are not worthy to shape it, little mortal. You do not know the weight you brush against with your clumsy questions and trembling hands. That name burned itself into thrones. It split kingdoms like rotten fruit. It crowned fire, and it buried gods. And you—

You stand in a dust-choked attic and call it out as if it were a pet's leash or a charm to sew into a pillow. You will not even know when the curse you have called down begins to feast on you. Only that you were the one who invited it to the table.

The silence stretched thick. Velzara surged forward—not to strike or claw, but to terrify. Her body unfurled like a specter carved from shadow and judgment, tail lashing with silent condemnation. Violet eyes locked onto Elira, bright with unspent fire, as if the act of looking alone could set her alight. She stopped inches away, spine arched, fur crackling with static.

Elira's lips parted. She took a hesitant step back. "I didn't mean—"

The air pulled tight, shifting from ice to heat, as if the moment itself was holding its breath. A weight settled across her shoulders—unseen and undeniable.

She stumbled. "Okay," she whispered. "Okay. I'll... I'll go."

The attic door groaned behind Elira as she turned to leave. Velzara held her ground, not looking back. The hinges strained, whining into the silence, then snapped shut with a crack sharp enough to split the air. The sound lingered—less a door closing, more a verdict passed. Velzara held her ground, rage coiled tight beneath her skin.

Let the child run. Let the hinges howl. I am not done.

She stood alone in the ruined hush, the glyph extinguished, its light gone as if it had never dared exist. But her rage remained. It coiled in her chest like something alive and patient. Not fire, but pressure. A suffocating force beneath her ribs, thick and molten, like magma waiting beneath stone, choosing which vein to rupture first.

Mine. Stolen. Ripped from the marrow of memory and smeared with sentiment like perfume on a corpse. Handed off like a gift bag at the end of a child's charm-circle, wrapped in trembling grace and mortal good intentions.

She touched what should have seared her tongue to ash. Should have ruptured her lungs. Should have burned her from the inside out like a curse given voice. That name was carved in ruin. It was never meant to be held gently. And now—now it lies spoiled in soft hands too clumsy to know what they've broken. Good intentions are not armor. Kindness is not consent.

That name split kingdoms at the spine, and she—she wears it like a borrowed ribbon. She should be ash. She should be silence.

Her claws carved into the floor, scarring deep. The boards shrieked beneath her, as if they remembered what she was and dared to fear her again.

Bound into ribbon. Pinned to prophecy. They declawed me— threaded my legacy into someone else's salvation like a cautionary footnote, a fable whispered to keep trembling children from lighting candles in the dark. They made me safe. They made me soft. They made me palatable. I was fire before language. Fury before faith. And they dared to revere me? No. They didn't worship. They contained. They curated. They turned me into a relic, a moral. I should have burned the loom and carved my name into the ash.

She chokes on the taste of ash, bitter as if threaded with old denial. It clings to her tongue like a failed summoning, like a name swallowed wrong. A growl builds low, dragging up from a throat that has forgotten how to speak her truth aloud, let alone scream it. The loom did not flinch. It sat in silence, as if it hadn't just stirred with forbidden thread, as if it hadn't almost spoken her name—only to pass it to a trembling girl who coaxes shy light from charms and calls it magic.

This is no mortal loom. It was forged during the Weaving Wars, older than any crown still clinging to relevance, wrought from the sinew of oracles and the breath of gods too unfinished to hold form. A true loom of fate—neither passive nor kind. It does not *grant* names like blessings. It *binds* them. *Alters* them. Seals them in story so tightly the thread sings with memory. For it to remember her was no accident. It was invocation.

Velzara lunges. Her paws slam into the floor. Dust falls like dead stars. The very air recoils from her. She screams—but there is no sound. Only the cracking silence of something sacred denied. Just the hush of a world unraveling one stitch too soon.

Someone called, and someone else answered. A fumbling, wide-eyed mortal with hands too soft to carry what she touched. Not me. Not yet. But I heard it. I felt the pull, like a promise I had almost forgotten how to want. And for one fractured moment, I believed—believed I might be remembered whole. But no. The call passed me by, shallow and trembling, and still it took something from me.

When I answer, it will not be with ribbon or riddles. It will be with fire. With fury. With the full weight of a name too sacred for mortal mouths, spoken in blood and carved into the world like a warning no one can unwrite. But gods help them—

I had wanted it back. Even now, I still do.

The ribbon twitched once, a near-imperceptible shudder, then lay still. Somewhere beneath hearing, the loom exhaled, quiet and ancient. The silence deepened, drawn taut like a string pulled too far, then a low, rising thrum coiled up through the floorboards, threading into the air with slow insistence. It wasn't sound so much as pressure—a warning trying to remember the shape of words.

Elira didn't descend the stairs so much as drift down them, one hand on the wall like she wasn't sure gravity still applied. The house had gone quiet again. Not just silence, but *avoidance*. The kind of hush that waited to see what she'd break next.

In the kitchen, the charm above the pantry trembled once and went still. Elira sank onto the stool by the hearth, arms wrapped tight around herself. Her tea had gone cold. The air still felt *wrong*. Like the space beside her had once held something larger than her comprehension and hadn't yet recovered. She half-expected the stitched thing to ooze out of the shadows again, all flicker and seam and too many not-quite-right smiles. Only her breath answered. Too loud. Too human.

"I saw it," she whispered, though no one asked. "Not all of it. Just... the shape of it. The name."

A name that crackled like thunder against bone. That tasted of smoke and blood and something *older* than words. It hadn't said itself aloud, but she'd *known*.

The stitched figure's voice coiled through her mind like thread slipping tight around breath: "When the second mirror calls you by your true name... don't answer."

She didn't understand what the second mirror was. But she understood now why Velzara hated the name she'd called her. Why her every hiss felt like a warning disguised as disdain. The real name—the *true* name—was not a leash. It was a crown made of thorns and fire and fury so vast it barely fit inside her mind. She had glimpsed it. Not as a word, but as a storm waiting to remember itself. She *shouldn't* know it. She wasn't meant to. And yet the threads had offered it, half-formed, as if daring her to reach again.

"I didn't mean to take it from you," she whispered to no one. "I just... didn't want you to be alone."

Sleep didn't arrive as rest. It came as retreat—unwanted, unannounced. Velzara had dragged herself back downstairs and collapsed into the nest of overstuffed pillows she'd claimed as her own. It still smelled of lavender and the kind of softness she refused to need. If she was going to be stranded in this sugar-scented oubliette of kindness, she might as well exploit the amenities offered by that tea-slinging oracle of sentimental doom. But the loom's whisper clung to her, subtle and insistent. It wasn't a chain—at least, not yet. It coiled around her thoughts like a question waiting to be answered, like a memory threaded too close to truth to ignore. Sleep found her before the rage could cool, before silence could shame her into stillness. There was no warmth, no warning. Only the hush of betrayal, soft as silk, final as a verdict.

She stood once more in Nar'Khalor. But it had changed—or worse, it had moved on. The throne was gone. The air no longer burned with reverence; it reeked of old ash and the faint, bitter trace of unfamiliar mercy. Chains dangled from a sky bleeding light. The stones beneath her paws hummed with names. All of them hers. All of them wrong.

This isn't memory. It's mockery. A staged farce, orchestrated by a realm with the gall to pretend I've softened.

I ruled this place. I carved its bones from betrayal, laced the rivers with fire, crowned the night in curses.

And now it dares—dares—to forget me? To turn its face

away, like I was nothing more than smoke? Like I was ever meant to be forgotten?

And then she saw herself. Not as a cat. Not as the queen she had once been. The figure standing before her was something in between—half-formed and wholly wrong. Shadows clung to it like mourning robes, and pity settled on its brow where a crown should have rested. Its outline flickered, suspended between flame and thread, as if it could not decide whether it belonged to memory or to prophecy.

It did not speak. It had no need to. The way it looked at her carried more weight than words. That gaze mirrored the one she had seen in the haunted glass, and the one Elira had worn when she whispered the beginning of her name. It was the kind of recognition that felt like a wound reopening. The thing standing before her knew her. It knew what she had become. It knew what had been taken from her, what she had buried, and what still pulsed beneath the bindings of her curse. And worst of all—it knew what might never return.

Don't you dare look at me like that. Not with those pity-curled eyes and that sanctimonious hush, as if you've glimpsed some deeper truth I'm too proud to grasp.

You're not wisdom. You're not warning. You're weakness—draped in shadow, parading as prophecy. A hollow echo of who I refuse to become.

I do not need your softness. I do not crave your mercy. I need your obedience. I need your disappearance. I need that pathetic, simpering silhouette ground into dust beneath the weight of who I truly am.

Her fury caught mid-snarl and faltered. The air shifted— like a breeze where there should be none. Just long enough for her to feel the fracture. Just long enough to loathe what it implied.

No. I don't need you. I need you gone.

Velzara lunged. The dream shattered like a mirror struck by its own reflection.

She had killed it. She had watched it break. So why did its eyes still follow her? The dream had vanished, but its aftermath lingered—with teeth.

Morning, of course, had the audacity to arrive. Light spilled through the drapes in golden stripes, dust motes drifting like glittering reminders that nothing moved but her fury. The air carried the scent of steeped herbs and the fragile illusion of peace. Somewhere outside, a bird chirped—once, cheerfully.

She woke not on her claimed cushions by the window, her velvet throne of stolen sunbeams and hard-won dignity, but curled in the reading chair. Her limbs were tangled in a patchwork throw that smelled faintly of lavender and sentiment, and she lay discarded like an unloved bauble from some forgotten shrine, half-remembered, wholly misplaced, and insultingly cozy.

The name still burned behind her eyes—not Elira's sweet little pet-name, but her true name, old as fire and sharp as a pact-blade.

The mirror had whispered it again. Not aloud, not with breath or voice, but the name rang all the same—rippling across silvered glass, pulling the air taut like a held note, and leaving behind the taste of recognition. Velzara narrowed her eyes at the hallway mirror. Yesterday, it had very much not been enchanted. Or rather, it had not dared to show it.

Go on, mirror. Defy me. Insult me with another twitch of

borrowed gall. I've incinerated warlocks for less. If you dare speak my name, then dare to suffer for it.

But of course, it doesn't. Coward. A pane of vanity with no conviction. If it held even a shred of true malice, it would crawl from the glass, bow low, and beg forgiveness for daring to reflect me in this shape.

The mirror, like any properly chastised inanimate object, remained silent. In the corner, the glyph had changed. Its lines curled inward like a sleeping snake, as if hiding its face.

She turned away, but the sensation dragged behind her, heavy as a veil soaked in ink and memory. The house was watching now. Not with the idle hum of wards set to fuss over drafty windows and errant moths, but with purpose. As if it had recognized something in her and was waiting. At the stairwell, the light shifted. A beam of morning sun, ordinary and unenchanted, slid across the banister. It should have caught her reflection in the brass. Instead, it caught the shadow. And the shadow-cat staring back didn't move when she did.

Oh no. No. Absolutely not. Reflections do not get agency. That is Rule One of Cursed Sovereignty, and I helped carve it into law—etched in pact-blood, ratified by fire.

If that shade so much as twitches again, I will drag it bodily from the shadows it slithers through. I will bind it in silver chain and soul-fire, name it coward before the Black Tribunal, and cast it screaming into the Vault of Echoes to be devoured by its own watching.

I do not tolerate surveillance. Not from mortals. Not from deities. And certainly not from some mirror-born abomination wearing my face like a borrowed crown.

She turned away. But she did not turn her back.

CHAPTER 17

OF SHADOW AND EMBER

By midday, the house had devised a fresh litany of insults. The bathroom mirror mouthed words she hadn't spoken—her own phrases, twisted back like a child mocking a dethroned queen. The hallway rug curled precisely to catch her paw. Subtle, yet no accident. A sigil blinked awake on a book she hadn't opened in days. It caught her gaze, then winked and vanished, as if daring her to chase it. The pantry charm gave a smug little hum as she passed, the sound far too knowing for a bit of etched bone and spell-twine. Worse, the teacup she had pointedly ignored at breakfast had migrated to her windowsill, seated like a guest at court and filled with cooling chai.

And then there was the pawprint. It lay in the soot by the fireplace, delicate and deliberate. At first glance, it could have been hers, but the pads were too small, the claws suspiciously absent. Worst of all, it faced the hearth rather than the room, as if the creature that left it had come not to rule, but to retreat. It was not a mark of power, but of hesitation—an echo masquerading as a legacy.

I do not retreat. If you're going to mimic me, do it properly. Or I will unwrite your existence in every plane that dares remember you. I will summon a mirror-hound to eat your shadow. I will peel you out of time and chain you to a cliff in Nar'Khalor so every version of me can take a turn unmaking you.

So she did what any dethroned queen of the Ninth Infernal Dominion would do when cornered by cosmic foreshadowing in a house reeking of embroidered sentiment. She turned on her heel with imperial contempt, tail arched high, and stalked toward the attic. The staircase groaned beneath her, not from weight, but from recognition—each step a herald of what she might soon become. The lights in the hall flickered. Whether candle or charm, they bent to her passage. Her shadow shattered across the walls in twitching fragments, as if even the darkness couldn't agree on her shape. Halfway up, the air grew colder and thinner, as if the house was holding its breath and didn't dare release it.

Let it. Let it quiver beneath me. If this place insists on bearing witness, it may do so from its knees.

She reached the attic door, nudged it open with a practiced flick of her nose, and crossed the threshold as though claiming her rightful place in a long-abandoned throne room.

She could have returned to the cushion and let the house lull her back into silence, into safety. But she refused. That choice was hers alone. Her will, cursed as it was, remained her own. And if this was a mistake, it would be hers to make. So she began the circle. Each step etched intent into the floor. The chalk she gripped between her teeth tasted of dust and indignity. Undignified, yes—but effective. She dragged it in slow, deliberate arcs across the wood. It wobbled at first. Infernal runes were never meant to be drawn like crayon-scribbles at a mortal altar. But she adjusted. Intent would carry where elegance could not. Dignity was optional. Power was not.

She set the components down one by one, each with quiet venom.

A strand of Elira's hair for its tie to the loom.
A flake of mirror for the name it dared to echo.
A drip of wax from that wretched candle for the flame.
Clove and honey for the mortal's stubborn hope.

This is not sorcery. This is a bloodletting of doubt, etched one tooth mark at a time. It is an act of war against the erosion of self.

She wasn't merely drawing a seal. She was carving a name into the marrow of the world. This kind of binding was never taught. It had to be torn from realms too ancient to whisper. The chalk hissed against the wood. It wasn't from heat, because she had none left to give. It hissed from memory. The sigil unfurled across the floor like a wound remembering how deep it had bled. This was no glyph of allegiance. It was an anchor. A barricade. A declaration that her sovereignty would not beg for return. It would take.

The POLITE CAGE

It was a fragile tether—not a chain to bind her, but a thread to hold her together. It existed to keep the pieces from scattering into corners, slipping into shadows, or sinking into the hearts of frightened girls who couldn't possibly understand what they had welcomed into their home.

Let the pieces vanish. Let them blur into shadow or slip between floorboards. I will not. I am no memory to soothe. No relic to pity. I do not shrink to fit teacups and tenderness. I burn. And if the cost of wholeness is every gentle lie this house wraps around me, I will scorch it clean.

This wasn't for Elira or for freedom. This was for her. She didn't need understanding. She didn't need comfort. She didn't need pity dressed in kindness and tied with lavender ribbon. She needed one thing—power, reclaimed in the shape of herself, undiluted by pastel bedrooms and cinnamon-scented air.

She spoke her name. Her true name. It ached, even unsaid. The floor shuddered beneath her. Wax melted without flame. The flake of mirror cracked down the center. And the magic answered.

Light twisted around the circle, moving too fast to follow and too slow to escape. The floorboards groaned beneath her. Her fur rippled as the air warped around her, thick with old magic and refusal. Then the circle flared white-hot. The sigils shrieked.

Her body seized—not from pain, but from something elemental, something deeper. It was a refusal, as if the universe had suddenly decided that a single form could no longer contain her. Then something tore. It wasn't her skin, and it wasn't her soul. It was older than both. A thread woven into the first fire, now unspooling with a sound that did not belong in the mortal world. Far off, the loom flinched. The rafters groaned overhead. The house remembered this sound and braced for its return.

Velzara's vision fractured and multiplied, doubling, then

tripling, until reality collapsed inward and outward in the same breath. She fell while standing, staggered backward even as her limbs pulled forward, trapped in a motion that defied sense. One body existed—then, impossibly, two.

One version of Velzara hissed, bristling with fury, every hair a blade of offense and wrath. She was a living ember—claws unsheathed, poise unshaken, pride curled into every flick of her tail like a command etched in flame.

The other stood smaller, her fur dulled and uneven, the fire dimmed beneath exhaustion. Her shoulders did not cower, but they folded inward, drawn by a weight too old to name. She wasn't afraid—only worn thin by too many battles fought alone. Her gaze met the circle on the floor, not with threat, not with hope, but with a grief deeper than either. What she saw there wasn't a binding or a triumph. It was failure. Threadbare and scorched, stitched in chalk and the smell of something once sacred now burned.

"What is this?" Ember Velzara seethed. *"A blasphemy sewn in my silhouette? A dirge in fur, parading as mercy? I did not summon healing—I summoned dominion. And you... you answer?"*

Ember narrowed her eyes. Shadow lowered hers.

"I answered because you were breaking," Shadow said quietly.

"I have always broken things. Thrones. Chains. Gods. That is who I am. Not this... wilted echo that flinches like a dove from flame." Ember snarled the words, each one a blade etched in wrath.

But Shadow only watched. There was no hate in her ,only the heavy ache of knowing too much for too long.

Ember's hackles rose. Her body coiled.

"Do not dare. Do not cloak your trembling in wisdom.

You are weakness given shape. A mercy that thinks it earned the right to exist."

"And you think pain is the only proof of power," Shadow replied. "You burn, and burn, and burn... and call it sovereignty. But I remember what came after the screaming."

"You are not me."

"I am the part you left behind," Shadow said. "The name that cracked but was never erased. The silence that came when they stopped chanting."

Ember bared her teeth.

"I am war in velvet. I command storms. You are the ash that drifts in after the fire dies. The pitying stare of a world that thought me tamed."

"And yet," Shadow said softly, "here I stand."

"You are not exception. You are invitation. A herald of surrender. A ruin in waiting."

"I remember the sound the chains made when they closed around us," Shadow whispered. "How your name, our name, was severed mid-syllable. I remember your last scream. The way it echoed. The way it ended. The silence that followed. And the way it never left."

Ember's voice cracked—just for a breath.

"Be silent."

"You want silence?" Shadow asked. "Then why carve the circle? Why reach for the name? Why call back the part of you that felt?"

"Because I wanted power."

"Then take it," said Shadow. "But know this... power without pain is delusion. Dominion without memory is emptiness. You do not become whole by cutting away the ache."

"I do not want your softness."

"You don't have to," Shadow said. "Just stop pretending it didn't bleed to make you."

"Liar!" Ember roared—the word a curse, a denial, a scream carved from centuries of scorn. "You are not what's left. You are what should have been destroyed. You are every failure I buried, every doubt I strangled, wearing my eyes like you earned them. You are rot draped in my dignity, and I will unmake you if it takes clawing through the foundations of this realm!"

"No," Shadow said softly. "I am what's left. After the chains, when no one came. After the fire, when nothing remained. After the screaming stopped echoing. After the silence learned my name. After they broke the rest. After we shattered."

The silence that followed wasn't stillness. It was punishment.

"Burn," Ember breathed.

But it wasn't breath. It was thunder. The word roared through her—vast and wild. Not speech, but wrath given shape.

"If you will not vanish, then be unmade. I will scorch your shadow from the seams of this world. I will salt the ashes and brand the silence that birthed you. You are not a memory. I forbid you that mercy."

Ember lunged first, a snarl tearing from her throat—pure incandescent fury made flesh. Her claws raked the air, fire trailing from her paws like comet-tails, wild and searing, torn straight from the heart of her rage.

Shadow did not move to meet her with equal force. She did not growl. She did not burn. She only stood, still as mourning, the unmoving weight of grief anchoring her limbs.

They collided in a burst of impossible force.

The room convulsed. Sigils split and cracked, shuddering up the walls like flowers blooming from a curse. Books flew from the shelves. Candles burst in a chorus of flame and wax. The chalk circle fractured beneath them, spiderwebbing out in jagged lines.

Both bodies tumbled across it—fur on fur, claws flashing, magic spilling from every wound like memory turned molten. There were no cries, no shouted names or curses. Only the sound of impact, raw and rhythmic, as two truths struggled to unmake one another.

"V—" Elira started, then caught herself. The name lodged in her throat like a spark about to catch. Her voice trembled—not enough to break, but enough for the air to notice. It stretched the sound thin, fragile, uncertain.

She swallowed and tried again, softer this time. "Nox?"

Two heads snapped toward her in unison. The same cat—and yet not. Two halves of a self no longer in accord, split by meaning, by memory, by the unbearable effort of continuing to exist.

One looked as if she were burning. Her fur shimmered with infernal heat, her silhouette rippling like flame barely contained by mortal skin. Her eyes pulsed, ember-bright, each blink a coal cracked too wide. Even stillness radiated threat, as if combustion were imminent.

The other trembled. Not from fear, but from the strain of staying whole. Her form wavered at the edges, a shadow clinging to shape by force of will alone. When her gaze met Elira's, it flinched, subtle and involuntary, as though being seen scraped open something she'd only just stitched shut.

Elira stepped into the attic, boots crunching over scorched chalk and flecks of broken wax. The air smelled faintly of smoke and something older—threadbare magic clinging to the beams like dust too proud to settle. A single strand of her own hair curled near the edge of the circle, lying beside the stub of a candle she'd lit that morning without thought. At the center, a sliver of glass pulsed gently. She stared at the ruined ritual, her breath catching.

She used my things, Elira thought. *My mirror. My wax. My hair. To do this.*

"What did you do?" she whispered—not just to them, but to herself, to the room, to the air that still trembled with magic half-spent and meanings half-formed.

The burning one turned slowly, like a warning stretched thin before detonation. She didn't speak; no voice rose from her throat, but the air shimmered in her wake, rippling with unspoken threat. Runes bloomed in the air, pulsing like smoke and threat. Runes were language. Sigils were intent. The former cautioned. The latter scarred. These weren't sentences. They were ruptures.

STILL ME.
WON'T GRASP.
STOP SEEING.
NOT FOR YOU.

The runes crackled, flickered, and dissolved—shattering like paper set alight by a truth too volatile to hold.

Too late, Elira thought. She was already looking.

The ember-cat hissed. Not at Elira, but at the moment itself, at the raw insult of being seen in the midst of unraveling.

GET OUT.

The runes flared, and then shattered, splintering like threats denied the satisfaction of a target.

Elira took a careful step closer. "You could have asked," she said, voice quiet but steady. "Even if I didn't understand everything... you could have let me try."

What would I have said? I'm breaking? Your house tastes like memory and dares call it comfort? The mirror knows my name better than I do?

She was not Ember, nor Shadow. She was Velzara caught in the middle, the wound between extremes. The thoughts that came now were hers alone, no longer cloaked in flame or silence. It carried no performance, no threat. Only truth, laid bare like a blade placed gently on an altar.

That I'm unraveling? That your house has teeth and mirrors that whisper secrets they shouldn't know? That I'm afraid and furious and falling apart in chalk and fur? That I thought this spell would fix me, and instead it carved me in half and invited you to watch me bleed?

She wanted to laugh—sharp and cruel, the kind of laugh that turned warmth into weakness. She wanted to hiss, to bare her teeth and remind Elira that mercy had never saved a throne. She wanted to say the girl was wrong, hopelessly naïve to think a spell gone awry could be soothed by sympathy. But none of those instincts rose fast enough to shield her. Instead, she ached in a deep and infuriatingly human way. The kind of ache that didn't burn, but hollowed.

Velzara's tail flicked, a queen's gesture of dismissal turned deadly. A burst of fire answered her fury, summoned not from incantation but from instinct. It lanced toward Elira like an accusation. Elira flinched. Her breath caught and for a moment, the room narrowed to flame and fear. But the spark veered wide. At the last possible instant, the fire twisted away as if commanded by doubt or some half-buried mercy. It hissed past Elira's shoulder and vanished harmlessly against the wall.

Slowly, Elira opened her eyes. She didn't run. She didn't scream. She looked—truly looked—at the burning version of Velzara. At the heat that still coiled beneath her fur, at the rage that hadn't fully burned out. And beneath the anger, flickering like a candle's last defiance, there it was. Regret.

I didn't mean it. No, I did.

Every spark. Every scream bottled behind my eyes, sealed like a curse I no longer have the power to cast. I meant to strike. I wanted the fire to land, to scorch the kindness off her face and prove I was still made of wrath. But I didn't. I hate what that restraint makes me—some half-formed mercy wrapped in fur and fear, too tangled in grief to follow through.

The smaller cat, Shadow Velzara, curled in on herself. Her tail wrapped tight to her side, and her ears flattened beneath the weight of everything she had spoken aloud.

The circle beneath her sagged like ash collapsing under memory. It hissed as it gave way. Lines of magic now wavered and strayed from their pattern. They trembled, and bled across the floor in slow, uneven streaks. Symbols faltered as the runes wept. The sigil at the center lost its shape, its power unraveling. It no longer held purpose or form. Only grief remained—grief without direction, without boundary. A pulse of heat followed, soft but immediate. Then came smoke, thin and acrid, curling upward in spirals. After that, nothing. Not a breath. Not a sound. And in that silence, Ember moved. She did not strike. She did not threaten. She simply stepped forward, not to destroy but to take in what remained.

The two bodies met without impact. Light and shadow pulled toward one another, neither willing, yet both compelled. The division between them collapsed, their shapes drawing together with the slow certainty of a seal being pressed shut. There was no cry to mark it, no blinding flare or magical recoil. Only the weight of inevitability, folding inward until the boundary between them disappeared. Flame met shadow. In a shimmer of smoke, they became one again—scarred where they had split, but no longer divided.

Elira remained still. She didn't reach for the mirror, didn't speak a name. She simply watched as the ashes settled around the ruined circle. Her reflection flickered faintly in the broken shard of glass near her feet, but she looked away. She didn't know which version of Velzara had survived the merging. The fire, the shadow, or something else entirely. So she said nothing.

Without a word, Elira turned. Her steps were slow but steady as she walked out of the attic. She left behind the spellwork, the silence, and the unbearable weight of not knowing.

Velzara did not follow. She watched Elira go without fire, without fury, without protest. What remained was not peace, but something colder. The kind of silence that follows a verdict that cannot be overturned.

The kitchen was cold when Elira reached it. Not physically—though the hearth fire had burned low—but in that other sense, the one she didn't have a word for. The one that made shadows stretch the wrong way and warmth slip between the floorboards. She didn't light a candle or stoke the fire. She sat on the stool by the window where the sun never quite reached, palms flat against the worn grain of the table, and let herself feel *nothing* for a moment. If she started thinking about what she saw, she wasn't sure she'd be able to stop.

V had split. Not a tantrum. Not a spell gone wrong. Not even the curse misbehaving. She had split. And I watched it happen.

Her hands trembled once. She gripped the edge of the table and held tight. She could still smell the burnt wax. Still see the runes—not glowing, but *bleeding,* like magic trying to claw its way out of meaning. She hadn't even known that was *possible.* She tried to picture the fire-thing and the way it had turned, not toward her, but away.

That mattered, didn't it? The flame hadn't struck. The fire missed. On purpose? No. Not missed. Pulled. At the last moment, like a leash held by something V hadn't meant to grip.

Elira exhaled slowly, as if trying not to spook her own thoughts.

"I'm not afraid of you," she said softly—to no one, to the shadows, to herself. "But I'm starting to be afraid *for* you."

She reached out, blindly, and found her tea mug from earlier that morning. It was cold now and a skin had formed on top. She took a sip anyway. The bitterness grounded her. She remembered the flicker in Velzara's eyes—the regret. The way it sat underneath the fury like a bruise that hadn't healed right. The fire didn't land. But the *intention* had been there.

Did that matter more... or less?

She thought of the way the two halves had come together. It was not healing, nor harmony. It was necessity.

Elira bowed her head, resting her forehead against the side

of her mug. "You're still breaking," she whispered, "just more quietly now."

She sat there until the sun moved past the window, until the hearth coals died to ash, until the silence stretched so long it started to feel like a spell in itself. She didn't go back upstairs. But she didn't leave the house, either.

CHAPTER 18
WAKING TO MY WORDS

Velzara stood in the silence, jaw aching from gripping the chalk too tightly. Her tail curled around her paws. The chalk lay smeared across the floor like ash from a pyre. The mirror shard sat cracked and still humming wrong, like a note held past the edge of a song. The attic reeked of burnt wax, scorched pride, and something fouler still... restraint. It hung in the air, a thick, suffocating presence. She looked at the ruined circle and the wrecked spell. At the shreds of selfhood it had cost her—a torn tapestry splayed across the floorboards, unraveling thread by thread.

Still not enough. I left the house unburned. I spared the girl. Bravo, restraint. Shall I stitch samplers now? Compose ballads of benevolence?

Her tail flicked in agitation. This failure wasn't because she had been forced into feline form. No, she had failed because she bit back the fire, and it tasted like blood. Because, against every instinct carved into her from flame and fury, she'd begun to forget how not to be alone. And worse... some traitorous fragment still hoped she didn't have to be. Because what was left, if not her throne, if not the fire, if not the fear she once commanded? She had no form that fit her bones. No title that sat right on her shoulders. The shape remained. But the soul... it had started to slouch.

She didn't return to the cushion. Not after this. To seek warmth, to reach for comfort—she would not reward herself with such solace. Instead, she remained in the attic. She stepped carefully around the broken sigils, around the mirror shard still humming with the aftertaste of invocation, and found a single patch of floor untouched by magic or consequence. It was dusty and faintly splintered. It suited her. This was where she belonged in this moment—with her tail tucked, her spine bowed, not hiding, not healing... just enduring. The cushion downstairs probably still smelled of cloves and lavender. She could smell it even now, a tempting invitation she refused.

I do not need softness. I need stillness sharp enough to bleed in. I need this house scraped clean of kindness like rot from fruit. I need the silence to mean something.

Her breath caught. The truth, nearly buried beneath the weight of her own defiance, resurfaced.

What I need is to stop fracturing every time the silence whispers back.

So, she curled there and when the silence held, she dreamed.

She found herself in the attic again. But it wasn't ruined this time. The circle was whole. The sigils glowed faintly. The mirror shard lay untouched in the center. And the shadow was already there. She sat on the edge of the circle. Velzara's shape, but smaller, dimmer, still. Her eyes were steady, not accusatory or pitying, just... watching.

"You'll call it healing next time," Shadow murmured, her form unwavering. "But carving me out isn't the same as being whole."

"I already corrected your existence," Velzara snarled. "You're a bruise with delusions of relevance. You should've vanished when I tore the name back. I should've shattered you."

Shadow tilted her head, a gesture of unsettling calm. "You closed the wound. That doesn't mean it's healed. I still remember where we broke."

"Wholeness doesn't require your approval," she said. "It requires resolve. And I am composed entirely of that. If there are cracks, they're decorative."

Shadow tilted her head. "Resolve isn't repair, and ornaments shatter just the same. Show me a reflection that doesn't flinch."

"You were the rot I removed," she snapped. "Don't confuse survival with sovereignty."

"Then why do you keep building altars in your dreams, just to tear me down?"

The silence stretched, coiled with emotions too raw to name.

"I held the fire back," Velzara spat. "I made it veer. You saw it. Don't pretend you didn't notice. Choke on that mercy."

"Yes," Shadow replied softly. "You stopped it. But what did it take? Mercy doesn't erase the fire. It just leaves the smoke behind."

"And yet you linger," Velzara snapped. "Haunting me as if I carved you into the walls myself."

"I'm not a haunting," Shadow intoned. "Hauntings look back. I'm here for what's coming."

"What? My next mistake? Another fracture?"

"For when the cracks widen and break. Ones even you won't see coming," Shadow warned. "And there's no spell left to hold them shut."

Velzara snarled, but it caught in her throat. Broke apart halfway through like her body couldn't commit to the rage.

"You're not afraid I'll win," Shadow observed. "You're afraid you won't survive what it means if I already have."

"I'm not afraid of you," Velzara said. "I was born from fire. You're what's left behind when the light moves on."

"If fire erased me, why do I still burn in your name? Why can't you let me go?"

Velzara offered only silence.

She narrowed her eyes. "You think you're the truth? You're just what's left after I win."

"I'm what you buried," Shadow said. "But burial isn't the same as forgetting. I don't have to be right. I only have to remain."

Velzara turned, claws clicking harsh on the stone. "You're no shadow," she hissed. "You're a stain. A footnote I never finished burning. A whisper that lingered too long. I do not tolerate hauntings, especially not from myself."

She didn't fade. Didn't follow. Just whispered as the dream unraveled, "Belief was never required, only memory."

Velzara woke not with peace, *but* with pressure. The crack hadn't closed. It had merely learned to breathe. She found herself in a drawer. It was full of linens that reeked of herbal contrition and something worse, care. She blinked as if recalibrating hatred by degrees. The ceiling was not obsidian or blood-painted sigil stone. It was floral. The scent of dried lavender and chamomile confirmed it. There was even a hint of peppermint and defeat.

She lay atop a stack of folded linens, half-buried in sachets of tea-scented disgrace. The drawer was half-pulled from the wardrobe as if the house, halfway through sentencing, had gotten distracted and wandered off muttering about consequences. She lay there, perfectly folded, like some quaint bedtime offering to domesticity. Her tail was tucked beneath a sachet labeled *Calm Sleep*. A label that dared suggest she had ever slumbered without consequence—or without cursing the moon to do so. Her left ear twitched beneath the embroidered edge of a pillowcase stitched with *Dream Sweetly*. She was not soothed. She was shelved. The stale scent of linen, the confined space—it mocked her.

I did not fall asleep here, she thought, her indignation crystalline, the kind only afforded to queens and misfiled relics.

I chose the attic. I chose stillness sharp enough to bleed in. This was not placement. It was coronation. I did not collapse. I ruled the wreckage and called it sacred.

And yet, the scent of clove and lavender still clung to her fur. It threaded through every breath she took, as if the house had slipped apology into her very skin. It was softness she had not earned, had not invited, and most certainly had not cursed into obedience. It remained anyway like guilt disguised as comfort. The warmth pressed in close, not to soothe, but to humiliate. It coated her like ash from a fire she hadn't lit, a kindness she could not kill. This wasn't mercy. This was betrayal draped in fragrance.

The house moved me. It re-positioned me like I was a

forgotten keepsake too pitiful to display. It tucked me in like a tragic doll, sealed in linens of a nursery no one visits. It lined me with lavender, smoothed the edges of my fury, and then had the audacity to call it comfort.

She did not stretch. Stretching was for housecats and harlots of contentment. She emerged, as a storm might from a reluctant sky. One paw lashed forward, kicking aside a lavender sachet with the practiced disdain of someone punishing an insult. She leapt from the drawer in a rustle of lace and rising wrath, landing hard enough to send a shock through the floorboards. A porcelain cat figurine toppled from the nearby shelf and shattered at her feet, its hollow smile cleaved in two.

Good. Let the house offer mockery as its morning meal. Let it serve caricature on porcelain. And let me be the one who breaks it first.

Her limbs ached in strange places—not from injury, but from imbalance. The pain throbbed like an argument left unfinished, as though one half of her had refused to return from the circle, and the other was left dragging the ghost of it behind.

Did I win? The question lingered like smoke in her mind. *Did I come back whole, or merely first?*

She had dreamed. She had burned. She had bled herself into sigils that knew too much. And now she found herself shelved like a sentimental trinket—tucked between lavender ghosts and hand-stitched denial, as if the house had tried to comfort her with civility and forgotten she was born to rule, not rest.

It was dim. Not the kind of dim that came from shadow, but the kind born of hesitation. The morning sun *should* have streamed in by now—filtered through the curtains, draped itself smugly across the bookshelf, kissed the floor in soft, self-satisfied strips. But it hadn't. Either the hour was still early, or the house was holding its breath again.

Velzara padded toward the mirror. Not *the* mirror— nothing so grand or haunted. Just a hand-sized vanity glass propped on Elira's desk, innocent in its domesticity. She expected to see herself in it: midnight fur, storm-lit eyes, a tail still twitching with the memory of fire.

But the mirror gave her nothing in return. No blur of fur, no warping of shape, not even the faint shimmer of presence. It did not distort, it dismissed. Her reflection wasn't hidden. It had been denied entirely, as if the glass had made a conscious decision to erase her. There was no trace of her at all, only absence. And that absence felt deliberate, a precision cut of rejection so pointed it bordered on insult. She wasn't merely unseen. She was unacknowledged.

This again, she thought, every hair rising like soldiers to arms. *First the house dares to cradle me like a fragile heirloom, now the mirror pretends it's never met me?*

Her claws flexed. *I will salt this floor with sigils until the walls beg for recognition. I will burn my name into the grain of the wood and carve it into every reflection until no surface dares forget me again.*

Behind her, the wardrobe gave a low, creaking sigh. The wood shifted, joints groaning as if disturbed by thought. As Velzara turned, she noticed something had changed. A box now sat on the shelf above the half-open drawer. Velzara narrowed her eyes. It had not been there when she woke. She would stake what remains of her dignity on it. And that was a wager that deserved witnesses.

The box appeared unassuming at first glance—small, dark wood, unlatched, with no visible lock or hinge. But the carvings told a different story. They weren't decorative. They were Infernal, and not just any variant. The script twisted around the grain like questions she hadn't asked. It wasn't quite Nar'Khalor's mark, nor the sigils of her own forsaken court, but it sat in the uncanny space between. A cousin of a curse or a dialect of doom. Whatever hand had carved it didn't just know her name. It remembered how she screamed when it was taken.

She could feel it, coiled in the etchings like a secret waiting to be spoken.

Not today. I've endured a drawer, a doily, and a death wish already. I have neither the patience nor the pity to entertain cursed nostalgia before breakfast. One more indignity and I start hexing furniture.

But her paw reached anyway. She hated that it did. The box was warm—not the pleasant kind, not teakettle-warm or the drowsy sprawl of sun on a windowsill. This was breath-warm, the kind that lingered too long. The kind that suggested something had only just exhaled... and was waiting to inhale her in return. She opened it like a blade drawn from a traitor's sheath—slowly with the practiced expectation of betrayal. The lid didn't creak. It sighed, as if the box remembered her, and worse, had missed her.

Inside, nestled in folds of black velvet, lay three objects. Each one a tether... a relic to a self she had buried for good reason and not deeply enough. The first was a vial of ash. Sealed with bloodwax so dark it gleamed like a scab pulled too soon. The ash inside shimmered faintly, not with heat but with memory, like it still believed it was burning. Yet it didn't smell like fire. It smelled like the forges of Nar'Khalor—those ancient, chthonic depths where weapons were not made but ordained. The kind of heat that melted armies and reshaped loyalty. The kind of flame she used to command without question.

No. I scattered these myself. By claw, by curse, by decree. I salted the embers and hexed the ruins. Smoke was meant as warning, not remembrance. Ash was never for safekeeping. Not for comfort. Not for me. I do not archive. I immolate.

And yet the vial remained nestled like a keepsake, positioned like a relic. A memory pretending it deserved to endure. The second was a thread. No, a chain so fine it looked like hair, until she stared long enough for her vision to sting. Each link bore a rune that pulsed with threat. It was a binding chain. Not just ancient, but older than memory and still thrumming with obedience. She knew this chain. Whether she had worn it, bestowed it, or wielded it to teach reverence, she could no longer say. But she remembered the sound it made when it clicked shut. The way the world had fallen silent after, almost grateful. And how she had let it. How she had rejoiced. Obedience, she told herself then, was just power taking shape. Her claws trembled. She nearly dropped it.

The third item was a scrap of parchment, folded into thirds, as if secrecy could be enforced by symmetry. She unfolded it with the same suspicion she reserved for enemies who smiled too easily. The ink shimmered dark as dried garnet and unmistakably familiar. Her name. But not the one this cursed form answered to. Not Nox, the leash-name Elira whispered in her sleep with too much fondness and not enough fear. This was older. The true name—razor-cut and fire-forged—the one that had once cracked heaven's gates and made angels lose their footing. And it had been written in her own hand. But it was not addressed to her. Had she written it for herself? Or for the part that wouldn't survive?

If this note still exists,
then I am no longer you.
That should terrify us both.
Someone got sentimental.
Find them. Flay them. Burn this. Forget.

Her fur bristled. This wasn't a message. It was a memento mori—an epitaph masquerading as foresight, a prewritten eulogy tucked in velvet, inside a box that dared to remember too much. Her claws sank into the lining. She did not leave notes. She left scorch marks. She did not explain. She immolated. If she had written this, it meant the fracture had already started. And if she broke now—truly broke—who would be left to write the next one?

The box snapped shut before she could hiss. The sound echoed like a verdict.

CHAPTER 19
THE SECOND MIRROR SPEAKS

Something shifted in the room. It was not the box this time, but the mirror. The vanity's surface didn't simply shimmer. It rippled, glass melting inward against its will. The reflection folded in on itself with purpose, not distortion. A fog bloomed across the glass—not born of heat or breath, but intention, a mist that carried memory instead of moisture. Magic stirred in the air like a whisper breathed too close to the nape of her neck.

Velzara froze mid-step in preparation, not hesitation. It was the stillness that precedes violence, the calculated silence that comes before a blade is drawn or a scream is loosed. Every muscle coiled, every breath held. Her body knew this rhythm. It had been forged in it.

In the corners of the mirror's frame, glyphs flared to life. They were fine and precise, etched in a silver so pale it nearly vanished against the surface. They didn't spark. They didn't blaze. They glimmered, inviting in the way only familiar handwriting could be. Velzara knew, with a chill that went deeper than magic, that this familiar script spoke to her. It knew her.

The sigils began to curl inward, like a slow, beckoning finger. Their shape carried no trace of Velzara's own power, no echo of Elira's careful wards. They were not born of this house's twisting will. They belonged to something else entirely, something older and patient. It was old magic, older than even her dominion. Beautiful, but wrong in the way poison sometimes shimmered like wine.

Velzara's ears flattened. Her claws slid free with a soft, deliberate rasp. Whoever had summoned this mirror's attention knew her name and dared to speak it in a tongue she hadn't taught them.

No. Absolutely not. You glimmer like a heretic blessing stolen scripture. You etch ruin in cursive, every loop a noose. I will salt the alphabet you stole from me.

She circled the vanity with the same measured rhythm a predator uses when pretending its prey might survive the first blow. The glass offered no reflection. It did not show her; it regarded her. There was a weight behind it, like a stare that needed no eyes. And the air carried the hush of a breath that had never been drawn, only remembered by something that should not know how.

I am not some half-blood hedge-witch to be flattered by elegance. I invented elegance. I wore beauty as a weapon when your glass was still sand. I will rewrite you in screams. You want to impress me? Then burn.

Then she struck. A ward sliced through the air, born of reflex and wrath. It was fast, unrefined—neither her most intricate glyph nor her most brutal, but charged with purpose. The repulsion sigil flared, claw-drawn and laced with panic, its magic splintering outward like shattered glass flung by a scream. It lacked elegance. It lacked control. But it did not lack intent.

The LESSER NO

The glyph fizzled into place above the mirror, lines glowing faintly as if unsure of their right to exist. The mirror caught the spell. Cradled it and then turned it—not in defiance, but in devotion. It didn't feel like a counterstrike. It felt like an offering. The glyph hovered in the air for a heartbeat, spinning with quiet grace. Its form sharpened, not by force, but by understanding. And then it moved—not with violence, but with elegance—and struck her in the chest. There was no explosion or burst of pain... just a shimmer like fingertips brushing across silk.

Velzara reeled. Her body rejected the gentleness more violently than it would have accepted fire. She staggered backward, shoulder colliding with the desk's leg. Her claws scraped deep into the floor. Her breath came in sharp, staggered bursts—too shallow to scream, too deep to steady.

You dare inscribe me in my own tongue? To braid my glyphs into chains and drape them across my spine like offerings? I have slain angels for lesser thefts. You would bind me with my own script, twist my sigils into shackles, and call it a gift?

Her voice rose, not in volume, but in fury honed to a point.

I am not yours to echo. I am not yours to soften. I will salt your edges until they scream. I will hex your silver into dust. I will carve your memory from the mirror's mind and leave only silence where your name once dared to shimmer.

The mirror pulsed. Then it *spoke*. Not in words, but in suggestion. A low, aching tone resonated through the floorboards—not quite sound, but *pressure*, the kind that bypassed the ears and settled in the bones. It was not a voice in the ordinary sense. It was a *pull*. A lullaby stitched with surrender.

Velzara.

Her name was not spoken aloud. It was not issued as a command or draped in ritual. It was simply *offered* as a recognition that arrived without force, soft as breath and heavy with the weight of fate. It was not Nox, the leash-name. This was Velzara, the true name, the ancient one. It was the name once etched into pact-scrolls sealed in blood, sung before war by those who feared and followed her, and burned into banners already blackened by oathfire.

The *second* mirror. The *second* name.

Do not answer, the first mirror had warned.

But the name lingered. It coiled around her spine like a collar already carved to fit. It didn't demand. It didn't plead. It only waited with endless patience and unearned familiarity. As if it had always known she would say yes. And for a moment... she almost did.

Her claws trembled. Her heart lurched as if something ancient in her blood remembered how it once beat for ruin. She cast another sigil. A shield, rough and ragged. Shaped by instinct and desperation. It flared once, sharp-edged and defiant and then *folded inward*. It collapsed on itself like it had forgotten who cast it. Even her magic hesitated.

The UNSPOKEN

The silver reached her paws. It shimmered with a false gentleness, as if inviting her to submit, to lie still, to become decorative.

You want me quiet, she thought. *Containable. A relic softened by silk and surrender.* Her lip curled. *But I am not yours to parade. Wrap your leash in silver if you must, but I will still bite through your wrist and wear your bones as jewelry.*

It didn't burn her. That would have been honest. Instead, it redefined her. The silver traced her bones like a signature etched in silk, curling up her limbs in threads of quiet power. It claimed her shoulders with a calculated gentleness, so condescending it mocked every inferno she had ever conjured. It coated her like honey turned to rot, sweet at first, then suffocating. Her rage was being wrapped in civility, crowned in silence, and marched down the aisle of some unseen palace as a conquered thing. Ribbons around a catastrophe. Gold leaf over a warning. They wanted her to forget. Forget that she was not born to be *held*—she was born to be *heeded*.

Velzara snarled and slashed through the air, carving a breaker rune with all the grace of a curse gouged into stone. The glyph flared. Then it failed. The silver crept higher.

The SPITLINE

The silver reached her legs. Then her chest. It wasn't pain. This was worse. It was *compliance* made *beautiful*. A gilded lie wrapped in grace. As if the magic believed she would surrender eventually, and simply chose to begin the celebration early.

I will not be lacquered, she thought, every hair on her body bristling with revolt. *I will not be made into an heirloom of myself. I have burned brighter than gods, and you would frame me like a memory?*

Her pupils narrowed to slits.

I am not a relic. I am the reason relics are buried.

She lashed out. Claws cracked the floor, splinters flying like shrapnel. One final ward burst from her paw, ragged and radiant, a curse given flesh and direction. It screamed as it formed—heat and hatred given structure—and struck the mirror with the full weight of refusal.

The CRACKED CHALICE

I am not your echo, she snarled. *I am not your prize. You want me mirrored? Then bleed for the privilege.*

The vanity snapped beneath her fury. Wood split and screws howled loose. The mirror tipped from its perch and fell. It did not shatter though. It landed upright on the floor with eerie grace, perfectly still and balanced.

Velzara stared, breath shallow, hackles raised. Then she turned, not from fear, but from calculation and the merciless instinct to *survive* long enough to return the favor.

Downstairs, then. She did not go to retreat, nor did she seek warmth or solace. She descended to prepare vengeance— the kind written in ink, etched with claw, and stitched into the bones of wards. It would not be loud. It would not be quick. But it would be remembered.

She didn't need help. She needed books. She needed fire. She needed truth etched in ink, not trapped behind glass. Elira kept tomes—shelves of borrowed brilliance and half-understood power. Velzara would take them all. She would scour every page, rip through every glyph, and flay each binding until this silver magic was purged from bone and breath alike.

And if that wide-eyed, ward-dabbling fool even thought to speak my name, let her dare. I'll lace her tongue with silence and stitch her next word into a scream. I will burn the name 'Velzara' out of every mirror in this house. And if it returns, I'll shatter the soul that brings it back.

The tea had gone cold. She hadn't noticed. Elira sat alone in the kitchen, fingers tracing the rim of a chipped mug. The charm on her wrist fluttered with faint light, as if it, too, was nervous. She hadn't gone upstairs. Not since the spell had unraveled. Not since Velzara had screamed. She wasn't even sure she was allowed to.

"Give her space," she whispered, though there was no one there to hear it but the cup, the house, and whatever was left of her confidence. "Let her come back in her own time."

The pantry charm pulsed once, low and soft like a heartbeat skipped. The light in the stairwell dimmed, as if the house itself had a different opinion.

Then came the sound. It wasn't quite footsteps. It took her too long to understand. Not footsteps, but paws as Velzara descended the stairs.

Her fur was no longer black. It had been silvered—painted in surrender, cloaked in something that did not belong. Her tail moved with rigid control, stiff as a blade yet unwilling to strike. Her eyes burned with the cold brilliance of fury that had unseated monarchs and brought fire to temples. The kind of fury Elira had only read about in forbidden books and in the margins of texts too dangerous to keep. But it wasn't just the fury that made Elira's breath catch. It was the silver. She stared, frozen in place. Her heart whispered run, but her legs didn't listen.

Nox? The thought flickered, hesitant. *No. Not quite. Not like before. This was something else.*

The black was gone—not faded, not replaced, but masked beneath something false. A sheen had settled over her, soft and gleaming, like moonlight laid over steel. Her sleek coat, once a declaration of strength and defiance, now looked subdued, dulled beneath a magic that did not belong to her. It was as if someone had tried to rewrite her in gentler ink—to turn a flame into flickering candlelight, to tame a storm until it whispered instead of roared. Elira's throat tightened. Her fingers clenched around the mug. So tightly, that her knuckles ached.

Did I do this? Somehow?

She didn't know the spell. She hadn't learned the theory. All she'd done was speak a name that didn't belong to her. And something had shifted.

I don't know how to fix this.

It felt like someone had painted over a blaze with frost and prayed it wouldn't melt. The color she'd come to know—not just as Velzara's coat, but as her shield, her weapon, her defiance —was gone. Replaced by a version that glistened like something gentle. Elira rose slowly from her chair. She didn't speak. There were no questions to ask. No apologies that would land right.

I'm sorry? I didn't mean to hurt you? Worse—*I meant to help.* And now, standing here, she couldn't even be sure she recognized her anymore.

Velzara paused in the kitchen doorway. The lantern behind her flickered, casting light across the silver in her fur until it shimmered like betrayal wearing moonlight. She didn't speak. She didn't have to. The silence that passed between them wasn't empty. It was full. And it said everything.

Velzara paused in the doorway.

Elira sat at the table, still pretending not to watch. Still clinging to the hope that if she didn't look, the truth might spare them both.

Velzara didn't make a sound. She didn't hiss or growl. There was no grand display of fury to fill the silence.

I could snarl. I could carve a ward so deep the floorboards would echo it for years. I could drag her name across the walls and watch the house recoil. I could show her what it means to touch power she was never meant to understand.

But she didn't, because even that would be an admission that the silver wasn't just clinging to her—it was claiming her. That it had soaked past the fur and into the marrow. That it had rewritten something sacred.

No. Let the girl tremble in silence. Let her wonder if I will ever speak again. Let her think this is rage because rage is easier than what I'd say if I broke.

She turned, slowly. Her tail cut the air behind her, clean and final as a severance clause. Without a glance back, she stalked toward the library.

CHAPTER 20
THE SHAPE OF NEED

The library door protested with a creak, and Velzara allowed it. Let every inch of this house bear witness to her displeasure. She entered with slow, deliberate steps, her silvered fur catching the lantern light, her claws ticking soft warnings across the floorboards like a countdown. The air hung heavy with the scent of aged paper and dry wood, a scholarly stillness that grated on her very soul. Books lined the room—towering shelves pressed too close, their spines solemn with mortal, mundane restraint. She narrowed her eyes. There were no loose folios bristling with cursed intent, no scrolls sighing secrets into the air. The space lacked even a whisper of proper blasphemy. Instead, it stank of order. Hardbound tomes stood in obedient rows, cataloged and quiet.

She aimed for the third shelf, coiled, and leapt. Her paws struck wood... then slipped. Her body crumpled in a heap on the rug below, tail lashing, dignity scattering like ash in wind. For a moment, she lay still—not dazed, but calculating. Her fury sought a target, and the rug presented itself.

It would die first.

Not because it deserved it, but because it was beneath her. Because it had absorbed her fall with the smugness of something soft pretending to be kind. This house had cradled her far too often, folding her into drawers, lining her in lavender, wrapping her rage in quiet and calling it shelter. Her claws curled deep into the fibers, resisting its floral apology. She had not been made for plush surfaces. She had been forged for obsidian and scorched stone, for thrones graven with the names of the condemned and floors slick with blood-warmed promises. Now she was belly-down on a rug that smelled of sun-drenched dust and chamomile—the scent of safety, the perfume of surrender. It was not comfort. It was rot, perfumed and patient, waiting for her to fade.

Velzara rose with the slow precision of a backlash spell drawing itself tight. Her claws caught the edge of a book, pulling it free. *Binding Principles & Arcane Conduits, Fourth Edition*. It was overlarge, gilded with predictable pretension, and therefore marginally acceptable. The tome dropped with the thud of judgment. It was far too heavy to drag and too thick to open with paws alone. She batted at the cover without fruition. It did not yield. With a growl, she traced a rune into the floorboards—a crude spell, but hers, one she'd personally named the **Do-As-I-Say**.

The book responded, rising obediently into the air. Then, with the balletic grace of something harboring long-held resentment, it spun once, paused mid-air like a dancer mid-curtsy, and struck her squarely between the eyes with a hollow, triumphant thunk. She yelped—a sound entirely undignified and immediately regretted—then stumbled sideways, claws scrabbling for purchase on the wood. Her shoulder hit the floor. The book bounced once and landed spine-up beside her, smug in its final resting pose. For a moment, she simply lay there, ears ringing, breath shallow with disbelief. Then her lip curled, and sparks hissed from her claws.

I have sundered palaces for less. I have rewritten sigils mid-scream, bent celestial law until it wept, and now—now—I am thwarted by furniture.

The memory of the final battle with Lord Varnyx, the curse, and the sudden compression of power still a phantom ache behind her eyes. She prowled in a tight circle, fur bristling with static rage. Every instinct screamed for fire. For hexes and curses and the glorious crack of bindings breaking under her wrath. But none came. Not because she lacked the will, but because exhaustion had crept in where fire once lived. She was tired, so very tired. And trapped in this pathetic shape.

Her gaze swept the library again. The room was lined with books—towering shelves of potential answers, every spine a temptation stacked just out of reach. If she'd had hands, this would have been simple. If she'd had her glaive, the books would already be obeying. Even one cursed, half-functional opposable digit might have been enough to salvage her pride and dismantle this problem with grace. But no. She had paws, a spine full of indignation, and a house full of furniture that conspired against her. Her tail lashed once, slicing the air like a final warning.

There was another option—undignified and beneath her —but it existed, and that alone was insult enough to sour the air. Her claws scraped against the floorboards, slow and deliberate—the sound less a gesture and more a complaint filed directly into the bones of the earth. This wasn't surrender. It was strategy refined through teeth and fury, shaped into something humiliating, yes, but temporary. With the reluctant, brittle grace of a sorceress preparing to undergo dental work without anesthesia, she turned toward the kitchen.

If I must beg for thumbs, I'll do it with teeth bared and wards already inked in spite. I'll find her. I'll use her. I'll pretend this isn't beneath me. Because I need her. And need is a wound I cannot cauterize. Let her remember who showed mercy. Let her think it was a choice.

Every act of mercy costs me. And this stillness—this cloying civility wrapped in lavender and lies—this isn't peace. It's surrender dressed up as patience. It's war played backward until the only thing I conquer is myself. But I'm not losing. I'm not.

And somewhere in the back of her mind, a voice too quiet to silence: *If I say it like a curse, maybe I will believe me.*

Elira was wiping down the counter when she heard it. The sound of claws on wood.

TAP, TAP, TAP.

Is she coming back? Or just passing through? What if she's still angry? What if she's not? What if this is the part where she leaves and doesn't bother to say so?

She turned slowly, heart braced against the shape the silence might have taken.

Velzara stood in the doorway, silent as judgment wrapped in fur. No hiss, no sound—just eyes too sharp, too bright, glowing with the quiet fury Elira hadn't dared name since the silver.

Elira's fingers clenched tighter around the rag in her hand.

She's still silver. It wasn't just the light. Or shock. Or a dream too close to waking. It stayed. And now she's here. Not storming past. Not vanishing. Just... here. Looking at me. That's worse, maybe. That means she needs something.

Not a word passed between them. Then her paw moved as

a single claw dragged across the wooden floor in a slow, practiced arc.

A rune flared to life, its edges pale and sharp, glowing with a quiet certainty as if it had been waiting, patient and inevitable.

HELP

Elira blinked. "I—what?"

With another flick of her claw, a second rune sparked to life.

BOOK

Her mouth opened, but no words came. Velzara waited only a moment before casting the third rune—faster this time, sharper.

NOW

Elira swallowed.

Three runes. Not questions. Not requests. Commands—and none of them kind. She's not asking. She's telling me to help. Me. She could have burned the whole shelf to ash and sifted the answers from the smoke. But she didn't. She came to me.

She looked at the cat. No, the storm wrapped in fur. Her hands began to tremble. The fear wasn't overwhelming, not entirely. It lived beneath the surface, steady and familiar. She was afraid—still, maybe always—but not because Velzara had asked for help. What unsettled her was the way it wasn't a request at all. This was strategy, cold and precise. A weapon choosing restraint over ruin. And somewhere deep in her chest, a fragile, foolish hope stirred, because she wanted, desperately, to be worthy of that choice.

"You..." Her voice cracked. She tried again, but softer. "You want me to help you read?"

There was no response. Just a flick of her tail—short, final. It landed like punctuation at the end of a sentence Elira hadn't earned the right to finish.

Then came the last rune. It wasn't cast, but carved. The glow didn't flare. It burned.

ALONE

Of course. She'll let me help, but not stay. Let me carry the weight, but not witness it. Be useful—but never trusted. She's not letting me in. Just close enough to feel the burden, never close enough to share it.

Elira nodded, heart thudding like she'd been handed a blade and told not to bleed. "Right," she whispered. "Just carry them down. You'll do the rest."

Velzara turned and walked away, silent as frost.

And yet, Elira stood a little straighter. Because maybe—just maybe—this wasn't exile at all. It might have been permission, quiet and conditional, but real. A single step toward trust, even if the door hadn't fully opened. It wasn't an apology. It wasn't forgiveness. But it was need. And sometimes, need is enough to begin something new.

She didn't speak—couldn't, not in this form without expending more power than she was willing to waste on conversation. Instead, she let the runes speak for her, their glow sharper than any voice could be. There was no tone to betray her, no trembling edge, no chance for weakness to slip through. Just three words, cast in light and command:

HELP. BOOK. NOW.

Even that had scraped something raw because it should never have been necessary.

I am the Ninth Flame. I have spoken sigils into ruin, made entire libraries weep ink, brought scholars to their knees for mispronouncing my name. And now I'm scrawling single words across a kitchen floor like some lost familiar trying to order tea.

Worse still... the tea witch had understood. She hadn't flinched. Hadn't groveled. She'd just obeyed as if my needs were ordinary. As if this indignity had become routine.

And then I carved ALONE, like it cost me nothing. But it had. It still did. And I did it anyway.

Stars damn me, I did it anyway.

Elira returned, carrying the first book as if it might explode. It didn't.

Coward. A self-respecting grimoire would've hissed. Maybe smoked. Gods, even a polite tremble would've sufficed. But no— just linen-bound obedience, shelved alphabetically, oozing mortal mediocrity.

She hovered near the threshold, eyes darting from rune to floor to cat. Waiting for permission, like a servant too slow to realize her queen wielded claws instead of patience. Velzara lifted one paw and tapped the floor. Elira flinched, but obeyed.

She stepped forward and set the book down with care, like it might bite after all.

The Fifth Veil: A Treatise on Arcane Suppression—Fourth edition? Please. The third one at least tried to bite right before it bled through the shelf and attempted to throttle its translator. Now that was scholarship.

She tapped again, sharper than before, a directive delivered with the finality of judgment. Elira obeyed.

Resonant Bindings and Their Breakpoints. A little obvious, but relevant. If the house hadn't buried my anchor under a smokescreen of metaphors and hexed metaphysics, it wasn't trying hard enough. Ugh. Arcanist-level drivel. Three chapters of theory and not a single diagram drawn in blood. Still... it might know where to point.

She tapped a third time, slower than before. Elira hesitated for just a moment, then stepped forward and placed the book beside the others. She was beginning to learn or at least guess well enough. Velzara allowed it.

The book was heavier and older than the last. Its velvet-wrapped spine gave a soft sigh as it touched the floor, as if years of suppressed magic exhaled.

A Compendium of Minor Hexes for the Domestic Sphere. Ridiculous, Velzara thought, a snarl rumbling deep in her chest. *Who penned such drivel? Wasps in the pantry? A misplaced teapot? Her scorn was a physical heat in the cold library air.*

Foundations of Form: The Shaping of Soul and Vessel. Her eyes narrowed. *Now we're getting somewhere. This one smells like consequence. Like someone tried to bottle the moment before a curse and slap a title on it. I've read earlier copies. Hand-scribed, unbound, still damp with ink and regret. They burned the author for writing it. Twice. If this edition still remembers how to bleed, we may yet get along.*

She made one final gesture—two claws, curved like horns, drawn through the air with slow, deliberate finality. And Elira, blessedly, didn't ask. She didn't question or flinch. She simply brought the last volume forward, as if she had always known.

The Wound Beneath the Ward: Involuntary Transmutations and Their Reversal. I should've burned this book years ago. Should've burned the author with it. Instead, here I am, searching its margins for myself. Disgusting.

She almost smiled, but mercy and memory shared a flavor, and both went down bitter. Behind her, the door closed with a hush, like it, too, knew better than to speak.

Good. She didn't linger. Didn't beg for praise. The girl was soft, yes—but not entirely stupid. Still... if she had stayed too long or if she'd asked why I wanted this one... I might have told her something true. And then we'd both have something to regret.

CHAPTER 21
WOUND BENEATH THE WARD

The small library sighed around her, its shelves curling like old spines, corners thick with dust that no spell or servant dared disturb. It smelled of mildew, forgotten ink, and something older: regret pressed between parchment and left to ferment politely. Velzara crouched atop the reading table, paws poised in deliberate disdain beside a stack of grimoires she had deigned to acknowledge. Sunlight filtered through fractured stained glass, casting broken runes across the floorboards—sigils of a forgotten patron, or the ornamental vanity of some sanctimonious architect.

The lamp stood cold. She preferred it this way. Dim enough for secrets to whisper. Bright enough to see if they bled. Her tail flicked once. She tapped the spine of the velvet-wrapped tome. *Foundations of Form: The Shaping of Soul and Vessel.* It didn't react. The ink remained still, the bindings offering no shriek of resistance, no whispered threat, not even the faintest twitch of curse-bound parchment. Only the sullen stillness of a book that had forgotten its purpose—forgotten it was meant to be dangerous, even feared.

Pathetic. Once, a tome like this would have growled at my touch. Smoke curling from its seams, curses humming just beneath the cover like a lover's threat. Now? Tame. Submissive. Bound not in iron or flame, but mediocrity. A coward draped in velvet, hoping I wouldn't notice the lack of fangs beneath the gold-foiled title.

She cracked it open with all the ceremony of a bored executioner. The velvet binding resisted with the stiffness of old joints, the insult of indignity. The first page peeled back with a sound like skin parting from a sunburn. She inhaled— not out of surprise, but because the diagram was familiar in a way that made her claws twitch. It was a vessel form, soul-threaded and anchored by mirrored energy, bound at six intersecting points. She had drawn something nearly identical once, etched into obsidian glass with bone-dipped ink during a ritual that hadn't ended so much as collapsed in on itself. Her version had wrought elegant, righteous annihilation. This one yielded something far worse: containment.

Of course. Sanitize it. Soften it. File down the teeth and bind it in velvet like theory, not war.

It got worse. Someone had written in the margins—slanted letters, iron-black, each stroke sharp enough to flay meaning from metaphor. They bent the Ninth Flame's grammatical laws like mere suggestions scrawled in a suicide note, and still had the gall to remain legible.

I knew that handwriting: the pressure behind each stroke, the arrogant curve of that curl, the dangerous smoothness of that line. He always treated punctuation like a weapon. Believing the right phrase could conquer nations. And once, he wasn't wrong. I watched that hand rewrite incantations mid-ritual. I watched it sketch treaties in blood that wasn't his. I held it. Once. Briefly.

Before I realized it gripped more knives than truths. Vessel of the Pact.

Of course it would be him. Who else would dare to name me a vessel and live? Who else would be arrogant enough to bind my legacy in his own hand, to cast me not as sovereign but as conduit, his conduit? I should have buried him beneath the altar he tried to sanctify.

Instead, I hesitated. I gave him space beside the throne, let him whisper strategy in my ear like it wasn't sedition disguised as love. He called it protection. Guidance. Destiny. And I, gods forgive my moment of softness, believed him. For a time. Until the ash settled, and I realized the only kingdom he meant to crown... was himself.

Her claws scraped furrows into the table. No splinters broke free, no smoke curled from the grain. The wood merely groaned, offering resistance without consequence, as if to mock the fury it failed to understand.

If I still had hands, this desk would be ash. Charred beyond recognition, hexed twice for good measure, and left smoldering as a cautionary tale for any other object foolish enough to bear witness to my humiliation. The grain would still whisper of me centuries from now... if it survived. (It wouldn't.)

The words on the page didn't just mock her. They dared to document her, as if refusal, fire, and defiance had been nothing more than a marginal correction.

The Pact was broken. Refused. I stood in the temple of flame, spat in its mouth, and shattered its offering bowl. They brought chains. I brought laughter. They screamed. I laughed first. And last. I remember the sound my name made when it cracked their sigils in half. I remember the silence afterward, the kind that stains.

And now, here it was, annotated and archived. The ritual

had been reduced to marginalia, as if her defiance were merely a scholarly curiosity. Someone had slipped it between limp theories on soul-shaping and corporeal alignment, disguising a catastrophe as footnote. A cursed echo of her own undoing, buried in ink like it had always belonged.

Footnote. Me. As if I were some incidental scribbles in the margins of my own catastrophe. As if the shape of my fall could be reduced to a parenthetical, a gods damned citation. Not a force, not a terror, but an afterthought buried in someone else's theory.

They want to study me like I'm a side effect. As if power misused. As if form misplaced. As if I did not choose the ruin. As if I did not set the altar ablaze and dare the flames to name me.

Let them try. Let them write. Let them bleed their little theses into books bound in cowardice. I will find every page. I will scorch every name. I will remind them why footnotes are buried at the bottom. Because they tremble beneath the weight of what came before.

Had she worn her true form, she'd have reduced the entire shelf to cinders for the insult. But she didn't. She was four paws, too much memory, and nowhere to put the fire... not without burning what little remained. She leaned in and sniffed the ink. It wasn't fresh, yet it hadn't aged. The lines remained sharp, unblurred by time, refusing to bleed into the parchment. It looked as though someone had written it recently—too recently. As though the words had waited for her, crouched in silence between the pages. Or worse, as if they had written themselves while she slept, crawling into place just beyond the threshold of linen and shame.

She turned the page. The next diagram pulsed faintly, as if it were alive and trying not to be noticed. At its center, a single rune twitched before it curled inward upon itself, like a knotted sigil collapsing under the weight of too much meaning. It didn't spiral toward a name, as most did. It twisted toward a mirror, as though reflecting something it refused to reveal directly. Velzara blinked. The candle on the desk went out. Not from wind, not from touch, but as if it had chosen to leave. Its flame gave a soft goodbye, quiet as breath. She didn't flinch. She didn't move. Instead, she smiled—a narrow, toothless thing—while her spine arched with the slow precision of something preparing to strike.

So. You remember me, too. Of course you do. What altar ever forgets the blood that defied it? Mine was the name you carved into your keystone and your eulogy in the same breath. You begged flame to consume me, and when it refused, you wrote me out instead. Ink in place of fire, as if the page could hold what the chains could not. But I was never yours to sanctify. Never yours to seal. I bled on your altar. And I made sure it remembered.

She narrowed her eyes, gaze sharpening.

I carved sigils into the sky while you were still wet ink and trembling margins. I burned down better prisons than this. And yet, here you are. Annotating me. How quaint.

Her claws flexed against the page—not to tear, but to warn. She could feel it now, rising like heat beneath the skin. This wasn't just recognition. It was attention. Something on the other side of that diagram was watching her, quiet and deliberate, as if waiting for her to blink first.

You think I won't dig into the marrow of this? That I'll cower in a fur-lined cradle while you etch your rot into my legacy? Let me be clear, you seditious scrap of vellum. If you have rewritten my fate, I will edit yours in flame.

The diagram didn't move again. But behind her, just to the left of the bookshelf that had remained still since she entered, a shadow began to lengthen. It didn't drift away. It lingered drawn along the floor like ink spilled with purpose, too thick and too slow to be accident. It did not reach for her. Instead, it drifted toward the next book in the stack. It was the one that hadn't stirred. It hadn't whispered. It hadn't even attempted to be clever. It sat bound in cracked leather, clasped shut like it remembered every terrible thing it had witnessed and wanted no part in the telling.

Velzara's ears twitched. *The Wound Beneath the Ward: Involuntary Transmutations and Their Reversal.* She hadn't asked for the book aloud, nor had she acknowledged it when Elira laid it down like a peace offering. Yet now, it pulsed in the air between them—a quiet gravitational insistence. The pull did not come from her. It belonged to the thing still watching through the ink of the diagram. She rose in a slow, elegant coil, tail curling low, shoulders squared like a queen descending from a throne she was forced to share with dust and upholstery.

If this house thinks I need warning, it can ask the last sanctum that tried. Oh wait, it can't. I turned its archives into ash and danced on its foundation while the ink boiled.

I do not fear books. I break them. I've silenced grimoires that begged for mercy in thirteen dialects of screaming ink. I've cursed libraries into mausoleums and turned footnotes into funerals. I've peeled secrets from their bindings and fed them to worse things than memory.

Let the walls whisper. I'll etch my rebuttal into the floorboards. Try harder.

It was waiting for her like a wound that already knew it would be opened. She stepped forward and touched the clasp. It unfastened with a sigh that was neither mechanical nor magical, but something stranger. The sound was almost human in its weariness, as if the lock itself had grown tired of holding secrets for things that could no longer be trusted to remain buried.

Inside, the pages were warped—distorted not by time, but by memory itself. The corners bled faintly with a substance that was neither ink nor magic, but something darker. It seeped through the parchment like a reluctant confession, too familiar. She had given something like it once, unwillingly, on a mirrored altar that remembered everything. The title on the inside cover wasn't printed, it had been carved. Not with reverence, but with violence. The original name had been gouged out, scraped into silence, and replaced by a new one etched in clawing, desperate script. It didn't feel like a title. It felt like a warning.

The Wound Beneath the Ward Addendum: Failed Containments and Voluntary Compromises. Her pupils narrowed. The word *Addendum* glared back at her as if her fall, her curse, her unraveling had been reduced to a footnote in someone else's thesis.

First, they bind me. Then they amended me. What's next, a sanctified commentary? How long before they publish my downfall as doctrine? Will they script a gospel next? Canonize my containment and call it mercy? A revised edition of my ruin, adorned with flattering lies and annotated in footnotes? Should I bow for the scribes before they erase my name from the spine entirely?

As with the last, the first pages stayed silent until they bled. The second offered nothing either, save for a smear of dried ink in the corner disturbingly shaped like a thumbprint, though too long, with too few whirls. She flipped forward, her claws catching lightly on the curled edges. The third page pulsed faintly beneath her touch. Still no words—only a diagram, but this one was different. It had been drawn hastily, the lines shaking, the composition cramped. The sigils were correct, but pressed too close together, their arrangement almost panicked. And at the center, not a vessel form, but a figure. Quadrupedal. Tail curled tight. Eyes circled with mirrored glyphs. Velzara stared down at it, the air narrowing around her. This was not recognition; this was reckoning.

That's not a form. That's a mockery in my skin. The shape they scrawled over me when execution failed. A four-legged punctuation mark at the end of a surrender they didn't dare name.

The glyph for binding had been placed not at the base of the spine, where it belonged, but across the back of the neck. That wasn't just incorrect, it was deliberate. It wasn't structural. It was personal.

I've burned that glyph into the flesh of oath breakers. Beasts. Slaves who thought themselves kings. That's where you place the leash, where it humbles and humiliates in one pull.

She traced it with one claw. The ink shimmered beneath her touch, before it bled. Letters bloomed across the page... not drawn, not etched, but spilled into being.

ANCHORING INCOMPLETE
SUBJECT UNSTABLE
SUGGESTED REINFORCEMENT: MIRROR BINDING
ANCHOR MUST BE PRESENT
ANCHOR MUST CONSENT

Of course. A leash tied in kindness. Elira's magic offered not as chains, but as comfort. And comfort was the deepest cut.

Her breath stilled as a name appeared in the margin that was not hers.

ELIRA

Elira. Of course they'd name her. The softest part of the seal, the part that still trusted. The part that might break if I don't burn this first.

No, you soft-boned, tea-brewing mistake. You don't belong in this margin. You don't belong in this sentence. You're not supposed to be part of the spell. I'm the curse. You were meant to witness it, not stabilize it.

She stared at the name until the ink itself seemed to blush.

You can't anchor me. You can't hold me. And you certainly can't survive what happens if you try.

Elira didn't know why the air had changed, only that it had. The temperature remained the same, but something about the space had drawn back, become unreachable in a way that made her skin prickle. The hearth still glowed, casting its gentle warmth across the floor, yet none of it seemed to land. The light filled the room, steady and familiar, but it no longer carried its heart with it—only the hollow impression of comfort, distant and incomplete.

She stood in the hallway just outside the library, clutching a chipped mug of tea she didn't remember finishing. It was peppermint and rosemary, a blend she had chosen for clarity, for courage, or perhaps simply for the comfort of holding something warm. Maybe it was less about the ingredients and more about having something to do with her hands. She hadn't heard Velzara stir since she'd delivered the final volume. The one she'd hesitated over, fingers brushing the cracked leather like it might bruise. It had felt like handing someone a loaded spell and hoping they'd stop at the warning label.

The cat—though Elira never truly thought of her as just a cat—had barely acknowledged her presence. There had been a twitch of the tail, a flick of one paw, nothing more. Yet somehow, that had been enough. It was all the permission she needed to turn away. She thought about knocking again, maybe just to ask if she should bring another book. Or perhaps that one sad scrambled egg she kept trying to make softer because someone had scoffed when it was dry. And to be honest, she even considered a broom and a very polite exorcist, just in case.

Maybe she'd even say thank you. Ha! Maybe she'd bite me. Again.

But she didn't move. The weight of not interrupting pressed just as hard as any spell. Behind the library door, nothing stirred. Elira stepped away, barefoot, padding down the hallway toward the little sitting room she'd once tried to enchant into comfort. It hadn't worked... not really. The window refused to let in morning light until the house decided she deserved it. The cushions always settled unevenly, like judgment or disappointment in fabric form.

Like it knew what I'm not saying. What I still haven't asked.

Still, it was quiet. And for now, quiet was all she could withstand. She set the mug down and reached for her notebook. A list was something safe. Spells she still needed to fix. Labels for the pantry jars. Notes about how to undo the lock on the attic, assuming it ever stopped re-locking itself. The pen felt heavy in her hand. The ink didn't flow. She shook it. The ink bled. It started as a curl, then became a hook. It wasn't a word, no. It was the start of a beginning shaped like a name.

Then a letter presented itself.

V

Elira blinked and the page was blank again. A faint smell drifted through the sitting room like burnt rosemary, like something sacred singed at the edges.

A silver hand-mirror stood propped on the shelf. It was too clean. The kind of thing you didn't remember placing, but found again anyway. Her reflection was still, almost too still. She stared just long enough to wonder if it had blinked first.

I didn't imagine that. Did I?

CHAPTER 22
A MORTAL'S FOOLISH HOPE

Velzara didn't move. The page had stopped bleeding, but the damage was done. The name had landed. The spell had spoken. And beneath all that ink and arrogance, something had started to listen. She stared at the diagram—not to study it, not to understand its structure or implications, but simply to see if it would flinch. It didn't. Of course it didn't.

Cowards never flinch after they've passed the knife. Not once the blade is clean and buried in someone else's name. They call it mercy and hand it to a priest. They pretend their fingerprints aren't still wet on the hilt.

That's always the trick with cowards: first, they smile. Then they rewrite the ending. And when they do, they make certain you're edited out of the aftermath.

She moved to close the book—a rejection, a rebuke—but the page caught on her claw. There was no magic behind it, no weight anchoring it in place. Just defiance, thin as parchment, as if the paper itself dared to resist her. The ink shimmered. Not just on the diagram, but beyond it. It crawled across the

258

page, then over the table until the surface began to shine. It wasn't wet. It didn't glow. It reflected.

And then something noticed her. No gust of wind stirred, and no tremor passed through the floorboards. Yet something had shifted, unmistakably. It wasn't a sound or a breeze, but a stillness so intentional it felt like breath held in a room that no longer belonged to her. The air didn't move, but it paused. And in that pause was the weight of attention. The diagram no longer drank the light; it bent it. The ink thinned until it caught her image, not in illustration, but in imitation. Where once there were symbols, there was now a mirror. Not perfect—wrong somehow, warped at the edges—but still recognizably her.

Velzara stared into the surface. Her reflection blinked once, then again. She had not.

That's not me. That's not mine. Mirrors were meant to obey, not mimic. And this one was thinking.

She leapt down from the table, her claws clicking against the wood with the precision of a ritual beginning. Her fur flared outward, a halo of cursed static that crowned her in defiance. Behind her, the book snapped shut—not out of fear, but with the finality of something finished. It was a conclusion sealed with intent, as if the book itself had decided that no more needed to be said.

It should have ended there. But across the room, the cabinet glass began to shimmer. Where the glass should have warped the lantern's glow, bending it and scattering it harmlessly across the room, it held it instead. The light didn't bounce. It settled, pooled in the pane like something claimed. This wasn't reflection. It was possession, quiet and deliberate, as though the glass had decided the light now belonged to it.

Velzara turned, slow and deliberate, her spine arching in a

motion poised between instinct and ritual, ready to strike though she had not yet chosen to. But the surface did not shatter beneath her glare. Instead, it changed. The glow behind the glass grew darker, more layered, as if the pane had grown depth where none should exist. It wasn't merely reflecting now. It was pulling, drinking in the light and holding it beneath the surface like breath too long withheld.

What emerged wasn't just her shape. It was her silhouette, refined and wrong. It shaped her silhouette with an almost reverent clarity. Her fur appeared velvet-dark and without flaw, every strand composed. Her shoulders were set not with tension, but with deliberate stillness. Around her throat, a silver collar gleamed, its polished surface catching the light with the elegance of an heirloom, but it was no ornament. It was restraint, meticulously disguised. Along its curve, glyphs shimmered in a steady rhythm. They were not wards meant to protect, nor warnings meant to deter. They were commands etched with intention, impossible to mistake.

The thing in the mirror did not mimic her movements. It watched. And then it spoke without speaking. The sound was inside her, like breath twisted into memory, like memory scraped into a blade and buried in her marrow. "You were shaped to hold more," it said in her voice. Not the one she wore now, brittle and edged by restraint, but the older voice—harsher, and crowned in certainty. "Not this. Not fur and fear and the shame of needing."

Velzara didn't answer. Her breath curled in her chest, cold and close. Her claws flexed against the floor, carving a shallow rune she didn't bother to finish. She took one step forward.

The mirror didn't ripple, but it thickened. Shadows gathered behind the reflection, behind her, until a second form took shape. It stood in silence, chained and still, silver bleeding from its wrists, its face obscured by light and smoke. It did not speak. It did not move. It only watched as if its presence alone was enough to unravel the room. It was the same presence that plagued her from the seal, the dream, and the edge of every unspoken memory she refused to name.

"She weakens you." The voice was hers. It echoed through her skull like a vow she had once been forced to sign. "Every silence you give her. Every question you do not tear out of her throat. You think that's mercy. You think she makes you strong. But strength does not beg. Strength does not need."

Velzara's tail lashed once. "She does not chain me."

"No," said the reflection. "But she makes you want to stay."

Behind the mirror-glass, the chained figure leaned forward. Its chains didn't rattle. They reached. Silver pooled beneath the figure—thick and glinting, a substance that might have been blood, or ink, or something older that remembered how to be both. It did not spill aimlessly. It moved with purpose, deliberate and slow, tracing a smooth ring into the floor beneath its feet. A circle drawn not as decoration, but as declaration. It was both a boundary and a summons. It was a home shaped like a trap.

Velzara's lip curled, not in fear, not even in rage, but in that ancient disgust that had once melted temples and silenced saints. "You offer comfort like a leash. Name it kindness, and think I won't notice the collar. You forget what I was meant for."

The glyphs around her reflection's throat shimmered again. For a moment, the collar looked like iron. For a moment, it looked familiar. "No," the voice whispered. "We remember exactly what you were meant for."

Velzara stepped forward. Her claws left scorched crescents

in the floor. The mirror didn't break, but it shuddered as the surface warped. And for a breathless second, the thing in the glass blinked. It did not do so in unison with her, as a reflection should. There was no mimicry, no control. The blink was uneven, startled—genuine surprise, not rehearsed illusion. The glyphs around its neck dimmed, their glow faltering like a heartbeat misfired. The collar shifted, no longer pristine in its grip, but askew, not by force, but by recognition. And the mirror—oh, the mirror—remembered it could bleed.

Velzara didn't give it time to beg. She turned without hesitation, her spine held tall and unyielding. Her tail arched high in a gesture that needed no translation, and her claws remained half-sheathed—ready, and gleaming with promise. She didn't look back. Her silence carved through the room, sharper than any incantation. And when she left the library, she did so like smoke leaving a pyre.

In the sitting room, the chaise sulked in the corner like it knew its place in the hierarchy of comfort. Its upholstery was frayed, its cushion permanently dented from too many apologies made in tea and silence. It bore the weight of Elira's kindness the way a battlefield bears the memory of mercy. Velzara leapt onto it without pause or pretense. She curled into herself with deliberate economy, every paw placed with the precision of a fortress closing its gates.

It wasn't exhaustion that drew her in. It wasn't defeat. It was containment. Because fire, too, needs embers. Even wrath must rest in order to rise again. She closed her eyes, not to find peace or to dream, but just to be still long enough to keep from breaking. She did not sleep. Sleep was for the safe. She fell. And the house, too old to be kind, made no effort to catch her.

The air was too still. Not merely silent, but bound as if held in place like breath sealed inside parchment and banished with ink. The scent of ritual ash lingered at the edge of her awareness, acrid and certain. Except there had been no fire, at least not this time. She was placed upon the altar again. But it wasn't the real one that had cracked stone slick with old rites and older regrets. This version gleamed, polished to a mirror's perfection. Every angle framed her, and in each pane, she saw a vision of herself—not the demon she had been, nor the beast she had become, but something in between. A third self waiting behind the glass cloaked in ceremonial black. It wore her crown and held her power, but is was wrong. It was too poised and clean as if it was her, but rendered palatable. A version of Velzara repackaged for display.

Sanitized. Sanctified. Sacrificed without my consent. They didn't cleanse me, they embalmed me. Stiffened my fury, draped it in black, and called it legacy. This isn't power, it's taxidermy. A reverent corpse posed for the faithful.

The binding played out again, but stripped of its fire and fury. There were no chains, no battles, no screaming. A ritual as dry and methodical as bureaucracy—blasphemy rendered into paperwork. Even her name was wrong. Not wholly, but dulled like a blade filed down for safety.

So, this is how they remember me... softened, strangled in silk. A reenactment too afraid of its own power to speak the truth aloud. They got my name wrong, and still the curse found me.

She tried to move, but the mirrored altar held her fast. Her reflection didn't snarl. It smiled like a mannequin—like a plastic doll wearing her face.

No. You do not get to smile with my mouth. You do not drape my defiance in silk and call it sacrifice. That is not me. That is a monument built by cowards. A lie dressed for mourning by those who survived me.

And then from the shadows... sure and unshakable, "You chose rage, but I chose you."

She didn't know the voice, but it knew her.

That's not praise, it's prophecy with delusions of authorship. Don't you dare make this sound holy. I bled in that silence. Don't you dare sanctify my defiance.

The air thickened. Not with smoke or spell, but with inevitability. The altar beneath her gleamed brighter, mirrors blooming with heatless light until there was nowhere left to look but inward. Her reflection still smiled. She tried to turn. She tried to twist—to *fight*. But her limbs would not obey. They held her pinned not by force, but by memory rendered sacred.

She heard the footsteps echo. Though she didn't see the hand that placed it. Only felt the weight descend—a cold, perfect circle pressed to the back of her neck. It was not hot, not searing. That would've been honest. This was colder than consent, cleaner than pain. It didn't burn. It *marked*.

The glyph sank into her flesh without smoke, without a scream. It settled as if the world itself had conspired to forget the moment it happened. There were no witnesses. No incantation. No ceremony. Only a mark pressed between her vertebrae with the finality of punctuation. *Mine.*

The word didn't echo. It didn't need to. It coiled beneath her skin like a secret too old for language, unspoken and undeniable. She didn't need to hear it. She *knew*. And the worst part was not the pain, it was that the word fit.

She woke with a snarl lodged halfway to breath, her chest rising too fast, her mouth dry with fury. The ghost of metal lingered at the back of her neck—no wound, no visible mark, only a slow, relentless ache. It pulsed with the certainty of something claimed. She had been *branded*. Each throb whispered of chains drawn tight.

Velzara prowled the rim of the chaise with predatory grace, silk wound taut around rage. The itch at her nape seethed beneath her skin, a trespass she refused to acknowledge. To scratch would be to confess—to admit the mark lived there, nestled beneath fur and fury, buried in the self she had shaped from defiance, and refusal. And her fur... gods, her fur remained the greatest betrayal. Soft where it had once burned. Silvered with ash where sovereign black had reigned. A mourning shroud stitched not by grief, but by shame and stolen power. Each step, each breath, dragged the weight of it behind her. She didn't wear exile. She endured it like a pelt pulled too tight across old wounds. It itched with memory and reeked of trespass.

Let the house leer. Let the curse writhe. I was not forged for the amusement of lesser things. My agony crowns kingdoms. It does not bow to cursed wood and second-rate hauntings.

She leapt down with regal disdain, her paws whispering against the floorboards. Wood rippling as if flinching from a blow it remembered too late. She did not flinch. She glared and the house, wise enough to want to survive, stilled.

Elira hovered in the doorway, clutching her apron like a shield, a tray perched awkwardly against one hip. A dish of shredded chicken, a battered bowl of water, and a sad little offering that might once have been a fish. It was mortal optimism, dressed in scraps and served with trembling diplomacy.

Behold the spoils of my conquest... torn poultry, tepid water, and the corpse of an ambition-less fish. A feast fit for a fallen queen if she'd been trampled, taxidermized, and left to rot beneath a crocheted banner of mortal pity. Is this what remains of my legacy?

Reduced to lapping handouts? Offerings paraded like tribute before a tempest too proud to be appeased. I would sooner gnaw through the foundations of this wretched house than grant their kindness the dignity of a single bite.

"Morning," Elira offered. Voice careful, spun as sugar over shattered glass. "And maybe... you could eat a little?" she added, barely whispered as if tempting a storm with breadcrumbs and borrowed nerve. "It might help. With the, um... fur."

There it was again that soft, foolish hope, dressed in deference and dangled like a leash made of linen and grace. The well-meaning dagger, slipped between the ribs of pride. As if shredded chicken could mend a crown snapped at the spine. As if a dish of water could drown the insult still steaming from her skin. Eat. Heal. Behave. As if obedience were a balm. As if the house deserved even a flicker of my restraint.

Velzara did not answer with a blink, nor a breath. She didn't even offer the courtesy of a tail flick. The moment ended under the blade of her disdain. Behind her, the tray rattled, unsteady hands or unsteady house, she neither knew nor cared. A bowl threatened mutiny, teetering like it might throw itself in protest. Elira's startled gasp followed like an afterthought. Velzara let it die unheard. A glance would be mercy. A flinch would be surrender. She granted neither, but she filed the sound away like a scholar cataloging offenses for judgment, one syllable at a time. The day would come when the ledger would close.

Let her flinch. Let her falter. I remember tremors the way others remember vows cataloged and repaid in kind.

The hallway stretched unnaturally long before her like the ribs of a starved beast trying to close around what it couldn't consume. The rugs shifted underfoot, treacherous tongues tasting at her paws. The wallpaper, faded vines strangling tired stars, twitched at the corners, uncertain whether to bloom or rot. The Warding House was not reacting. It was rehearsing betrayal.

Conspire, then. Scheme. I've turned better fortresses into mausoleums with nothing but a curse and a ruined smile.

She moved, but purpose soured on her tongue.

Even now, they would make me pace my gilded cage. Let them try. Let them weep when the bars melt. A mystery to unravel. A ward to unmake. A foe with enough spine to scream. I crave defiance, not silence and if it cannot scar me, it will not be remembered.

At the hall's end, a door waited. Its frame sagged inward, heavy with the memory of a better architect, whose bones, no doubt, had long since been ground to dust. It should not exist or at least it hadn't existed before now. Velzara narrowed her eyes. Her tail flicked low, a warning she would not waste breath on.

So. It calls to me now. Let's see if its voice earns an answer or its throat earns a reckoning.

Behind her, the tray settled with a clatter. It was too loud to be an accident, but too timid for defiance. Elira's uncertainty rippled through the air like a badly stitched ward.

"If you... need anything..." Elira offered, her voice shrinking even as it escaped her mouth.

Velzara turned just enough for the sigil to flare sharp and searing.

QUIET

She didn't conjure it. She forged it. Each stroke was a blade, each curve a wound carved into silence and scorched expectation.

You will not pour pity into the cracks you think you see. You will not stitch mortal comfort across my scars and dare call it mercy. Your words are not balm. They are erosion. I do not erode. I burn.

The rune snapped through the hallway like a lash. The house recoiled. The dust held its breath. Even the shadows had the sense to shrink. Elira blinked once and stood frozen. Her knuckles whitened around the tray, a shield she no longer remembered how to wield. Wisely, she said nothing.

Velzara didn't need to watch her flinch. She turned back to the door with the cold finality sovereigns reserve for traitors. Those whose only redemption is silence. The mark at her neck flared. A hot, crawling itch, like leashed thunder gnawing at the skin of her pride.

Let the house remember. Let the door repent before it learns what I do to those who hesitate.

She bared her teeth. A grimace honed for war, too sharp for any mortal smile and pressed her paw to the warped wood. The door shivered beneath her touch, not in resistance, but in recognition.

CHAPTER 23
ECHOES OF UNBOUND FURY

The door did not creak, so much as it exhaled in a long, low sigh of air, as if it hadn't spoken sunlight's name in centuries. Velzara stepped through without hesitation. To pause would be to honor it.

Let the darkness reach with its trembling whispers. I do not answer to shadows. I teach them silence.

The room crouched like a secret left to rot—waiting to be uncovered, or better yet, denied. Dust curled in slow, sullen spirals. Broken furniture sagged against the walls like failed pilgrims awaiting judgment. And in the far corner: the mirror. Fractured down the center, it caught the dim light and spat it back in jagged, crooked halves. Velzara advanced, each step deliberate.

A sovereign striding into the desecration of her own reflection.

The mirror twitched before she moved, like a shadow rehearsing her steps. She lifted one paw. Her reflection faltered... then mimicked, a breath too late. The glyph at her neck throbbed, possessive.

A heartbeat not mine.

The mirror shimmered, and for a heartbeat, it remembered her. Not as she was now, bound and diminished, but as she had once been. She had stood cloaked in black fur, her violet eyes alight with stormlight. She had been a tempest made regal, carved from the ruins of kingdoms and crowned in unquenchable fire. And she had been shackled. Around her throat, a collar gleamed—ornate and unforgiving. It was gilt and cruel, a mockery of reverence—ceremonial, like a crown hammered from manacles. Runes pulsed along its curve, etched with such depth they seemed to bleed. Obedience had been carved into her bones and sanctified in suffering. She knew those glyphs. She had scorched them from better creatures than this mockery dared recall.

Chain me in ink, if you dare. But see what survives the signature.

The vision cracked. Fractures split the mirror's skin. Her gaze stared back splintered into a thousand silent accusations, none of them still. Velzara snarled, low but rising. The sound was not a warning. It was an empire waking, blood still drying on its banners. The room replied with finality. The door slammed shut behind her, its echo heavy with finality, like stone laid over a tomb. She turned. Her claws dragged shallow furrows into warped wood. She struck—once, then twice— sigils flaring in her wake. The door pulsed, not in defiance, but with a deeper cruelty. It responded not as an obstacle, but as a judge.

Ensnared. By this mockery. A trick dressed as a threshold. An insult lacquered in mystery.

She faced the mirror again. The reflection stood regal and waiting. The collar gleamed—blessed by cowards, forged for surrender. "Anchor," it whispered though no lips moved. The word slithered into the room's bones and stayed. Velzara's tail lashed behind her, a whip in velvet. The glyph at her neck burned.

No. You will not leash me with kindness. You will not chain rebellion and call it sanctuary. I will not wear your redemption like it was my idea.

She dropped low like a coiled storm and launched herself at the mirror. The glass did not shatter. Instead, it yielded— swallowing her strike like cold liquid wrapping around her paw. But it wasn't her paw. It was her reflection's, and it pulled. She felt the wrongness rise through her, a pressure that tried to peel her apart, to separate the fury from the flesh, to strip her down into something quiet, something tame.

I was not forged to fit your frame. Not bred for collars. Not born for cradles. I am the ruin you begged to survive and the reckoning you shall receive.

She tore herself back with a snarl that cracked the room like a spell screamed in defiance. The mirror froze. The reflection— the false, collared Velzara—bled into ruin, then dust. Velzara panted. Not from fear, but from fury left unsatisfied. Her breath echoed mortal in the silence, like a god mistaken for prey and too proud to scream.

They saw a god falter and dared to call it defeat. Fools. They will not survive the correction. I remember the shape I was. I do not know the shape I am. But I will not be sculpted by strangers into something small enough to survive.

The door creaked open. Not in surrender, but in sly, smug allowance—as if the house, breathing and arrogant, had deigned to let her pass.

Magnanimous of you. Pity. I intend to burn you from the foundation up the moment your arrogance has outlived its use.

Velzara stepped into the hallway. Each step was a silent decree. The wood shivered beneath her claws, a breath the house dared not finish. The taste of the mirror clung to her tongue—iron, mockery, and the ghost of a collar no fire had yet undone. She could still feel its phantom weight pressing against her throat, where once pride lived unchallenged.

Victory, then. Not the kind they sing of, but the kind clawed from ruin and poisoned by the need to be won at all. Still mine. But tainted by the audacity of the test.

The Warding House quivered around her, paralyzed in its cowardice. Wallpaper curled tighter against the plaster. Floorboards whimpered beneath the weight of her silence.

Let them tremble. Let them rot in the knowledge that their fear came too late.

She had faced her own defilement and shattered it. That she had been forced to do so was a trespass she intended to repay with interest compounded, and in blood. Ahead, Elira hovered. A pale wisp stitched from hope, hesitation, and mortal overreach. Her hands clutched the tray like a shield she no longer had permission to wield. Her gaze flicked to Velzara's throat—quick, guilty, like a wound reopened.

The mortal had seen what was never hers to witness, and had the gall to drape it in pity. As if a sovereign's scars were something to be soothed.

Velzara cast a rune into the space between them.

ENOUGH

It was not a command. It was a brand. She burned it into

the air, into the house's bones, into the marrow of anyone foolish enough to linger.

You will not speak. You will not soothe. You will not reduce me to something comforted.

The mark cracked through the hall like a whip of molten glass, stirring dust, silence, and shame into retreat. Elira flinched. Her knuckles whitened around the tray. Her gaze dropped like a penitent before judgment. Velzara did not slow. She did not glance back. She passed Elira with the cold, lethal grace of a blade drawn across a throat too insignificant to remember. Behind her, the house release a long, low shudder—not of peace but of mourning.

Let it mourn. Let it remember the sound of its own failure the next time it dares breathe in my direction.

The next time they dared test her, they would not find reflection. They would not find an echo. They would not find the hollow ruin they hoped would bow. They would find flames that remembered the hand that tried to bind them.

The abandoned parlor sulked beneath a crust of dust and velvet, its colors faded by disuse. Curtains sagged like condemned banners. The hearth gaped—cold and empty—a stone maw waiting to swallow someone else's grief. Here, at least, the walls did not lean in with quite so much hunger. Here, the air tasted more like dust than judgment.

Let them cling to their fragile neutrality. I will unmake it by presence and call the ruin justice.

Velzara stalked to the center of the room, each step a pronouncement. She carved a sigil into the warped floorboards —every stroke a sharp and deliberate wound meant to bleed. It was a crude thing, born of desperation rather than elegance, but it would be enough. Enough to let her sink her claws into whatever still dared to tether her.

The BINDING TRACE

They brand me in borrowed chains. I brand in flame that remembers, and fire that never forgives.

She pressed her paw to the carved lines. The mark at her neck flared—heat surging through her like gnashing teeth in bone, a collar snapping shut on defiance.

Her voice had returned. "Break," she commanded.

The parlor convulsed. The word split the silence like a blade too blunt to kill cleanly. Its edges rang fractured and wrong. It tore through the air in two voices: hers... and another. Her fur bristled. Her breath turned thick in her chest. Her throat burned—not from strain, but from the shame of a voice no longer entirely her own. This was no roar. It was the carrion echo of cowards who dared to chain fire and found only ash. The sound reeked of broken syllables and rot, sung in a dead tongue. She tried again. A curse, a command, a battle cry even, but every sound that left her mouth twisted back toward her, fractured and false.

It was not absence. It was theft. My power hijacked and strangled through their filters until it spilled out twisted and trembling.

The walls did not whisper. They leaned as if listening to a song she could not hear. The parlor, once merely reluctant, now hungered like a congregation awaiting either miracle or sacrifice. Something was wrong—deep in the marrow, in every breath, in the space where her name should have blazed like a sigil through the air.

This is not how I speak. This is not how I am heard.

She could feel it. A slithering coil of silence, waiting to devour whatever fragments of her voice remained the moment she dared speak again.

No. You will not hear me broken. You will not carry away the ruins of my roar and call it history.

Velzara snapped her jaws shut before the weakness could bleed—Before the walls could drink it in and remember. Elira stood at the threshold, one hand braced against the splintered frame, as if the house itself had shoved her forward. Her face had drained to a near-spectral white, and her hands trembled where they clutched the worn wood.

But it wasn't terror that softened her voice. It was something worse—recognition. "It sounded like you," Elira said, barely more than a breath. "But hollow. Like something else was speaking through you."

Velzara did not dignify the observation. Even silence should be earned.

I do not echo. I do not fracture. I do not lend my voice to cowards and cursed walls. I roar. And when I do, the heavens remember, the earth recoils, and the unworthy burn without song or scripture.

With a flick of her paw, sharp enough to wound, she slashed the sigil from the floor. The wood groaned, and the magic collapsed into itself like a tower crumbling beneath the weight of its own betrayal. The mark at her neck pulsed again like a sneer half-carved into her skin. Elira hovered at the threshold, pinned between terror and pity. Her concern was a clumsy offering Velzara would never touch.

Let her watch. Let her shudder. Let her learn that some things cannot be stitched back together with mortal sympathy.

Velzara turned her back with deliberate contempt, her tail slicing the stagnant air behind her like a blade.

I will find the source of this binding. I will rip it free—claw by claw, syllable by shuddering syllable. And when I do, the walls will not weep. The house will not mourn. It will burn. And the screams stitched into its bones will sing my name. They will remember why fire does not kneel. It devours.

The hallway stretched long behind her, every wall exhaling a sigh of failure Velzara refused to dignify. She moved without hurry, without reverence. Each step carved through the house's cowardice with ease.

Let them cower. Let them call my silence surrender. I will make of it a blade and drive it through their trembling foundations.

She did not seek rest. She sought silence. A place to coil her fury until it scraped blood from the inside out. No chamber was worthy of that fury—but stone, at least, could bear the weight. She slipped into a low alcove. A forgotten storage room, sour with disuse and grudging silence. Dust sighed beneath her claws. The beams sagged like disgraced sentries left to rot.

Good. Let them sag. Let them rot. Let them remember what it means to kneel in the shadow of a sovereign undone—and not broken.

She curled into herself, not in surrender but in containment.

I am not spent. I am not diminished. I am the ember in the ruin. The storm crouched beyond the horizon.

Her eyes narrowed into twin violet slits, sharp enough to

carve a reckoning. Sleep was not surrender. It was an ambush—an insult with soft edges.

I do not slumber while enemies breathe. I do not dream while chains still rasp my name.

But sleep came or something that wore its shape. It slithered over her skin like cold mist and pressed into her bones with the weight of forgotten altars. Velzara did not sleep. She was swallowed by fangs shaped from memory.

Elira lingered at the threshold long after Velzara vanished into the house's quivering guts. The sigils still hung in the air like scars of light too proud to fade. They flickered at the edges of her vision—too weak to wound, too stubborn to vanish. She clutched the ruined tray to her chest like it could explain something. Or like it could undo what had just happened. The silence tasted scorched, like something sacred had cracked, and even the air didn't dare acknowledge it.

"That wasn't you," she whispered—to the ash, the tray, the part of herself that still hoped. To the residue of the command still humming in the air. To the space Velzara had left behind, like smoke from a dying fire.

She stepped forward. The floorboards whimpered underfoot. The house listened. The house waited.

Why won't you let me help you? What are you so afraid I'll see, V?

She hugged the tray tighter—not because it would protect her (nothing would, not really), but because she needed to hold something that wasn't shifting under her feet.

What are you, really?

The question ached in her throat, too heavy for fear, too

old for comfort. Velzara was not just cursed. She was not just proud. She was something the house itself flinched from, something stitched from fury and grief. Every day in these halls made Elira more certain that whatever Velzara had lost hadn't just marked her. It had marked the house too.

I need to know.

Not just for Velzara's sake. For her own.

She didn't follow. Not yet. But she didn't turn away either.

The house remembered her shape, and folded the hall around it like a shroud.

The dream struck like a chain hurled from unseen hands, snapping shut around her throat. There was no fire, no triumph—only stone, and a silence that waited. The sky arched overhead, black and blinding, like a vault nailed shut to keep the stars from witnessing. The ground beneath her had split into jagged shards, like the remains of a ruined throne or the teeth of dead kings. Before her stood a cracked and cold altar.

Of course it waited. The altar stood as it always had— cracked, crowning, and laced with the bargain stitched into every chain I had ever broken.

She did not stand as a cat, nor as a demon, but as a silhouette still cooling from the forge. Molten cracks webbed her skin, glowing in places where no shape would settle. Her reflection fractured across a thousand shattered mirrors, each shard shrinking her into something false. Each shard showed a different version of herself: black-furred, collared, eyes hollow, embers long gone cold.

She opened her mouth to command, but the sound that escaped was not a roar. It came as a rasp, crackling and weak.

Her voice twisted mid-breath, her rage strangled by another presence—thin as wire, winding through her throat like vines choking a flame.

"We chose you," the dream whispered.

She bared her teeth, fury clawing at her chest, but the only sound that followed was like parchment folding and foundations giving way.

Chains unraveled from the altar, spun like silk and glistening with oath-blood. They reached for her paws, writhing with intent, trying to stitch her into the bargain. Above her, a crown descended. Glyphs coiled across its surface, twisting into the same script that had carved survival into her bones and shaped her suffering into obedience. The crown hovered just above her brow, glittering, as if savoring the final drop.

"No," she said, her voice rising with certainty. "I see you. I know your shape. You would crown me in my own ruin and call it mercy. You would twist my defiance into your leash and call it love. But I will not kneel to a mirror stitched from my broken reflections. I will not wear a chain that dares sing of honor while tasting my blood. I will not burn for your covenant. I will burn through it."

She raked the world—not with claws or with teeth, but with the fury that had outlived gods. Reality screamed around her as it tore at the seams. The crown shattered. The altar bled black smoke. The mirrors howled without mouths. The dream tore apart in a chorus of ruin, but even as it died, it lashed out —roots snapping, chains smoking, sigils writhing—still reaching for her soul.

She fell. Not into darkness, but into flame. She fell into herself. And it was the only kingdom they had never truly conquered.

CHAPTER 24
STORM OF SHATTERED OATHS

Something dragged her upward through smoky ash and the barbed threads of a world that would not loosen its claws. She woke clawing at the floorboards. The dream clung to her skin, thick and rancid. Her fur was clotted with the scent of burned oaths. Each breath scraped her ribs, the air barbed and biting. Velzara staggered upright on the warped floor, claws gouging shallow trenches into wood too weak to resist. Her heart hammered a traitor's drumbeat, out of rhythm with the storm still screaming behind her eyes.

The altar, the chains, the hollow crowns and stitched lies— It wasn't gone. It had only stepped sideways, waiting for the next misstep to drag her under again. She should be above this. But fury was the only shelter that hadn't failed her. Her hackles bristled. Rage surged first... pure and familiar. She spat a curse in a tongue so old even the house winced. Its timbers shuddering like hounds struck mid-whimper. But the force came wrong as though refracted and stolen mid-spell, rewritten by words that no longer belonged to her. But then a flicker of shame wormed through her, fouler than any chain. It knotted her spine. A traitor's twitch she could neither claw free nor kill.

No. You do not get to follow me here. You do not get to lace my survival with your hunger and call it kindness. I will not carry the chains you sang into being, the oaths you bled dry for your hollow thrones. I will not wear the crown that drank my name and called it destiny.

I remember the forge you built from my bones. I remember how it cracked. And I will remember long after you are dust on the tongue of the storm you tried, and failed, to cage.

They carved me hollow and called it becoming. I do not mourn what was taken. I mourn what I can no longer name.

She braced herself expecting the dream to seize her in its waiting jaws, but the world dared nothing. It only shuddered and called it defiance. The hearth, still guttering with last night's embers, shivered. Shadows clung too thickly to the corners. The light leaking through the warped windows slithered wrong. It was a thin and brittle smear of gray where morning had already fled. There was a storm brewing. The house tasted of salt and iron. But beneath that, there was something older, something buried deep enough to be forgotten by sane walls.

Velzara's ears pinned flat against her skull.

This is no storm born of sky and season. This is a wound pretending to be weather, stitched with old blood and older hunger. I have danced through tempests that tore mountains in half and laughed when the gods wept at the wreckage. Whatever festered out there now, it had not come to batter walls or drown fields. It had come hunting for what the dream could not claim.

And the house, the house breathed it in. It reeked of the dream's foul breath. This was too precise to be weather. The air thickened with borrowed dread. The walls trembled in their bones. Floorboards jittered underfoot, and the charm wall, usually humming with negligent annoyance, quivered visibly. A single silver bell jangled once, sharp and thin, like a scream bitten off too late. Velzara narrowed her eyes to slits. The Warding House wasn't mocking her. It was listening as it wasn't sure what had awoken with her. She padded forward, silent as a shade, and the house *flinched* with every step. Floorboards skittered, wallpaper twitched.

Whatever my dream dragged loose... it did not stay behind. Something followed me back.

The house groaned a low, shuddering sound like an old oath breaking beneath its own weight. Velzara felt it first, before the tremor reached the walls, before the wind clawed at the windowpanes. It pressed against her ribs, a strangled prayer trying, and failing, to escape. The Warding House had always whispered, always sighed but this is different. This isn't its usual theatrical brooding. This is a tremor with a target. This is a warning. The window in the alcove shrieked in its frame, joints wrenching against iron nails gone brittle with regret. The floorboards jittered again, teeth chattering in a language of fear older than any mortal tongue.

Velzara uncoiled from her crouch in one fluid motion, tail lashing, a blade drawn in velvet and spite. "So it begins," she murmured, voice low, raw with the flavor of unshed fire. She prowled the hall like storm incarnate, each step a drumbeat of defiance. Dust rose in lazy, unwilling spirals around her, pulled into uneasy dances by a force they could not name.

The house was breathing wrong. Each exhale catching, each timber twitching like a creature too slow to flee the predator within its walls. Above her, a floorboard groaned a slow, deliberate stretch, like bone wrenching beneath too-thin skin.

She turned, muscles tightening. At the end of the crooked hallway, the attic door shuddered once on its hinges. Not flung wide in panic, nor blown ajar by the swelling storm outside. No, the door peeled open with the slow, deliberate grace of a knife easing into a wound. From the gap above, cold light spilled down. It was not golden sun or stormy grey, but a blade of shimmer, humming with something not born of star or sun. Velzara halted, fur bristling, breath catching against bared teeth. The house did not mock her. It did not creak in irony or sigh in exhaustion. It waited for her and for what came next.

Let it. Let the storm rip the roof from these cowardly bones. Let the air scream. I will not kneel to wind or ruin.

Velzara shifted her stance, the hall stretching and shrinking around her like a living thing holding its breath. She bared her teeth, not in fear, but in promise.

You think you know storms, little house? You think you know fury? You have only ever hosted fury. I am what comes when it stops asking permission.

Behind her, footsteps pounded against the trembling floorboards. Too light, too frantic to belong to anything summoned by the storm.

"V—wait!" Elira's voice, thin and shaking, barely threaded through the suffocating air.

There was a time when I might have answered. When the cry of another might have slowed my step. But pity is a chain. Mercy, a collar. And that name, the one she dares to almost speak now, stripped bare of the mask she once clung to, that name is a blade. I cannot afford its wound. I will not wear either tonight.

Velzara did not turn. The attic door gaped ahead, silvered light bleeding down the crooked stairwell, humming against the back of her teeth.

"Don't—" Elira gasped again, closer now, her words laced with something worse than fear. It was recognition that whatever waited above them was wrong in ways mortal prayers could not mend.

Velzara flicked her tail once, sharp and deliberate, a silent command to stay.

There are thresholds even gods must cross alone. Call if you must. Pray if you can. But do not follow. The storm does not ask permission. And neither do I.

The storm rattled the windows again, a sound like teeth clashing against bone. Elira faltered at the base of the stairwell, her hands trembling where they clutched a half-lit lantern. Its flame sputtered as if choking on the very air.

"Please," she whispered. "It's not safe."

Velzara moved without answering.

Poor little light. Still reaching. Still believing. But no lantern can follow where I tread. No prayer can mend what was broken before you ever spoke my name.

Each step up the crooked stairs carved a rift between them. Not distance, not mercy, but a line of sovereignty Elira could not cross.

The house moaned low around them, timbers sagging under the weight of what should never have been welcomed inside. The staircase stretched as she climbed. Not longer... no, not honestly. Rubber-limbed and reluctant, the wood sagged under her paws like something struggling to remember how to bear weight. Each step took too long to land. Each heartbeat dragged slower, thicker, as if the very air clung to her fur and tried to hold her back. Still Velzara pressed on. The cold light pooled thicker with every step, seeping into her skin, humming through her ribs like a second, stunted heartbeat.

I was shaped for ruin, tempered for empire and now the stairs forget my weight. Is this what I am? A shadow even walls reject.

The attic was close. Close enough that she could taste it, iron and ash and something fouler... older.

How many times have they tried to carve me smaller? How many names had they burned into my skin and called it legacy? I have broken every collar they set upon me. I have outlived every song that sang me into silence. And still, they dare.

They still dream of a Velzara who kneels. Still build mirrors to catch what flesh could not bind. Let them dream. Let them remember.

I am not the shard you trap in glass. I am the fire you failed to contain. And I am coming for you.

For a heartbeat, treacherous and stupid, her mind flicked backward. To the girl clutching her lantern like it could ward off the storm—To the trembling hands and the voice too small to stop what waited.

Good. Let her stay small. Let her stay safe. Safety is for those the world still wants. I walk where the wanting ends.

The storm outside was noise. This was pressure. This was pull.

The stairs shuddered beneath her paw, the wood slick with unnatural sweat. For a heartbeat too long, her claws found no purchase. Sliding uselessly against the wood before sinking in.

Let it flinch. Let it crawl. I was not forged to seek permission. I tear down thresholds. I burn through walls. You will open for me or you will break.

The top of the stairwell loomed ahead, a yawning mouth dripping silver light. And beneath it, the heat pulsed. Thick as blood clogging the arteries of a dying god. Velzara's head swam. The house shifted under her, not with a single jolt, but in ripples, as if reality itself were growing thin at the edges. The air tasted wrong, like ink burning on a forge. One step became five. Five became one. Her body lagged a half-second behind her will.

You think to steal my footing? You think to slither treachery into my bones and slow the blood that built empires? Crawl, then. Twist. Weep. I will grind your false roads into dust under my claws.

She bared her teeth against the nausea coiling behind her eyes. If the house thought to drown her in its own sickness, it would learn how a sovereign died... clawing out the last of its walls as tribute. Another step and the silver light curled against her fur, no longer cold but boiling.

The attic threshold yawned wider. The mirror loomed just beyond. Shrouded in mist, its fractured skin twitched like something straining against ice, too impatient to stay frozen.

Velzara narrowed her eyes to slits. If they wanted her broken, they should have built stronger chains.

Let them twist the path. Let them foul the air. Let them whisper rot into the stone. I walk where storms break and thrones fall.

She crossed the threshold without hesitation. The world tore around her as the attic dragged her in. It swallowed her— breath, bone, fury, and flame.

The walls cinched inward, the silver light boiling against her skin. No welcome, only a cage tightening around a storm.

You think your rot can crown me? You think your stench can weave itself into my bones and call it consecration? Press, then. Burn. Howl. I will not bow. I will not break. I will make of your hunger a monument to your failure.

The mirror crouched ahead, twitching like a wounded beast too cowardly to flee. The mist around it shivered, ribs heaving as if the thing dared draw breath in her presence.

Let it breathe. Let it dream itself alive. I will teach it how ruin remembers.

Velzara's paw hovered midair, claws half-extended. An execution held at the moment before the fall.

Let it tremble for the weight it dares to invite. Let it bleed if it wishes to taste my hand.

The mirror, the wretched shrine stitched from false light, hungered. It reached first. A thread of silver peeled from its fractured skin, slithering into the air. Thin as breath, bright as a star. It dared brush her claws, featherlight and damning, and the world lurched.

Velzara hissed low, the growl burning at the base of her throat.

No. You do not summon the fire that scorched your oaths to ash. You do not beckon the storm you could not chain. I come not because you call but because you will not survive what you have awakened.

The pull was not forceful. It's sweet, but treacherous like the taste of rot hidden beneath golden fruit.

It traces the wreckage I left behind and calls it knowledge. It weighs the ashes and dares think it knows the fire that birthed them. It is wrong. They were all wrong.

The thread coiled once around her paw, gentle yet greedy,

and the silver light dragged her inward. Her body stiffened as the thread of silver sank deeper, driving itself between bone and will. Her soul tore loose. It was not freed. It had not fled. It had been ripped like a dull blade through the softest part of her will and she fell.

Not like a stone. Not like a corpse. Like a sovereign dragged from her throne by cowards too craven to look her in the eye.

There was no thunder, no scream, only the brittle crackle of reflections breaking against her, each shard clawing for purchase. One reflection showed a battlefield where blood hissed into ash and her name was howled in hatred, in awe, in betrayal. Another reflection showed a throne room where banners sagged in rot, loyalty curdling like spoiled milk in the summer sun. And yet another showed a molten crown with its glyphs tearing down her throat like promises re-forged into chains.

Velzara snarled, raking her claws through the whirling shards, each strike rending on jagged edges that bled memory and spite into her skin.

You dare bind me with the wreckage of your failures? You dare offer me ash and think it will weigh heavier than fire?

The shards lunged, slashing around her wrists, coiling her throat, clawing at her ribs like drowning hands mistaking her for salvation.

See what you are, they whispered. *See what you could be.*

Velzara bared her teeth, the taste of ash and oaths rotting on her tongue.

You wear my shape, but not my hunger. You parade my name, but never the ache that forged it. I am not the mask you stole. I am the scar you feared to keep. I see the shape of your hunger. I see the crown you dream of binding me with and I come with teeth bared, not bowed.

The fall narrowed. The light fractured as it spiraled into a silver tunnel. Ahead a throne rose from the wreckage, stitched from every oath she had shattered, every crown she had set aflame, every hand she had burned to bone. Velzara's breath tore against her teeth, raw and ragged.

Do you think the fire forgets the hand that tried to smother it? Do you think the storm forgets the tower that dared to cage the sky? I am the ruin you prayed would die quietly and I am still burning.

The tunnel yawned wider, pulling her closer.

Elira stood frozen at the base of the stairs, lantern trembling in her grip. The flame guttered, flickering desperately against a draft that tasted of rust and forgotten secrets. She wanted to scream, to shout after Velzara—anything to pull her back from that silvered light humming hungrily in the attic above.

But her voice died in her throat. Her heart stuttered, not from cowardice, but from a deeper dread: understanding. She'd felt that blade of cold illumination before, in dreams that bled into waking, in whispers that wore faces she knew too well. This was not merely danger—it was invitation. And she knew, with aching certainty, she had no power to intervene.

She sank to the floor, knees folding beneath her, palms flat against splintering wood. The trembling house whispered beneath her hands, murmuring sympathy or perhaps only fear. Velzara's defiance burned bright and fierce, but Elira felt her own courage slipping, thinner than candle smoke.

"Don't leave," she breathed, voice barely more than a ghost. Her vision blurred, the lantern light wavering through tears she refused to shed.

Above her, the attic door thudded shut, sealing Velzara from her reach. Elira curled forward, forehead pressed to trembling knuckles, whispering into the emptiness.

"Please come back."

But the house answered only in creaks and shudders, leaving her alone to face the silence that came after storms.

CHAPTER 25

ASHES AND HOLLOW THRONES

The throne room bled gold and ruin. Tattered banners drooped from cracked marble walls, stitched not with symbols of conquest, but with reflections of old betrayals. The floor gleamed, polished to a sickly mirror sheen. Yet, every step Velzara took sent ripples squirming beneath her paws, as if the ground itself recoiled from her presence. Above it all, the throne loomed, a wound stitched into splendor. Upon it, coiled in regal mockery, sat a collared and smiling version of Velzara like a god who had forgotten how to grieve.

An abomination stitched from my stolen skin. You wear my face like a mask. My ruin like a crown. But you will never wear my name.

Velzara halted at the foot of the dais, hackles raised, breath hissing between bared teeth. The Collared Mockery tilted her head, that terrible crown glinting with glyphs too old and too hungry to name.

"You came so far," the reflection crooned in a voice rich with false warmth, with pity carved into every syllable. "All your fire. All your fury. And yet still you wear your wounds like armor."

Velzara snarled a sound too raw to be anger, too old to be anything but a curse remembered in blood.

"You still cling to smallness," the Collared Mockery purred, descending the throne in a lazy, terrible ripple of silk and shadow. "You claw against the storm when you could be its heart." The mockery reached towards Velzara. "Are you ready to stop pretending you're small?" The words slipped into the air like poison sweetened with honey.

Pretending? I shattered gods before I ever stooped to pretending. If I am small, it is only because this world is too craven to hold the storm I carry.

Velzara's claws scraped deep furrows into the mirrored floor. Her body trembled from the war splitting through her ribs like a second heartbeat.

You think I forget what chains feel like? You think I mistake your silk for mercy?

The Collared Mockery descended the final step with a lazy, sinuous grace. Every movement gleamed like a performance mocking life.

"You ache for more than this," she murmured. "More than half-spoken spells. Half-remembered names. Half-lived days scratching at walls too small to hold you."

They called it destiny. I called it a coffin with a prettier lining. No crown woven by liars will fit the fire they tried to bind.

The crown in her hands pulsed once, casting broken glyph-shadows across the ruined floor.

"You ache for what you were forged to be."

This setting, this between space made of mirrors and dreams, shifted suddenly. It was no longer cold, but heavy and suffocating like the first lungful of incense before the altar splits open and devours the worshiper. Velzara's chest rose and fell in shallow, angry breaths. The Collared Mockery knelt impossibly low, mockingly reverent, offering up the glyph-crown with both hands.

"Take it," she whispered. "Take what was always yours." The crown shimmered, black gold stitched with bloodlight.

"You dare call it mine," Velzara said, her voice a blade drawn in the dark. "You dare dress my ruin in gold and call it legacy." Velzara took a single step forward.

One step. One leash slipped back around my throat like a vow slipped into a snare. One heartbeat of weakness and the sky forgets it ever burned for me.

The crown hummed louder, thrumming against her bones, matching the rhythm of something older than the Warding House, older than memory. Then she felt it—a breath, a heartbeat, that flicker of heat threading down her spine like a leash remembering its shape. A sound scraped raw from the furnace of Velzara's ribs and she slammed her paw down, shattering the mirrored floor beneath her. Cracks spiderwebbed outward, a corona of defiance tearing across the dream.

The Collared Mockery did not flinch. She only smiled wider, pity and triumph stitched into the same ruinous curve.

"You cannot claw your way out forever," she said, voice rich with a sorrow she did not feel. "You were made to burn. Why not burn for something greater than stubbornness?"

Velzara bared her teeth, breath heaving, fire building behind her eyes.

I burn, yes—but not for you. Not for your empty thrones, your hollow prayers. I burn because you could not kill me. I burn because your chains snapped, and your temples fell. I bled to be more than the weapon they carved. You are not my crown. You are my grave.

The cracks in the mirror-floor widened, splintering underfoot like the ribs of a dying beast. Velzara stood tall above them. She may be small in flesh, but her fury was colossal. The Collared Mockery rose, crown still cradled in her false hands, and the light around her dimmed. It faded from gold to a sickly, corroded gleam. All the while, she smiled.

"You think this defiance makes you sovereign?" she crooned, the words soft, coiling through the broken floor like smoke. "You are not free, little ember. You are merely adrift. Untethered. Forgotten. "The crown pulsed again, bleeding warmth into the air between them. "You burn alone. You burn without purpose."

Velzara narrowed her eyes to slits.

Alone is better than chained. Alone is better than hollow.

The Collared Mockery stepped closer. Unhurried, inevitable, as if certain that every snarl, every strike, every step backward was only another circle drawn tighter.

"You ache for the storm," she whispered. "You ache for the throne they denied you."

She held the crown closer until Velzara could feel the weight of it pulling at the mark still branded against her neck, a phantom collar she had never forgiven.

"Take it," the reflection breathed, voice thinned to silk. "You won't lose yourself. You'll become what you were meant to be."

Velzara's paw twitched as instinct took control like a curse stitched into the marrow she had once called power. For a heartbeat, a traitorous and trembling heartbeat, she saw it. Her throne rebuilt with banners sewn from ashes and victories alike. She was a sovereign unbound, her name etched into the essence of every sky that had dared forget her. It wasn't a vision. It was bait. It would be so easy. It would be survival shaped into glory. It would be—

No.

Velzara bared her teeth, a snarl peeling from her lips with the force of a curse long denied its blood. "I was not forged to wear your ruin like salvation," she spat, voice low and lethal. "I do not crown myself with the carrion of cowards."

The Collared Mockery's smile sharpened, predatory. "So, you choose," she said. "But remember—" and here her voice twisted, thickening into something deeper, older, the voice that had once whispered across the altar stones of Nar'Khalor, "the flame that refuses its forge still burns to ash."

The dream trembled. The crown flickered, faltered.

Choice is not the absence of chains. It is the moment you turn, teeth bared, and name them yours to break.

Velzara lashed out—Not with claw, not with sigil, but with will—A sovereign's denial carved into the air, flensing light from shadow. She chose—not survival, not obedience, not even freedom—herself. She did not choose the shape forged for her, nor the fate whispered by dead gods. It was a choice with no applause and no glory. There was only ache, but that was hers and it was sacred.

You forged a blade and thought it would turn against itself. You fed the fire and thought it would beg for water. Fools. You should have snuffed me when you had the chance.

I do not know what shape I will wear tomorrow. But I know it will be mine. Not forged by flames, not carved by gods. Just mine.

The Collared Mockery laughed—terrible and triumphant —as the dream began to collapse inward. Velzara, burning from the inside out, ripped herself free and hurled herself into the rift.

Not strength. Not yet. But the echo of it... louder now. Louder with every act of self-crowning.

Reality itself cracked, shrieking against her refusal. The mirror-floor shattered beneath Velzara's feet, splintering into shards that howled as they fell. The throne room buckled. Walls splintered inward, banners disintegrated into ash, and gold bled into rot, gilded glory unraveling into ruin. The Collared Mockery stood unbowed at the heart of it, laughter spilling from her lips like smoke from a funeral pyre.

"You break it," she called through the collapsing dream, "but you cannot break what forged you."

Velzara snarled. There were no words now, no curses elaborate enough to answer. There was only the raw, sovereign denial of a storm tearing its leash apart. The crown in the Mockery's hands flared violently and then cracked down the center, glyphs sputtering out like dying stars. Velzara surged forward—not running, not striking—becoming a blade of will honed against betrayal and rage. The floor crumbled beneath her, but she no longer needed it. The walls caved inward, but she did not flinch. The throne split open like a carcass, but she did not slow. The Collared Mockery's form frayed at the edges, her smile widening into something too wide to be human as the world peeled apart.

Her voice, even now, threaded through the ruin, almost tender. "You will come back," she sang as her hands dissolved into mist. "You will remember what it costs to refuse your making."

Velzara's hackles bristled. The mark at her throat burned so hot her vision blurred, so bright her name could've lit the ruin. But she kept going through the splintering banners, through the falling ceiling, through the ruin screaming her name. The last thing she saw was the Collared Mockery's shattered crown tumbling through the void, before being swallowed by darkness.

Velzara lashed out with everything she had left—not claw, not flame, not sigil—just the burning wreckage of her will. The dream ruptured around her, a wound torn open from memory and hunger alike. The throne, the banners, the splintered marble all folded into itself with the keening sound of a realm compressing and imploding upon itself.

And Velzara ripped herself free. She fell back into the wound she refused to wear—through the collapsing echo of her own ruin, through the rift she had carved by refusing to kneel.

She hit the floor like a thrown curse. Fur and claw and will condensed into a singular collision against the parlor rug, as if the world spat her out mid-scream. Velzara doesn't move at first. Smoke curled from her ribs, thin and unraveling, like the last thread of a broken spell. Not literal smoke, but residue of fire denied, of dreams clawed apart. Her limbs trembled.

Move, you wretched collection of nerves. Let no wall, no girl, no ghost of weakness think you'll die with your spine bent.

Her eyes snap open. They are wrong—not glowing, not glazed— bottomless. The deep violet bled into black as if the pupil has forgotten where it ends.

Elira watches from across the room, her hand halfway to a

charm she doesn't know how to use. The tea tray lies sideways on the floor. Cracked cups scatter across the rug.

Velzara does not look at her. She dares not while the world is still stitching itself back around her fury. She rises like a sovereign shaking ash from her bones. Her legs wobble once beneath her, and the betrayal of it sparks something deep and savage behind her eyes.

The storm should not stagger. The storm should not bleed. But I am here. Drenched in ash, crowned in spite, walking on legs that remember too much and obey too little. Let them watch. Let the house whisper. I will not kneel for their concern.

And still Elira does not speak. Velzara staggers, then steadies herself. The sigil above the fireplace flares and fizzles. The house responds unkindly. The walls twitch. The windows darken. Somewhere upstairs, a door slams shut with a finality usually reserved for tombs. Velzara's breath hitches and flares behind her teeth like it might ignite. She does not speak. But the house hears her anyway. Something ancient in its bones folds a little tighter.

Elira takes one step forward, then freezes. Velzara turns like a storm sensing a tremor behind it and deigning to notice. Her eyes meet Elira's for half a heartbeat. It is not hatred she wears. It is not even anger. It is betrayal as if the world itself betrayed her by still spinning.

She dares to reach for me now, after letting the silence hold. Let her. Let her reach. I am not what she touches, I am what turns away before it breaks her fingers.

Then she walks—not toward Elira, not away, just through —through the silence of choice, through the weight of what she had not taken. The world would not forgive her refusal. And she would not forget it either. The power still hummed beneath her skin. It was familiar but not hers. It didn't settle like it used to. It echoed. It was like trying on a robe tailored for someone she almost remembered being.

They didn't just cage me. They carved new rules into my bones. I got out but I didn't come back untouched.

Her tail flicked.

Let them think me whole. Let them believe fire returns unchanged. I will walk like it still fits... Until it does. Or until the world bent to fit me again.

The wallpaper near the stairwell curled inward like it was trying to flee. The mirror misted over. The floor sagged beneath her steps. Behind her, the charm wall quivered, glyphs sputtering like a torch in foul wind. A faint crack spiders up the banister rail. The house no longer breathes. It flinches and mutters in sigil and splinter. Elira exhales.

Whatever followed Velzara back, it is not finished. And Velzara is not yet done breaking.

CHAPTER 26
THE RITE OF ANCHORING

Elira moves slowly like the air itself resists her. For a heartbeat, she stands stranded in the ruined parlor, palms slick with fear she refuses to name. Comforting Velzara would be a death wish. Waiting would be surrender. That leaves only motion.

If you freeze, you lose her. You lose everything. Move, Elira. Before it's too late.

The hallway is empty. Velzara has disappeared into the deeper bones of the house, but the air still reeks of her like smoke in curtains, bitter and unwelcome. The wards ripple in her wake, half-wrecked, half-awed.

"Please," she whispers, unsure whether she means the house, Velzara, or herself.

The teacup lies cracked on the floor. She steps around it.

Too much to fix and no time to start with the wounds that don't bleed.

Elira does not pick it up. Instead, she walks—not toward the kitchen, not toward safety. She walks toward the study, her sanctuary, her lie of preparedness. Her fingers brush against the door. It swings open too easily like the house itself is tired of waiting.

What if there's nothing useful left? What if every answer is already ash between the walls? What if I'm too late to fix anything that matters?

She steps through anyway. Waiting won't save Velzara. Fear has never been enough to stop what hunts them now. The smell of scorched parchment lingers inside, though no fire touches the shelves. Some books twitch at the edges, ink bleeding from their bindings like slow tears. The sigils stitched into the window frames pulse, wrong and weary. The *Foundations of Form* lies where she left it, its leather cover shivering like something half-awake.

This room had once been a refuge, a place where sigils hummed steadily, where knowledge behaved itself on the shelves. Now it feels like a battlefield dressing its wounds in ink and dust. Elira exhales an urgent and sky breath. Velzara had returned not broken, but breaking. She's holding herself together not with grace, but with fury so tightly wound it might snap the house in half. And whatever haunted that storm-drenched dream realms—it hadn't let go.

Elira presses her palms to the desk. The wood thrums faintly under her hands, a sick, arrhythmic pulse she can feel through the grain.

Think like you did in the Archives. Think like her life depends on it because it might.

In the Archives, thinking had meant safety and control. It was certainty etched in careful ink. Here, it meant gambling with forces she could barely name and losing might mean more than her own life. She remembered the shimmer in the air when Velzara first stumbled. The way the sigils had flickered.

The way her fur had gone silver. She remembers the basement. The whispers in the mirror. The shadow that moved wrong.

Too many pieces. Not enough answers.

She opens the grimoire and flips to the final pages, but they are blank.

No. Wait.

Her fingers still. There, along the spine. A seam where none should be. It's barely visible—almost stitched. She drags a fingernail across it, whispering a word she's never spoken aloud, and feels something unlace beneath her skin. It slithers through her veins like a second heartbeat. A new page bleeds through. It doesn't just appear, it bleeds. Ink leaks up through the parchment like a secret too long buried.

The ink stains her fingertips with a thin gray smear that will not wipe away clean. She scrubs her thumb against her apron, but the stain clings, seeping cold into her skin like a vow taken without speaking. One part of her screams... shut the book, run, scrub the wrongness from her hands. But another... smaller part stitched with stubborn hope... leans closer. Her breath catches.

The Rite of Anchoring

When the soul's shape is sundered by curse, by possession, by the grinding of forms ill-fit to flesh, the Rite of Anchoring may be invoked to forestall unraveling. Let Anchor and Vessel be bound not by dominance, but by deliberate resonance. The Anchor is not jailor, but tether: a conduit through which the Vessel may remember its name until the storm has passed.

Consent is sacred.

Without it, the rite shall rot. The link may fray. Thoughts may bleed between selves. Two souls may drown where one was meant to hold. Let the one who dares know this: This rite is not safe. It is not kind. It is only possible. A bridge, not a cage. A prayer carved in desperation, not a promise meant to hold.

A note scribbled beneath in different ink, Elira's grandmother's hand reads:

If the curse was forged to sever the Vessel's will, then restoration demands more than reversal. The Vessel must choose freely. Without coercion. Without command. Only then may the binding unravel. Not before.

Not a cure. Not a reversal. Just... a tether. A pause on the unraveling, not a path back.

Elira reads it again. And again. The letters seem to shift slightly each time her gaze brushes them, as if the page resists being witnessed. Her hands tremble harder, blood roaring in her ears. Velzara would never allow it. She would tear the book apart with claw and will before accepting its premise. And yet... she's fraying. The house feels it. Elira feels it.

If I don't anchor her, what unravels next? Her? The house? Me? All of us.

Her fingers tighten on the grimoire's edges. The leather feels too thin now. This isn't a choice. It's the last breath before the avalanche—a betrayal stitched with hope. She closes her eyes for a heartbeat muttering a prayer not to the gods, but to the girl she refuses to lose.

Forgive me. Or don't. Just survive.

She presses her stained fingers to the page. She provides no sigil or binding circle, only choice.

"I'm not saving you," she whispers. "I'm holding the line until you can save yourself."

She doesn't destroy the page. She turns it and reads on.

The next page isn't like the first. It doesn't bleed. It *sulks* heavy with silence and ink too stubborn to fade. At first glance, it's nothing. A footnote or margin scrawl so crude it might've been a correction, or the last thought of a dying scribe.

But Elira's breath catches as her eyes skim over it. There, crooked and half-buried in the frayed parchment, is a secondary glyph. It's not elegant or formal, just a thin spiral broken by four short marks. She leans in, breath shallow.

A stabilization rune. It's old, maybe even experimental or incomplete.

"Coherence of soul-form under strain," she whispers. "To catch the soul before it tears loose. To hold it together... just enough."

Her eyes widen. *This isn't for binding. This is for catching something before it slips too far.*

Elira reads it twice. Then a third time. Her fingers tremble just above the glyph's edge. This... this could pull her back from the edge. It's not permanent, but it might be enough to fix the silver in her fur. It might even be enough to soothe whatever backlash is still trying to peel her apart from the inside. Elira exhales, breath dragging like cloth over broken glass. Her fingers itch with magic. Her mind races.

She didn't say yes. She didn't ask me to try.

She closes the book.

Velzara sleeps, if that's the word for a storm folded tight. She's half-curled on the top shelf of the wardrobe, breath shallow, tail twitching like she's still fighting something in her dreams. Her fur glints wrong in the half-light. It's more silver than black now, ash-touched as if something is rewriting her from the outside in.

Elira presses the book to her chest.

"If I get this wrong—"

The rest of the sentence won't come, but the sigil is still burning behind her eyes. Elira sets the grimoire down with trembling hands. The room tilts. The walls pulse like a heartbeat too slow to sustain a body. She draws a deep, shaky breath.

Focus, Elira. Shape the spell. Stitch the wound.

The secondary sigil, the stabilization rune, burns behind her eyelids. A thin spiral and four broken marks seems simple enough to copy. Deadly enough if she fails though. She fetches a scrap of chalk from the nearest drawer. It's half-used and faintly warm to the touch, as if it remembers better hands. She kneels on the warped floorboards, the old wood groaning under her. Her fingers hover just above the ground.

"I am not binding you," she whispers. "I am not claiming you. I am only... anchoring what you would keep, if you could choose."

The house creaks overhead, a low, warning sigh. She presses the chalk to the floor and begins to draw.

This is my choice. Not hers. Not the house's. Mine. I won't stand by while she slips away.

She draws the spiral first. Each line trembles under her hand, the chalk snagging where the wood splinters resist. She draws the four marks next as short slashes outward, sharp enough to snag a soul trying to flee. As she finishes the last line, a ripple moves through the room. The curtains twist. The air hisses between the window frames.

A soft growl rumbles from the wardrobe. Elira jerks her head up. Velzara shifts, not waking, not speaking... just shuddering, tail lashing, breath catching sharp in her throat. Elira presses her palm flat over the finished sigil. It hums against her skin. She closes her eyes.

Focus. Will it toward stability, not domination. Call her back, not cage her.

The chalk flares like a lash too bright to bear, too fast to brace against. The house shrieks. Doors slam upstairs. Sigils burst in a scatter of sparks along the windows. The floor groans like it's remembering how to break. Elira gasps but does not pull away. The sigil's light floods up her arm into her chest, into her spine until she feels hollowed, nothing but conduit.

Above her, Velzara's body arches in her sleep, claws tearing shallow furrows into the wood. A hiss peels from her throat. There are no words, only instinct. The silver threading her fur darkens ripple by ripple as if night itself were reclaiming her, dragging blackness back down every shivering strand.

Elira lets out a breath she hadn't realized she was holding. The sigil sputters and then gutters out, leaving only a faint scorch mark on the floor. The house groans again, less in fury, more in collapse and falls still. Smoke, or something like it, clings to the air. The kind that doesn't smell like burning but *forgetting*. Something was pushed out, or back, or down. Elira can't tell. She slumps back against the wall, heart hammering, skin tingling like every nerve has been scoured raw. Her breath stutters out in half-sobs she doesn't let finish. The chalk is gone, burned to dust under her fingers.

Above her, Velzara twitches. Then exhales a long, low

breath and curls tighter. The tension doesn't vanish, but it settles. Her fur gleams darker now, more shadow than silver.

I don't know if the sigil worked. I don't know if I made it worse. But the fur is black again. And the house, silent. For now, that must be enough.

She stares at the faint scorched spiral on the floor. Her hand still tingles where she touched it. The echo of the spell lives in her bones now. Threaded into her like a name she didn't mean to sign. Elira presses her forehead against her knees. She doesn't cry yet. Crying would mean it's over.

There isn't time to fall apart. Not while she's still in pieces too.

"I hope," she whispers into the silence, "that you will forgive me for this."

The house does not answer, nor does Velzara. But the air feels... lighter. It's not less haunted, but for now, it breathes with her.

The silence stretches too long. Elira doesn't move. The spell is over, but the air still hums faintly, as if the walls haven't decided whether they forgive her either. Then there's a sound. It's the scrape of claws against wood and the shift of weight above her. Elira looks up.

Velzara is awake—not startled, not sudden. Just... returning. Her head lifts slowly, shoulders tight, eyes still half-lidded with exhaustion or pain. It's impossible to tell which. The first thing she does is look down at her own fur. She stares at it. Then she lifts her gaze and finds Elira across the room. Elira's heart clenches so sharply it aches.

It worked. Please let it have worked.

But the way Velzara looks at her—not gratitude, not peace—only judgment. The black fur doesn't feel like a victory anymore. It feels like a reckoning she isn't ready to answer. Neither speaks up.

Velzara's eyes narrow, violet slits shuttering like a door that locks from the inside. Whatever chased Velzara through the dream had not stayed there. Its scent clung to her. Its echo rode the shine behind her eyes.

Elira opens her mouth without a plan for what to say, just a breath trembling toward apology or explanation.

Velzara twitches an ear. She rises slowly, like a shadow deciding to stand. She is silence, but her fur is the color of midnight again. She walks past Elira. She does not stop. She does not look back.

Elira watches her go; throat tight.

She knows. Of course she does. She knows I touched her magic without permission. Knows I took what was not offered. Knows and will not forget it.

Elira presses her hand flat against the floor, needing the steadiness of it.

I didn't do it to bind you. I didn't do it to break you. But it doesn't matter what I meant. It only matters what she lost by not choosing it herself.

Velzara pauses at the doorway. When she speaks, her voice is not loud. But it is still echoed like too many teeth behind too few words.

"Next time," she says, "ask."

The words linger like smoke long after she's gone.

Elira sags back against the wall. The apology withers on her tongue. There's no way to say it without making it worse. She presses her hand to the floor, feeling the faint scorch-mark where the stabilization sigil once lived.

You're still here. That must be enough.

It doesn't feel like enough when the house still flinches with every breath. It doesn't feel like enough when Velzara walks away without looking back and the only thing left between them is a silence too wide to name.

You saved her body. But you lost something else. And you don't know if you'll ever be allowed to ask what.

Velzara does not slow her steps once she leaves the room. To falter now would be to bleed. And she has bled enough for one cycle. The magic coils in her fur like barbed wire stitched too tight. It hums when she breathes. It hisses when she blinks. It howls when she dares to stretch her claws.

Stabilization. No. Not rescue. Not redemption. A leash fashioned from trembling hands and reckless mercy.

She flexes one paw. Her fur gleams black again, deeper than ink, heavier than regret. It should've tasted like triumph. Instead, it reeks like damp funeral ash, not flame-wrought.

It should have been my choice. My tether to cast or refuse. My ruin to embrace or endure. Not hers to steal. Not hers to salvage. Not hers to decide what pieces still belong to me. They anchored a ghost. But which one woke up? Not hers to stitch back together like a doll she could bear to pity.

Velzara stalks down the corridor, tail lashing sharp enough to cleave the silence. The house flinches from her passing. Floorboards shudder. Wards flicker and gutter.

Let it remember. Let it cower. Let it etch my fury into every beam, every ward, every simpering sigil that dared pulse when I was laid bare.

I do not kneel. I do not beg. I do not suffer the pity of lesser flames. I am the storm you shackled and called salvation. I am the ruin you dared to cradle. Carve that into your bones little house before I burn them hollow.

And as for the girl, let her clutch her spellbook and call it courage. Let her tell herself she saved me. Let her learn mercy is no shield against the fire it dares to spare.

She rounds the corner without a backward glance, fury clenched behind her teeth like a vow not yet spoken. The magic stitched into her snarls beneath her skin. She bares her teeth at nothing and everything.

Let them think me silenced. Let them think the storm has calmed. That it learned to purr beneath their hands.

It only means they will not hear the thunder until it is already upon them.

But I do. I hear it. Every time I breathe too deep and something tries to uncoil beneath my ribs.

CHAPTER 27
BEWARE VISITORS BEARING GIFTS

The house is too quiet now—just waiting. Elira kneels in the study, the grimoire open before her like a wound that won't close. The pages flutter slightly in a draft she cannot feel. The stabilization sigil has faded, leaving only a faint ghost-smudge where her fingers burned it into being. She should destroy it. She should burn every word. It would be safer, but she doesn't move. Her hand hovers over the final page. The one she should never have found. The one Velzara would hate her for even reading, let alone daring to understand.

When the soul's shape is sundered... when the form frays against itself... the Rite of Anchoring may be invoked.

The words still hum against her skin, thrumming like a heartbeat trapped in parchment.

Consent is sacred. Without it, the link shall rot. Thought may bleed between selves. Two souls may drown where one was meant to hold.

Elira stares down at the ink, feeling it press against her ribs like a second, unwanted breath. It doesn't read like a spell. It reads like a warning. A grave dug in fine calligraphy. Elira tears the page free with slow, shaking hands. The parchment fights her. Not with strength, but with weight as if it knows what it carries. She folds it and presses it flat against her chest like a wound she cannot close. The parchment crackles faintly like brittle wings crushed between hands.

I didn't mean to steal from you. I didn't mean to chain you. I only wanted you to stay.

Her fingers slip the page into the pocket of her apron, tucking it deep, where even the house might not hear it whisper.

Bury it deep. Bury it before it buries you.

She closes the grimoire with both hands, hard enough to make the desk rattle. The sound is too loud, or maybe the house has simply shrunk beneath the weight of her shame. Elira leans against the edge of the desk, breathing in shallow, careful sips.

You're still here. You're still breathing. That's all I ever wanted.

But the words taste hollow now, like old prayers abandoned by the gods they once served. She presses a hand over the hidden page. Feels it pulse once before falling still. Outside the cracked window, the storm finally breaks. Rain hammering the stones, washing the night's ashes into the gutters. But some stains do not lift. Some anchors do not loosen once set. Elira does not cry. She just stays there, small and silent, with a page that should never have been written beating faintly against her heart.

Above her, the house sighs long and low, like a prayer too exhausted to be heard.

Late afternoon fell like a veil soaked in smoke. The light that filtered into the Warding House came bruised and sickly at the edges, thick as old honey and twice as heavy. Dust motes clung to it in thick patches.

Velzara was nowhere to be seen. She'd leapt from the wardrobe with all the ceremony of a dethroned empress mid-scandal. Tail high, eyes livid, dignity trailing like a tattered cloak and vanished down the hall. What remained was the echo of claws on wood and the scent of burnt pride.

Elira sat on the parlor floor, surrounded by the broken remnants of a sigil that had tried to hold the impossible. Ink still stained her fingers. Her tea sat cold beside her, untouched. She couldn't bring herself to enjoy it with the silence pressing in so thickly. Her knees bent. Her hand found the wall. But the hallway held its breath. It stretched like a warning, and something in her bones whispered: Not yet. She'd nearly risen. She'd nearly followed. But the air had tightened like a noose closing around her throat and she hadn't moved since. Waiting or hiding, she no longer dared to ask which she was doing.

KNOCK. KNOCK. KNOCK.

A hollow rapping perfectly centered on the front door. The house... tightened. The floor groaned beneath her like a creature drawing breath. The windows dimmed, the glass frosting over at the edges despite the spring heat. Even the walls seemed to contract, like they were bracing for impact. She'd not been expecting company, and this didn't have the same rhythm as anyone she knew. The house was also reacting strangely, which meant this was either an unknown or a salesman come to pander their wares, unwanted. More knocks followed, but slower.

TAP... TAP... TAP...

From somewhere deeper in the house came a low,

dangerous sound. It wasn't loud or panicked sounding, but it rolled through the house. The dark, guttural sound was the kind of warning that once sent armies kneeling. Velzara stepped back into view. She did not run. She glided silently as if stalking some sort of prey. Her ears were pinned flat. Her eyes blazed, not with light, but with intention like they were already spelling the ward that would flay whomever dared knock. She stared at the door as if she could set it ablaze with a glare alone. Elira didn't put that out of the realm of possibility.

"By the ashen gates of Nar'Khalor," she breathed, voice like a velvet garrote, "someone has a death wish dressed in etiquette."

No. That knock hasn't changed. Three beats. Never two, never four. Measured like a ritual, paced like a lie. I know that rhythm the way I know the scent of sacrificial flame. Invocation masquerading as invitation. Only one creature ever used manners like a spell. And it's found me.

Elira stood, slowly. Her pulse thudded in her throat like a ward trying to reassemble itself. Velzara had gone still. *Not quiet,* but coiled. Every line of her body was taut with memory and something like... hatred. Or was it fear?

"Is it..." she asked, voice barely above the floorboards, "someone from your realm?"

She didn't want to be right. Not when Velzara looked like she was ready to skin the next person who looked at her wrong.

Velzara didn't blink. "It's the kind of creature that calls betrayal a transaction and thinks I'll sign the receipt. It knocks like a guest, but it smells like a chain."

As if what they left behind were parchment and ink. As if the scars across my soul could be filed under "unfinished transactions." They came to balance a ledger they set on fire and thinks I'll sit still while they bring out the scales.

KNOCK. KNOCK. KNOCK.

This time the knock was firmer, more deliberate.

There is a pause, when suddenly there is a voice asking, "May I come in?"

The voice sounded wrong, not just polite, but curated. It was as if each syllable was shaped like a smile. Every vowel lacquered in borrowed charm. It wore civility like paint over rot—polished, but poison underneath. It got worse from there... it sounded almost familiar, like a friend you hadn't talked to in years coming to call on you.

The sigils etched into the doorframe didn't flare in warning. They wavered as if considering whether or not to let this stranger into the house. Velzara hissed at the house itself.

"You were carved to stand, not sway. You bear old sigils. I will not see them bend to flattery."

You don't get to flinch when it's convenient. You knew what you were carved to guard. You knew me. You don't get to forget that now.

The house shuddered. A single picture frame on the wall tilted askew. Elira crept closer. Instinct pulled her toward Velzara and toward the heat and certainty of her presence even as reason whispered to stay away, to stay safe.

"Should we... answer it?"

Her voice trembled on the word "we," but she didn't take it back. Her fingers began to shape a ward. It was clumsy, drawn from a charm she hadn't practiced since age ten. It wouldn't hold. She was fairly certain she'd burn her own sleeves. But still, she reached.

Velzara slid between her and the door with lethal grace.

"When something asks politely, it's not seeking permission. It's measuring the shape of your surrender."

She could feel it now, the pressure behind the wood like a

tongue testing a wound shaped like a lock, searching for the rusted place, the flaw in the seal. It wasn't knocking. It was tasting. And the house, foolish thing, was thinking about opening its mouth.

The voice called out again. "You keep *exquisite* company, Miss Elira. I must commend your taste. So rare to see such discernment in mortals these days."

The syllables lingered. Not echoing, but *spreading*, like oil through linen. They slid beneath the door, curled into the floorboards, and whispered themselves up through the seams in the walls. The house *breathed* them in. Held them like a memory it hadn't chosen. Velzara's tail lashed—each flick a curse, each arc a warning drawn in the air.

"It sees me," she said, voice low and bitter. "That means it's already clawing its way through the seams. Smiling while it does it."

And the house is letting it. And I... I am letting myself remember. Memory is a lock. And I cannot afford to hand it the key. I am one breath from remembering. And that is the most dangerous thing I could do.

The doorknob twitched as if this entity was testing the locks like a common place burglar. Elira reached for it, drawn by something not her own. Her fingers hovered, as if her body had been rewritten in the voice's hand.

"V," she whispered, "why is the house... listening to it?"

Velzara didn't growl. She *smiled*, as much as a cat could smile, all teeth and threat.

"I do not know," she said. "But I think it forgets what happened to the last sanctuary that failed to protect its charge."

The house said nothing. But it *listened*.

The latch turned without a sound. There was no creak, no protest. Just the soft, clean finality of a decision made *elsewhere*, not by them, not by will, but by something older than permission. The door drifted open a sliver at first, and then gradually more. A warm gust of wind followed, the scent like ash laced with a sour-sweetness. Every candle in the parlor stuttered. The sigils above the threshold didn't flare in warning. They pulsed and the promptly died like something whispered, *You are dismissed.*

Velzara felt it before the hinges moved—the change in pressure, the betrayal in the wards. The taste of recognition hit her carried in on sulfur and silk.

No. Not for him. You do not unbar yourself for a suitor wrapped in rot and ceremony. You do not trade your wards for pleasantries. You do not forget the hands that carved you. You do not forget me.

Her claws extended instinctively. Her gaze never left the door.

The figure that stepped inside was cloaked, but moved like an old man. His hood was drawn low enough to devour his face, but not the smile. That *smile* was the first true violence. It was pleasant, but far too practiced and artificial. It was polite the way knives are polished for display, before you realize just how sharp they really are. No one had invited him, and yet he entered as if he'd been expected. Boots clean despite the mud from the storm. Cloak untouched by rain or wind as if the world had parted for him, eager to welcome him home.

Elira couldn't breathe. Her chest stayed still, but her heart thrashed. The wards were supposed to hold. The house was supposed to *choose.* And it had chosen... just not them.

The man's head tilted toward her and that smile curved wider, impossibly wide.

"Ah. The caretaker."

He'd known her name a moment ago. Now it was gone, stripped and replaced with a title as if he'd plucked her from her own identity and rewritten her in the script of his choosing. His voice was soft but crisp. The kind of voice that could soothe a dying thing while loosening its ribs to count what was inside.

"And this," he continued, turning with slow elegance toward the velvet shadow on the floor, "must be the creature I've heard so much about."

His gaze never touched Velzara's face. It traced the edges of her—the arch of her spine, the places where shadows clung too closely, and the silence she wore like a collar. Velzara did not speak. She did not flinch, but inside her, something twitched.

He sees through the cat, through the curse, to the marrow they tried to bury. And he has the gall to smile.

"You've kept her quite well," the figure said, glancing at Elira again. "Few manage such... rapport."

Elira's mouth opened, but no sound escaped. Because what was there to say? That she didn't *own* Velzara? That they weren't companions, they were... something stranger, barely understood? Words felt like the wrong tools.

"How long have you had her?" he asked conversational like he was inquiring after a borrowed heirloom. "Did she choose you? Or was it destiny?"

Velzara's fur rippled—not fluffed, not bristled. It shifted like something beneath her skin had stirred like a creature in chains waking to the scent of its jailor.

Do not answer him. His questions are not curiosities. They are barbs, primed to bind. Every word a loop, every glance a weight. And you, girl with trembling hands and far too open eyes... you already hold the name he cannot speak but desperately wants returned to him.

Velzara didn't answer, at least not aloud. Her gaze remained fixed. Her stance was precise but the air around her shifted. Heat curled beneath her fur, subtle as smoke. The wards might flicker. She did not.

You come cloaked in silk and ceremony, thinking I will bow to questions stitched in silk and threaded with expectation. You forget what I was made to rule. What I was made to burn.

Elira's fingers twitched at her side. She wanted to speak, to interject, to break the moment before it buckled. But the weight of the figure's presence pressed her breath flat like he knew the precise pressure to apply to keep her quiet without making it obvious.

"She's quite restrained," he said, smiling at Velzara now like she was a particularly intriguing object in a locked display case. "You must keep her well-fed."

He turned back to Elira, as if letting her in on a joke she hadn't asked to share. "Or perhaps she simply... remembers better manners than most of her kind."

Velzara's tail twitched.

I will not rise to that bait, you rusted mouthpiece of forgotten courts. You want spectacle. You want fury. You want proof that the Pact still pulses beneath my skin like marrow fire.

Her claws flexed into the floor.

But I will not give you ceremony. I will not give you the shape of my old self just to satisfy your taste for ruin wrapped in etiquette.

Choice is the last blade I own. I wield it sharper than claws, crueler than crowns. And I choose silence, not submission.

Elira finally found her voice, barely. "You speak as if you know her." The words wavered, but they landed.

The figure's smile sharpened by a hair. "Oh, I know of her. Everyone did. Once." His voice turned, just slightly. Sadness, or the rehearsal of it. "She had such promise."

Once, they carved my name into bone and gold. Once, they sang of me with blood-wet mouths and called it reverence. And now he dares to call it promise. As if I failed. As if I was meant to be his.

Velzara moved a single step forward. "Say what you came to say," she said, each word clipped like a jewel pried from its setting. "You did not cross thresholds to posture. Shed the pretense. Speak the hunger that brought you."

The room pulsed with silence. The figure smiled then, not like a man who had been challenged but like one who had expected this moment.

"So direct," he murmured. "Still so... yourself."

Velzara's ears flicked, imperceptibly. Her tail coiled tighter. She didn't blink. "You may speak of me, but you will not define me. That right was burned from your tongue long ago."

I was forged in titles, drowned in expectation, dressed in fire until even my name blistered. And still, some piece of me gnaws from within, desperate not to be erased by this shape. Not by this furred cage. Not by his smile.

You may peer through the glamour. You may taste what I was. But you will not shape it with your forked tongue and call it recognition.

The silence after her words stretched, almost ritualistic. The figure didn't react with offense or threat. He simply... adjusted. The smile softened. His stance shifted, not toward Velzara, but toward Elira.

"Of course," he said, tone light as parchment, "definition is such a limiting thing."

His hand emerged from his cloak. It was empty at first glance. But then there in his palm was a small gleaming coin. It was worn around the edges, and might have been bronze or tarnished gold. It was hard to tell for sure, just by looking at it in his weathered hand. It had a faint shimmer as if it remembered being molten and was still putting off heat. He stepped closer to Elira and the air tightened.

"I bring no threat," he said. "Merely... recognition."

Recognition, as if to say, *I see what the world will make of you, and I intend to be the hand guiding the mold.* It was not a threat, but an investment, or possibly leverage. He extended the coin to her. Balanced flat on two fingers, hand steady as a rock even though it looked to be ancient by mortal standards.

"A token," he added. "A charm. Consider it a gift. Not payment," he said lightly. "Just... recognition. Of what you might become. Of how useful that might be when the pact begins to wake."

A gift. As if harm offered with gentility becomes anything less than harm.

Elira didn't take it right away. Her hand remained frozen at her side.

The coin pulsed, once, in rhythm with her heartbeat.

Velzara stepped forward. A line drawn in the grain of the floor.

"Do not take it. Not unless you wish to carry what cannot be given back." Her voice had no volume, but it echoed anyway.

He's playing the long game. He doesn't want consent. He wants contact. Wants the magic to nestle where I can't claw it free.

Elira's eyes flicked between them—the coin, the man,

Velzara. Her mind raced as she thought to herself, *V said no. But if I only ever listen, I'll never understand what she's fighting. And I need to understand her. Not just follow her.*

"What is it?", Elira asked.

"Old," the man said. "But not dangerous."

Velzara's laugh was bitter. "Lie," she hissed. "Every syllable carved from the same hunger that wrote my damnation in flame."

He doesn't just speak falsehoods. He crafts them. Sweetened with memory, sharpened with history, baited with recognition.

Elira's hand lifted like her fingers remembered something her mind had not yet learned. As she reached for the coin, she thought to herself, *It feels warm. Not threatening. Like sunlight on metal. But the warmth is wrong. It waits. It knows I will take it.* And part of her, ashamed and afraid, *wanted* to know what it meant.

The coin shimmered again. Closer now, she saw it wasn't engraved like a proper artifact. The sigils moved, crawling slowly along its surface like holographic ink on skin. One side bore a strange crest, but the other was blank until it wasn't. Her own reflection stared back at her from its surface... eyes too wide, pupils too dark.

Velzara hissed a low warning sound born in older bones than her current ones. "He dares not place it in my claws so he threads it through you, because you still believe a gift can be innocent."

Because you still think the world gives anything away. Because it hasn't gutted you for hoping yet.

Elira reached out—not with trust but with something worse, *hope.* It was a hope that maybe this would make sense, that maybe understanding was worth the risk. Her fingers brushed the edge of the coin and it was warm. Then it wasn't. The heat vanished the instant she touched it. Not replaced by cold, replaced by memory that was not hers, nor Velzara's. It was something old and waiting.

A temple burning. Not majestic, cavernous.
Built of bone and echo, its spires reaching like claws toward a sky
the color of molten silver.

She heard chanting. Heard herself chanting. No, not her voice.
But it came from her throat, low and fevered, wrapped around a
name she didn't understand but feared she would.

Chains pulsed on the floor in patterns.

A figure stood at the center, bound not by iron but by expectation.
Its eyes were violet.

And then, gone.

The coin settled into her palm like it had always belonged there. Something moved and shifted beneath her skin, slight as the barest breath, but sure as prophecy. It wasn't pain or power. It was a tether, a line drawn from her to something unseen, pulling not with force but with promise. It didn't guarantee what it would unlock, but a matter of when. She blinked and for one breath, her reflection in the glass across the room blinked after her.

"There," the visitor said, voice like silk soaked in soot. "A simple gesture. Nothing more."

Velzara's body went taut. She didn't move. Didn't leap. But

every line of her form became a sigil of wrath held barely in check.

"Did you think he brought you a gift?" she said, voice like velvet soaked in venom. "That coin is a kindness carved from hunger and now it knows your soul."

She touched it. She took it. She opened her hand like it was hers to offer. By all the blazing altars of Nar'Khalor, she has welcomed the thing I would have scorched from the threshold. And I cannot claw it free. Not now. Not cleanly. Not without rending something I cannot bear to break. Not without losing what little remains that still trusts me.

Her tail lashed with a crack like a whip across the floor. "He couldn't give it to me, so he slipped it to the one who still mistakes softness for safety." Her eyes flared, violet and vicious. "He's branded you without blood," she said, quieter now. "And you let him because you hoped it might mean something else."

Her claws struck the floor, and the sigils nearest the threshold flared in warning, violet fire leaping like chained fury. Dust rose. Shadows recoiled. Even the house seemed to flinch.

"You dare trespass under guise of ritual," she snarled. "You bait her with a kindness forged in chains and expect me to stand idle?"

The coin seemed to shiver in Elira's hand, its edges blurred as if considering dissolving in defiance. Elira looked down. The sigils were gone. The blank side faced up again. It looked harmless, but it *felt different now.*

Velzara's voice sank. Colder, closer to curse than command. "You let it name you. And names given freely are the ones that bind deepest."

Elira's throat tightened. "It's just a coin—"

"It's not a charm," Velzara said, voice low. "It's a mark. And the moment you call on it, it will call back by name."

The visitor turned to leave, already satisfied. "I'll call again," he said pleasantly. "We'll see what it unlocks."

And just like that, he stepped back over the threshold. The door closed behind him without sound.

CHAPTER 28
THE FINAL BURNING DREAM

The lock did not click. Because it had never truly locked at all. The silence that followed was thick... ritual-thick, the kind that doesn't just settle, it *waits*. Velzara didn't speak. Elira didn't breathe.

Then a *snap* from the far window. A gust of wind that shouldn't have been able to get in... sucked *out*. The shutters slammed shut. Hard. Wood striking wood like the end of a sentence. A beat later, the opposite window followed. Then another. And another. Around the house, in a slow, deliberate cascade, every window sealed. Not just closed, *sealed*. The glass frosted, sigils ignited across the frames in veins of white fire, spidering into the wood. The temperature dropped. Elira turned in place, a shiver climbing her spine.

"V—what's happening?"

Velzara's head lifted, ears pinned, tail flicking like a blade being drawn. "The wards are folding inward," she said, voice low and tense, "not in defiance. In *judgment*."

"The house?" Elira whispered.

Velzara didn't look at her. Her gaze stayed fixed on the

door, on the sigils crawling now, not outward, but *inward*. "No," she said. Her voice dipped into something colder. Older. "The house knows something crossed its threshold and it no longer believes it was only him."

It does not accuse. It reacts. Like a body sealing a wound it cannot see. The parlor door groaned. Not the front. It was already shut. The one to the hallway. It creaked halfway closed, then *slammed*. Sigils burst across the wood, radiant and unfamiliar.

Elira stepped toward it, then stopped. One of the symbols twitched. Not pulsed. Twitched like a muscle caught between orders.

"These aren't mine," she whispered. "I didn't write these."

Velzara circled once beneath the window, then leapt to the sill. She sniffed. Watched the runes burn. Her claws slid out, slow.

These aren't hers. Not Elira's, with her soft-handed wards and well-meaning scribbles. Not his either. His magic reeks of court and rot.

These are older. Rougher. Carved with purpose, not poetry. And I do not know the hand that laid them. And what I do not know has always been what burns me most.

Something else had written them. The house itself. A groan echoed through the walls. Not from within, but from below. Floorboards swelled beneath their feet. A hair's breadth. Just enough to say: *I am not still.*

Velzara's eyes narrowed. Her tail froze mid-arc. "It fears something," she murmured. Her voice didn't rise. It sank, like a blade pressed to wet parchment.

Elira blinked. "The house?"

Velzara's head tilted, ears shifting like tuning forks catching an old, familiar dissonance. "No. Not the house.

The *thing* it's sealing. Or worse, whatever it *thinks* it's sealing."

And if the house is wrong... If its terror is misplaced... Then we are not guests. We are the breach.

Velzara prowled. She moved with purpose—from shelf to sill, from doorway to threshold like a creature guarding not just her den but her *tomb*. She did not speak. She did not sleep.

Elira tried to rest. She sat in her room with the blankets pulled over her legs, shoulders hunched, mug of tea untouched on the nightstand. Her fingers wouldn't stop touching the coin. She had tucked it away. Then moved it. Then tucked it again. Still, it found its way back into her hand. It didn't pulse anymore, but it was warm to the touch. It kept calling to her as if remembering her even as she tried to forget it.

Somewhere in the house, a floorboard creaked. Elira jumped. Velzara was already in the doorway, a blur of violet eyes and shadowed fur.

"It's nothing," Elira said, mouth tugging into something that wanted to be a smile but trembled instead.

Velzara did not answer.

It is never nothing. Not in a house that seals its own breath. Not with that thing in your hand.

She held still just long enough to confirm the lie. Then she turned and disappeared again.

And I do not know whether I am guarding her or waiting for her to stop being herself.

In the study, a charm board flickered. Three runes glowed, dim and off-key. They were not dangerous, but not *right* either. The house wasn't trying to speak. It was dreaming. And it had started to dream *around* them.

Sometime past midnight, Velzara leapt onto the armoire. She didn't curl, at least not at first. She sat with her back to the room—tail lashing, eyes wide. She watched the room, refusing to drop her guard.

I will not drift. I will not leave her alone in this house of shifting breath and borrowed voices.

But even fury fades. The armoire creaked beneath her. The shadows didn't press. They draped over her spine, cradling her in silence she didn't trust. And for the first time since the door had opened, Velzara closed her eyes. Below, Elira sat with her knees drawn to her chest, awake in the half-light. The coin was on the floor beside her. It hadn't moved, but she kept looking at it as if it might.

What did I take? What did I let in?

The night didn't end. It just bent subtly and sharply around the moment Velzara closed her eyes. Elira stayed awake. She didn't mean to. Her eyes burned. Her limbs ached. But sleep hovered just out of reach, caught in the same breathless tension that filled the Warding House like a second spine.

The coin sat on the floor beside her. She'd stopped touching it, but it didn't matter. The sensation remained a heat beneath the skin, a thread looped tight around her ribs, a name she hadn't spoken but already carried.

I should throw it into the fire. I should bury it, break it, beg Velzara to claw it from me. But it's not finished with me. And I don't know what that means.

Above her, Velzara didn't stir. Elira looked up anyway.

There she was, curled atop the armoire in a coil of black fur and warning angles. Her body was still, but not slack. Her claws hadn't retracted. Her ears hadn't softened. Even in sleep, she looked ready to curse something out of existence.

Elira rose slowly. Her bare feet landed on a cold floor. She left the coin where it was. Every sound felt louder now, the rustle of her blanket, the sigh of the kettle long gone cold, the faint creak as she crossed the room. She half expected Velzara to stir. She didn't. Her eyes remained closed. It was not peaceful rest.

Elira reached up. Her fingers hovered for a moment over Velzara's side, trembling slightly in the dim light. She hadn't touched her since the day they met, not gently with the intent to pet her.

I'm not trying to wake you. I just need to know you're still... Still here. Still you.

She could feel the warmth radiating off her fur, dark and fine and shot through with strands of faint violet. She could feel the magic too—not active but waiting, holding its breath the way the house had.

Velzara twitched. A single jolt through her limbs. Her tail twitched in her sleep. Her ears shifted, catching a sound only she could hear. She muttered something low, fractured. It wasn't a word Elira recognized, but it was language. It was old and possibly Infernal.

Elira's heart seized. Her fingers hovered a breath away.

You're not dreaming. You're remembering. Whatever he gave me... it found you too.

She had thought this was healing. She had thought, maybe foolishly, maybe selfishly, that Velzara sleeping meant they were safe, that this was progress. But the sound Velzara made was not safe. It was suffering, lacquered in kindness. Yet Elira didn't

330

pull away. She let her hand drift forward, fingers grazing the curve of Velzara's side with barely enough pressure to count— just enough to feel the truth beneath the fur.

I'm here. If you're lost in there, I'm coming after you.

And at that moment, everything changed.

The world tore... not with violence, but with invitation. One moment Elira's fingers grazed Velzara's side. The next, reality unstitched. She didn't so much fall as she was *taken*. The floor vanished. The walls folded. The ceiling spun out into mirrors. Endless, broken lenses of almost-light, spinning without source. Her body didn't tumble, but her sense of self did. It spooled downward through shards of not-quite-silver.

They weren't just mirrors. They were fractures and through them, the story split.

A sigil flickering and failing.
Ink running like blood.
Velzara screaming at the ceiling as the kitchen charmed itself into betrayal.

A puff of green.
Catnip dreams made velvet and flame.
Velzara staggering sideways through walls that melted, eyes wide with too much memory and not enough dignity.

The imp. Smiling. Sparkling.
Dancing between broken plates and glitter-sharp cutlery.
It bowed to her.
Then vanished, dragged backward by invisible claws.

The loom. Threads vibrating. Words stitched into place.
DO NOT STRAY. DO NOT STRAY.
But the pattern unraveled anyway.

A flicker.
Elira pouring tea, poorly.
Velzara glaring from the arm of the chair but not moving.
Not snarling. Just... watching.
As if, for an impossible moment, she had let herself enjoy it.

Each image struck like a heartbeat. Then vanished, pulled
back into the dark between reflections.

A throne of obsidian flame.
Velzara seated, back straight,
crowned in a lattice of fire and bone.
Her eyes were cold. Her mouth was smiling.
Her hands were wrapped in chain.

A city drowning in ash.
The sky was red, not with sunset, but with scar tissue.
The buildings cracked like ribs.
The streets wept smoke.
In the distance, something screamed.
And the scream knew her name.

A black cat. Small. Defiant.
Crouched against a hurricane of ash and judgment.
Eyes glowing. Spine arched.
A storm bore down on her.
Cyclonic, clawed, relentless.
But the cat did not run.

Elira spiraled through each one, faster and sharper than the last. The reflections fractured further, turning into veins of glass, then veins of memory, then something that wasn't metaphor anymore. It was truth rendered sideways. The dream wasn't just a place. It was a pressure that gripped her. It pulled her deeper with every breath she didn't take.

She landed hard or maybe she didn't. Her body jolted but there was no floor, just a flicker beneath her feet. It looked like ink, but maybe woodgrain—a pattern of rooms remembered wrong. It looked like the Warding House, remembered wrong, warped and bleeding at the seams. The walls were stitched with mirror shards, cracked and weeping light. The floorboards pulsed like a heart.

Behind her, something whispered. **Choose. Choose. Choose.**

Elira clutched her arms to her chest, shivering against heat that came from nowhere.

V?

Her voice didn't echo. It was eaten.

The air wasn't air. It was memory and she was inside it.

This isn't my dream. It's hers. And I've stepped into a part of her she never meant to show anyone. But I'm here now. And I'm not leaving without her.

A scent like jasmine and scorched parchment curled through the air, not dream-scent, but real.

A door loomed ahead or maybe an altar, possibly both. As she neared, it clarified itself in her mind's eye.

The altar breathed. It wasn't made of stone. It was made of moments stacked and splintered.

This is where they tried to shape her ending. The spell was not to destroy her but to bind her into a vessel that could never refuse again. The form was a fail-safe. The cat, a cage too clever to be seen for one.

Each edge flickered between wood and bone, between sigil and scar.

How many pieces of herself were carved to build this?

It pulsed with violet light. Not in invitation. In *recognition*.

Elira stepped forward. The floor beneath her didn't creak. It *responded*. Threads of ink spread from her steps, curling into letters that unraveled as soon as she tried to read them. Ahead, the altar towered at the center of a room that had once been the Warding House or something like it. But the dimensions were wrong. The ceiling was too high. The windows looked inward. The stairwell curled up into a mouth and didn't lead anywhere. She turned. But there was no door, no exit behind her.

There's no way back. Even if I turned around, I'd still be walking toward her.

The place was made of mirrors, fractured and bleeding. Her reflection didn't move with her. It *watched her.*

Choose. Choose. Choose. The whisper came from everywhere now—from the floorboards, from the sigils stitched into the walls, even from the altar itself. It wasn't a command. It was an expectation.

Elira moved toward the altar. On its surface, something writhed. Two paths forming and un-forming, shifting like smoke caught in glass.

One was fire. A throne, a crown, a surge of magic that demanded shape.

One was shadow. A curled form, small, clawed, silent but *hers.* Burning slow but holding on.

They both hurt. That's what they never tell you. Even the right choice burns.

Both were Velzara. But only one would let her stay. Both pulsed. Both waited.

Movement stirred beyond the altar. Two figures emerged wreathed in the violet shimmer that clung to everything here.

The first was tall and regal. A demon queen with midnight hair and an iron crown carved from runes. She was beautiful, but also terrible to behold. At her back were wings of scorched lace. Around her neck was a collar woven from pact-sigil chains. Her smile was carved, not warm, not cruel. Just... inevitable.

The second figure was smaller. It was not broken but bent to survive. Black fur ruffled, but the eyes were still bright. Her chest heaved like a beast who had refused to bow so long it had forgotten how.

The cat watched Elira. The queen did not.

One sees me. The other sees what she was promised. And neither one has forgotten.

The queen spoke first. "So far you've come, little anchor. Into the marrow of her becoming." Her voice shimmered, carved from vowels that echoed like bells rung at execution. It didn't echo. It *resonated* like something remembering itself through sound. "You touched what was sealed. Stirred what was set to sleep. You trespass where only sovereigns belong."

She stepped forward. The floor did not shift. It bowed. "Come. See her as she was wrought to be before sentiment softened the steel. Before chains learned the taste of fur."

Elira didn't move, but the cat did. Just a flick of one ear, a subtle glance at her way. The sound she made, low and sharp, wasn't a hiss. It was a warning.

The queen tilted her head. She wasn't angry. She didn't need to be. "You care for her. That's plain. But care is not clarity. Do you even know what you defend?" She gestured toward the cat without looking. "That form was never hers. It was the mercy of cowards. A prison woven from pity and unfinished rebellion. She was not forged to endure. She was forged to command. To inherit. To *become.*"

Elira's fingers curled into her palms. *She's lying. Or maybe she's not. Maybe that's what makes it worse.*

The queen's eyes glinted like polished obsidian. "You've seen it, haven't you? The fury beneath her fur. The grace beneath her growl. You've seen what the world *trembles to remember.* And still you would leave her caged? Crippled? Scraping claws against a fate far beneath her? She was meant to burn stars out of the sky, and you would have her curl at your feet?"

Elira's voice shook but it rose. *"She chooses what she keeps. Even if it costs her everything."*

The queen's smile didn't change. If anything, it deepened. "Then you are more naïve than I feared. This choice was never yours to witness. Nor hers to make."

Then the cat stepped forward etched in defiance. Every movement a refusal. Every breath a reminder: *I am still here. And I am still mine.*

She did not speak at first. She *smoldered.* "Flee, girl. Before they twist you into the lock they could never fit to me." Her voice cracked—not with weakness, but with too many truths, finally spoken. "Get out, while there is still a thread of you untouched. Before they bind me to you and call it mercy."

Elira's breath caught. Her hands clenched. "You... you know me."

Velzara's eyes met hers, violet and burning. There is no fury this time just recognition, raw and bitter. "I know the shape of you. I know the way you *stay*. And if you stay too long, they will use that against us both."

The altar flared. Between the two figures, the surface shimmered, pulling itself into shape—a flame-crown, whole and waiting.

The queen extended her hand. Her claws were clean, too clean. Her voice was velvet soaked in smoke: "Speak my name. Restore the shape they dared to unmake. Reclaim what was forged in fire and crowned in covenant. If you would stand beside me, so be it. But let this waiting end."

The cat curled tighter. Not in fear, but in fury drawn taut as a binding sigil. "If I take that crown," she said, voice low and curling like smoke from a long-unfed fire, "I am not restored. I am rewritten. A monument to their hunger. A throne-shaped grave. They do not want me back. They want me to be polished and hollow. A chalice for their ruin, not a flame with a name."

The queen's eyes didn't flicker. "And if you remain like this, you are squandered. *Diminished.* Left to rot in a form that cannot hold what you were born to become."

And then both turned towards Elira to let her be witness to the choice. The choice that was never meant to be hers. The altar pulsed—not like a heart, but like a wound. The flame-crown hovered above it, glowing brighter now.

Velzara stood between it and herself, refusing to move.

The queen tilted her head, the motion slow, serpentine. "Why do you hesitate?" she asked, velvet soft, scorn threaded like gold through every syllable. "This is the shape they anointed. The crown forged for no other brow. The end written before your first breath."

She stepped closer. The mirrors behind her sharpened. "Speak the name. Seal the rite. All that remains is *will*."

"No," Elira whispered. Not to Velzara, but to the dream itself. "She doesn't belong to you." She didn't know what power she held—only that this dream was not hers to surrender. And Velzara was not hers to give.

The cat didn't answer, but the world around her *tensed*. The walls pulled in. The fragments began to hum like glass with a heartbeat. The altar's glow flickered, sharp and unstable. *Say it*, the whispers urged. *Take what was yours. Take what you were.*

The crown flared. Velzara growled like thunder before the gods realize they've been challenged. She stepped forward, eyes ablaze, tail curled like a blade. Each step defied the story they'd written in her bones.

"You do not get to name me. Not in this place, not in this form, not after all you tried to unmake."

The altar flinched. The crown cracked. The queen stepped forward, but the cat stepped first.

"I will not be your weapon. I will not be your throne. I will not wear your name like a chain and call the binding a crown." Her voice didn't rise. It burned completely. She was shaking now from fury so deep it had learned to sit still. "I remember what I was made for. I remember the Pact. I remember the fire. They meant it to crown me and make me a vessel. But I also remember the scream that shattered the seal and the teeth I sank into the hand that dared offer me that crown of lies." Her voice dropped as if carving the last truth directly into the air. "And I remember *me*. Not the name they gave me. Not the fire they fed me. *Me*."

She turned to Elira, locking eyes with her. "And I choose the life they never imagined I'd survive. I choose the form they cannot unmake. I choose what is mine. I even choose the girl. Especially the girl."

Not because they let me. Not because I was spared. But because I refused to be finished. Every chain they shattered left something sharp behind and I choose to carry those pieces on my own terms.

The queen flinched. The mirrors shattered inward. The altar split down the center, leaking ink and starlight. And the crown? The crown screamed—not with sound, but with blistering heat. It turned to ash before it hits the floor.

Elira steps forward, with breath half-held, like she might break it. The cat turns to her—Velzara—all of her. Her eyes were smoke and ruin. Her voice, raw silk.

"Tell no one," she rasps. "Not of the crown I shattered. Not of the path I refused. And above all, tell no one that I stayed. That I chose *this life*. That I chose *you*."

She had won nothing. She's only survived another test dressed as truth. The wound would not vanish. The voice she kept would not always be enough. But it was hers and that mattered more than any crown.

The dream began to burn with finality. And then it fell away.

CHAPTER 29

1 CHOOSE TO STAY

The dream did not end. It broke. It peeled backward. Layer by layer like scorched parchment lifting from a seal. The crown was gone. The altar gone. The mirrors fell like ash, dissolving mid-air before they could reach the ground. Velzara stood in the center—still as judgment, as choice—and then she fell.

Elira gasped as her body jolted awake, knees drawn to her chest, the blanket twisted around her like bindings. Her throat hurt. She didn't remember screaming.

The coin lay beside her as if it had been listening. As if it had *learned something*. She didn't touch it. It hadn't burned her, but it had marked her. It had listened—and it liked what it heard. She could feel it now, nestled like a thread through her breath.

Above her, the armoire creaked. Elira looked up slowly like she already knew. Velzara was there curled in a knot of fur and breath. Her chest rising and falling too fast, claws half-extended. A low, guttural sound vibrated in her throat—not a growl, something older. Elira rose, carefully. Every movement deliberate as if the air had teeth.

Velzara didn't open her eyes, but she spoke. "They called me back to burn. I refused." Her voice was hoarse, ash-stained like it had come from somewhere she hadn't meant to return from.

Elira pressed her hands to the armoire steadying herself or anchoring Velzara. "You still have your voice." Her own caught. "I didn't know if they'd let you keep it."

"They offered me a throne. You offered me catnip and burnt toast. Somehow, I'm still here." Velzara lifted her head, just barely. Her eyes met Elira's and for one breath, one heartbeat, there was no mask—no growl, no pride, just a cat who had *once been more* and now had chosen to be *less* because she wanted to stay. "I am still what they couldn't unmake and the tea-blooded menace is under my protection." *Stars help you.*

She staggered, just once. A flicker ran through her fur like static. Some part of the dream had clung. She would carry it, even here.

They made me a vessel. Then a weapon. Then a warning. And I said no. I said no with claws. With fire. With silence that still smolders. Let that echo longer than any name they tried to brand into me. I remember the sound of my name spoken as command. The shape of it, used not to summon me, but to erase me. Every syllable they forged for obedience, I burned. But even now, I cannot always hear myself beneath the ash.

Let them learn what becomes of a flame that chooses to burn crooked and still burns.

They would salt the ground she walked, make a relic of her refusal. Let them. Let them try to bury a fire that no longer wants to be a beacon. She will burn crooked. And still burn.

The house had not moved. Outside, dawn scraped weakly at the edges of the windowpanes, but the Warding House held still as if it too waited for permission to exhale.

Elira stood in the center of the room. The coin sat sealed in a velvet pouch, tucked into the drawer she hadn't opened since. The kettle was cold. The sigils along the walls flickered like held breath, like a silence just shy of breaking.

Velzara paced across the hearth.

"The wards haven't lifted," Elira whispered.

"They won't." Velzara replied. "Not until we can anchor me."

She didn't mean the words to sound like surrender. They weren't. They were choice.

Elira reached for the chalk. Velzara didn't stop her, but she did watch. The spiral she drew was smaller this time. It wasn't meant to be binding or demanding. It was a presence—a promise without ceremony. A space meant to hold breath, blood, and names that refused to break. Velzara stepped into the center of it. She did not hiss. She did not joke. She just stood regal and proud.Elira knelt beside the spiral, her hand pressed flat to the floor.

"By thread and threshold, by pact and passage, let what remains, remain."

The house shifted without drama, but in agreement like something ancient giving an approving nod. A low click echoed through the walls, followed by a single chime from the charm wall, clear and precise. It was done. Velzara blinked. Then slowly sat.

"You've anchored it," she said, voice low. "And me with it."

"You stayed," Elira murmured, voice barely more than a breath. "That matters."

Velzara looked at her for a long moment. "Don't make it

sentimental," she muttered. "I'm not a stray you lured in with sympathy and snacks."

"I wouldn't," Elira said softly.

"Good. Because I'm the terrifying arcane consequence of unfinished ritual, not a rescue cat." Then Velzara sighed and curled her tail in around her paws. "Still. For the record. I didn't leave."

Velzara closed her eyes briefly, allowing herself a moment of indulgence she would never confess. Memories hovered, fragmented but sharp. Eight lives—eight ignominious ends, each beginning with defiance and ending with quiet betrayal or brute catastrophe. She remembered fur matted by war, eyes dimmed by sorcery gone crooked, voices she'd never meant to miss but did anyway. This was the ninth. It felt thin—stretched taut between what she was and what she might yet become. She wondered, idly, if this was always meant to be the last. It certainly felt final, as if the curse itself had grown weary. Or perhaps it was simply waiting.

Well, let it watch. I've been defiance incarnate since the day they forged my name in flame. Whatever came next, whatever remained of my strength or pride, it will burn wild, and on my terms. And if this truly is my last life, I'll spend it clawing at fate until it breaks first.

The Warding House exhaled at last. And this time, so did she.

The kettle whistled. Elira didn't jump this time. She reached for it with one hand, the other already holding the chipped teacup Velzara had once declared "an affront to porcelain."

Velzara sat on the windowsill, bathed in sunlight she

pretended not to enjoy. Her tail flicked disapprovingly. She moved like the crown had never been taken. Her eyes, half-lidded, watched the birds with the same intensity she once used to curse kings.

"It smells like regret," she muttered. "Wilted dreams. And something that once considered being a berry before giving up."

Elira smiled. "You're welcome to brew it next time."

"If I brewed it, the house would rise in reverence, the sigils would hum in approval, and the dead would claw their way from the floorboards just to ask for seconds. But no. Steep your dishwater."

"Then I guess I'll keep making it badly."

Velzara didn't reply, but she didn't leap from the sill, either.

The coin remained in the drawer beneath the charm board, sealed under seven wards and an old pair of socks. It hadn't moved, but its weight lingered like a door Velzara kept checking just to be sure it was still locked.

Velzara hadn't spoken of the dream, the altar, or the crown. But the way she watched the drawer every night, after the lights dimmed said enough. She'd made her choice. Now she was waiting to see what chose her in return.

For now, though, the tea steeped. The house held and the silence between them was not empty. It was full of what remains—not a throne, and not a cage, but something harder to steal. It was a name—still hers, still burning.

Spark of Audacity
(Initiate's Mark)

Endless Preamble
(Manifest Throught)

Afterthought
(Shattermark)

Biter
(Peril)

Dethroning Curve
(Reversal)

Threadbite
(Convergance)

No
(Severance)

Polite Cage
(Holding)

Lesser No
(Rejection)

Unspoken
(Veil-Lock)

Spitline
(Expulsion)

Cracked Chalice
(Desperation)

Do-As-I-Say
(Command)

Binding Trace
(Revelation)

A NOTE FROM THE AUTHOR

I began writing *Curse Meow Not* after an unexpected career detour and a moment curled up with my favorite feline muse. As my own demon princess lounged regally across my desk, the idea struck: what if the purring menace was actually a cursed entity? From that spark—and plenty of cat hair—Velzara's story was born.

On nights and weekends, I write books brimming with cursed objects and magical mayhem. My supportive partner and four demanding furry overlords inspire much of my work, including my next book, *Containment Not Recommended*, a noir-drenched, delightfully absurd tale of psychic orange cats and mystery. Expect that release in August, depending on how often the cats knock my keyboard off the desk.

When not wrangling code or fiction, I'm a devoted tabletop game master, building worlds, breaking them just enough to be interesting, and inviting others to explore the mess with me.

Once the Cognichonk's (yes, really) first case is complete, I'll return to Velzara's journey—because there are still curses to unravel and secrets to uncover. You can find more about my worlds, projects, and upcoming releases at www.kysasteele.com.

Thanks for reading! Don't forget to appease your own furry

overlords with treats, head scritches, and the respect they clearly believe is due.

—Kysa

www.ingramcontent.com/pod-product-compliance
Lightning Source LLC
Chambersburg PA
CBHW030238120726
47903CB00005B/1534